MW00773024

THAT DARN SQUID GOD

ALSO BY NICK POLLOTTA

Bureau 13: Judgment Night
Bureau 13: Doomsday Exam
Bureau 13: Full Moonster
Illegal Aliens (with Phil Foglio)
Tequila Mockingbird

FORTHCOMING

Bureau 13: Damned Nation
The Bureau 13 RPG Handbook (with Richard Tucholka)

THAT DARN SQUID GOD

NICK POLLOTTA
& JAMES CLAY

WILDSIDE PRESS

THAT DARN SQUID GOD

A section of this novel was originally published as the short story, "Turnabout."

A publication of
Wildside Press
P.O. Box 301
Holicong, PA 18928-0301
www.wildsidepress.com

Copyright © 2004 by Nick Pollotta and Phil Foglio.

All rights reserved

Cover art by Fastner & Larson

No portion of this book may be reproduced by any means, electronic or otherwise, without first obtaining the written consent of the author. For more information, contact:
www.NickPollotta.com

ISBN: 1-59224-097-6
First Wildside Press edition: 2004

DEDICATION

To our wives.

And a very special thanks to Nick's sister,
Kathi Somers who proofread the novel.
Any mistakes still found are entirely my own.

ONE

Swirling fog ruled the London night.

Stepping from a horse-drawn carriage into the thick mist, Professor Felix Einstein paused on the pavement, briefly consulting the small glass globe in his hand. Trapped in the middle of the crystalline sphere was a mummified Egyptian tarantula that remained motionless under his hard scrutiny, and the professor relaxed at the sign that there was no evil magic in the immediate vicinity. At least, for the moment.

Satisfied for the nonce, Prof. Einstein tucked the talisman away once more into his great coat. Dressed like a Bow Street banker, Einstein was sporting an Inverness cape over his gray-striped suit and Oxford school tie, with the mandatory small porridge stain. His craggy face was deeply tanned, and the silver highlights in his wavy hair almost perfectly matched the silver lion head of his ebony walking cane. The inner pocket of his coat bulged with an Adams .32 revolver and looped across his waistcoat was a gold watch chain with a petrified shark tooth dangling at the end as a fob. Jutting from a pocket of his vest was an embossed case containing numerous calling cards that merely listed his name, address, and a few dozen of his titles. His real profession was not among them.

Starting to address the waiting cabby, Prof. Einstein frowned as he caught a gale of merriment coming from the nearby building. Eh? In the expert opinion of the professor, a tribe of Zulu warriors performing the Mexican hat dance could not have been more incongruous than the loud laughter, which came from the ground floor windows of the five-story brownstone building dominating the block.

In the past few weeks, Einstein had noticed that the weather patterns of the entire world were steadily becoming worse; snow in Egypt, tornadoes in the Amazon jungle, bright sunshine in Liverpool, and such. Yet those were merely side effects of the coming apocalypse.

So who could possibly be laughing at such a dire time as this? the professor demanded irritably. *Surely not my fellow club members! Maybe the fog was distorting the noise of some distant party so that it seemed nearby? Yes, of course, that must be the answer. How obvious.*

"Best stay sharp, Davis," Prof. Einstein said, reaching upward to shake hands with the burly driver. The complicated procedure took a few moments as thumbs, fists, knuckles, tickling and slapping were involved. It seemed more of friendly fight between the two men than a salutation.

"I'd recommend a routine number nine," Einstein added as they eventually let go.

"My very thought," Davis whispered, checking the iron cudgel tucked into his wide leather belt. The 'Liverpool Lawgiver' was worn from constant use, and appeared as formidable as a consort Navy battleship. "Just you look for me, and I'll be there, governor."

"Good man."

Giving a wink, Davis shook the reins, and started the two draft horses away from the curb at a gentle canter. The cab vanished into the billowing clouds, and soon there was only the rattling echo of its wooden wheels on the cobblestones that ghostly faded away.

Shaking off his uneasy feeling, Prof. Einstein checked the loaded pistol in his pocket before starting along the pavement towards the giant brownstone. Then the odd laughter sounded again, louder this time, and most definitely from the club. Outrageous! With an annoyed snort, Einstein began to stride impatiently towards the towering downtown mansion.

Reaching the front of the huge building, Prof. Einstein ambled up the worn marble stairs with his mind still on the strange laughter. Einstein was quite aware that at any given time one could be almost sure of the leader of some newly returned expedition regaling the assembled members with their latest tales of derring-do, heavily embellished with sound effects, visual aids and the unwilling cooperation of the nearest staff member. In point of fact, the London Explorers Club was the only establishment in England that was forced to offer its servants combat pay. But raucous laughter when the world was on the brink of destruction? Professor Einstein frowned in consternation. Most unseemly. He had sincerely hoped that at least some of the other members would have been able to read the portents of the coming apocalypse. Perhaps he was wrong.

Pushing open the brassbound mahogany door, Einstein entered the mansion and handed his Inverness cape, hat, and cane to a doorman, who in turn passed them to a liveried page. Taking a deep breath, the professor stood for a precious moment to let the warm air seep into his bones. The pungent atmosphere was thick with the homey smell of wood polish, pipe smoke, and cordite. *Ah, home, sweet home!*

Just then, another burst of laughter arose only to be abruptly cut off by a man's stern voice. Einstein tried to catch what was being said, but it was rapidly drowned out by a new upswelling of mirth. The noise seemed to be coming from the Great Hall. In spite of the urgency of his mission, the professor was forced to admit that this was becoming interesting. There was an unwritten law in the club that one had best know when to stick to the truth and when one could embellish a story a bit. A law that many bent, but few actually broke. Sadly, there was always a significant number of expeditions that encountered nothing more exciting than fetid jungles, smarmy natives, and dull animals that were so patently stupid that they would wander directly in front of you and politely wait while you dug the old .577 Martini-Henry bolt-action out of your haversack and did them the favor of blowing out their brains. But those were tales hardly worth repeating.

Proceeding quickly down the center passageway, Professor Einstein turned left at a suit of Spanish armor and entered the Great Hall. No exaggeration had been used to name the room, as it was a good three hundred paces long, its oak beam ceiling an arrow flight away. The four'n square wood floor was dotted with a hundred islands of India rugs and velvet smoking chairs, while in the center of the room, a tiered Italian fountain quietly burbled and splashed. Lining the walls were mammoth bookcases containing over a million leatherbound tomes, most of them first editions, or handwritten journals. High above this grandeur on the second story balcony was a beautifully sculptured bronze bust of Marco Polo, the patron saint of explorers, dutifully keeping watch over his modern-day students.

Crowding around a blazing fireplace, a group of club members was surrounding a display table. Placed prominently on that scarred expanse of dark oak was a small wooden ship, barely a foot in length. A single low cabin was in the middle of the deck of the tiny vessel. No sails or masts were visible, and the rudder was broken.

"By god, Carstairs," Lord Danvers laughed from underneath a bushy Royal British Marine moustache. "You'll have to do better than that!"

"Rather," Dr. Thompkins snorted, dipping his red nose once more into a half-empty whiskey glass. "Balderdash, I say. Violates the unwritten law. Noah's Ark, indeed."

In righteous indignation, Lord Benjamin Carstairs rose to his full height, and no hat was necessary for him to tower over the other members.

In cold scrutiny, Prof. Einstein could see the fellow must be over six feet tall, and maybe two hundred pounds in weight, with not an ounce on fat on the heavily muscled, almost Herculean, frame. The giant was dapper in a three-piece suit of a brown worsted material that perfectly complemented his stiff white shirt and striped Harvard tie. His lantern jaw was painfully clean-shaven, while the pale brown hair and blue eyes clearly announced a Saxon heritage.

Oh well, nobody's perfect, the Norman-descended Einstein observed wryly.

"I stand on my earlier statement, sirs," Lord Carstairs said calmly, resting a tanned hand on the little craft. "You have seen my journals and read my analysis. This ship was found on the peak of Mt. Ararat, hidden in a stratified gully just below the snow line. It is made of 4,000-year-old gopher wood and sealed with crude pitch. To scale, it is of the proper dimensions, and perfectly matches the description of the craft in the Book of Genesis, chapters six through ten. I believe that it was constructed by Noah Ben Lamech, as a working model, before he built the actual sea-going ark itself."

Once more, guffaws filled the air and some rude soul added a juicy American raspberry.

"Good evening, gentlemen," Professor Einstein said loudly, interrupting the brouhaha.

In prompt response, the boisterous crowd stopped making noise and turned smartly about.

"Felix, old boy!" Baron Edgewaters shouted, his bushy beard appearing to weigh more than his prominent belly. "Excellent timing as always. We've got a real wowser for you this time."

"Lad claims to have found a relic off of Noah's Ark, by gad!" Lord Danvers chortled, taking another healthy gulp. "Thinks he can fool us like Thomson did in '74 with his 'continent under Antarctica' theory. Haw!"

"How wonderful," Einstein snorted, dismissing the matter with a gesture. "He found Noah's Ark. My heartiest congratulations. But I have even more pressing news to convey."

"I said a model, not the ark itself, sir," Carstairs corrected primly.

The professor shrugged. "Whatever you wish. It is of no consequence."

"Indeed? And what could be more important than this?" Lord

Danvers demanded, stroking his moustache. "The end of the world?"

Eagerly opening his mouth to speak, Prof. Einstein was cut off by Lord Carstairs.

"And exactly who are you, sir?" the lord asked.

"Haven't you two fellows ever met before?" Dr. Thompkins gasped in wonderment, rising from a chair.

"No," they replied in unison.

"But this calamity must be corrected with all due haste!" Colonel Pierpont declared, adjusting his pince-nez glasses and assuming an authoritarian pose. "Carstairs, might I introduce Professor Felix Einstein of the International British Museum, a private concern. Einstein, may I introduce Lord Benjamin Carstairs of Heather Downs, Preston."

With both hands clasped behind his back, Lord Carstairs nodded in greeting. "A pleasure, sir. I have read your books on archeology with the greatest of interest. Particularly your monograph on the feasibility that Stonehenge is a form of solar calendar."

Impatiently, Einstein accepted the compliment with what grace he could muster under the circumstances. "A minor work. And I have more than a passing acquaintance with your own journals, sir. Your theories on the possible Aztec origin of the Easter Island statues are most impressive."

"Thank you."

"And if it will speed things along, as a senior member of the club, I officially acknowledge and congratulate you on your find," Einstein continued. "For this is not a model as you suppose, but the actual ark itself."

The roomful of explorers went stock-still at that as if a live woman had entered the club.

"A-are you crazed, Felix?" Sir Lovejoy erupted in shock, going even more pale than usual. "The craft is barely a foot long! How in the name of Queen Victoria could that *toy* carry seven and two of every animal on the face of the earth?"

"Explain yourself, sir!" Dr. Thompkins demanded.

Quite exasperated, Prof. Einstein closed his eyes so that nobody would see him roll them about. Ye gods, plainly no other topic of conversation would be considered until this trifling matter was resolved. So be it.

"Jeeves!" the professor shouted over a shoulder.

Instantly, the liveried butler appeared in the doorway as if he had been waiting for the explosive summons. "Yes, sir?" he drawled in proper English servitude.

"Fresh gasogenes, please," Einstein commanded, thoughtfully rubbing his lucky shark's tooth. "Every bloody one we have."

This gave Jeeves pause. There was a barely used soda water dispenser on the liquor cart right beside the man. Why would he wish additional reservoirs? And every one? For a club like the Explorers, that meant several dozen, at the very least. Then the butler went cold. *Oh no,* he prayed fervently, *not another re-enactment of the Amazon rain forest. Anything but that.*

"Wasn't aware that you've recently been to the Amazon, Felix," Lord Danvers said, refilling his glass as the somber butler shuffled away.

Ignoring that comment, Prof. Einstein stolidly waited until Jeeves returned moments later. Experience being a bitter teacher, the butler was wearing a Macintosh overcoat and rubber boots as he pushed along a trolley loaded with several small wooden crates full of gasogenes soda water dispensers. Plus, an umbrella and a bucket.

"Thank you, Jeeves," Professor Einstein said politely, taking a gasogene from the trolley. The umbrella and bucket were a wise precaution, but unnecessary in this particular instance. "Now please give one of these to everybody in the room."

As the butler distributed the dispensers, Einstein moved the display table to the center of the hall. Now armed with gasogenes, everybody waited to see what would happen next. Felix Einstein had a well-deserved reputation of pulling rabbits out of his hat. That bizarre museum of his was a prime example.

Exercising extraordinary care, Prof. Einstein aligned the tiny ship so that its keel was directed length wise down the room. The wood felt dry as dust to his touch and his fingers stuck slightly to the craft, which certainly seemed to substantiate his theory about its origins. With extreme fastidiousness, the professor made one last minute correction in the ship's placement. Yes. Good enough.

"On my mark, gentlemen, hose the ark with water," Einstein said, assuming a firing stance. "Ready, aim . . ."

The encircling crowd was plainly delighted beyond words, while the stunned Lord Carstairs lowered his gasogene. "Are you sure this is prudent?" he asked in real concern.

"Fire!" Prof. Einstein cried, triggering his dispenser. A sparkling gush of effervescence splashed onto the minuscule craft. The stream of water hit it squarely, yet not a single drop of liquid rolled off the vessel to land on the table. Then an ominous creaking sound came from the wooden boat.

"All of you! Act now!" Einstein barked, over the hissing spray of carbonated water. "Spray quickly, or the ship will tear itself apart!"

It was more the whipcrack tone of the professor's voice than anything else that made the other members comply. In an orchestrated attack, several streams of carbonated water went gushing onto the relic, washing over it from stern to bow and back again.

As the pressure in the gasogenes eventually become exhausted, the rush of soda water slowed to a trickle, the last dribbles falling from the spouts to spot the India rug.

"Astonishing," Duke Farthington whispered, staring at the little boat. It was barely damp. Definitely, something strange was going on here.

With a bizarre sucking noise, the pools of moisture around the craft disappeared into the hull, and before the startled eyes of the club members, the desiccated craft began to swell like some impossible sponge. With incredible speed, the expanding ship outgrew the display table, the enlarging pushing aside a vacant chair and smashing a lamp.

"Get back!" Colonel Pierpont cried out, throwing both hands skyward and accidentally knocking off his pince-nez glasses.

No further prompting was needed for the startled club members to dive for safety. With a loud crack, the display table broke apart and crashed to the floor. Rapidly, the ark continued to increase in size in every direction, all the while creaking and groaning as if was being tortured on the high seas. Five yards, ten, twenty yards in length it reached, before the rate of growth noticeably slowed.

"By Jove!" Baron Edgewaters roared, crouching behind an ottoman. "Look at that! The bloody thing actually is Noah's Ark!"

"Indubitably," somebody said from the other side of the craft.

"This is dehydration on a scale unheard of in the entire civilized world!" added another unseen member from the general vicinity of the prow.

"Or England," a patriotic chap added, from behind the window curtains.

"Congratulations, Benjamin!" Lord Danvers boomed from under the liquor cart.

Wriggling from their hiding places, the entire assemblage gathered around Lord Carstairs and gave him a thunderous round of applause.

Beaming in unabashed pleasure, Carstairs suddenly took on a pained expression and pointed in horror. Everybody turned just in time to see the still slowly expanding prow of the vessel nose into the trough of the bubbling fountain.

"Bloody hell," Prof. Einstein whispered, taking a step backwards.

There came a loud slurping noise, closely followed by a mighty groan of tormented wood, and the ark exploded into double its size. More than fifty yards in length, the vessel loomed over the scrambling men as it continued to grow, rapidly filling the Great Hall. With the sound of shattering stone, the fountain noisily collapsed and the ship settled over the stony remains, precipitating a great column of water that washed over the ship and yielded yet another massive spurt of growth.

"The mains!" Lord Carstairs shouted to the staff members who were staring in wonder through the doorway. "Turn off the water mains!"

Obediently, one of the servants spun about and dashed down the hall.

His mind swirling with dire mathematics, Prof. Einstein could only scowl at the monstrosity forming before them. *Two and seven of every animal on the earth. How big would the Ark get? Answer: too damn big. This was definitely not good!*

Like a wooden express train, the traveling prow violently rammed into the fireplace, smashing the hearth, and tilting the oil painting of Her Royal Majesty. As it fell, the stern of the ship slammed into the far wall, shattering the plaster and causing the bust of Marco Polo to rip free from its pedestal on the second floor balcony. As the massive bronze statue plummeted straight towards a horrified Jeeves, Lord Carstairs surged forward to shove the man aside. The heavy bust crashed onto Carstairs instead, the savage blow driving the lord to his knees as he barely managed to deflect the three hundred pounds of metal onto a 7th century pirate's chest. Even over the creaking of the Ark, the splintery explosion of the chest from the meteoric impact was clearly discernable.

White-faced and trembling, Jeeves had trouble speaking for a moment. "Y-you saved my life," the butler finally stammered, his nerveless fingers dropping the umbrella to the floor.

"Think nothing of it," Carstairs panted, flexing his hands to stop the stinging. "I'm sure you would have done the same for me."

Tilting his head, Jeeves glanced at the quarter-ton of metal explorer laying in the splintered midst of what had once been a sturdy steamer trunk. "Quite so," the manservant remarked in dry sincerity.

Now from beneath the Ark there came a series of squeaks and a banging metallic rattle. Its growth immediately slowed and with a final groaning lurch that shattered the eastern skylight, the titanic craft went thankfully still.

"By Gadfrey!" a member whispered askance, wiggling free from between the broken rudder and a bookcase. "And I thought Williamson's recounting of his trip to Lake Geneva exciting."

Battered, but undamaged, the explorers slowly crawled out from under the furniture, and dusted themselves off while staring at the impossible vessel. Going to the remains of the liquor cabinet, Lord Danvers poured himself a stiff drink.

Prof. Einstein straightened the Queen's portrait back on the wall. *Better.*

"Damnation, sir," Duke Farthington cried out, clapping Lord Carstairs on the shoulder. "But you're a hard act to follow!"

Breaking into nervous laughter, the younger members began clearing aside the assorted debris, while the senior members contemplated the Biblical behemoth filling the hall.

"Of course, how we will get it out of here is another matter entirely," Lord Danvers observed, finishing his whiskey.

"Damned inconvenient holding meetings with this hanging above our heads," Judge Foxthington-Symthe stated, thoughtfully stroking one of his many chins. "We could always just tear down a wall or two and ease it out into the back courtyard. Make a fine gazebo, it would. Impress the neighbors no end."

All work paused as everybody turned to stare at the judge.

"Outside?" a man asked.

"Where it *rains*?" another questioned.

The entire group of explorers paled at those words and looked at the Ark with growing expressions of horror. Exactly what were they to do with this thing?

Clapping his hands, Prof. Einstein got the members moving again and eventually a path was cleared to the doorway, allowing the staff to rush in with brooms and dustpans to begin the Herculean job of straightening the hall. Leaving them to the task, the disheveled club members now gathered round Carstairs and Einstein.

"Members of the Explorers Club," Duke Farthington shouted in his best Parliamentary voice. "I give you, Lord Benjamin Carstairs!"

A formal round of applause came from the members, and the British lord made a sweeping bow. "Thank you, gentlemen. I am most gratified." Then Carstairs turned to address Prof. Einstein in a quieter voice. "And thank you, sir, for saving my reputation. If ever I can return the favor, pray inform me."

"Now would be a good time," Einstein said bluntly. "I came here to find two or three men to assist me on an extremely dangerous expedition." The professor smiled at the dapper young goliath. "But then, it appears that you are two or three men."

As the observation was hardly original, Lord Carstairs accepted the statement complacently. "Pray tell, what is the nature of this expedition?"

"To save the world from total destruction."

Taken aback in surprise, Carstairs blinked a few times at the outlandish statement. "Are you quite serious, Professor?"

Einstein nodded. "Absolutely, Lord Carstairs."

Since honor was on the line, the decision came instantaneously. "Then I am at your command, sir," Lord Carstairs said, extending a massive hand.

As gingerly as if grasping a spring-loaded bear trap, Prof. Einstein accepted the offer and they shook.

"Excellent, lad!" Einstein said, glancing about at the scene of turmoil about them. "But this is no place to talk. Come, I'll tell you the details on the way to my home."

"Indeed. Why the hurry? Is the matter pressing?"

"Yes, time is of the essence."

"Accepted, then."

As the two men walked from the room, Lord Carstairs took the opportunity to add, "Is there any chance that we may be back from wherever we're going by early next month? Several friends and I had planned on taking another crack at locating the elephants' graveyard in Africa."

Starting a caustic reply, Professor Einstein paused and then spoke tactfully. "Lad, if our expedition is not successful, then you won't have to worry about such matters."

Frowning darkly, Lord Carstairs uneasily chewed upon that cryptic statement. "Indeed, sir," he murmured.

In the foyer, the liveried page gave their coats to the doorman, who in turn primly passed them to the owners. In the background, there could be heard a great deal of cursing and hammering from the ruin of the Great Hall.

Donning their outer garments, the two men departed from the club, and walked down to the curb. Placing two fingers in his mouth, Prof. Einstein gave a sharp whistle, and from within the billowing fog there came the crack of a whip, a horse whinnied and a brougham carriage into view with Davis at the reins.

Climbing inside, the two explorers seated themselves comfortably as Davis set the carriage into motion. As the cab moved into the deeper recesses of the river mist, a group of hooded figures stepped from the shadowy alleyway alongside the Explorers Club. Shaking the broken window glass from their robes, the men adjusted the scarves masking their features, pulled knives, and swiftly followed the departing vehicle. Oddly, their hard-sole boots did not make a sound on the granite cobblestones of the city street.

TWO

Clear and strong, the mighty Big Ben began to chime the midnight hour as somewhere in the gray mist a muffled foghorn moaned in warning to ships on the Thames River.

Inside the jostling carriage, Lord Carstairs reclined in the sumptuous leather seating. "That was a spot of good luck to locate a cab this quickly on so poor a night," he commented. "Perhaps it is a good omen for our journey, eh what?"

"Nothing of the sort, lad. I had it waiting for me," Einstein remarked, checking the time on a gold Beugueret pocket watch.

"How unusual," Carstairs noted, stretching out his legs. "You must pay the driver exorbitantly for such a service. Or is he part of your staff?"

"Merely professional courtesy," the professor corrected, showing an ornate signet ring on his left pinky.

Arching an eyebrow, Lord Carstairs studied the unusual bit of jewelry. "You're a member of the Cab Drivers Guild?" he asked incredulously.

"The Coalition of the Street we prefer to be called, but yes, I am an honorary member," Einstein said, breathing on the ring before polishing it on a trouser leg. "Quite often in my work I have found it highly useful to belong to as many private associations and restricted clubs as possible. One can never tell when the assistance of a fellow member will be highly desirous."

"That certainly seems to make sense," Carstairs replied politely.

Resting the ebony cane across his lap, the professor smiled ruefully. "So far, the only society that has totally refused me admittance is the Daughters of Lesbos."

Unsure if that was a joke or not, Lord Carstairs leaned back and reached inside his coat to produce a gold cigar case. Snapping it open, the lord politely offered an assortment of hand-rolled Cubans to the professor. Einstein stared at the leafy cylinders with dismay.

"An imported Havana mixture," Carstairs said encouragingly. "My own private blend."

Recognizing the futility of arguing health with a confirmed smoker, the professor relinquished his usual adamant position and joined his associate in lighting a slim panatela. Soon, the atmosphere inside the cab was as thick as the air outside and, in spite of his scientific abhorrence of the practice, Einstein was forced to admit that it really was a damn fine cigar.

From the front of the carriage came the crack of a whip and a horse whinny, and the vehicle angled sharply about for a tight turn. Almost losing their seats, both men grabbed hold of the convenient leather straps set next to the door and fought to stay upright.

"Incompetent bounder," Lord Carstairs muttered angrily.

"Evasive tactics," Prof. Einstein corrected.

"Are we being pursued, sir?"

Inspecting the end of his cigar, Einstein said nothing.

Allowing the pungent smoke to trickle from his mouth, Lord Carstairs turned to glance out a window. Even through the dense river fog, he could see the vast halls of Parliament, the great stone building still encased in a maze of scaffolding.

"Appears they're almost done with the repairs," he remarked with pride, the smoky words momentarily visible in the air.

Puffing contentedly, Prof. Einstein nodded. "A nice job too, considering how much damage it received in the–"

"Troubles," Carstairs interjected, gesturing with his cigar.

Furrowing his brow, Einstein scowled in irritation. "It was war, damn it. War! Why can't anybody just admit that?"

"Tact," the lord replied simply.

As politeness was the backbone of civilization, the professor had no possible retort to that. Angrily, he flicked cigar ash out the window just as the fog briefly parted, admitting a wealth of silvery moonlight into the cab.

Gesturing with the smoldering stub, Einstein indicated the misty sky overhead. "Well, is polite society willing to talk about the moon?" the professor demanded. "Or is that also something else people decline to discuss?"

"Not a bit of it," Lord Carstairs replied, shifting the cigar to a new location in his mouth. "I heard about the phenomenon before I left the continent. The Royal Astronomical Society is completely foxed about the whole thing."

"As so they should be, lad," Prof. Einstein said, blowing a smoke ring at the crescent. The fumes joined the fog and moon was gone again. "By celestial mechanics beyond our understanding, the moon is revolving to show us its long hidden face. What do you think of that, eh?"

Inhaling deeply, Carstairs gave the matter a few minutes of somber thought. "Be a nice change, I dare say."

"What? Is that all it means to you?" the professor asked, staring agog.

The lord shrugged. "Honestly, sir, considering the state of the world, I don't see how this development can be of any real importance. Except perhaps to poets, and a few painters."

"Indeed," Einstein said sounding disappointed, his fingers drumming on the coach seat. "Lord Carstairs, how familiar are you with the mythology of the Dutarian Empire?"

Lord Carstairs thoughtfully puffed on his cigar before answering. "Only vaguely," Carstairs replied honestly. "It was a small secluded city/state in the Sumatra region, founded around 3000 BC. They were a rather vigorous empire with a pronounced reputation for bloodthirstiness. They were on the rise for slightly over a hundred years until they suffered some sort of natural disaster and completely disappeared."

Tapping the excess ash from the glowing tip of the cigar, Carstairs replaced it to savor another deep puff. "As to religion and myths, they worshiped some sort of fish, I believe. Don't remember anything about the moon." He focused his attention onto the professor. "I assume there is a connection."

Although he tried not to show it, Prof. Einstein was extremely impressed. Most university scholars would have had to consult numerous volumes to unearth the information this man had so casually tossed off. Obviously, Einstein had made the correct choice in an associate.

"Absolutely there is a connection. And the Dutarians did not worship a fish, per se," Einstein corrected, "but a giant squid. The Squid God, they called it, although demon might be a more accurate translation. It was supposed to be a horrific beast that had a thousand tentacles, a dozen mouths, and was totally invulnerable to man-made weapons."

"And it fed on human blood."

His cigar drooped as Einstein eagerly leaned forward in the smoky cab. "Great Scott, you've heard of the creature?" he demanded.

"No, but it would have been a rather unusual deity for a warrior state to revere if it didn't," Carstairs said, puffing away steadily. "Rather reminds me of that Aztec god of war, Huitzilopochtli. He required massive amounts of the stuff to make the dawn come."

"Ah, but in the sun god aspect of Tonatiu, he was perceived as a bringer of life," Einstein noted with a raised finger. "The Squid God was known only as a destroyer, just barely controlled by the Dutarian priests who summoned it and, in the end, not even they could do so."

"You're talking as if the thing really existed," Carstairs chided, flicking his cigar butt out the window. "And that is patently absurd, sir."

"As absurd as Noah's Ark?" Einstein asked quietly.

The British lord closed his mouth with an audible snap and, for the next several seconds, conflicting emotions battled for supremacy across his handsome face.

"Oh, at least as absurd," Carstairs conceded with a smile. "However, sir, you actually saw my proof."

"And soon," the professor said, leaning back into the seat to gaze out the window, "you shall see mine."

* * *

With a clatter of hooves on cobblestone, the brougham carriage came to a halt at the curb in front of a simple brick mansion bordered by a high wrought-iron gate. Exiting the cab, Prof. Einstein tried to pay Davis, who adamantly refused. Sensing a battle of wills was in progress, Lord Carstairs took the opportunity for a good stretch after his confinement. The lord was still in the same position when the professor joined him on the pavement.

"Something wrong?" Einstein asked, taking the fellow by the arm.

"The International British Museum for *Stolen* Antiquities?" Lord Carstairs said reading the huge sign above the front door. "Good lord, Professor, isn't that laying it on a bit thick?"

With a cavalier gesture, Prof. Einstein completely dismissed the matter. "Purely advertising, lad. It gives the patrons a vicarious thrill. You should have seen the newspaper headlines on the day we opened shop."

"But still," Carstairs hedged uncomfortably.

"And it's not entirely true," Einstein continued, unlocking the front gate and holding it open. Carstairs walked through and the professor securely locked it again. "Well over twenty percent of our exhibits have been legally purchased."

Quite impressed, Lord Carstairs gave a whistle. "As many as that? My apologies."

"Think nothing of it," Einstein said, unlocking the front door and swinging aside the heavy oak portal.

Entering a vestibule, the two men dodged round a group of velvet ropes set to direct patrons to a ticket booth, and continued past a sturdy brass turnstile. The foyer was lined with various old world maps; some on parchment, others on papyrus or sheepskin. Each was highly illuminated with imaginative renderings of the creatures that supposedly lurked in the deep waters, waiting to devour anybody rash enough to venture beyond the safety of land.

As they proceeded through a curtained alcove, brilliant light washed over them and Carstairs gasped in astonishment, while Einstein snorted in disgust.

"Owen must have forgotten to turn off the bloody lights again," Prof. Einstein complained. "Damned gas bills are going to bankrupt me. William Owen is a bright student and a good lad, but he has no sense of propriety."

"Indeed?"

"Well, he's Welsh, you know," the professor added, as if that explained the matter.

Looking over the museum, Carstairs dumbly nodded in agreement. The building was a single colossal room that stretched the length and breath of the property. The entire Explorers Club could have easily fit inside the cavernous structure!

Everywhere were rows of exhibit cases and display racks of a thousand different types. Rainbow-colored tapestries lined the walls and precious Ming vases stood secure inside a row of gleaming glass pyramids. Dominating the entire west wing was the elaborately carved skeleton of a Tyrannosaurus Rex, poised as if ready to attack. Next to the dinosaur stood a squad of brightly lacquered Oriental armor in proud formation, guarding a gilt-edged sarcophagus, its glass top displaying a perfectly preserved Egyptian mummy inside.

In the east wing was a completely restored Viking long boat, a Roman galley, and an Imperial Chinese barge, each resting in stout mahogany dry docks sporting delicately engraved brass plates that detailed their histories and attributes.

Adorning the ceiling was a painted panorama of the Milky Way, with round glass skylights depicting the eight known planets, plus two theoretical worlds. Directly below the panorama hung a huge pair of feathered wings joined together by an ancient leather body harness. Even the floor seemed to be an exhibit, the black fleck marble underlain with strange runes and geometric patterns. In somber deference, Lord Carstairs removed his hat.

"I am speechless, sir," he finally managed to croak, throat tight with professional admiration. "It is totally unlike any museum I have ever seen before!"

Busily tying the curtains closed, Einstein glanced up at that statement. "What, this rubbish? Bah. Mere baubles to amuse the idle tourist. The real museum starts on the other side of that brass door."

Lord Carstairs turned. The door in question was located alongside the mammoth Tyrannosaurus, set into a hinged section of the wall that obviously served as an access portal for the larger exhibits.

"Might we take a moment?" Carstairs asked eagerly.

The professor gave a bow. "Certainly. It's on the way to my office."

"Splendid!"

Walking side by side, the two men briskly strode across the museum. Prof. Einstein noted that the cases had been properly cleaned, while Lord Carstairs observed the bewildering assortment of material, which included stacks of ancient coins, jeweled hairpins, golden whips, plus an array of highly ornamental crowns from as many countries as centuries. The riches of a hundred kingdoms were on display with no apparent guards or protection of any sort.

"Professor, do you have much trouble with thieves?" the lord finally asked.

"Not at all," Einstein remarked. "The glass in every exhibit case is specially tempered and veined with hair-thin steel wires, quite invulnerable to anything short of a sledgehammer. Plus, at night the grounds are patrolled by Hans, Dolf, and Inga."

Carstairs nodded sagely. "Ah, pit bulls no doubt, or perhaps you use mastiffs. Nasty dogs. My gilly makes use of them for my country estate."

"Dogs?" Professor Einstein said as if he had never heard the word before. "Nonsense, lad. Even the most vicious *Canis Familiaris* are far too gentle to serve as protectors of my establishment. I use the much more brutal and bloodthirsty *Felis Tigris*."

"B-Bengal tigers?" Lord Carstairs gasped, coming to a halt.

"The biggest you have ever seen," the professor added with a touch of pride.

Suddenly staring into the darkness, for a split second Lord Carstairs was back in the wild bush of Africa, with the thunderous purring of the huge killer cats coming from every side at once.

"Is this prudent, Professor?" the lord asked nervously, fingering the area on his chest where a bandoleer of shells would be if he was on a safari. "Bengal tigers are notorious mankillers!"

"Oh, they quite happily eat ladies, too," Einstein grinned, "although, that is pure conjecture on my part. Occasionally, I find the gnawed bones of some burglar strewn across the floor when I open shop in the morning. No way in Heaven of ever telling the gender of the would-be thief by then."

"Egad. Whatever do you do?"

"Notify the cleaning staff and don't feed the cats any lunch that day. By Gadfrey, there's nothing lazier than a fat tiger."

"I shall take your word on it, sir," Lord Carstairs demurred, surveying the labyrinthine museum. Loosening his collar, the man started to walk forward once more, this time with renewed vigor. Bengal tigers as house cats? Interesting idea, actually. He wondered if they might like the English countryside.

Reaching the brass door, Prof. Einstein strolled on through, while Lord Carstairs was forced to duck to achieve passage. Fumbling on the wall to his left, Einstein threw a large switch and there was an audible clunk as electric lights in the ceiling crashed into life. Lord Carstairs was braced for anything, but despite the grandeur of the artificial illumination, in contrast to the glitter and polish of the show place they had just left, this room seemed drab and almost utilitarian. It was a plain square brick room with a concrete floor. Several large marble tables were covered with a mishmash of old junk, and dusty objects lined the wall shelves.

However, catching the lord's attention was a massive stone slab, slightly cracked and covered with several lines of deeply carved figures in some kind of a flowery script.

"Fascinating," Lord Carstairs mused, studying the stone with great interest.

"Ah, we're particularly fond of this exhibit. Can you read any of it?" Prof. Einstein asked, with a hint of teasing in his voice.

Sensing a friendly test, Carstairs applied himself with fervor, struggling to dredge up the most obscure languages at his command, until at last the cryptic symbols began to make sense and sentences slowly unraveled. Why, it was a modified form of Hellenic! "Contribute? No, deposit, your money . . . in the Bank of . . . Atlantis! We are . . . as firm . . . as the . . .

ground . . . you stand on. Good Lord!" the explorer cried, rocking back on his heels.

"It was probably true once," Prof. Einstein sighed, sadly running a finger across the proud facade of the bank lentil. "Behold how the mighty have fallen."

"Pity about the crack," Lord Carstairs added after an appropriate moment of silence.

Einstein shrugged. "Yes. Well, nothing's perfect."

Turning about, hoping for more artifacts from the lost continent of Atlantis, the British lord slowly arched an expressive eyebrow as he drank in what else was on display. Over in the corner was a shimmering steel sword thrust into an anvil atop a moss-covered boulder. *No, impossible.* Suspended from the ceiling was the skeleton of a winged human infant still clutching a tiny bow and quiver of pink arrows. In a small alcove was a crimson book positioned under a weighty glass bell jar, its fluttering pages held closed with an iron C-clamp. Beyond that was a five-yard tall copper coin, embossed with the face of a recently assassinated American president and an impossible date. Then came another glass jar holding two fig leaves marked 'His' and 'Hers' in ancient Hebrew. This was followed by a pillar of salt in the shape of a woman sticking her tongue out at somebody. Next was a battered sailor's sea chest, the name **D. JONES** on its lid barely visible beneath a coating of barnacles. There was an iron pot of gold coins that shone with a rainbow effect, and more, and more items, *ad infinitum.*

Soon, Lord Carstairs felt his head began to swim and he was forced to call a halt. Taking the big man by the arm, the professor courteously escorted him towards a second door partially hidden behind a coat of many faded colors.

"Forgive me, Carstairs, but I've had a lifetime to ponder the revelations this room represents," Prof. Einstein said. "To ask anyone to try and comprehend it all in a single viewing was sheer foolishness on my part."

Pushing aside an Oriental screen, Einstein ushered Carstairs into a narrow room pungent with the tangy smell of carbolic acid.

"My workshop," the professor announced, guiding the British lord to sit on what appeared to be some sort of weird porcelain throne.

Strangely, the place felt like home to Carstairs. It was nearly identical to the workroom at his estate. The floor was strewn with excelsior packing, and stacks of wooden crates shipped from around the world stood about waiting to be opened. In the center was a battered table covered with bits of an alabaster urn lying on a white linen cloth, along with a dozen brushes, two notebooks, a magnifying glass mounted on a brass stand, and a glue pot that looked infinitely older than the urn itself. The walls were lined with shelves crammed to bursting with ancient bric-a-brac, rusty lumps of metal, books, and loose papers. Across the workshop was a chemical laboratory occupying a granite-topped bench. To Carstairs' surprise, there was no mysterious bubbling experiment in progress.

Going to a locked cabinet, the professor returned with a pair of laboratory beakers containing an inch of swirling, caramel-colored liquid.

"Napoleon Brandy," Einstein said, handing the lord a glass. Then the professor took a seat in an overstuffed chair. "My own private stock."

"How interesting," Lord Carstairs said, looking at the liquor dubiously. "I was of the opinion that every drop had been lost in The Troubles."

"Not every bottle. I managed to save a few."

After a first hesitant sip, Carstairs nodded in full approval. "Exemplary, sir! Well, sir, after seeing this museum, if you were to tell me that the mythical Realms of Fairy were about to invade Scotland, my only question would be . . . when?"

"Tomorrow at noon," the professor snapped.

Caught in the middle of a swallow, Lord Carstairs gagged at the news and sprayed brandy into the air.

Feeling a bit sheepish, Einstein handed the dripping lord a handkerchief. "Sorry, lad, I couldn't resist. Besides, I need your mind at its sharpest, not befogged with awe. Feeling better?"

"Ah, yes, thank you," the lord murmured demurely.

Securing the bottle of brandy once more, Einstein refilled the lord's beaker to the very brim this time in apology.

Lord Carstairs took a fresh sip and carefully swallowed before speaking. "Now tell me more about this Dutarian god."

"I'll be brief," the professor said in a somber voice, placing aside the bottle. "Sometime around 3000 BC, the priests of the city of Dutar summoned forth a magical protector to aid them in their battles against the local hill people who were constantly stealing their goats. The monster responded as requested, eating the hill folk, and the goats, but then it refused to depart. Indeed, it threatened to consume the people of Dutar unless other food, human food, was provided. Obtaining these, ahem, 'provisions' was the reason behind Dutar's two hundred years of conquest and expansion. The forging of the Empire was a mere side effect."

While Lord Carstairs chewed that over, the professor took a sip from his own beaker. He would need a drink for the next part. "Eventually, the population grew tired of endless battles and tried to destroy the demon. However, even with the entire military might of a warrior empire to draw upon, the fight went badly for them. Their doom seemed certain until the descendants of the very magicians who had summoned the monster in the first place cast a spell that they had been working on for the last two hundred years."

"And?" Carstairs prompted, swirling the brandy in his glass beaker to savor the lush bouquet.

Leaning forward, Einstein spoke rapidly. "And it damn well worked, after a fashion. A volcano erupted directly under the Squid God's temple, shattering it to pieces and destroying the city of Dutar. This marked the end of the Dutarian people as a force to be reckoned with, and the end of the Squid God. Or so it was thought. At the height of the eruption, the Squid God and its temple vanished. The priests were trapped inside and everybody assumed that they had also been killed. But, some ten years later, one of them reappeared. He was quite mad, but coherent enough to reveal that the Squid God was still alive, though horribly burned. Yet even more terrifying was the information that the monster was undergoing a bizarre regeneration, leaving its damaged old body for a fresh new one, supposedly even more powerful than the first. The priest was a bit vague on when this miracle would occur, but he swore that the unmistakable warning sign would be given by a new face on the moon."

The ticking of the clock on the mantle was the only sound as the professor took a long pull of the brandy and emptied the beaker. "It seems to have taken a bit longer than anybody had expected," he said placing it aside. "But to a demon, what's a few thousand years, more or less, eh?"

In wry rumination, Lord Carstairs mulled over the story. "And this is the foundation for your belief that the world is about to be destroyed?"

"In a nutshell, yes."

Still holding his beaker, Lord Carstairs rose and began pacing about the room. "A truly fascinating story, sir. But if apocryphal stories are what you want, then the procreation myths of the Uldon lizard tribes would keep a man happy for years. Surely, there is some material proof to back this theory."

Hesitantly, Einstein stood. *Here we go.* "Only circumstantial evidence, at best, I must admit," he said, going to a shelf containing numerous papyrus scrolls. Choosing a specific scroll, the professor unrolled it with a crackle.

"Read this," Einstein instructed, "third section down."

Placing aside his beaker, the lord peered at the scroll. "A thousand armies of a thousand men each were naught but toys to the dire squid," he read slowly. "Interesting. Hyperbole by a fanatic priest?"

Moving closer, Prof. Einstein pointed to a purple seal at the bottom of the page. "Military report from an enemy general."

Lord Carstairs gave a slow nod. "A good start. Anything else?"

"Yes, but brace yourself, lad." Reaching under a worktable, the professor brought forth a large object wrapped in linen cloth.

Carefully, Prof. Einstein placed it on top of the table and folded back the covering. As the stone tablet was unwrapped, Lord Carstairs went pale and dropped his beaker, the laboratory glass shattering on the floor.

Covering the upper part of the tablet, Prof. Einstein said, "There is an inscription under the, ahem, picture."

Summoning his pluck, the lord forced himself to look once more. "The mighty Squid God at its noon feeding of . . . blind orphans. Souvenir of Dutar City." Carstairs swallowed with difficulty. "Don't miss the b-baby d-d-decapitating festival in the spring."

Slowly, Einstein started to fold back the next cloth to reveal the next section.

"Enough!" Lord Carstairs cried, averting his eyes. "This is an abomination against man and nature!"

"Absolutely," Prof. Einstein agreed, quickly wrapping the tablet again and tucking the artifact away. "And we must do everything within our power to see that such a hideous occurrence is never repeated."

"Yes, yes, we must," Carstairs said with growing resolution, straightening his shoulders. "Sir, I must confess that I am not wholly convinced of this danger. As you said, only circumstantial evidence at best. But to protect the world from *that*!" He gestured at the empty table where the tablet had just been. "I will gladly join you on any expedition, even if it be a fool's quest."

"Thank you," the professor gushed in relief, his voice shaking with emotion. "I can ask for nothing more."

"So what is our first step?" Carstairs asked, reclaiming his throne. "If this creature is as powerful as believed, then even a modern battleship might mean nothing to it."

"Well spoken, lad," Einstein grinned. "But the monster has an Achilles' heel. It has yet to be born!"

"I beg your pardon?" Carstairs asked with a profound frown. "What was that again, please?

"Not born yet," Prof. Einstein repeated slowly. "The Squid God will not be re-born until the new face of the moon looks upon the earth. I estimate that we have slightly more than two weeks in which to find and destroy the temple in which the creature rests."

"Which will spoil the magical spell and prevent the creature from regenerating," Lord Carstairs finished in a rush of excitement. "But that is simplicity itself!" Defiling sacred relics was something British explorers were especially good at doing. "I'm surprised that you asked for assistance on such a trivial matter. So where is the temple anyway? Ceylon? Tibet? The South Pole?"

Under the lord's honest gaze, Prof. Einstein squirmed uncomfortably. "Ah, well, that is the hitch, lad. Because, you see, I have absolutely no idea."

THREE

"But I do know how it can be found," Prof. Einstein said quickly, before any possible denouncements could be voiced.

Lord Carstairs made a temple of his fingers. "Meaning that you have a map, which has a piece missing?" he ventured for a guess.

"Very close, lad," Einstein acknowledged. "The map is a cryptic puzzle, but I possess the key: a copper bracelet in the shape of an engorged squid. On the inner side, there are hidden markings that only become discernible under a solar eclipse, or the artificial light of an electric lamp. I purchased it thirty-six years ago at a flea market in Amsterdam. I had always planned to solve the puzzle, but there always seemed something more important to do."

"Of course, I understand fully," Carstairs agreed. "Merciful Heavens, you should see some of the things I have gathering dust in my workshops." The lord loosened his Oxford school tie. "So let us begin. Have your boy, Owen, fetch us a pot of black coffee, bring out the documents, and let's get cracking."

Walking to the doorway, Einstein and tugged on a bell-pull hanging over his desk. Going to the shelves, he then removed a small wooden box. "The map itself is in the vaults, but the bracelet is here; you'll see why I first purchased it." Lifting the lid, a frown crossed his features. "Odd, this box is empty."

Replacing the box on the shelf, the professor drew another. "This must be it." But, as he opened the container, a large blue beetle attempted to fly out. Frantically, Einstein snapped the lid shut, successfully trapping the insect inside. With an angry gesture, he shoved the box onto the shelf and reached for another. In short order, several other boxes were examined, but the bracelet was in none of them. By now, the professor was visibly annoyed.

Suddenly, Einstein smacked a hand to his forehead. "Of course! That confounded girl must have cleaned again. Lord Carstairs, please follow me."

Unlatching a small door at the rear of the room, Prof. Einstein led the way and the two men walked along a dimly lit corridor. Numerous side passages led off in several directions.

"She?" Lord Carstairs asked. "Your wife, perhaps?"

"My niece," the professor explained. "Mary Einstein. She has been threatening to straighten my workshop for some time and it is my feeling that she's actually gone and done it!"

Placing a hand to his heart, Lord Carstairs appeared properly scandalized. His staff was under strict orders, upon pain of dismissal, never to touch anything in his work area. The only exception was his manservant, Crainpoole, who labored single-handedly to prevent the lord from being buried alive under several growing tons of prehistoric debris.

As the explorers reached a door completely covered in cork, the professor violently shoved it aside and shouted, "You cleaned my workroom!"

Bent low over a filing cabinet, a young woman continued at her work sorting folders. Dressed in a starched red-and-white striped blouse and a long dark skirt, her hair was a magnificent auburn and was gathered into a simple, but elegant coil.

"I have done no such thing, Uncle Felix," she replied, standing straight and rifling the folders cradled in her arms. "Whatever you've lost is probably exactly where you left it, six months ago."

"But you must have, Mary," the professor insisted, entering the office. "You said you were going to do it, and now I can't find a very important document!"

Raising a hand, the woman halted the outpouring. "I suggested straightening that rat's nest you call a workroom exactly once, over seven years ago, when I first came here. Your subsequent hysterics immediately convinced me to never broach the subject again."

Juggling the folders, Mary slid the last one into a drawer and pushed it closed. "Now what was it you were searching for?" she asked, turning around.

Unable to breathe, Lord Carstairs found himself drawn into the most magnificent pair of blue eyes he had ever seen. Mary Einstein was a goddess. Her features were flawless, culminating in a jaw that displayed a strength of character that would have put off a lesser man, but which Carstairs found deliciously refreshing.

Caught unawares, Mary blushed under the frank appraisal. "Forgive me; I didn't know that we had guests, Uncle."

Crossing the room, Prof. Einstein started rummaging in the drawers of the desk, opening and slamming them shut in rapid order. "Guests? What guests . . . oh yes. Mary, this is Lord Benjamin Carstairs. Your lordship, may I present my niece, Mary Elizabeth Victoria Einstein. She's responsible for the actual day-to-day running of the museum."

Feeling as if she was dressed in rags, Mary's eyes widened slightly as she studied the handsome stranger. After a long moment, she gracefully extended a hand.

"Welcome to our home," Mary said in unaccustomed shyness.

Lord Carstairs started to shake a greeting, then changed his mind and gallantly raised her hand to his lips.

"Enchanté," he murmured, holding her hand fractionally longer than convention required.

"Sir," she replied softly, her blush deepening.

From behind the desk, Prof. Einstein gave a rude snort. "Mary, I can't locate that bracelet I was working on this morning."

Nervously checking the lace at her throat, Mary took a moment to organize her thoughts. "Do you mean that hideous copper band that resembled a squid with indigestion? Try the red wooden box."

"I did. It's not there!"

"Oh."

Not exactly sure what to do with his large hands, Lord Carstairs stuffed them into his pockets. "Perhaps your lad, Owen, moved it," he suggested.

Scowling darkly, the professor slammed a drawer shut so hard the table lamp rocked. "Good lord, no! Billy is most conscientious," Einstein stated. "Then again, where the devil is he anyway? I rang for that boy ages ago."

"Come to think of it, so did I," Mary added, biting a thumbnail. "I had forgotten. He was supposed to move that old exhibit down into the basement and must still be working."

"Lazy blighter," the professor muttered. "How long can it take to shift a dozen swords?"

Mary arched a scolding eyebrow. "Knowing the exhibit in question, Uncle," she said, "I think it would depend on whether or not they wanted to go."

In recollection, Einstein's dark face brightened. "Ah, that does explain the matter. Well, it's not that important, I transcribed the symbols from the bracelet when I first purchased the thing. We can just as easily work from that."

"Would you and Lord Carstairs care for some refreshments?" Mary asked, moving towards the door.

"Thank you, my dear," the professor smiled, his stomach rumbling at the mere mention of food. "That would be capital!"

As the woman left the room, Prof. Einstein went to a filing cabinet and opened the top drawer. With brisk efficiency, he went through the folders, paused, then repeated the search slowly. Stepping away, his face was a mask of vexation.

"Strange," Prof. Einstein mumbled half to himself. "I could have sworn the Dutarian map was filed under 'D'."

"Mayhap you have it under 'E' for Empire of Dutar," Lord Carstairs suggested, attempting to be helpful.

Prof. Einstein seemed doubtful, but burrowed into another drawer with the same lack of success.

"Where ever could it be?" the professor demanded, then gave a finger snap. "Of course! 'M' for Maps!" Going to that drawer, his strong hands ruffled the manila folders like a deck of cards.

"No," Prof. Einstein reported sullenly, easing the drawer shut. "It's not there either. Miscellaneous, perhaps?"

"I will check 'S', for Squid God," Carstairs said, joining the search and pulling open the appropriate drawer.

"Good man, I'll try 'G' for God and 'T' for Temple."

"Righto!"

* * *

A few minutes later, Mary returned, wheeling in a serving cart filled with the necessaries of high tea: a steaming hot water pot, six types of tea, milk boat, cups, saucers, spoons, napkins, scones, muffins, biscuits, butter, and an assortment of jams. It was several times the amount of food she usually served, but she assumed that Lord Carstairs must support a Herculean appetite.

"I thought we might as well eat as we work," Mary began gaily, her voice fading away, only to come back strong. "What in the Lord's holy name is going on here?"

With papers fluttering in the air, the usually neat office was a total shambles, manila folders and envelopes strewn everywhere. Einstein and Carstairs were both elbow-deep in the files, haphazardly throwing documents over their shoulders as each proved fruitless.

"Have you tried 'P' for Puzzles?" the professor shouted, his nose buried in a collection of travel brochures.

"Of course," the lord retorted hotly from behind a mass of nautical charts. "Plus, 'U' for Unsolved, 'A' for Amsterdam, 'F' for Flea Market and 'L' for Lost!"

Professionally incensed, Mary walked around the cart with its array of steaming food. "If you are referring to the Dutarian cipher you transcribed off of the bracelet, I filed it under 'D' for Dutar. Is the transcription alone missing or the whole folder?"

"Transcription, folder, and my collection of notes," Einstein snorted in ill temper. "Including my telegrams, correspondence, and calculations on the turning of the bloody moon!"

From behind the sheath of charts, Carstairs jerked his head into view. "Please, Professor, your language! There's a lady present."

"Really, where?" Einstein asked in confusion. "Oh, you mean my niece? Bah, she's heard worse, lad. Been with me on a dozen expeditions to India, Africa, and even New Jersey."

Waving a hand to brush aside the minor concern, Mary smiled benignly. "Your concern is appreciated, Lord Carstairs, but my sensibilities are not that delicate."

"As you say then, Miss," Carstairs acknowledged courteously, returning to his task.

Stepping to the desk, Mary began shifting through the mountains of paper to see if the men had accidentally overlooked the goal of their search. "Uncle, is there any chance that Billy has done something with the transcript?"

"None," the professor cried, slamming a metal drawer shut and almost catching a finger. "He knows it would mean the sack."

"Are you quite sure the folder was here in the office?" Lord Carstairs asked, probing for possibilities. "Do you have any other files? In the library perhaps? Or your reading room?"

"Of course not!" the professor fumed. "That information was far too important for me to leave just lying about like a pair of old shoes. Oddbotkins! You should only know what I went through to get that map!"

"Wait a minute, Uncle," Mary interjected, pausing in the excavation. "What about the vault downstairs in the cellar? That's where you keep the duplicates, isn't it? Might you not have placed everything there for safekeeping?"

"Feasible," Prof. Einstein admitted hesitantly, toying with his lucky shark tooth. "Imminently so. Let's find out. Bring the desk lamp!" Turning on a heel, the professor hurried from the office.

"An actual vault?" Lord Carstairs queried, gathering the heavy oil lamp. "An unusual practice. Do you keep silver plate in the house?"

"A little. Some of our exhibits have to be purchased in hard cash," Mary replied, trying to control her breathing. Odd how warm the room was. "But mainly it's for the daily receipts from the museum. Aside from assisting my uncle on his expeditions, I also run the financial aspect of the museum, which is quite considerable."

"Indeed, miss," Carstairs spoke, very impressed, and he made bold enough to step closer. "Archeologist, secretary, and accountant. You are a woman of many talents."

Tingling at his nearness, Mary Einstein made no effort to step away until a familiar voice from down the hallway called for their attendance.

"We have to go now . . . Benjamin," she dared to add, almost askance at the overt brazenness.

"I am yours to command, milady," he acknowledged *sotto voce.*

Blushing uncontrollably, she blessed him with her eyes.

Proceeding along the hall, the couple encountered an open doorway with painted wooden stairs leading downward. Letting Mary go first, Carstairs held the lantern high to illuminate the way. Beneath the floor beams, the cellar walls were constructed of block stone on the style of old Roman forts.

"How very interesting," Carstairs muttered, momentarily lost in curiosity. The museum was actually an exhibit itself. Then a muffled scream reclaimed his attention.

In a flash, Lord Carstairs vaulted over the railing and landed beside a pale Mary. Surrounded by stacks of crates and barrels, Prof. Einstein was kneeling on the earthen floor examining the sprawled body of a man who lay face down in the dirt. An oddly shaped knife protruded from the dead man's neck and the soil was darkly red. Lord Carstairs set the large oil lantern down next to a small bull's-eye lantern lying on its side in the dirt, the glass flue a spiderweb of cracks. Near the still body was a strongbox, its sides bound with wide iron straps. The lid was ajar, a padlock and thick chain dangling broken and bent.

"Owen?" Lord Carstairs asked softly.

The professor nodded. "Dead, but not for long."

Suddenly, the lord was starkly alert, feeling as if he was back in the deep jungle with savage natives on every side.

"Professor, is there any other way out of this cellar?" Carstairs whispered, glancing around in the darkness.

In a rush of comprehension, Einstein felt cold adrenaline flood his body. Good god, there wasn't! "Mary, my dear," he said in a strained voice trying to sound perfectly normal, "do please go upstairs and call the police."

At those words, there was a curse in the shadows and out rushed a gang of hooded figures brandishing long curved knives, the wicked blades gleaming evilly in the harsh light of the oil lamp.

"Ambush!" Lord Carstairs shouted, stepping in front of his friends and raising both fists.

As the first wave of the attackers came close, the lord grabbed hold of the overhead rafters, lifted himself off the floor, and shot both his feet forward. His hand-cobbled shoes rammed into a pair of hooded faces and blood sprayed from the brutal impact. Gurgling horribly, the two figures dropped limply to the floor. Impossibly, they rose again. Lord Carstairs bitterly cursed as he recognized the reactions from his days in India. The blighters were some form of hashishin; murdering fiends drugged into a wild frenzy that made them nigh on invincible to pain and fatigue. Summoning his resolve, Carstairs grimly waded into the masked figures, his mighty fists punching and jabbing like steam pistons.

Two more of the cloaked killers darted around the imposing lord and charged at the elderly Professor Einstein just as he drew his pistol. The weapon was knocked aside and vanished in the blackness. With a smooth motion, the professor knelt, yanked the blade from the warm body of his manservant, and swung it in a glittering arc to parry a knife slash aimed at his throat. Swiveling his own blade inward to protect his vulnerable wrist, Einstein thrust his arm forward, the razor-sharp edge slicing one attacker across the cheek, the pommel thumping between the eyes of the other. Reeling drunkenly, the masked man rotated once and fell down with a thump.

Squealing as theatrically as possible, Mary dashed across the cellar, hoping that at least one of the mysterious intruders would stupidly follow her. Three of them did, howling for blood. As Mary reached the far wall, instead of collapsing in a faint or cringing in fear, she threw open a closet door and yanked out a broom. With the wooden shaft twirling like a baton, the woman began expertly pounding on the attackers, their bones cracking under each whistling blow of the makeshift quarterstaff. However, her foes seemed impervious to the disabling wounds and steadily advanced, their blades cutting ever closer until snippets of cloth fell from her clothing.

Sidestepping an axe swing, Lord Carstairs rudely smashed the jaw of the assassin with an expert jab. As the tooth-spitting figure stumbled off, Carstairs grabbed the wrist of another cloaked figure, twisted it to the breaking point, and then yanked the screaming fanatic over his shoulder in a Judo throw, the ancient secret art of Japanese wrestling. The body hit the ground with a grisly thump, bounced back onto its feet, and insanely came at the lord again. Wasting no more time with simple maiming tactics, Carstairs slammed his right fist directly into the dimly seen face of his enemy with every ounce of strength he possessed. The attacker flew backwards from the triphammer blow, the dark cloak spreading out like wings, fully revealing the person beneath. In stark horror, the lord saw that his adamantine foe was a woman! Sickened at the thought of striking a female, Lord Carstairs never the less knocked the woman back down again and then pinned her to the floor with a packing crate marked 'Meteorites'. Although trapped, the woman tried to wiggle free.

Startled by the sight, Carstairs almost did not hear the rush of footsteps from behind and barely turned in time to sidekick a cloaked figure charging at him with an 18th-century pike. The attacker went airborne minus most of his teeth, but the lord frowned deeply. It was damned inconsiderate of the professor to store dangerous weapons in the cellar. With a soldier's grace, the lord nimbly dodged another deadly thrust. Then again, it was also a pity that Einstein hadn't thought to store just a few more of them for friends to use!

In the meanwhile, Professor Einstein had dived forward and managed to bury his knife blade into the stomach of one of the cloaked figures. He pulled it out, trying for a deadly lateral rip in the abdominal muscles, but failed, merely slicing open the rib cage. Dancing about, Einstein cursed his clumsiness. He had grown soft sitting on his hindquarters and lazing about in the museum for too long. It had been years since his last real fight. Dodging a knife thrust that would have removed his throat, the professor put his boot into the fellow's groin and proceeded to kick the man mercilessly in the torso, trying to shatter as many bones as possible, while slicing another attacker with a deft backhand slice. *By God, he was weak. Old and weak and feeble. Perhaps he could join a gymnasium.*

With the sound of splintering wood, Mary's broom handle broke over a hooded skull. Temporarily defenseless, she retreated to the wall. As a snarling figure brandished a knife and moved in for the kill, she nimbly dodged out of the way, the blade shattering as it struck the stonewall. Vaulting over a steamer trunk full of her childhood toys, Mary pulled a shovel from the mountainous pile of coal alongside the furnace and whirled the heavy iron implement over her head in the manner of a Viking war hammer. The cloaked figure stumbled over another to avoid the makeshift weapon, and a chance blow from the shovel tore a fist-sized hunk out of a nearby wood support beam.

Shouting something in a foreign language that none of the English scholars could understand, a tall masked figure snatched the desk lamp off the barrel and hurtled it to the floor. Fire erupted from the crash, the pool of burning oil rapidly expanding across the hard packed dirt.

With a roaring whoosh, a pile of Christmas decorations ignited, sending angry tongues of orange flame to lick at the wooden ceiling. Within seconds, thick smoke was everywhere and the masked invaders could be dimly seen struggling to reach the safety of the stairs.

"Come on, lad," Prof. Einstein cried, grabbing the fallen pike. "We've got them on the run!"

"Tally ho!" Lord Carstairs lustily answered, his broad face flush with battle fury.

"Stop! Let them go!" Mary shouted, tossing aside the shovel. "This fire could spread to the museum!"

That horrifying thought galvanized both of the men into instant action. Ripping off their jackets, Einstein and Carstairs started beating at the flames while Mary began shoveling dirt upon the growing inferno.

* * *

Stumbling more than running, the seven cloaked figures burst into the main hall of the museum, the bang of the brass door echoing throughout the corridors and galley. Instantly alert, with a rumbling purr of delight, a trio of Bengal tigers darted out of concealment to flow across the floor of the museum like striped blurs.

Stuffing a broken arm into his belt for support, one of the bleeding invaders saw the jungle cats and calmly pointed. Nodding agreement, another removed his hood and quickly made a complex gesture in the air. As rainbow light washed over the tigers, they froze motionless, then frantically turned around and scampered back into their hidden den whimpering in fear.

"B-bar the door!" a limping man ordered, gasping for breath. "T-that will h-hold them for awhile."

"Block it with what, fool?" another robed man demanded hotly. "You know that everything in this room is bolted into place."

"By the Great Squid, my brother, we'll never get away," a third man panted, holding a stained handkerchief to the bloody ruin of his nose.

Sporting a number of wounds, the leader of the group grunted in reply. "We must and will. Our only chance is to use a portal."

A chorus of delighted gasps greeted this announcement.

"Brilliant," a disheveled woman stated, cradling a broken arm.

"That's why he's the leader," a toothless fourth man mumbled, his left eye already beginning to swell shut.

"But the moon is not full," the second speaker reminded. "The power yet sleeps. A sacrifice will be needed."

Grimacing in pain, a woman nodded in agreement, the simple act making a well of blood ooze from within her ripped cloak. "Kill me, brother," she volunteered, "and make good your escape."

"So be it, sister," the leader spoke, drawing his bent knife. "And the blessings of the Great Squid upon you."

Ripping open the cloak, she exposed a bare throat and the wicked knife slashed forward in a single swift stroke.

* * *

It only took a few minutes for the fire in the cellar to be beaten into submission and, once more, the explorers took up the interrupted chase. Bursting onto the first floor, they found the office deserted, as were the workroom and storage room. That left only the museum.

Grabbing express rifles from a weapons cabinet, the armed explorers charged into the main building of the museum, Lord Carstairs, the professor, and Mary Einstein ready for battle. But they found nothing except a small crimson pool of fresh blood on the floor. Jumbled sets of footprints led from the ghastly puddle for a single yard and then stopped, almost as if the people making the tracks had simply vanished into thin air.

FOUR

The Einsteins and Lord Carstairs spent the next several hours dealing with the inquiries of the local constables who had arrived to investigate the ruckus at the museum. The police had assumed it was merely another burglar meeting his ultimate fate under the claws of the big cats, and were horrified to learn about the death of the professor's assistant.

Draped in a sheet, the body of Billy Owen was removed from the premises by a sleepy police surgeon, everyone present bowing their heads in respect as the still form passed by.

After that, a full search of the museum was made to make sure none of the masked assailants was hidden anywhere, but the building proved clean. It was four in the morning before the last police officer left the establishment. Although thoroughly exhausted, the three explorers knew by wordless agreement that sleep would be impossible for the time being.

After locking the building tight, Felix and Mary led Lord Carstairs out of the museum and along a flagstone path to the living quarters located in the rear of the massive building. Going directly to the kitchen, a weary Prof. Einstein made the tea, while Mary silently produced bread and cheese from the larder and Carstairs dutifully set the table. Once their mugs were filled with steaming brew, they each took a seat and let peace and quiet rule for a while.

Fatigue blurring the sharp edges of his social graces, Lord Carstairs slowly stirred his tea with a soup spoon, the transgression completely unnoticed by the others.

"The police were remarkably perfunctory with their questioning about the body, I thought," the lord remarked at last, feeling the need to say something, anything, to break the thick silence.

"Yes, well, you are a member of the House of Lords," Prof. Einstein replied, adding lemon to his tea. "While I am an honorary member of Scotland Yard."

Stifling a yawn, Mary set her half-empty mug down. "What with all the excitement, it's just sinking in that poor Billy is dead." Her eyes welled up and a tear flowed down her cheek. She dabbed it away with a cloth napkin. "He was a good friend."

Exhaling from the very depths of his soul, Prof. Einstein slumped his shoulder. "Aye, that he was, old girl. But come-come, my dear, don't cry; Billy wouldn't have wanted tears."

"True enough," Mary murmured with a sniffle.

"He was Welsh, you know," the professor said to Carstairs.

"So I understand," the lord replied, pulling an enormous handkerchief out of a pocket and proffering it to Mary.

She accepted it thankfully. "I believe you'd have liked him, Lord Carstairs," Mary whispered, dabbing at her eyes.

Having lost close friends before in The Troubles, Carstairs reached into his coat and produced a silver flask bearing his family crest. "Then talk to me about him," he urged, placing it upon the table. "Tell me all about Billy."

In understanding, the professor uncapped the flask, liberally enhancing his tea with the strong whiskey, and even Mary did the same. After sampling the powerful drinks, they both shuddered, then visibly relaxed.

Loosening his starched collar, Prof. Einstein noisily cleared his throat. "Well, I first met him in Egypt, of all places. He had this crazy theory that the ancient pyramids were not constructed by thousands of slaves hauling vast blocks of stone, but by being poured, out of a substance similar to cement."

"Really?" Lord Carstairs cocked an eyebrow. "I know that the Romans invented cement, but the pyramids were constructed thousands of years before that."

"Quite right," Mary said, between sips. "Anyway, he was determined to try to duplicate their efforts and had this vast collection of bubbling chemical experiments laid out around this desert oasis."

"Indeed?" Carstairs said, taking a sip. "Tell me more."

Now Prof. Einstein leaned forward, a smile of reminiscence tugging at his face. "Well, nobody had bothered to inform my camel drivers about this, so when the fireworks from Athens arrived . . ."

* * *

The dawn began coloring the sky. The three people were still laughing around the kitchen table, immersed in drunken conversation, with Lord Carstairs feebly trying to stop the others so he could catch his breath. However, Einstein and Mary plowed gamely on, each determined to top the other's tall tale about the misadventures of William Owen.

". . . so when poor Billy tries reading the forbidden book, out of the clear blue sky comes a bolt of lightning that strikes the two of them down!" the professor said in a dramatic voice. "Naturally, the Mandarin was killed instantly, but Billy survived because he was still wearing the conquistador helmet!"

Sloshing his tea-flavored whiskey onto the table, Lord Carstairs guffawed and almost fell off his chair. "W-was the p-poor lad hurt any?" he finally managed to gasp.

"Not a bit," Mary denied wobbling in her chair, making the empty hip flask fall over sideways onto the table with a clatter. "Oh, metal filings had a habit of sticking to him for a week or so, but there was no permanent damage."

"Welsh, you know!" they all finished in unison.

This time the laughter was gentle, and slowly wound down to another prolonged silence. There was only the gentle crackle of the fire in the hearth, from somewhere outside a horse gave a whinny, and then a dog barked.

With a sigh, the professor used a napkin to wipe tears of laughter from his eyes. "William Henry Owen was a good worker and a fine friend," he said softly. "And I, for one, shall miss him greatly."

Both Mary and Lord Carstairs murmured in agreement and raised their mugs high. The professor joined them in the gesture.

"To Billy," they toasted, draining what little remained in the cups. Then the trio all cast their mugs into the fireplace, the ceramic containers shattering like broken dreams.

In the powerful stillness that followed, Prof. Einstein mopped the sodden table with the napkin and clumsily stuffed the damp cloth into a pocket. "I think a few hours of sleep are what we need now. Please stay, Benjamin. We have a splendid guest room, and we can send a carriage for your things at the Club."

Unable to stop himself, the lord gave a bone-cracking yawn. "Thank you, sir," Carstairs mumbled wearily. "I think that is wise. The tea, you know. Very strong stuff."

"Quite, so, lad! Quite so."

Utterly embarrassed, Mary tugged on the sleeve of her uncle's coat. "He can't stay there," she whispered, "the guest room hasn't been aired out for weeks!"

"Piffle," Carstairs said with a slurred chuckle. "In my current state, unless the bed is actually on fire, it will not interfere with my sleep in the slightest."

"As you say, Benjamin," she murmured, feeling very small and girlish for no discernable reason. "Then may I wish you a good night."

Tender words rose in Lord Carstairs' throat. Glancing at the professor, he choked them off and merely reiterated the sentiment. Rising stiffly, Prof. Einstein showed the lord to the guest room, while Mary stumbled down the corridor to her own room. Sleep came on swift wings to the emotionally exhausted people, and the gods were kind, as their slumber was without dreams of any sort.

* * *

In the morning, Lord Carstairs woke feeling a hundred per cent better. The bed had been excellent and a few minutes of exercise got his blood pumping and cleared the cobwebs from his mind. The accommodations had proved to be more than adequate. Oh, his boots had not been polished, nor was there a fresh *Times* waiting for him, but the sure knowledge that Mary was beneath the same roof dispelled such minor considerations.

However, his mouth was filled with the taste of a dead vole. What dementia had compelled him to poison perfectly good Irish whiskey with English breakfast tea? Bleh.

Thankfully, there was a basin of lukewarm water waiting for him on the dresser, along with one of his travel bags from the club. Excellent! After getting clean, the lord rushed downstairs with joyful thoughts of seeing Mary once more filling his mind. Entering the steamy kitchen, Carstairs found a plump woman cheerfully kneading a pile of bread dough.

"Good morning, your lordship!" the cook sang out. "Breakfast is waiting for you in the dining room. You just sit down and I'll bring in a nice cuppa tea."

"Ah, thank you, miss . . . ah . . ." he faltered, and spread his arms in sublimation.

"Katrina, sir," she supplied, slapping the dough into a pan.

Lord Carstairs smiled. "Thank you, Katrina. Any chance of some coffee instead?"

Respectfully, she curtsied in return. "Of course, your lordship," Katrina replied, placing the dough aside to rise. Then she began to bustle noisily about in the pantry.

Hearing voices on the other side of a set of sliding doors, Lord Carstairs pushed them aside to find the dining room. Bending over a long table, the professor and Mary were conferring about a pile of papers that appeared to be train and steamship timetables.

"Good morning, lad!" Prof. Einstein called robustly, looking upward. "How do you feel?"

Following a tantalizing smell, Carstairs went over to the sideboard and removed a steaming cover to reveal a plate of kippers. "Fit as a fiddle, sir," he said, taking a double portion, then made it triple. Lifting the lid on another platter, the lord discovered cold eggs and damp toast. Ah, just like Mother's cook used to make! How homey.

With his breakfast plate properly loaded, Lord Carstairs took a seat at the table across from the uncle and niece.

"And good morning to you, Miss Einstein," the lord smiled, tucking a napkin into place. "I trust you slept well?"

"Considering the circumstances, yes," Mary smiled sweetly. "Thank you."

Searching for a fingerbowl, Carstairs saw none about, and decided simply to do without. The explorer had plenty of experience roughing it in the wild. "And what are our plans for today, Professor?" he asked, digging into the mound of food.

"We'll be on the road within the hour, lad," the professor said from behind a steam line timetable. "So eat up."

His heavily laden fork pausing in midair, Lord Carstairs swallowed a mouthful before replying. "Excellent!"

At that moment, Katrina came in with a clean cup and a fresh pot of steaming coffee. The rich aroma was heavenly, and all three of the explorers filled their mugs.

"Will you be gone long, Professor?" she asked, gathering a few of the dirty plates off the table. "If so, the staff could get the spring cleaning started a little early this year."

Already back studying the timetable, Prof. Einstein glanced sideways. "What? Oh, yes, several weeks probably."

"Where will you be going this time, sir?" Katrina asked curiously, closing the lid on the sugar bowl to keep out the flies.

Lowering the steam line chart, Prof. Einstein gave her a long, hard, cold stare.

Completely unaffected by the show, Katrina snorted in amusement. "Ah, more secrets," she chuckled. With a flounce, the cook left the room, closing the sliding doors with a slam of her rounded hip.

"And where will we be going, sir?" Lord Carstairs asked, liberally buttering a piece of toast. By then, he had already consumed half of the farmer's crock on the table; his father had always said that food was sleep. "Without the map and bracelet, I thought we were stone up a tree."

"Utter nonsense, lad," Prof. Einstein denied, stuffing some papers inside his coat pockets. "Initially, we go to France; and no, my dear, as to your earlier question, I don't believe it would be wise for us to take the London ferry. We must avoid the obvious. These Squid God chaps know far too much about us already, attacking us right here in the museum."

"Circumspection is the key," Carstairs munched around a mouthful of food.

"Quite right, lad," Prof. Einstein agreed, circling times on a schedule with a pencil stub. "We'll take the 10:30 Southern railroad to South Hampton and leave on the noon ferry."

Trying to appear casual, Lord Carstairs digested this information as he savaged a perfectly prepared kipper. With a touch more tact than was natural, he asked, "And will Mary be accompanying us on this trip?"

"I'm afraid not," she answered, wiping her mouth on a napkin. "Somebody must stay here to guard the museum. We can't be sure those brigands got everything they wanted, and I know the museum better than anyone does. Isn't that correct, Uncle?"

Folding a map, Prof. Einstein nodded. "Definitely. Somehow they managed to get past the cats and that alone worries me enough that it seems prudent for one of us to stay behind. Sort of a rearguard."

"But sir!" Lord Carstairs cried aghast, dropping his fork. "A woman, alone and unprotected?"

From under the table, Mary coolly hoisted a .32 Adams pocket pistol into view. The long barrel of the oiled weapon glistened in the morning sunlight. "Alone, but not defenseless," she growled dangerously.

"And a crack shot, too," Prof. Einstein added proudly, stuffing more papers into various pockets. "Much better than me, in point of fact."

Strangely excited, Lord Carstairs stared boldly at the armed woman. "Then I shall eagerly look forward to the day of our return."

Holstering the weapon, Mary paused before brazenly returning his look with all of her heart. "And I, sir, shall fervently pray that day shall quickly come."

Feeling nauseated, it took everything Felix Einstein had not to retch at this romantic exchange. *Oh dear Lord, please save me from the anguish of young love.*

* * *

In short order the men were fed, washed, dressed, armed, and bundled into a waiting brougham carriage. Lord Carstairs half-expected Davis at the reins once more. But it was a new man, a skinny fellow with a droopy moustache, and bald as a poached egg. As the explorers climbed into the cab, the driver merely touched his cap at the passengers with no particular display of camaraderie. Interesting.

As the cab rattled off round a corner, Mary Einstein stood on the cobblestone street and watched as it vanished into the heavy London traffic. She stayed that way for several minutes, then returned to the museum. Carefully, she closed and locked the gate of the iron fence, then hung a small hand-lettered sign from an iron picket, before going inside and closing the front door.

Whistling tunelessly, a strolling chimneysweep chanced to glance at the sign and stopped in his tracks. '*Closed for the duration?' That was the kind of sign you'd expect to see during a war. How very strange.*

* * *

Crowds of noisy people pushed and shoved across the busy train station, toffs and guttersnipes mixing freely, while shouting vendors sold meat pies, and mudlarks dove into the gutters squealing in delight when they found a dropped coin.

"What did you just say?" Professor Einstein roared again, dropping his portmanteau onto the floor with a loud thump.

"All sold out," the ticket agent repeated from behind the grating of the cashier window. "You'll have to take the next train at 4:40."

"B-but that's too late," the professor stammered, almost flustered. "We'll miss our connection to the channel ferry!"

"Not my problem, mate," the man calmly replied, then looked past the two explorers. "Next, please!"

Blocking the rest of the people in line with his sheer bulk, Lord

Carstairs loomed over the ticket agent. "See here, sir, I am a member of the House of Lords, surely something can be done."

"Sorry, governor," the clerk said with a shrug. "But there's nothing to be done if you were the Queen herself. All-sold-out means, all-sold-out."

Having dealt with the lower classes before, Carstairs blithely retrieved a wallet from inside his jacket and fanned a few dozen five-pound notes in the air. "Speaking of Her Highness, you don't collect pictures of the royal family do you? I posess a few dozen spares that I could let you have."

Staring at half-a-year's wages, the agent wiped a bit of drool from his chin. "Cor blimey, for a gentlemen like yourself I surely wish I could," he gushed. "But the honest answer is still no. Booked solid, she is, with a contingent of Royal Army Engineers."

Prof. Einstein jerked up his head at that. "But of course," he cried in delight. "Come along, lad. We're leaving."

Hauling away the confused Lord Carstairs, the professor stepped outside on the crowded platform and headed for the front of the long train. All of the windows in every carriage were filled with grim people shouting at each other. Lord Carstairs started to ask a question, but his words were drowned out by the volcanic hissing of the steam engine mixing with the loud talking from the passengers, and the summoning call of the conductor.

"Don't worry, lad, I'll get us on," the professor stated confidently, as the deafening rush of steam faded away. "Let's go talk with the engineer."

"But what good will that do?" Lord Carstairs asked, puzzled. "The engineer has no control over passenger allocation."

Radiating mystery, Einstein gave a contemptuous smirk. "Just wait and see."

Inside the open control booth of the massive steam locomotive, the engineer and his assistant were busily checking over the hissing gauges and ticking meters, while the muscular stoker was steadily shoveling coal from the black mountain of anthracite in the rear carriage and transferring the fuel into the open door of the blazing firebox under the huffing engine.

After waiting a polite interval for their attention, Prof. Einstein gave a diplomatic cough, and then loudly rapped the silver lion head of his cane on the iron plate floor.

"Yeah? An' what the Hell do you want?" the grizzled engineer snapped, mopping sweat from his brow with a dirty bandanna.

The assistant engineer glowered at Einstein and Carstairs in open hostility, while the stoker ignored them completely, concentrating on his endless task.

"Hello. I just wanted to inform you, sir," the professor said in an astonishingly friendly manner, "that my friend and I have a most important boat to catch at South Hampton and needed to take this train."

Further down the platform, an oiler proceeded along the length of the train, touching up the wheels with his long-necked can of lubricant. Right behind came the conductor who closed the carriage doors as a final preparation to leaving.

"And what's that to me, ya toff?" the engineer growled rudely, pulling a lever to balance the mounting pressure in the pistons. White steam hissed from jointed pipes on the iron chamber, the leakage filling the cabin with hellishly hot clouds.

"Well," Prof. Einstein said, rubbing his hands together in an odd manner as if they were numb. "I was just wondering . . ." His right hand held his left elbow while the professor dusted off his lapels. "If there was anything . . ." He smoothed his hair and fixed an invisible string tie. ". . . you might be able to do for us, as we are lost travelers from a distant land."

Halfway through this rigmarole, the engineer and his assistant began smiling. By the end, they were practically beaming with pleasure.

"Why, of course! No problem!" the engineer cried in delight. "You can either ride in the caboose with the staff, or stay up here with us. The wind'll be a bit nippy, but I've got a bottle we can share to stave off the cold."

"That would be fine, thank you," the professor said with a grin. Stepping in close to block Carstairs' view, Einstein shook hands with the fellow for some thirty seconds.

"Grab our bags, lad," Prof. Einstein instructed, hoisting a foot upon the metal step that lead to the cabin. "It is not first class, but I think you will find the company infinitely more entertaining."

"So what are you all, Freemasons?" Lord Carstairs whispered, passing up a brown leather Gladstone. He vaguely remembered reading an article in the *Gazette* that seemed to imply that most engineers, architects, and scientists belonged to the secret society.

Accepting the toiletry bag, Einstein appeared to be shocked. "Lord Carstairs, surely you are aware that The Society of Freemasons has been declared illegal by the British government and that membership in the illicit order is punishable by jail?"

The engineer and his assistant vigorously nodded in agreement.

"Why, so it has, Professor," Carstairs replied, struggling to maintain a neutral expression. "My mistake, sorry."

Then on the sly, Prof. Einstein gave the man a knowing wink. Hiding a smile, Lord Carstairs began relaying their numerous bags and portmanteaus onto the cabin, barely finishing in time to hear the conductor yell his ancient summoning.

"Next stop, South Hampton!" the professor cried in victory.

* * *

The large stone room was cold, lit only by the harsh light of a single oil lantern suspended from a greasy ceiling beam. Kneeling on the ground, a swaying crowd of robed figures maintained a low chant as they watched the thin man at the head of the room. Their leader was dressed in an ornate red robe and wearing an elaborate crown that he constantly shifted about while he studied a very modern map of central Europe.

"Yes," the High Priest hissed between clenched teeth, a bony finger tracing a crooked path along the brilliantly colored surface of the paper. "This is lovely. Lovely! I couldn't have asked for a better place to stage a death trap."

At those words, the crowd stopped chanting.

"Speak, and we shall heed thy words, oh beloved priest," a hooded woman voiced, and the rest of the throng chorused a willing assent.

"Then listen well, my brethren," the priest instructed. "Listen, and obey in the name of the Squid God."

Ceasing their pendulous swaying, the crowd paid close attention to their master.

"Using a portal, the first team will be waiting for the Orient Express to stop at Milan, and will board the Italian Central train in disguise with the rest of the passengers traveling to Rome," the priest intoned sternly. "They are to do nothing until just after the train passes the town of Codogo; then they are to attack, killing everybody on board."

"Everybody?" a man asked, puzzled. "Even the women and children?"

"Our enemies might be traveling in disguise," the priest said judiciously. "Leaving no survivors assures our success."

Mutterings vows of obedience, the people bobbed their heads in unison. *Ah, wise was the High Priest of the Squid God.*

"Meanwhile," the priest continued, adjusting his crown, "a second group will be waiting to explode a dynamite bomb at the Apennines Bridge." His finger stabbed at the map. "The blast will destroy the support columns while the Central Express is passing by overhead, tumbling the train, and any surviving passengers, four hundred yards into the icy waters of the Po River."

"But, Holy One," interrupted a fellow with a great swatch of bandage across his nose, "shouldn't we attack immediately and, if they fail, send in another group, and then another after that?"

"We will drown the defilers in our blood!" an undulating zealot shouted.

Patiently, the High Priest smiled at his minions. Ah, they were such children in the wicked ways of the world. "An admirable plan," he said. "But, no. If we should fail, our quarry might leave the train and travel by some unknown route, seriously hindering our efforts to kill them. No. Our greatest strength at that moment lies in their illusion of safety. Besides, a long wait will lull them into a false sense of security and thus, when we attack, they will be taken completely by surprise!"

Approving murmurs rose from the Squid God worshipers at this clever strategy.

"There is no way that they can escape," the High Priest smirked, raking a skeletal hand across the map of Italy. "From the moment they board the Italian Central, Professor Einstein and Lord Carstairs are dead men!"

FIVE

The train ride down to Southampton was uneventful for Prof. Einstein and Lord Carstairs, aside from a minor disturbance involving a prostitute, a rabbi, a Texan, and a Chinaman with a blind parrot. In the subsequent pandemonium, Einstein and Carstairs managed to make their ferry with only seconds to spare.

However, the channel proved to be unusually choppy, and the French schooner they rode constantly bucked and pitched with each crashing wave. Many of the passengers clinging to a rail, or with their faces in a bucket, voiced loud complaints on this subject. Alternately, they blamed it on arctic winds, sub-sea currents, the Parisian captain of the ship, and/or the British Parliament.

The sailors operating the sailing ship felt that the rough sailing conditions had something to do with the revolving of the moon. The lunar orb was said to cause the tides, so if it was behaving strangely, why shouldn't the sea as well? Other passengers chimed in with growing reports of freakish atmospheric phenomena across the globe. Throughout the varied conversations and diatribes, Einstein and Carstairs kept steadfastly mum.

When the steamer docked at Le Havre, Professor Einstein's first name basis with the local officials of the seaport hastened their passage through Customs. But it was the imposing appearance of Lord Carstairs that earned them a cab at the height of rush hour in the bustling city. Le Havre was a madhouse with traffic everywhere, almost as bad as South Hampton during rush hour.

The details of their travel plan were finalized by the two explorers on the three-hour journey to Paris, the City of Lights. Upon reaching the Parisian train station, Einstein and Carstairs openly purchased tickets on a train scheduled to leave for Morocco early the next morning. They then left the station, donned disguises of heavy beards, and returned to obtain tickets on the fabled Orient Express, destination Istanbul. Then they covertly sent most of their luggage on board under assumed names.

Next, as surreptitiously as possible, Einstein and Carstairs retired to the Men's Room of the train station and, several minutes later, a burly stevedore and a Dominican priest exited. Separating in the crowd of other passengers, they bought second-class tickets for the Simplon Express, which was leaving in ten minutes for Milan. The two men maintained a discreet distance from each other until boarding, and took their assigned seats, each carrying but a single piece of baggage. Prof. Einstein and Lord Carstairs casually sat across from each other and pretended to read an incredibly French newspaper until the train slowly pulled out and left the station behind.

As the hours and the miles rolled by, nothing worse than boredom occurred to the men on their trek through the lush vineyards of the French countryside, then the soaring mountains of Switzerland. Yet it wasn't until they were deep into the Italian hills that the two explorers finally allowed themselves to relax, secure in the knowledge that they had completely foiled any attempt the Squid God worshipers might make at following them.

Switching trains at Milan, Einstein and Carstairs decided it was safe to drop their theatrical pretensions and purchased proper first-class tickets on the Italian Central, an inland service that would take them directly to Rome, almost to the very doorstep of their ultimate destination.

Feeling more resolute wearing their own clothes, Einstein and Carstairs reclined in the plush velvet seats of a private compartment and lit fresh cigars. Almost immediately, a porter came to take their lunch request. Literally starving after being forced to subsist on French cooking, the famished explorers ordered with true working class gusto from the extensive menu. The Italian Central was justly famous for both the speed of its powerful 408-cycle steam engines, and for the fact that the plump staff served six meals a day, plus late night snacks. After the porter had gone, the explorers locked the door and returned to their cigars.

"I dare to say that we should be safe from any further interference by those damn Squid chaps," Prof. Einstein puffed contentedly. "Your idea of booking passage on several trains was splendid. Simply splendid."

Before answering, Lord Carstairs let streams of pale blue smoke trickle from his nose, savoring the long-denied treat. *Ah, delicious!*

"Old hunters trick," the lord said humbly. "Learned it from my father, Sir Randolph Carstairs III, when I was just a lad. But those delightful costumes were what made the whole plan workable. Where ever did you get them?"

"Actually, the stage clothing was supplied by my niece, Mary," Einstein admitted sheepishly. "She thought we might need to travel in a clandestine manner, as it were. Clever lass."

"Really?"

"In point of fact, she is a member of the Actors Guild."

"No!"

"God's truth."

The British lord puffed away in silent contemplation. His future wife was an actor? The ladies on the London Social Register would be absolutely scandalized! Of course, that was a big point in its favor.

"The scamp," Carstairs admonished, secretly amused by the notion of the woman's boldness.

"Runs in the family, I dare say," the professor noted, with a fleeting suspicion that something important had just happened, but he wasn't exactly sure what it was.

Refusing a second cigar from Lord Carstairs' seemingly endless supply, Prof. Einstein produced an oiled cloth from his valise. Twisting the silver lion head on his ebony cane, the professor withdrew a long steel blade and energetically began to polish it. When the Italian border guards accidentally discovered the blade, the deadly weapon had caused a great disturbance, until the explorers discovered that the stout fellows collected pictures of the British Royal Family, at which point the sword was returned with gushing apologies.

A knock at the door made the British explorers freeze. But then the familiar voice of the porter requested admission with their meal. Already? Excellent! With a flourish, Einstein ceased his absolutions and deftly returned the silvered steel to its ebony sheath. Once the blade was out of sight, Lord Carstairs opened the door and stepped aside so that the porter could roll in a serving cart. The white linen top was dotted with a collection of silvered domes from which wafted the most delicious and tantalizing aromas.

"Ah, real food at last," Prof. Einstein sighed, uncovering a dish and breathing in a lungful of the fragrant steam. Double portions of Beef Wellington, with the crust golden brown to perfection. What obstacles could not be surmounted with a healthy serving of that staunch repast in a man's stomach? The asparagus in Hollandaise sauce, potatoes *au gratin*, and brandy pudding, while eminently edible, were deemed secondary at best in comparison.

Pulling some loose bills from his vest pocket, Lord Carstairs generously tipped the porter, who departed gushing his thanks and love for the British. After securely locking the door, Carstairs used a pocketknife to cut the red wax seal on a bottle of wine, popped the cork, and filled the glasses.

"What is it?" Prof. Einstein asked, lifting the pear-shaped bottle. "Chianti? Never heard of the stuff."

"No?"

"I'm more of a coffee drinker."

"Ah. Well, this is a locally grown vintage, a dry red wine possessing a remarkably robust bouquet."

"Pours well," the professor admitted, twirling his glass to watch the crimson fluid cling to the sides.

Lord Carstairs beamed in pleasure. "Chianti is wonderful stuff. It would make quite a hit once a decent supply reached England."

Taking a judicious sip, the professor's face lit up with pleasure. Bloody Hell, that was good! "Any chance of smuggling some home?" he asked hopefully.

"Professor! I'm shocked," Lord Carstairs replied haughtily, then smiled. "And ten cases are waiting for us back in Milan marked as 'industrial boot polish'."

"Good show, lad!"

Sitting down to the enormous meal, the starving men got busy and, for the next thirty minutes, the compartment was filled only with the sounds of silverware on china, along with the comforting, monotonous, rhythm of the train wheels from underneath the wooden floor. In short order, the main course was demolished and Einstein and Carstairs were making headway into the pudding, when a muffled scream of terror was heard from down the corridor. The cry was closely followed by the crackle of small caliber gunfire.

"Bandits?" Prof. Einstein asked, laying down his spoon.

"We can't take that chance," Lord Carstairs stated grimly, dashing his napkin to the floor and pushing the table aside.

Stepping out of their compartment, the two men listened to gauge the direction of the earlier cries. As another faint scream sounded, the men burst into action, sprinting down the narrow corridor towards the rear of the train.

The passenger car behind theirs proved filled with frightened people, but nothing else. Placing decorum aside for the moment, Einstein and Carstairs rudely shoved their way through the nervous crowd, ignoring the endless multi-lingual requests for information on what was happening.

Easing open the exterior door, the two explorers were buffeted by the rushing wind as they carefully stepped over to the next carriage and threw open the door. Inside was a scene of horror. A group of hooded figures was still in the act of plunging knives into the screaming passengers, a score of bodies already sprawled lifeless on the bloody floorboards. Turning at the sound of the door, a hooded man balked, then howled an unintelligible cry at the sight of the two British explorers.

"It's them!" another killer added in colloquial English. "Praise be the Great One!"

The Squid God worshiper pushed aside a dead woman and raised a deadly LeMat pistol. Moving fast, Lord Carstairs grabbed a nearby fire bucket of sand from a niche in the wall and hurled it at the killer with all of his prodigious strength. The impromptu missile was still flying across the carriage when Prof. Einstein whipped out his Adams pocket pistol and fired.

The impact of the bullet knocked the gunman aside, and the heavy bucket sailed by to smash into two of the robed murderers, sending both of them crashing through the rear door in a hail of splinters. The buffeting wind carried away their very brief screams as the Squid God worshipers tumbled to the tracks and had an unpleasant confrontation with the wheels below.

Only grazed on the shoulder, the first robed man tried to stand, then made a horrid gurgling noise and crumpled into a heap to the dirty floor, quite obviously dead.

Utterly bewildered, Carstairs could only stare at the professor as the few remaining passengers scurried past them towards the safety of the next carriage.

"Poisoned bullets," Prof. Einstein explained, brandishing the Adam's .32 pocket revolver. "Rubbed with the venom of the Golden Arrow Frog from South America, the most deadly poison known to modern science."

Just then, a robed assassin armed with a hatchet dashed in through the smashed doorway at the far end of the coach. Without hesitation, Lord Carstairs brushed aside his tweed jacket to draw a massive revolver and pull the trigger. The deafening boom of the weapon nearly burst the professor's eardrums and, minus a head, the Squid God worshiper collapsed into a vacant seat, instantly rendered no more dangerous than his deceased predecessors.

"Webley .455 British Army revolver," Carstairs reported, waving the barrel of the military pistol to disperse the smoke pouring from its gaping maw. "Poison would be superfluous."

"Most definitely, lad," the professor agreed in clinical admiration.

Over the cold wind, a cry of pain sounded from the caboose, and the explorers surged forward. Hopping from one rattling car to the next, they kicked open the door to the caboose with their weapons drawn and ready. But the caboose was a slaughterhouse; the dismembered bodies of the relief engineer, cooks, and porters lay neatly arranged to create some form of ghastly pentagram on the bloody floor. Nobody was alive in that nauseating hell, aside from the twenty hooded figures that now gleefully advanced while howling their indecipherable cry.

Firing their pistols in unison, Einstein and Carstairs retreated to the passenger car. While Lord Carstairs held off the Squid God worshipers with his booming Webley, the professor lay down to release the locking mechanism that held the two railroad carriages together.

Suddenly, the caboose began to fall behind the rest of the train. One Squid God worshiper tried to dive across the widening gap and failed completely with grisly results. But then several more of the robed lunatics appeared with crossbows and started shooting. The first quarrels went wild, but the next slammed into the woodwork directly alongside the two explorers.

Assuming a firing stance, Prof. Einstein emptied his revolver at the retreating enemies while Lord Carstairs quickly reloaded. Every man the professor hit, no matter how small or trifling the wound, twitched once and dropped stone dead.

Then Carstairs took over and the booming Webley sent the robed fiends running for cover as this was a danger they could understand.

"Bloody cowards," the lord snorted, standing in plain sight. But by now, the caboose was beyond the range of the crossbow arrows, and the huge explorer turned a contemptuous back on the murdering dogs. Then he went stiff in shock.

"Professor, behind you!" Carstairs cried, as a hooded figure leapt out of the Water Closet behind his friend.

With the old man directly in the way, the lord could not risk a shot, but Einstein ducked and both men fired their weapons together. The Squid God worshiper hit the floor a yard from his shoes, his toes already curling into death.

"That was dirty pool, eh what?" Lord Carstairs grumbled in disdain.

"Quite true, lad. But I find all of this much too easy," Prof. Einstein observed, removing the lone spent shell from his gun. "I really expected better."

"Agreed," Lord Carstairs said, cracking the heavy cylinder of the Webley to reload again. The empty brass fell to the floor with musical tinkling sounds. "Perhaps we killed off the leader in the last attack."

"Doubtful, lad," Einstein said, taking a glassine envelope from his coat pocket. Inside was a single .32 bullet, the lead tip streaked with an oily yellow substance.

"How do you milk the frogs for the venom?" Lord Carstairs asked curiously, thumbing in fresh .455 rounds.

"Tickle them with a warm goose feather right behind the–"

A crashing shower of glass interrupted the dissertation, and a screaming hooded figure flew in through the window to their left. Dropping his pistol, Carstairs grabbed the assassin in midair and added his strength to the woman's momentum. As graceful as a trapeze artist, the surprised killer continued to fly across the passenger car, smashed through the window to the right, and disappeared into the rushing forest.

"Well done, lad," the professor complimented, closing the cylinder on his revolver with a neat click.

"Thank you," Lord Carstairs replied, retrieving his own pistol. Then he scowled. "Sir, I've just had a rather nasty thought. Might this clumsy attempt be a diversion to keep us busy while the real attack happens in another location?"

"Of course! The Po River Bridge!" Einstein exclaimed, smacking himself in the forehead. "Quick, lad, to the engine!"

At top speed, the pair of men raced back to the middle carriage, pausing only for second at their compartment for Lord Carstairs to grab his travel bag.

Reaching the lead car, Einstein and Carstairs impetuously shoved a hysterical conductor into a closet to get him out of the way, and then stepped outside the lead carriage onto the small platform. There were no more carriages to use. Directly ahead of them was the riveted steel aft-end of the coal car.

Gauging the top as too high to reach with a jump, the men separated and each stepped around the corner of the coal car to place a shoe onto a slim catwalk running along the exposed side of the fuel carriage. Holding onto a smooth iron railing, they swung around and started slowly edging forward. The footing was treacherous, but this was the only access route to the engine. The wind whipped their clothing about painfully as the men inched along; the rushing ground below their feet was only a blur that they desperately tried not to think about, having already seen the grisly results of somebody falling off the train.

Inches of distance slowly became feet, then yards, and finally they reached the end of the catwalk. Pausing to draw their weapons, the explorers swung around the corners and stepped into the engine cabin ready for anything! The startled engineer and shoveler both cried out at the sight of the armed British men. But the Italians proved to be alone and unharmed.

While Prof. Einstein conversed with the quaking men in idiomatic Italian, Lord Carstairs leaned out the open side of the cabin to check ahead of the train. He still had the feeling that there was more to come in this attack.

Squinting against the blurring effect of the onrushing wind, the lord could just barely see the rapidly approaching Apennines crossing and the wooden trestle of the Po River Bridge. He started to relax, but then noticed something on the side of the bridge trestle about midspan. Oh hell.

"Professor!" Lord Carstairs cried over his shoulder, pointing ahead of the train. "See there! Midway on the superstructure!"

Rushing to join his friend, Einstein raised a hand to soften the pressure of the wind, then cursed in four languages as he spotted several robe-clad figures crawling along one of the main support columns.

"Planting bomb!" Prof. Einstein shouted over the screaming wind. "Must stop train!"

His hair whipping madly about, Lord Carstairs shook his head. "Too fast! No time!"

"What do we do?"

"Follow!"

Stepping out of the rushing air stream, the lord tore apart the lid of his travel bag and withdrew a heavy wooden stock. Deft as a palace surgeon, Carstairs expertly began to attach a long steel barrel to the stock, then slid in a single-action bolt. In stunned surprise, Prof. Einstein watched as his friend nimbly assembled a Holland & Holland .75 Nitro Express elephant rifle in mere seconds.

"But you'll never make it, lad!" the professor cried. "The train is rocking and the wind shear is impossible to calculate!"

With steadfast resolve, Lord Carstairs slid in an eight-inch long cartridge and worked the bolt. Without comment, the British lord leaned out the window, squinted, aimed, and pulled the trigger. There was a thunderous report from the weapon that momentarily overpowered the strident wind, but nothing else seemed to happen.

* * *

"Okay, pass me the . . . ugh!" cried the Squid God worshiper as his chest exploded, and he flew off the support column like a puppet yanked by invisible strings.

"By The Great Squid!" the tall hooded man gasped, as the body of his comrade disappeared into the misty abyss of the river chasm. A moment later, artificial thunder boomed across the yawning abyss.

Hurriedly, the short man glanced at the approaching train, which, instead of slowing for the crossing as per regulations, seemed to be increasing its speed. "Light the fuse!" he ordered frantically.

With a grim nod, the tall man struck a match and instantly sprayed blood from both sides of his chest. A second later, another rumbling boom arrived as the screaming man dropped into the depths below.

In raw desperation, the last Squid God worshiper strapped the dynamite bomb to his stomach and struck a match. As the wind blew out the flame, there was a loud crack and an overhead strut exploded into splinters, followed by another roll of thunder. Praying for divine assistance, the Squid God worshiper tried again. The second match flared, and died, as another beam in front of him disintegrated.

"Protect me, Mighty One!" he beseeched, and emptying the entire box of matches into a hand, scratched every one simultaneously across the striker. The bundle flared like a miniature volcano, the flames bent to the wind, but did not go out. *Yes*! Touching the crackling fire to the fuse, the man whimpered in ecstasy as the gunpowder string hissed into life.

Success! In triumph, the Squid God worshiper clenched a raised fist at the rapidly approaching train just as one more wooden strut behind him cracked, closely followed by the expected rumbling explosion.

Not a very good shot, the killer thought smugly. *Those first two hits must have been pure luck.*

Then he abruptly changed his mind as the disconnected section of the trestle began to bend away from the bridge. The assassin could only hang on to the wooden lattice as it snapped free completely and began to plummet. His last thoughts were not very complimentary to either his dark master or to the now-proven accuracy of the unseen rifleman.

* * *

Still accelerating, the train was in the middle of the weakened bridge, traveling at twice the recommended velocity, when the falling bomb detonated. The force of the violent blast shook the entire trestle and the Italian Central swayed dangerously as it continued to rocket onward.

With the support beams of the bridge creaking and groaning in protest, the Roman engineer threw the throttle lever to the floor and the 408-cycle steam engine lurched forward in a burst of raw power. This jerking surge of the iron wheels caused a fresh rain of struts to begin dropping from the damaged section, and the bridge began to sway dangerously.

Putting aside their weapons, Einstein and Carstairs joined the panting shoveler and used their bare hands to throw coal into the firedoor. The pressure gauges rapidly rose to the danger level as the screaming train raced across the sagging bridge.

All across the support trestles, the breakage was spreading like some horrible disease, timbers and columns falling away in a growing deluge of splintery destruction.

The engineer started to pray, and the shoveler to curse, as the rails began to buckle, the bridge to writhe, and the whole world shook around the steaming locomotive. One of the pressure gauges shattered, a pipe cracked releasing precious steam, their speed dropped, but then the howling engine went level as it shot off the bridge and onto firm ground! Now the locomotive doubled its speed and started pulling the rest of the carriages to safety like fish on a stringer.

But the exact second the last car of the Italian Central cleared the river chasm, the disconnected caboose appeared at the other side of the bridge. Taut above the carriage was a crude sail made of swords and hoods, and a swarm of naked Squid God worshipers cheered as they rolled onto the bridge in hot pursuit of their escaping enemy. That was when the entire wooden structure gave a mighty groan and collapsed.

Tumbling over sideways, the caboose full of startled men joined the avalanche of timbers and beams cascading down into the rocky Po River. If the Squid God worshipers screamed, it could not be heard above the deafening barrage of destruction. In less than a heartbeat, there were only the wobbling iron rails and wooden ties of the railroad track itself remaining to span the wide river valley; then those also broke apart and fell away.

In joyous victory, the engineer sounded the whistle and the exhausted shoveler stood to light a cigarette, as the sweaty passengers on board the train stopped their praying and commenced cheering.

"Magnificent shooting, lad," Prof. Einstein exhaled, wiping a film of coal dust from his sweaty brow. "Especially from a moving platform. Where the devil did you ever learn to do that?"

"On safari," Lord Carstairs calmly replied, trying to disassemble the prized rifle with his dirty fingers. "Often I've hunted lions while riding on the back of an elephant. You must shoot the beast through the eye, or else ruin the head for a trophy. It's all a matter of timing, sir."

"Good thing that trestle was made of wood," the professor noted, hesitant to voice his opinion of hunting for recreation. His personal views were so out of touch with the times. "Probably just another temporary structure erected until they could replace the original granite bridge destroyed in The–"

"Trouble," the engineer interrupted, wiping his grinning face with a dirty rag.

Tolerantly, the professor eyed the older man, and sighed. "Yes-yes, as you say." Then after a moment, Einstein grimly muttered, "Although, I dare say they'll put up a proper bridge now."

"On the other hand, I bally well want to know how the squiddies found us," Lord Carstairs demanded, working the belt tight to cinch closed his travel kit. "We did everything possible but turn invisible!"

"Quite right, lad, it is a puzzler." Pensively, Prof. Einstein toyed with his sharktooth watch fob. Its vaunted good luck seemed to be operating rather spottily these days. "The Squid God worshipers are either hot on our trail, or even worse, have deduced our destination. I can only pray that we're not too late."

Now the professor turned and spoke with passion, "Lord Carstairs, we must get to the Vatican as fast as humanly possible!"

SIX

"And here we are at the Vatican!" Prof. Einstein declared, as their horse-drawn carriage raced around a street corner.

A rosy dawn was beginning to illuminate the towering spires of a hundred cathedrals across the great city of Rome. Countless church bells were slowly ringing, their strident tones mixing into a clarion song of joyous music.

"Made bally good time, too," Lord Carstairs noted, "what with paying off the railroad and customs to get all of our weapons through."

Sitting in the rear of the open cab, the lord was keeping a hand firmly on his hat as the driver whipped the team of horses ever onward. In Italy, when passengers asked for all due speed, that is precisely what they received! People on the pavement and side streets were only a blur, and twice they had plowed straight through a loaded fruit cart, the professor and Carstairs tossing a handful of lira over their shoulders to pay for the destruction in their wake.

"Money is the language of the world, lad," Prof. Einstein added, swaying from side to side as the horses swerved over a brick fruit stand far too resilient to go through.

"Quite!" the lord chuckled. But then Carstairs frowned as the driver began to slow the cart. Blast!

After checking their luggage into a small hotel, the two explorers had headed straight for Vatican City. Their chosen carriage made good time through the narrow streets and alleys of Rome until approaching their final destination. But now, just as they got within sight of the Vatican, the bustling crowds of people slowed the rushing vehicle to a crawl. The delay was causing Prof. Einstein to fume and curse under his breath. Diplomatic as ever, Lord Carstairs leaned forward to speak with their driver, a stout round-faced man dressed in an old red shirt, hired mostly because of his remarkably good grasp of English.

"*Scusi, signore,*" Lord Carstairs said, tapping the fellow on the shoulder. "But is there some religious festival, of which I am unaware, taking place?"

Tilting a battered cap, the driver scrunched his face. "No, *signore.* Why you ask?"

Waving a hand, Lord Carstairs gestured at the milling throng. "It's just that I don't remember the Holy City being quite this crowded."

"Ah, you mean the pilgrims," the driver smiled, displaying oddly perfect teeth. "Yes. It is the bad weather that makes them come. Seas are rough, fishing bad, and the crops, they fail. Some blame it on the turning moon. *Pazzesco*! Strange events frighten people. So they come to pray."

"I see," Carstairs demurred, taking his seat once more. "*Grazie*, thank you."

In the universal language of all cabbies, the driver eloquently shrugged. "*Siete benvenuti*," he said calmly.

Itching with impatience, the explorers forced themselves to stay in the carriage as walking would not have gotten them to the Vatican any faster. This close to the Holy City, the crowd was a single mass of people, moving in waves and eddies like some impossible Sea of Humanity. And everybody seemed to be praying. It was soon difficult to hear anything above the constant murmuring and steady clicking of rosary beads. But slowly, almost interminably, the driver guided his horses to force a path through the milling throng and eventually brought the vehicle to a glacial halt across the street from the famous city-within-a-city.

Bursting with energy from the confinement, Prof. Einstein leapt to the pavement even before the vehicle had completely braked. Arms waving, the professor impatiently tapped his foot as Lord Carstairs paid the driver and bid the friendly Italian a good day. Whistling contentedly, the cabby drove off at the merest crawl, his next passengers stepping into the carriage from the mobbed streets without bothering to wait for it to stop.

Turning to face the Vatican, Einstein and Carstairs only briefly glanced over the world famous colonnade that encircled three fourths of St. Peter's Square; four rows of marble Doric columns supported a walkway some ten yards in the air, lined with life-size statues of various saints and notables. They had seen it all before, and under better circumstances, too.

Summoning their pluck, the explorers started pushing their way through the packed street. Reaching the colonnade, they took a breather near one of the columns and relished the deliciously cool shadow giving a momentary respite from the blazing Italian sun. This close to the Vatican, Einstein and Carstairs noticed the hundreds of liveried Swiss Guards lining the enclosure, resplendent in their flared steel hats and crimson plumes, polished steel breast plates and striped pantaloons stuffed into matching high-top boots. Razor sharp halberds were held at attention by the big guardians, and tasseled swords dangled from every hip. But despite the quaint garb, the guards were clearly more than ceremonial and they closely scrutinized the crowds with the hard gaze of professional soldiers. The swarms of people paid the Swiss Guards no attention, unless it was to ask directions, or to inquire about the history of something.

With the smooth art of jungle explorers, Prof. Einstein and Lord Carstairs joined the busy throng once more, using elbows and hips to keep moving constantly forward. Reaching the concourse, Einstein and Carstairs found themselves surrounded by a mob of priests, monks, friars, and nuns of every order, each walking with a quiet serenity, the feeling seeming to dominate the entire complex. As if in a world of their own, the clerics seemed immune to the jostling mob and the marble square was quieter than the cobblestone streets of Rome, the chatter and bustle expected from a crowd this size mostly absent. Once more, it was possible to hear the occasional bird singing in the trees, and the air was filled with the smell of sweet incense and spring water.

By mutual consent, the two explorers stood still for a moment, the sights invoking a sense of wonder and awe. The towering spire of an Egyptian obelisk some twenty-five yards in height rose dramatically upward from the center portion of the square, flanked on either side by gushing fountains. Dominating the square was St. Peter's Cathedral, majestic even in its present ruined condition. A complex array of scaffolding framed the row of giant marble columns, the mighty stone towers that supported the famous upper balcony and the dome designed by Michelangelo Buonar- roti. Scores of sweating workmen were everywhere; hauling lumber, laying brick, painting, and performing the most delicate of stone carving.

The passing of the centuries was tangible here, almost to the point of becoming a physical force, firmly reminding them that this was a major focal point of world history on a regular basis. For every archeologist and historian alive today, this was a holy place, although for entirely different reasons than those of the Catholics. With a supreme effort of will, the Englishmen finally moved on.

"So, Professor," Lord Carstairs said, keeping his steps slow to match the pace of the smaller man, "where is the tablet located?"

Looking about, Einstein pointed towards a busy staircase alongside a magnificent church whose soaring spires reached for the stars. "To the right, just past the Papal post office, is the ground floor entrance to the Sistine Chapel. Go up the winding steps and follow the signs to the library. I shall wait for you across the street at that little coffee shop we passed."

Glancing downward, Carstairs arched an eyebrow. "Aren't you going to accompany me, Professor?"

"Ah, no," the professor mumbled, "I don't think so, lad. Maybe next time."

"But why not?" Lord Carstairs asked puzzled. "What with time being of the essence, surely the presence of an academician of your stature would simplify things to no end."

Shifting his stance uncomfortably, Prof. Einstein forced an innocent smile on his face. "Well, normally, yes. But the Pope and I had a bit of a tiff once."

"A papal tiff?" Carstairs said with a frown. "Involving what, may I ask?"

His eyes searching the sky for divine inspiration, the professor gave a delicate cough. Then another.

"Involving the tablet?" Lord Carstairs guessed sagely.

In mock embarrassment, Einstein nodded. "They refused to allow me access to the Dutarian stone, so I, well, borrowed it."

"Borrowed? And exactly when did this event take place, sir?" Lord Carstairs inquired, the implications becoming frightening clear.

"Oh, about three in the morning."

"*You burgled the Vatican*?" Carstairs cried aghast, then quickly lowered his voice as the nearby crowd turned in response to the cry. "B-but that is unpardonable, sir!"

"Well, the Pope certainly thought so," Prof. Einstein agreed wearily.

A woman with a baby rushed by, parting the men for a moment. In her wake, they stepped close once more.

"So, did they catch you?" Lord Carstairs demanded.

"Me? Ha! Certainly not," the professor sneered, then added, "Although in retrospect, that was what seemed to annoy them the most."

Feeling slightly ill, Lord Carstairs slumped onto an ornamental railing around a fountain. Holding his head in both hands, the big man appeared to be at prayer, and several hurrying priests gave him a brief benediction in passing.

"Did you ever return the stone?" Carstairs asked hopefully, from behind his hands.

"Of course, lad!" Prof. Einstein said, sitting next to his friend. He patted the lord on the shoulder. "Why, I even gave them a splendid copy of my rubbing from the Amsterdam bracelet. But for some reason they still consider me *persona non grata.*"

Spreading his fingers, Lord Carstairs peeked down at the grinning professor. That wasn't lasagna he smelled now, but an East London rat.

"And why is that?" the lord demanded in a low rumble.

"Well, I did charge them a modest fee for postage and handling," Einstein admitted coyly.

"Professor!"

"Seemed like the thing to do at the time," Prof. Einstein demurred, shifting about uncomfortably on the bench.

Now massaging his temples, Carstairs made a small noise of pain.

"Oh, and lad, you'd better let me have your pistol," Einstein added, holding out a handkerchief.

Wearily wary, Lord Carstairs scowled at the cloth. "Merciful heavens, why? You're not going to use it to steal some of St. Peter's Gate or something?"

With a flippant gesture, the professor snorted in disdain. "Bosh and tish, I already have a piece. No, the reason is that the Swiss Guard is notorious for its total lack of humor involving foreigners bearing weapons anywhere near the Papal residence."

"Understandable," Carstairs acknowledged, reaching inside his coat. "So be it." Wrapping the massive revolver in the linen handkerchief, he transferred the Webley.

Tucking the mammoth pistol inside his own coat, Einstein then rummaged around in his vest before producing a small jewelry box. "Just in case there are any problems about getting into the occult section," he said, passing it over, "offer them this."

As if accepting a bomb from a mad German revolutionary, Lord Carstairs inspected the jewelry box, then flipped open the lid. For several moments, he studied the contents in puzzlement until a sudden burst of understanding washed across his features and the lord stared in awe.

"No. This isn't . . . it couldn't be!" Carstairs said, having trouble getting out the words. "No. It is impossible!"

"To the best of my knowledge, that is real," Prof. Einstein sighed, starting to reach for the box, then slowly lowered his hand. "So don't fritter it away, lad. Use it only as a last resort to get that tablet!"

"Absolutely, Professor," Carstairs muttered, reverently closing the box, and tucking it deep inside his clothing. "Although, technically, I suppose this belongs to them as well."

"Balderdash, lad," Einstein snorted. "Finders, keepers, that's my motto."

Just then, an eddy in the swirling throng opened wide showing a clear path directly to the front entrance of the Vatican.

"There's your cue, lad," Einstein said, gesturing onward. "Good luck, and be sure to keep your wits sharp."

"Righto," Lord Carstairs replied, squaring his powerful shoulders. Standing, the dapper lord strode away, the tiny box still tightly clenched in a scarred fist as the mob filled the square once more.

Watching the head of the tall man move over the milling crowd like a coconut floating at sea, the professor cast a nervous glance at the papal home and hurried at his best speed for the nearest exit. The Pope was famous for many things, and his boundless wrath towards successful thieves was one of the Top Ten.

Leaving the square, Prof. Einstein wriggled his way to a nearby piazza, the pleasant Italian invention of an open-air restaurant. Taking a seat facing the Vatican, the professor placed an order with a handsome waiter for cappuccino, and settled down to begin his vigil.

Slowly time ticked by under the warm Mediterranean sun. Two cups of strong coffee and a plate of sugared zeppoles later, Einstein was still waiting for word from Lord Carstairs and starting to develop a dilly of a case of heartburn. In idle amusement, the professor fed a bit of his pastry to one of the innumerable cats of Rome. Julius Caesar himself had brought the creatures over from Egypt and, as far back as the fifth century, historians had noted the large number of the furry beasts stalking the city. In wry humor, the citizens of Rome referred to them as 'The Little Kings' and gave them free reign.

With casual efficiency, the waiter removed the luncheon menu from the professor's table and replaced it with one for dinner. Einstein barely had a chance to glance at it before a different waiter appeared, bearing a fresh cup of coffee.

"Is everything to the English gentleman's satisfaction?" the waiter politely asked, placing the tiny cup and saucer on the checkered tablecloth.

"Absolutely, the cappuccino is delicious," Prof. Einstein said, taking a fresh sip. "Don't know why we can't get this at home."

"The purchase of a special brewing machine is necessary," the waiter explained helpfully, wiping his hands clean on a white apron tied about his waist.

"Interesting. And I suppose none are available for sale?"

"*Excusa*, no, *signore*."

Relaxing in his chair, the professor gave a bemused smile. "I see. It is a clever way to make sure the customers are forced to return. Are you British, by any chance?"

"Pure Sicilian," the waiter smiled, giving the word the proper pronunciation. "Oh, there was another matter, sir."

Licking his sticky lips, Einstein lowered the drained cup. How strange. The waiter's command of English had just drastically improved. "Yes?"

"The lady at table eight wishes to express her thanks," the waiter said, gesturing with a towel-draped arm.

Raising an eyebrow, Prof. Einstein glanced at the woman in question. He had noticed her upon arriving, if only for the striking beauty of her features, which were evident even behind the black lace veil. Her style of dress declared her British, as did the quiet refinement of her movements. But as far as the professor could tell, she had never once looked in his direction.

"Her thanks," Einstein repeated curiously. "Whatever for?"

Now the waiter leaned in closely and softly whispered, "Why, for drinking your drugged coffee so very quickly, Professor Felix Thaddeus David Einstein of the International British Museum."

With a surge of fury, the professor tried to stand but his head went reeling. Pawing for the pistol in his pocket, Einstein discovered his fingers were numb and useless as cordwood. *Great Scott, he had actually been drugged like a shanghaied sailor!* Desperately, the professor opened his mouth to shout for help and the waiter stuffed in a warm zeppole.

Trying to chew his way to freedom, Einstein felt the piazza begin to spin madly about and, somewhere in the distance, there were bells tolling. Bells? No, that was the blood pounding in his ears.

As the swooning professor slumped forward onto the table, his last conscious thoughts were of the sugared zeppole and his own forthcoming doom.

SEVEN

In slow stages of foggy delirium, Felix Einstein gradually awoke, feeling just awful. His temples were pounding louder than jungle drums and an angry porcupine seemed to be nesting in his stomach. Plus, there was a taste in his mouth of sour mash and tin, as if the professor had tried to out-drink a Welsh miner. *Bleh.*

Attempting to stand, Einstein quickly discovered that his wrists were individually tied to the arms of the wooden chair he occupied. Coils of rope circled his legs from ankle to knee. More rope was wrapped about his middle, and still more wound around his throat. Despite the seriousness of his predicament, the professor had to admire the thoroughness of the binding. This was the work of a true expert. This meant that he was in very big trouble indeed.

Breathing deeply to regulate his pulse, Prof. Einstein forced himself to take stock of the room. It was small and well lighted, with plain, whitewashed plaster walls, two windows and a single door. The floor was carpeted and there were fine lace curtains on the windows. A hotel, perhaps, or a lady's private chambers. Unfortunately, he could see nothing outside except empty blue sky. *Blast.* The only furnishings were a carved mahogany washstand with a matching wardrobe and a beautiful four-poster bed with a stunningly lovely embroidered quilt of superior quality.

Reviewing his escape options was a short and depressing process, as Einstein spotted his personal belongings lying on the quilt some two yards distant. Prominent among them were his sword cane, pistol, pocketknife, and Lord Carstairs' huge Webley, still partially wrapped in the linen handkerchief bearing the Einstein family crest with the Latin motto: *Cre do qua ab sur dum est!*

A creak caught his attention, and he turned to see the door swing aside and admit a lone hooded figure, its arms and face hidden by the voluminous folds of the dark cloth.

"So you took me alive," Prof. Einstein snarled rudely, feeling better by the moment, which was very odd indeed. No known anesthesia could detoxify out of a human body this rapidly. *A bit of magic here, eh*? That made sense, seeing *who* it was they were fighting.

The masked figure said nothing in reply.

"What now?" Einstein continued. "A bribe to stop our quest? A bit of torture? Or am I a hostage?"

"All of those and more," the person said in a husky feminine voice. "But first, conversation."

"An unusual tactic for dullards," Prof. Einstein snapped as insultingly as possible, even though his captor was obviously of the opposite gender. Biologically a female, but certainly no lady! "I have nothing to say to the likes of you!"

"Mayhap you do not understand what it is we offer," she countered, crossing her arms under an ample bosom. "After the initial cleansing bloodbath, the world will be at peace, with the undesirables removed. What advances science and art could make with the politicians and bureaucrats gone!"

"The undesirables removed," the professor repeated, the words bitter as the aftertaste of the knockout drugs. The phrase made Einstein think back to the Dutarian tablet in his museum and he shuddered. "Never! I will never comply!"

"Oh, but you were never counted among them!" the woman cried, clearly misunderstanding his reaction. "A man of your knowledge and abilities? We admire you greatly. Indeed, that was why . . ." The woman literally bit her tongue and Einstein realized that he had just missed getting important information.

"Still not interested," the professor stated flatly.

Placing both hands on her wide hips, the woman tilted her head as if in contemplation, then straightened it, obviously making a decision.

"Besides the unlimited money, power, fame, and freedom to do your research," she continued undaunted. "You are also offered . . . me!"

With a whirl of her cape, the woman removed the flowing garment and stood brazenly before the bound man in her street clothes from the restaurant. Minus the veil. A man as well as a professor, Einstein was impressed by the sheer beauty of the woman. Her face was classically beautiful, the skin smooth and unmarred, except for matching dimples. Her eyes were blue as the Aegean Sea, her lips lush as a plump Scottish lass's.

Incredulously, the professor watched as the woman deliberately lifted the hem of her skirt and teasingly revealed a sweetly shaped ankle. Then she wiggled it!

The hussy! A proper Victorian gentleman, Prof. Einstein felt his mouth go dry at the raw sexual display. H-he c-could almost see her actual leg!

Dropping the hem again, her slim fingers now slowly unbuttoned her blouse, exposing a full inch of swelling cleavage.

Desperately fighting not to rise to the carnal bait, the professor tried juggling algebraic equations and logarithms in his head. *Euclid, save this mortal wretch!*

Tossing her long auburn curls over a shapely white shoulder, the animal temptress leaned in closer to the sweating man. "I have also read many of the forbidden volumes on intimate man-woman relationships," she purred warmly in his ear. "Such as the Tibetan Book of Love."

At that point, Einstein could not stop the mathematical equations from abruptly turning into geometric calculations on rods and spheres.

"My favorite is the Kama Sutra," she said running the pink tip of her tongue over scarlet lips. "I am particularly fond of position #37."

Pouring sweat, the tumescent professor tried to think of his dearly departed mother and paying taxes. *Position #37. That was almost as good as his personal favorite, #52.*

"Although, my personal favorite is #52," the seductive trollop giggled lustfully, slowly tracing a dainty hand along the coils of rope around the professor's thigh. "In my private collection, I also have a dozen Japanese Pillow Books."

He swallowed hard.

"They're illustrated, you know," she added, thrusting her torso forward and breathing deeply with the most delightfully astonishing results.

A sudden tightness in his undergarments told the professor that unless he did something fast, his own body would betray him. Einstein was a man of science, but still a red-blooded man. There was but a single defensive weapon remaining for his use that had any chance of success, and the professor had to unleash it immediately! Closing his eyes to the vision of loveliness, Prof. Einstein regulated his breathing and became very still.

At first, the woman thought Einstein had succumbed to her charms. But as nothing happened, she began to wonder if the elderly man had suffered a heart attack. Placing an ear upon his chest, she not only heard his heart beating strongly, but a faint humming as well. It only took her a few moments to recognize what it was. Snarling furiously, she slapped the prisoner hard across the face, stomped away in disgust to exit the bedroom, and loudly slammed the door in her wake.

"Well, Yolanda? Has he talked yet?" a burly fellow asked, lounging against the wall of the corridor, cleaning his fingernails. He was dressed entirely in white laboratory clothes and there was a small medical bag on the floor.

"No, Adolph, he has not," the woman replied testily, buttoning her blouse closed. "And in my opinion, he will not. The little British fool has resorted to humming 'God Save the Queen.'"

"Damn," Adolph muttered, tucking away the knife he had been using to clean his nails. "The one thing we feared! Our employers will be most vexed."

"And they paid us a fortune to get what they need," Yolanda muttered, straightening her starched collar. "A fortune!"

Glancing at the closed door, Adolph looked hopeful. "Then, I suppose this means we must . . ." He let the sentence trail off expectantly.

Running fingers through her wild hair, Yolanda tossed her head from side to side to get the desired effect, then gazed steadily at her brother with burning eyes of hatred.

"Do it," she growled. "All of it. Everything!"

"Excellent," Adolph purred, grabbing the medical bag. "Do you wish to watch?"

Taking a chair, Yolanda sat down heavily and massaged her ankle. "I am in no mood for entertainment," she said wearily. "He was my first failure, and I am truly depressed. But you have a good time."

"Thanks, I shall!" Whistling a happy tune, Adolph swung open the door and entered the bedroom.

His eyes shut tightly, Prof. Einstein continued humming in patriotic fervor as the whistling Adolph locked the door and dragged the washstand over to the prisoner. The musical counterpoint disrupting his concentration, Einstein dared to sneak a peek. The woman was gone, replaced by a tall man with a thin, cruel mouth. The fellow was emptying a black medical bag onto the washstand, laying out an array of shiny steel surgical instruments. *Uh oh.*

Next came a small metal container that was ingeniously transformed into a tiny brazier, already full of red-hot coals. Some branding irons followed, along with pliers, knives, shears, eye-gougers, testicle crushers, and several unearthly looking apparatus that sent chills down the elderly professor's spine. In his college days, Einstein had experimented on animals in his medical classes, but he had always been polite enough to make sure the subject was thoroughly deceased first. However, it did not appear that courtesy was going to be afforded to him in return. *Lord Carstairs, where the Hell are you?*

"My name is Adolph Gunderson, and you are an admirable adversary, Professor," the fellow announced, placing both of the branding irons into the hot coals. "You have also earned my deepest admiration. There are few men who can resist the siren allure of my sister, Yolanda."

Minutely adjusting the array of steel on display, Adolph waited for the expected response, but as it was not forthcoming, he continued. Let the poor fellow save his voice for the screaming.

"However, if you will not talk willingly," Adolph added, raising a knife to inspect the edge in the red light of the glowing brazier, "then I must rip the information my master desires from your quivering flesh."

Sweat trickling down his back at this pronouncement, Einstein swallowed hard. This was no idle threat, but the deadly serious announcement of a master craftsman about to begin his hellish work. A dozen escape plans flew through the professor's mind, each critically flawed by the fact that he was thoroughly bound, and speech was the only weapon remaining to him, with the topics of conversation not his to choose.

"What is the information they desire?" Prof. Einstein asked, stalling for time.

Every second of life offered the possibility of this Adolph person making a fatal mistake or of Einstein outwitting the man. The weapons were on the bed, so if the professor got a hand loose, that would be the direction Adolph would naturally block. So Einstein would go the other way, throw the water pitcher through the window, and grab a shard of glass as a makeshift dagger. Yes, it could work! If he had a hand free. Just one hand was all he needed!

Placing aside the knife, Adolph grinned. "First, let me remove any thoughts in your mind of these being mere threats." And without any further preamble, he picked up a sharp-tipped glowing iron rod and shoved it against the professor's left ear lobe.

With a brief sizzle, the needle seared through the flesh so quickly that Einstein could only gasp in shock at the horrible sound. Then the burning pain arrived and the professor ground his teeth together as the agony blossomed on the side of his head. Bloody buggering Hell!

"You will never leave this room alive," Adolph droned on, barely audible through the fog of agony. "I am the last person you will ever see. Mine is the last voice you will ever hear. Your cooperation will only decide how quickly I give you the sweet release of death. A release from the unimaginable agonies you are about to experience."

The professor fought to bring air back into his lungs, and made no reply.

"Nothing personal," Adolph added in a friendly manner, removing the larger branding iron from the brazier. "Just business."

As his last great act of defiance, the professor summoned his every ounce of pluck he possessed and spat forth the most astonishingly vulgar phrase that he knew, crafted from a lifetime of exploring the vilest pestholes on the face of the globe and associating with the sub-human scum who thrived in those beastly environments.

Recoiling in shock, Adolph dropped the glowing iron back into the brazier, creating a small explosion of swirling sparks. He had never heard anything even vaguely like that before in his entire existence!

"Sideways, in your hat," Einstein added as a fillip, knowing there was nothing to lose.

With ill controlled fury, Adolph bared his teeth and his face contorted into a feral mask of insanity. "Now it is personal!" Adolph snarled, grabbing the professor's shirt. With a quick jerk, buttons went flying as he ripped it open, exposing the pale silver-hair on the chest underneath.

As the glowing iron advanced, Prof. Einstein mentally said goodbye to his niece and prepared to meet his Maker with what dignity and courage he possessed. He would wait, until the very last second, and then thrust himself forward onto the iron, piercing his own heart, and ending the torture long before his mind was broken. These foul bastards would never learn the location of Lord Carstairs! Death before betraying a fellow club member! Oh yes, and saving the world, too. That was also rather important. But the club came first, naturally.

"I hope you never tell us the location of the Sword of Alexander!" Adolph added hatefully, taking up the blade once more to warm the tip in the crackling fire. The edge began to glow a dull orange.

But the odd words brought icy clarity to Einstein's mind. "The what?" the professor demanded loudly, leaning forward against the binding ropes.

Caught off guard by this reaction, Adolph took a step away from the scowling prisoner. "The Sword of Alexander," he repeated. "You stole it from the New York Metropolitan Museum and they want the relic returned."

Blinking away the sweat in his eyes, Prof. Einstein licked his dry lips several times before speaking. "Is that what all of this folderol is about?" he demanded furiously. "That bloody damn sword I won in a poker game from the German Explorer's Club? You're not a Squid God worshiper?"

"Poker game?" Adolph blinked in confusion. "Folderol? Squid God?"

Relaxing in the chair, the professor felt a wave of relief wash through his body. "Never mind, old man. The Germans stole the sword from the Metropolitan, and now New York wants it back? Fine. It is yours. I gave it to the Royal War Museum of Spain."

"Gave?" Adolph squeaked aghast, dropping the knife. It fell to the floorboards with a thud and stayed in place, a tiny wisp of smoke rising from the charred wood.

"Well, I had to," Prof. Einstein said with a small shrug. "It was useless for my research. The sword was a fake. A good job, but as Grecian as a Cockney bootblack."

In furious disbelief, Adolph narrowed his eyes to tiny slits. "You lie," he growled, grabbing the branding rod again.

Once more, hot iron was applied to bare flesh, but for much longer this time and the hissing stink of roasted meat filled the bedroom. Eventually, Prof. Einstein could take no more and he cut loose with a raw throated scream of pain that seemed to last forever.

"Oh please, feel free to make all of the noise you wish," Adolph said brightly, laying down the cooled iron and picking up a pair of jagged-edged scissors. "This room has been completely soundproofed and your cries will not be heard a foot outside these windows."

"Really?"

"Absolutely," Adolph grinned, but then paused. Wait a minute, that voice had not been the professor.

Groggy from the pain, Einstein had just come to the same conclusion and opened his eyes in time to experience the most beautiful sight in his life. A tall dark man with a bristling black moustache stepped out from a hole in the wall behind the wardrobe. His face was blackened with charcoal and in his hands was a sleek crossbow, the quarrel tipped with a razor-sharp barb.

Muttering a curse, Adolph clawed under his surgical gown and extracted an old-fashioned Newark .66 pistol exactly as the stranger fired the crossbow. The quarrel slammed into Adolph's throat, the barbed head going completely through his neck and coming out the other side. Hot blood gushed from twin wounds staining his white garments a spreading crimson. Hacking for breath, Adolph stumbled backwards against the dresser and two more shafts slammed into his body.

Gurgling something incomprehensible, Adolph shuddered and went limp, but he did not drop to the floor as he was pinned to the heavy piece of furniture by the steel shafts.

"If we had known the room was soundproof, we would have used our pistols and not wasted time getting these," the dark man stated in apology, brandishing the crossbow.

Dizzy from the pain, Prof. Einstein tried to speak, "Who . . ." But his inquiry dissolved into a ragged series of coughs.

Slinging the crossbow over a shoulder, the Italian man with the big moustache blinked in surprise. "*Ma don!* Do you not remember? You joined our organization several years ago, taking the *ometra* with my cousin, Nunzio."

Ometra, a blood oath of brotherhood. Einstein quickly rifled through the vast catalogue of his brain. Of course, the Italian resistance fighters struggling for political freedom against a brutal and oppressive Sardinian government. How could he have forgotten them?

Drawing a slim knife from his boot, the dark man began slicing through the ropes. "There has been a great deal of inquiry about you recently," he said, cutting with speed and care. "Inquiries from most unusual people. When you arrived in Rome without even stopping to pay your respects, we decided to keep an eye on your movements."

"Who are you?" Prof. Einstein managed to mumble.

Sheathing the blade, the dark man smiled in gentle reproof. "You may call me Guido."

"G-grazie."

With a shrug, Guido tossed the ropes aside and started to apply a soothing ointment to the puckered burn on the professor's chest and ear. "At first we thought, perhaps, you were having an assignation," he said, as more men armed with crossbows poured from the hole in the wall. "You English are so strange in these matters of sex. But when the truth became clear, we moved with all due haste."

"Much a-appreciated," the professor said with a weak smile, buttoning his vest in an attempt to hold his shirt closed. The pressure on the blisters was painful, but the merest trifle compared to what he had just been rescued from. Besides, the Italians would look upon any complaints as a sign of weakness, and Guido would lose face. It would be unthinkable to insult his host in such a manner.

Just then, the door swung open and in stepped a young, muscular giant, nearly the size of Lord Carstairs. "*Padrone*?" he rumbled like distant thunder.

Gently as possible, Guido assisted Einstein to stand. "Yes, Angelo?" he asked, without turning around.

Pursing his lips, Angelo glanced thoughtfully at the professor. "We caught the woman," Angelo said in Italian. "The one who drugged our compatriot. She was attempting to flee on horseback."

"You killed her?" Guido answered in English.

Brushing back his slicked hair, Angelo appeared puzzled, then gave a gesture of compliance. "Of course," he said in English. "Should I have the bodies dressed as beggars and tossed into the river?"

"Si."

"No," the professor countered in perfect Italian, clenching and unclenching his fists, trying to make the shaking stop. "For all of our sakes, it would be best if these particular bodies were never found."

"Never?" Rubbing his jaw with the back of a hand, Guido nodded. "Angelo, has the foundation been laid for the new building next to your brother's olive oil shop?"

"Si, padrone. Yes. They are working on it even as we speak."

"It is a fascinating process. Perhaps the *signora* and her friend would care to see it close up. Tender our usual compliments to the foreman and his crew."

"At once."

"Buon! Good."

Meticulously, Guido examined the dressing on the professor's ear and seemed satisfied. Upon his orders, several more men entered to carry the weakened Einstein down a long set of stairs and into a small courtyard at the rear of the private house. The purple grapes were full upon the arbors, and colorful flowers filled numerous clay pots. It was the most utterly beautiful garden that Prof. Einstein had ever seen, and he treasured every smell, every sight.

Placing the professor on the ground, a short man in a striped shirt passed over a small corked bottle.

"What is it?" Prof. Einstein asked groggily, weighing the container in a palm. It was heavy and cool.

"A powerful stimulant," Guido replied, tugging on his moustache. "Its effects will not be pleasant, but afterwards it will stop your shaking, and bring clarity to the mind. Pain is an old friend to us, and we know how to handle its many aspects."

Summoning his nerve and holding his nose, the professor drained the tiny vial in a single swallow. The men in the garden seemed impressed by the action. Prof. Einstein found out why as a few seconds later his stomach did a flip. Then a flop. Then it did both. Glancing about frantically, the professor spotted a small brick kiosk with a door marked by a crescent moon, the international symbol for Water Closet, and he dashed across the garden at Olympian speed.

A very long time later, Prof. Einstein stumbled out of the privy as pale as wax, but his movements were strong and sure once more.

Sitting on a stone bench under an olive tree, Guido laid aside the piece of cheese he had been cutting pieces from as a snack, and watched closely as the professor approached. The other men were also still present, several passing around a bottle of Chianti, while others were sharpening the tips of their crossbow quarrels on whetstone.

"Feeling better?" Guido asked, laying aside a cheese.

"I'll live," Prof. Einstein replied, wiping his mouth with a sleeve. The smell of the cheese made his stomach tremble, but that was all. "And it is a statement I would not have been able to make without your timely intervention."

"Grazie. Your belongings," Guido said handing over the wallet, pocket watch, cane, and pistols. "I sense that this affair has nothing to do with our smuggling organization?"

Filling his pockets, Einstein checked the load in the .32 Adams pistol, making very sure not to touch any of the bullets with a bare finger. "That is correct. This is connected with my work outside your country."

In Sicilian elegance, Guido displayed his innocence in the matter by showing both of his open palms to God in Heaven. "Then I am sorry that we can only protect you here in Rome. Our organization is small and even for a *ginzo*, we can only do so much."

With true heartfelt thanks, Felix Einstein shook the man's hand. "You have already done infinitely more than I ever had a right to expect. I thank you again, *padrone*."

The expression of extreme respect did not go unnoticed and the nearby group of armed men murmured in approval. Standing slowly, Guido gave no sign he heard the word. "My pleasure, Professor. The rights of the innocent must always be protected."

Heading for the wrought iron gate of the garden, Guido called over a shoulder, *"Andiamo, i miei amici!"* With a stiff-arm salute, the Italians blended into the shadows of the lush arbor and were gone.

Taking a few moments to build his strength, Professor Einstein sat on the bench and breathed in the fragrant air of the garden. Then looking about to make sure he was alone, threw the cheese as far away as possible.

Einstein realized that he would carry the memory of Guido coming out of that closet to save him for the rest of his life. By Gadfrey, they were such brave men fighting for a just cause. He had thought the group destroyed in the turmoil of The Trouble, and was very glad to see that they survived. But as a student of history, Einstein hoped that if they won their struggle, the victory over the hated kings of Sardinia would not make them corrupt over time. They were such good fellows, and he would hate to see the Mafia go bad.

The length of the shadows on the ground caught his attention, and the professor checked his watch. Gadzooks! He had to get back to the piazza before it closed. Shuffling out of the garden, Einstein stopped a moment to wipe the latch clean of any fingerprints with a handkerchief, and then hastily made his way along a brick alley to the main cobblestone street.

At the corner, the professor hailed a carriage and returned to the cafe. The traitorous waiter was thankfully gone. With a weary sigh, Prof. Einstein sat down at the same table as before. Soon, another waiter arrived to take his order of a sealed bottle of wine and no glass.

Sipping the blood red Chianti, Einstein savored the sounds, sights, and smells of the living city. But as the cathedrals began to ring their bells for evensong, the professor glanced at his pocket watch and frowned in apprehension. Lord Carstairs was taking an inordinate amount of time for a relatively simple task. He certainly hoped the lad hadn't also run into trouble.

EIGHT

In bold sure steps, Lord Carstairs strode up the wide granite stairs leading into the main building of the Vatican complex. Everywhere pilgrims bustled, tourists gasped, nuns counted their rosaries, and priests scurried about with their arms loaded with books.

Turning north at the Sistine Chapel, Carstairs proceeded through the world famous Vatican Library. The room was so spacious and quiet that his footsteps echoed slightly on the worn marble floor. The broad walls and vaulted ceiling were adorned with breathtaking frescos, but the lord saw only the rather dull brown filing cabinets that held the wisdom of a thousand years locked within their reserves.

Turning left into the main exhibition hall, Carstairs stooped to pass through a tiled arch and entered the Vatican Museum. Every inch of every wall was decorated with rare paintings, a forest of bronze statues stood on a multitude of ornate pedestals, and miniature marble statues filled the alcoves that topped each door lentil. Not so much as a postage stamp could have been fixed anywhere without covering a priceless work of antiquarian art.

Gawking pilgrims stood about in clusters, the magnificence of the holy museum making them seek the comforting solace of others for company. Numerous soldiers stood on guard throughout the museum, but Lord Carstairs continued unmolested through the numerous galleries until he entered a small side corridor closed off with a velvet rope. Beyond that was an iron door flanked by two more of the ever-present Swiss Guard. But rather than the callow youths helping the tourists, these were scarred and burly men. The sergeant sported an eye patch, while the younger private possessed a puckered scar that bisected his entire face. Both of them were obviously veteran fighters, and these guards did not hold antique halberd spears, but very modern day, bolt-action, Vetterlis 6.5mm carbine rifles, ominously outfitted with long sharp bayonets. Very nasty little barkers, indeed.

In cold scrutiny, the somber guards watched Lord Carstairs approach and crossed their weapons to bar his way.

"Halt, *signore*," the sergeant said in flawed English. "This section of library closed to public."

Smiling diplomatically, Carstairs replied in perfect Italian. "So I understand. However, I am Lord Benjamin Carstairs, a member of the British Parliament and a member of the London Explorers Club. I wish to speak with your curator."

"A scholar?" the private said in Italian, starting to raise his rifle. "Then pass, sir."

"Excuse me, but we must ask for proof of this," the sergeant interrupted, using his one good eye to give the private a stern look of disapproval.

Performing the necessary ritual, Lord Carstairs dutifully produced his wallet and showed them his membership card to the Explorers Club, a buyer's certificate from the Royal Museum, and a British Passport bearing his family crest. The last item caused a noticeable warming in the attitudes of the soldiers.

"Thank you, sir," the private said, swinging his rifle aside. "You may pass."

"Just a moment," the sergeant added, barring the way again with the Vetterlis carbine. "As you will be very close to the living quarters of his Holiness, I must ask if you are carrying any weapons." The guard repeated the phrase as if he said it a dozen times a day. However, that did not stop him from studying Lord Carstairs in the manner of a tax collector scrutinizing a known cheat.

"None, but these," the lord said, innocently extending his huge hands. As expected, the guards broke into laughter.

"Such fine weapons they are," the private acknowledged, his scar contorting the smile into a snarl. "I would not wish to try and confiscate them."

"Pass, sir," the sergeant chuckled. "The curator's office is through this door, down the hallway, to the left."

"Grazie."

"You are most welcome, Lord Carstairs."

Following the directions, Carstairs soon found a dour nun working as a receptionist at an intricately carved Berouzzi desk. Removing his hat, Lord Carstairs repeated his request for the curator. After examining his credentials carefully, the sister excused herself and went down a side corridor. A few minutes later, she returned with a plump priest in tow. The man was of indeterminable age, mostly bald, clean-shaven, and wore a simple brown cassock.

"Blessings upon you, my son," the priest said in halting English. "I am Father Tullio. It is a pleasure to meet you. Our library has several works by both yourself and your esteemed father. How may I help you?"

"Thank you, Father, may I speak with your curator, please?" Lord Carstairs again responded in Italian.

Both hands clasped in piety, the cherubic face of Father Tullio radiated pleasure at hearing his native tongue used so fluently. "There are several curators," he said. "Which department of the library are you in need of assistance?"

"The private closed section," Carstairs said tactfully.

"But the Vatican Library is open to any who ask," Tullio answered with a quizzical expression.

In a conspiratorial manner, Lord Carstairs lowered his voice. "What I wish to see is the occult museum."

"I do not understand," Father Tullio replied, nervously fingering his rosary. "An occult museum? I assure you that the Vatican has no such a division. Perhaps you mean the Secret Archives? Permission from his Holiness, the Pope, is normally needed for an outsider to enter. But I'm sure for you an exception can be made."

Not born a fool, Lord Carstairs knew when he was getting a runaround and decided to try a direct frontal attack.

"Father, I know of the existence of the occult section because I have had the honor of talking with others who have been there," he stated forcibly. "Gentlemen whose word I trust implicitly."

In ragged stages, the plump features of the priest slumped. Without a word, he took Carstairs' arm and led him into a nearby office. Closing the door, Father Tullio hardened his expression.

"My son, you have caught me in the commission of a venial sin," Tullio admitted without much shame or remorse. "There is indeed an occult section to the library, but it has not been closed off capriciously. There are books and objects of heresy and abomination that could cause untold strife within and without the church if they were revealed to the general public."

Lord Carstairs nodded in agreement. "I understand completely, Father," he said. "The object I wish to study is for my own private research. You have my word as an Englishman that I have no intention of publishing anything that would make the church regret allowing me access."

Taking a seat, Father Tullio drummed his fingers on the arm of the chair. "Church of England?" he finally asked.

"Yes, Father. Will that be a problem?"

"Not in this life, my son," the priest said benignly. "Very well." Reaching to an overflowing shelf, Tullio pulled down an ancient leather-bound book and opened it creating a small cloud of dust. With great ceremony, the father donned a pair of very modern pince-nez glasses, cut a fresh point on the nib of his quill pen, and uncapped a small crystal bottle of ink.

Laboriously, Tullio wrote Lord Carstairs' name, address, and academic degrees on a blank page. After the pen finished transcribing this last bit of information, Father Tullio asked, "References?"

"I beg your pardon?" Lord Carstairs asked in a small voice.

The priest removed his glasses and tapped them on the book. "I need your references, my son. You claimed to have talked with somebody who has been inside the occult section. We require the name of that confidant, whose admittance we shall verify. It is how we assure ourselves that only worthy scholars are allowed entrance."

"Oh."

Poised expectantly, Father Tullio kept his pen above the page. After a minute, the priest lowered the quill stylus. "Is there a problem, my son?"

Seeing the expression on the priest's face, Lord Carstairs racked his mind searching for the correct words. "Truly, I have a legitimate reference, sir. It is just that, at the moment, he does not enjoy much favor with the church."

In gradual stages, the expression on Father Tullio cleared. "Ah, I understand. Yes, there have always been those who have abused the trust that we have placed upon them. The fact that you are aware of the person's indiscretions will hopefully act as a check to any indiscretions to which you might be tempted."

"Oh, I say," Carstairs said in great relief. "That's awfully decent."

"Well, we are in the forgiving business, no?" the father smiled. Once more, he picked up the pen. "So who is your reference, please?"

"Well," Lord Carstairs said, pausing to clear his throat, "Ahem. Professor Felix Einstein."

"Guards!" Father Tullio screamed, leaping from his desk, and yanked open the door. "Guards!"

"Wait!" Carstairs cried, spreading his arms. "I'm prepared to make reparations for the professor!"

"Ha!" the priest sneered. "With what?"

The sound of running boots grew in the corridor, and suddenly a full squad of armed soldiers and several nuns packing heat appeared at the doorway. Father Tullio pointed to the stunned Carstairs. "Arrest him! Jail him! Export him! Shoot him!"

Growling menacingly, the soldiers steadily advanced and worked the bolt on their Vetterlis 6.5mm rifles. The nuns drew smoothbore pistols and cocked back the massive hammers. In frantic speed, Lord Carstairs dug into his pocket, produced the jewelry box, and flipped back the lid.

Everybody flinched, as if half-expecting an explosion. But when nothing happened, Father Tullio cautiously leaned forward and peered inside. Lying on a cushion of blue velvet was a large splinter of dark wood.

"And what do you claim this is?" the priest asked, his tone dripping suspicion.

"I make no claim, father," Lord Carstairs stated in all sincerity. "And I ask no favors. Freely do I give this to you, with no obligations attached."

The ritual words stopped the priest cold. Once again, Tullio bent forward to examine the contents of the box, and now a sweat broke out upon his brow. Rather hesitantly, the priest reached out to take the box, and closed it tight with a snap. Turning about, Father Tullio passed it to the nearest nun. Tucking the pistol up her wimple, the nun genuflected and scurried away. The other sisters followed close behind, surrounding her for protection.

"Your men may also go, captain," Father Tullio said, sounding almost regretful.

Shifting his grip on the rifle, the officer frowned at that, then finally saluted. Turning about on a heel, he strode from the office with the rest of his troops close behind in tight formation.

"This way, Lord Carstairs," the priest directed, taking the explorer by the elbow. "The occult library is down in the catacombs."

"*Grazie*, father," the lord sighed in relief. "Thank you."

Although Father Tullio answered in the affirmative, his heart really didn't seem to be in it.

* * *

Going from hand to hand, and pocket to pocket, the little box eventually made its way to a secret part of the Vatican not on any map. The splinter was removed from the box and minutely examined by an unseen figure beyond a massive iron door. Suddenly there was a cackle of glee, the splinter vanished from sight, and the door was slammed shut with a hollow boom.

Beyond the door, a paneled room was lit by thousands of candles in tiny wall niches. Several black-hooded figures scuttled over to the newcomer, a white-robed figure, who bore the splinter on a silk pillow. As the pillow moved about, the others examined the splinter with sounds of pleasure. With regal dignity, the tiny sliver of dark wood was laid upon a vast limestone table covered with a pristine white cloth and adorned with thousands upon thousands of similar splinters, each bearing a small card with neatly written numbers. In the midst of the room was a dais of blue marble, upon which was a hollow trough lined with millions of similar splinters, all painstakingly fitted together into the vague shape of a tall, man-sized, capital letter 'T'.

* * *

Taking a locked stairwell down into the cellar, Father Tullio and Lord Carstairs followed a subterranean path that wound its way deeper and deeper into the bowels of the Earth. Lord Carstairs knew that this was only the tip of the catacombs of Rome. They were a nigh endless series of man-made tunnels, grottos, and burial chambers that once held the entire population of old Rome.

The rough-hewn tunnel was well lit by alcohol lamps, the blue flames giving an eerie illumination. As the two men progressed deeper, they passed dozens of doorways gaping wide, their interiors only dimly seen in the flickering light. But more than a few passages were sealed with bronze doors, securely closed with iron padlocks.

"What is it exactly that you seek, my son?" Father Tullio asked, unlocking yet another iron grating for them to pass through. Afterwards, he firmly locked it once more.

"A stone map, circa 1500 BC," Lord Carstairs replied, ducking his head to avoid a low support beam. "From the city state of Dutar."

Arching both eyebrows, Father Tullio almost tripped. "The Dutarian temple map?" his voice squeaked in surprise.

"Yes, I heard that the Vatican had it, along with the deciphering key, some sort of a bracelet."

"We do not have the bracelet," the priest averred, "only a rubbing."

Lord Carstairs already knew that, but did his best to act surprised. "Ah, more than satisfactory."

"The Dutarian map," Father Tullio mumbled, looking at the British lord sideways. "And you are a member of the London Explorers Club. I might have guessed."

For a while more, the men tramped along the stone tunnel until stopping at an innocuous door marked in Medieval Latin. Fumbling in his cassock, Father Tullio produced a key and unlocked the bulky padlock holding the old-style hasp shut.

"Broom Closet?" Lord Carstairs read aloud translating the sign.

As the heavy lock came undone, the plump priest gave a half-smile. "An innocent ruse to detour the unauthorized, eh?"

"Better than using tigers, I suppose," Carstairs muttered softly to himself.

Not quite sure what that meant, Father Tullio shrugged in response and pulled on the door. But it remained firmly in place as if nailed there. Taking hold of the latch with both hands, the priest tried once more to move the door, with the same lack of results.

"How curious," Tullio muttered softly, releasing the latch.

"Allow me, sir," Carstairs offered. Taking hold of the handle, the British lord applied more and more strength, but surprisingly the portal resisted even his efforts.

"It must be jammed," Father Tullio suggested, touching the cross around his neck. "This section of the catacombs is over a millennium old, you know."

"No, I don't think it's jammed," Lord Carstairs answered, placing an ear against the door. Very faintly, he could hear a whispery wind on the other side, steadily rising in tone and volume.

Leaning closer, Father Tullio copied the position. "Now whatever can that be?"

Although, Lord Carstairs did not know what was happening, he felt a definite tingling on the back of his neck, exactly as if he was on safari and a lion was about to drop on him from a tree branch directly above. Instincts honed in a thousand fights flared to life, and adrenaline surged through his body.

"There's trouble afoot. Stand back, sir!" Lord Carstairs snapped, and turning he kicked at the portal. The wooden planks cracked at the blow, but the door stayed in place. Striking twice more to no result, the lord then threw his entire body against the barrier in a full Rugby tackle, and the door exploded off its hinges with the sound of splintering wood.

As Lord Carstairs released the wreck of the door, a violent wind swept through the underground corridor, blowing away the dust of ages. Inside the room was a sort of hurricane, or dervish, a vortex of wind howling through the chamber bringing every book on the shelves alive with fluttering pages. The floor and ceiling were solid banks of fog, and filling the far wall was some sort of a hellish whirlpool, its misty center apparently extending forever.

Lord Carstairs could only stand and stare dumbfounded as a smooth rectangle of stone floated from one of the wall shelves and began to drift through the air towards the vertical tornado, the tornado's rim crackling with lightning. The explorer had no idea what he was looking at, but he recognized the floating stone tablet as the Dutarian map from Prof. Einstein's description. *This must be more dark magic from those dastardly squid chaps! And right here in the very bowels of the Vatican! Outrageous*! Lunging forward, the lord grabbed the stone block in both hands and held on for dear life itself.

"Go for help!" Lord Carstairs shouted over the strident wind, trying to dig his heels into the stone floor.

Hitching his cassock, Father Tullio departed with Olympic speed, already yelling for assistance and guards.

Exerting every ounce of his phenomenal strength, Carstairs tried to pull the Dutarian map away from the rushing matrix of colors. But the block continued to move relentlessly forward, as unstoppable as the tide.

Frantically searching for any purchase, the lord spread his legs wide on the rough-hewn floor and leaned backwards. Leverage was the answer, and the more, the better! The brutal, sucking wind whipped his clothes about with stinging force and the lord's arms seemed to creak audibly under the awful strain of the magical tug-o-war. Resolutely as a 500-point man at Eaton, Lord Carstairs put his entire body into the task, roaring in unbridled rage. The irresistible force was meeting the immovable object. But the stalemate did not last long, and soon the implacable forces holding the map began to drag him closer to the heart of the savage tornado.

In spite of everything he tried, Lord Carstairs was forced to grudgingly yield a step, then another, and still another towards the heart of the maelstrom. Bloody hell! Without warning, he crossed an invisible barrier and was engulfed in the turbulent zone of effect. Now he could all but see the magnetic-like attraction of the yawning pit ahead. Hooking a leg about a marble column gained Carstairs a brief respite, and he dared to stare directly into the magical abyss. Blinding sheets of lightning crashed in the distance, each deafening thunderbolt causing static-electric charges to crackle painfully over his skin. The tiny discharges blistered his hands and arms. But through the strobing light and hellish noise, Carstairs could faintly discern a rocky hill cresting to a castle made of jet-black glass. It was a horrid soaring fortress with flaring towers and jagged walls, a somber abode of inhuman madness that bade welcome to none. Nothing else of the landscape was visible, yet Carstairs somehow received an overwhelming feeling of death and desolation.

"For Queen and country!" Lord Carstairs shouted redoubling his efforts, and he actually managed to take a step backwards. *Yes! He was winning!*

As if enraged by the success, the lightning of the whirlpool struck at the man, the crackling discharge slammed him across the room, crashing him into the wall with bone-cracking force. Momentarily stunned, the lord lost his grip and the Dutarian tablet was yanked away to tumble and twirl off into the whirlpool of flashing colors.

Using a most ungentlemanly phrase, Lord Carstairs struggled forward after the tablet as it flew towards the black castle. Then from somewhere in the chaos he could hear a faint mocking laugh.

"Coward! Blackguard!" Lord Carstairs roared, brandishing a bruised fist. "Face me here and now!"

The laughter came once more, and the wind vanished as if it had never been. Caught by surprise, Carstairs stumbled forward to find himself all alone in the wreckage-filled room, with only the certainty of total failure for company.

* * *

Escorted by a full company of armed Swiss Guard, Lord Carstairs was shown off Vatican property, and given a heavy bill for the damages incurred. Weary with defeat, he paid the cashier on his way out and shuffled listlessly through the milling crowds of pilgrims. Heading down the street, Carstairs went to the piazza and found Prof. Einstein sitting at a corner table sipping wine and checking a pocket watch. The knowledge that the professor had been sitting about and having a fine afternoon did nothing to improve the lord's sour disposition. Then he glanced at the older man again.

"What happened to your ear, Professor?" Lord Carstairs demanded in real concern.

Reaching up to gingerly touch the injured earlobe, Prof. Einstein tried to force a joke about getting a gold ring and joining the navy, but the woebegone expression on his friend's face negated any such levity.

"It's not important, lad," Einstein said, gesturing at a chair. "I'll tell you later. Did you get to see the stone?"

"Oh, I got to see it, sure enough," Carstairs snarled, taking the seat. "That is, after I convinced them not to shoot me. But then the map was stolen from my very hands by some kind of, well, a sort of magical tornado."

"Big swirling thing full of color and noise?"

"Quite so, Professor!"

"Damn and blast. A dimensional vortex," Einstein identified with a frown. "Egad, those squid chappies are really pulling out all of the stops."

Reaching for the wine, Lord Carstairs poured himself a glass and drained it in a single draft. "And on top of losing the Dutarian map, afterwards I had to explain to several cardinals what happened, all of whom remembered your previous midnight visit to the archives in excruciating detail."

In apology, the professor hastily ordered another bottle of wine. After several more glasses, some of the edge had been taken off the lord's temper and Carstairs was able to relate the adventure in more detail.

"So they have beaten us," Lord Carstairs finished glumly, slamming aside his empty glass. "I never would have believed it possible. I mean, we're British, for God's sake!"

"Beaten? What nonsense, lad," Prof. Einstein snorted, gingerly massaging his sore chest. "We're far from beaten."

"Whatever do you mean?"

"Yes, the matter is dire. But we have a single hope remaining. It is a shot in the dark. A fool's gamble! But it just might work," Einstein said, clapping his hands together. "Actually, I've been looking for an excuse to try it for years. Even brought along the proper materials, just in case we came to an impasse, as we surely have. Preparation is all, lad!"

"Better and better," Lord Carstairs acknowledged, feeling a glimmer of hope once more. "What is it?"

"First we need to rent a boat."

"A boat?" Lord Carstairs echoed in surprise. "What kind of a boat?"

"A ship, actually. As large as possible," Einstein said with a glint of mischief twinkling in his eyes. "And then we must place an advertisement in the local newspaper. A full page in the evening edition should do nicely. I wonder if we can get the inside spread on this short a notice?"

"How very interesting," Carstairs said slowly, resting an elbow on the table, and placing his jaw in a palm. "And, pray tell, what precisely is it that we will be advertising? Our own staggering incompetence, or the imminent destruction of the world?"

Slapping the larger man on the shoulder, the professor gave a laugh. "Neither, lad. The advertisement will be a call to gather a brave crew of sailors to join us on a journey to destroy the temple of the Squid God."

Although temporarily unable to speak, Lord Carstairs' expression quite eloquently stated his heart-felt opinion that Professor Felix Einstein had obviously gone absolutely and utterly insane.

NINE

Thousands of miles away, a lone robed figure stood motionless in a hurricane of wind and thunder, droning forbidden words of arcane power.

With both clenched fists raised as if ready to strike, bunched muscles stood like knotted rope on his arms, tendons and veins painfully extended on his neck, and his flushed face was ablaze with the hideous tattoo of an engorged squid. Its devil eyes overlaid his own, giving the design a horrible semblance of true life, the suckered tentacles seeming to move inside his sweat-drenched skin.

Damp clothes clinging to his shaking frame, the robed man increased the tempo of his chanting, the tongue-twisting words causing the robed crowd of onlookers to fidget in discomfort. Protectively surrounded by the people was a large black cauldron of bubbling red blood. The pungent steam rising from the vessel entwined about itself, and angled over and seeped into the back of the shouting man, the spot of entry glowing like a white-hot wound.

The brick and mortar wall of the basement had been replaced by a horizontal vortex of swirling clouds, the border a seething oval of energy that filled the cellar in wild bursts of color. Inside the strident matrix was a black castle atop a barren hill and in the distance was another magical vortex with a small object moving about inside.

With a shout, a Squid God worshiper excitedly pointed. Quickly, the others craned their necks and squinted against the crackling pyrotechnics. A glad shout arose as they saw the faint speck arcing into the sky over the castle. It was the ancient stone tablet! At the apogee of flight, a bolt of lightning transfixed the Dutarian tablet, exploding it into fragments that disintegrated into dust as they fell away.

A cry of victory rose from the assemblage and an expression of confidence crept into the features of the droning man.

"Success, Brother Carl!" a woman cried in delight. "You beat the infidel!"

Just then, the cellar door slammed open and in walked the bony High Priest. Rather than his ornate robes of station, he was dressed in the simple garb of a shop clerk; yet his mere presence filled the crowd with fearful apprehension.

"Stop, Carl!" the High Priest bellowed, his face distorted with rage.

"Cease this at once, or die!"

At the interruption, Carl Smythe slowed his chanting and the vortex faded away until the wall was composed of simple brick and mortar once more. Gradually, the colored lights dimmed, and the oil lanterns automatically flared into life as a gentle wind swept about the cellar rustling papers. Then all was still. Even the cauldron stopped its ominous bubbling.

"'Do not disturb the old man,' you probably told them," the High Priest sneered, advancing step by step towards the quaking robed man. "'We can handle this ourselves. Who needs him?'"

Pushing back the cowl of his robe, Carl turned to face the approaching High Priest. The tattoo had already faded from his skin and he appeared a normal human being again.

"But, Holy One, I succeeded!" Carl replied confidently. "The ancient map is destroyed! The Englishmen can never find the temple now."

Stepping forward, the priest violently slapped Carl across the face. Worried murmurs came from the attending crowd.

"Fool! Idiot! Poltroon!" the High Priest snarled contemptuously. "You did not 'handle' the situation. You did nothing but waste some of our precious reserve of magic. You have weakened the Pool of Life specifically created to bring back the Great Lord Squid!"

Wincing in pain, Carl touched his face and the fingers came away covered with blood. "But there was no other way to stop them from getting the map!" he whimpered.

"We couldn't take the Vatican by force, Holy One," somebody said in the crowd. "It is far too heavily guarded."

"Magically and physically," a fat man added.

His eyes barely human in their anger, the High Priest gazed at the cowering Carl. "No? Well, I can think of four other ways the objective could have been reached, without resorting to magic."

Utterly forlorn, Carl hung his head in shame. "I am heartily sorry that I failed you, Holy One. If you wish, I shall remove my mantle of authority and join the ranks of the new believers, there to serve in any way asked."

"Did you really think to get off that easily?" the High Priest demanded in cold fury. "By the Great Lord Squid, you are a fool."

New sweat poured down Carl's pale features. "Sir?"

"Kill yourself," the High Priest ordered.

The onlookers started to gasp, but cut the sound off in the middle.

"Have mercy!" Carl begged, kneeling down to grab the cuff of the High Priest's trousers. "Mercy!"

The High Priest looked down upon the man in marked disdain. "No," he stated, the single word spoken in a tone that broached no further discussion.

Releasing the cuff, Carl slowly stood, but kept his head bowed in shame. "Then please, grant me the boon of adding my blood to the life pool for the Great Squid."

Tilting his head, the High Priest chewed a lip while considering the suggestion. Lifting a hand, he flipped it back and forth while weighing the single failure against a lifetime of obedience. "Granted," he said at last.

A cheer rose from the robed crowd and tears of happiness mixed with the sweat on Carl's face. "Oh, thank you. Thank you!" he gushed happily. "Blessings of the Great Squid upon you!"

Impatiently, the High Priest waved the fellow away. "Cease that blubbering and go kill yourself."

"At once, your holiness!" Carl chortled in glee. Rushing over to the cauldron, the man drew a knife from inside the sleeves of his robes and calmly slit his wrists. Hot blood spurted out to splash into the reeking cauldron.

Led by the High Priest, the crowd began to chant a prayer as Carl grew pale, and as the blood ceased to flow, he finally toppled to the floor in a dead heap.

"Death for life," the High Priest shouted. "Life for death!"

The crowd took up the chant until a pounding came from the ceiling.

"What's going on down there!" a woman's voice demanded.

Extending a bony finger, the High Priest pointed at one of the Squid God worshipers. Stepping into the middle of the cellar, the man cleared his throat. "Ahem, terribly sorry about that, Mrs. Smiggins, we, ah, the cat tipped over a lamp!"

"The rules say no pets, Mr. Wicker!" the voice beyond the ceiling rasped angrily.

The man called Wicker glanced about in confusion, then rallied. "Oh, it's not a real cat, Mrs. Smiggins. I meant the fellow in the cat costume!"

"The rules say no costume parties, Mr. Wicker!"

"It's not a party, Mrs. Smiggins," he said desperately. "We're practicing a skit."

If it was possible, the stern voice grew even colder. "And the rules, Mr. Wicker, most explicitly state, no actors or other livestock."

Stepping to his side, a woman whispered into Wicker's ear.

"Oh, they're not professional actors!" he shouted with a chuckle. "That would be disgusting! Our church group is just putting on a skit . . . for the orphanage!"

There was a pause. "Very well!" the woman barked. "But this is the last time I shall tolerate any noise!" There came the sound of heavy footsteps, closely followed by a slamming door.

Everyone in the cellar gave a sigh of relief.

"Cor' blimey," Wicker exhaled, slumping his shoulders. "What a nasty old witch."

"If only she were," another man sighed.

"S'truth! If the old biddy is such a problem, brother, why don't we just kill her?" a woman asked, pulling a dagger from her sleeve and testing the point on a thumb.

"Because this spot is our fixed locale of power," the High Priest answered in annoyance. "Killing the legal owner of this land would taint the pool of power, and it would take us many weeks to tap into the dimension of magic again. Time we can not spare."

The Squid God worshipers got long faces at that, and shuffled their shoes on the ground.

"However," the High Priest added after a moment, "when the time is right, Mrs. Smiggins will be the first to die."

"Hallelujah!" everybody whispered in chorus.

* * *

Bursting through the front door of the London Explorers Club, a panting telegram boy delivered an envelope to a liveried page. The page tipped the errand boy a penny, then placed the telegram on a silver tray, and primly carried it down the main corridor and into the smoking room, a quiet haven of gun cabinets, chess boards, and humidors.

Clustered about a poker table, several of the senior members were puffing cigars while they studied a complex diagram depicting a complicated winch hoisting an ark-shaped object. Faintly in the background could be heard the steady hammering of a busy work crew building the new waterproof wing of the club.

Appearing from nowhere, Jeeves Sinclair intercepted the page at the doorway and accepted the telegram. Minutely adjusting the formal black suit of his butler's uniform, Jeeves walked to the men at the poker table and politely coughed twice to announce his presence.

Removing his cigar to tap the ash into a crystal bowl, Colonel Pierpont glanced up from the diagram. "What is it, Jeeves?"

With uncharacteristic boldness, the butler walked into the room, apparently impervious to the dense clouds of tobacco smoke. "Telegram, sir," he announced.

"For whom?" Dr. Thompkins asked, recapping a whiskey bottle on the shelf behind the mahogany bar counter.

Examining the outside of the envelope, Jeeves blinked in surprise, then did it again. "Why, it appears to be for me, sir," he muttered, sounding embarrassed. "How very strange."

"For you?" Colonel Pierpont asked, putting the cigar back into place. It was always faintly disturbing to realize that the staff had lives outside of their work.

Extracting a tiny folding knife from his vest, Jeeves began to slit open the telegram envelope. "If I may, sir?"

"Certainly, by all means," Lord Danvers gestured magnanimously. Courtesy cost nothing, as his dear mother used to say, while a good servant was priceless.

Pocketing the envelope, the butler remained impassive as he read the brief message twice.

"Deuced strange our butler receiving a telegram," Baron Edgewaters muttered, stroking his Royal British Marine moustache. "Smacks of socialism to me."

"Oh, be quiet," another man chided, doodling notes on the diagram with an engineer's pencil. "Everything smacks of socialism to you. Including my billiard playing."

"Quite!" Baron Edgewaters laughed. "Quite so!"

"Is it bad news?" Dr. Thompkins slurped, his red nose lodged comfortably inside a glass tumbler filled with good amber whiskey.

With exaggerated care, Jeeves folded the telegram and tucked it into the same pocket as the envelope before replying. "I am afraid so, sir. I must ask for a leave of absence."

A murmur filled the smoking room and the explorers crowded around closer.

Removing his pince-nez, Colonel Pierpont polished the lenses on a sleeve. "For how long?"

"Indefinitely, sir," Jeeves answered.

Finished with the spectacular ablutions, the colonel slipped his glasses back on again. "Indeed. May I ask why?"

"It's my aged mother," the butler said sadly. "She's had a remission and is on her sick bed."

Sympathetically, the colonel nodded. "I understand. When do you wish this leave to be effective?"

"Immediately, sir."

This time, anguished cries sounded from the members present. The London Explorer's Club without Jeeves? But that would be like cricket with no wicket! Why, Jeeves Sinclair had been a part of the club for as long as anybody could remember!

"Egad, man!" Lord Danvers cried, coming as close as he ever had to dropping a full glass of whiskey. "But what ever shall we do without you?"

"With your consent, I shall have a temporary replacement sent over from Buckingham Palace," Jeeves replied, closing the lid on a humidor that was not in use by anybody. "I have a cousin there, Carl Smythe. You should find him most satisfactory."

"By the way, what is lunch today?" General MacAdams creaked from a chair by the fireplace. The old man was almost completely covered with a thick military blanket. "Soup again? Or more of that damned curry?"

"Prime rib in wine sauce," Jeeves announced softly. "And cook's special treacle pudding."

The general smiled vaguely, "The kind with the little butterscotch fishies?"

Using a handkerchief, the butler wiped some drool off the wrinkled chin and tucked a stray bit of blanket back under the aged military officer. "Just so, sir. Lots and lots of little fishies."

"Excellent," General MacAdams whispered, falling promptly to sleep.

Arising from his chair, Sir Lovejoy waddled forward. "I say, must you really leave so hastily?"

Primly proper, Jeeves brushed a speck of lint off the velvet collar of his black morning coat. As always, he was the perfect picture of the ultimate butler. "The summons was urgent, sir. I fear that I must be gone within the hour."

"So be it," the knight said. Then after a brief pause, Sir Lovejoy impetuously offered his hand to the servant and they shook. "Best of luck, old top."

Turning to leave, Jeeves found himself waylaid by an endless series of glad-handing and well wishing.

"Take care," Baron Edgewaters added, his voice thick with emotion.

"Let us know if you need anything," Judge Foxington-Symthe ordered, his eyes filled with unaccustomed mist. "Anything at all, old man."

"The sentiment is truly appreciated, gentlemen," Jeeves said softly, his features masked by darkness as he stepped into the shadows of the main corridor. "But I can absolutely guarantee you that this matter will end in death."

TEN

Powerful waves crashed across the prow of the *Bella Donna* as the Italian steamship knifed through the cold water of the Tyrrhenian Sea.

Although the weather had been fair this morning, the sails were furled tight, and the cargo hatches were lashed closed, as if the stout craft was prepared for a major storm. The bridge was set on top of an island of workrooms and private cabins. Behind its wide glass windows big men in heavy coats could be seen standing at the wheeled helm, scanning the horizon with binoculars, and checking navigational charts with frantic intensity. Rising directly aft of the bridge was a tall riveted flue spewing out great volumes of dense black smoke.

Since dawn, the rented craft had been under full steam, yet in spite of carrying a working crew of two hundred sailors, the decks were deserted except for two sodden figures standing at the extreme forward point of the bow. The crashing waves constantly spraying them with chilly seawater, the men expertly swayed with the motion of the hurtling vessel and continued to check over the weapons in their hands.

Frowning in concentration at their task, Prof. Einstein and Lord Carstairs were dressed in quilted traveling clothes, Macintosh rainslicks, and sealskin boots, and had bulky canvas bags draped over their shoulders.

On the horizon, the sky was growing dark as clouds began to blot out the sun. However, the sea was preternaturally calm, and unnaturally vacant of fish. Since the *Bella Donna* had sailed from port early this morning, the explorers had seen nothing alive moving in the sea, and these waters were normally famous for their rich variety of sea life.

With a scowl, Lord Carstairs finished loading his Webley and tucked the pistol into a military-style shoulder holster. "Do you really think this will work, Professor?"

"Do you know of anything else we can try, lad?" Prof. Einstein asked, nervously twisting the silver lion head grip of his sword cane. The Adams .32 pistol was snug in a belt holster, and a deadly French stiletto was tucked into his right boot.

"If I did, sir," Carstairs rumbled, "we would not be here."

"Then check the distance, please. Precision is important."

Reaching into the canvas shoulder pouch hanging at his side, Lord Carstairs withdrew a brass sextant and squinted at the dark sky through the device. Briefly, there was a cloud break and the lord caught the sun to do some fast mental calculations.

"Done, sir," Carstairs reported, returning the sextant to its cushioned box in the pouch. "We are past the twelve mile limit and are officially in international waters."

Straightening his cuffs, Einstein took a deep breath. "Then this is it. Are you ready?"

Loosening his collar, Carstairs answered with an affirmative grunt.

Cupping both hands to his mouth, the professor turned away from the sea and shouted at the top of his lungs towards the ship, "THE SQUID GOD ISN'T FIT TO BE A DOG'S BREAKFAST!"

Instantly, there came a wild scream and a snarling sailor waving a large knife sprang from behind a lifeboat to charge at the Englishmen. Assuming a firing stance, Lord Carstairs triggered the Webley and a single booming round brought the sailor crashing to the deck.

On the bridge, men dropped things and pointed, their mouths flapping wide in shock.

"Well, sir?" Carstairs asked, the big bore pistol still smoking in his fist.

Hurriedly reaching into his coat pocket, Prof. Einstein pulled out a small crystal ball clutched in a mummified tarantula. Slightly embarrassed, he touched the crystal with the tip of his tongue.

"Anything?" Lord Carstairs asked eagerly.

Lowering the crystal, the professor sadly shook his head.

Resting a fist akimbo, Lord Carstairs gave the older man a skeptical look. "You are sure that thing is working?"

"Definitely. If there is an undead presence out there, I will definitely be able to detect it." Absent-mindedly, Einstein stroked the globe and the spider twitched in response. "This talisman has proved itself useful innumerable times in the past. I have no doubt that the Witch Doctor who owned it previously was most vexed at discovering its absence. Although, I did leave him a splendid picture of the Queen in exchange."

"More than adequate compensation," Lord Carstairs acknowledged. "Then the question becomes one of whether or not there is something, anything, out there."

Holstering the pistol, the lord extracted a Royal Navy telescope from his canvas bag and scanned the horizon. "And so far, sir, we seem to be alone."

"Well, it was only an idea," Prof. Einstein demurred uneasily.

"An idea that has quite probably gotten us trapped on a ship staffed entirely with squid worshipers," Carstairs reminded harshly. "If any innocent sailors had answered that advertisement to sign aboard and 'destroy the Temple of the Living Squid God,' I should imagine that they would have shown to investigate that gun shot by now."

As another crashing spray washed across the bow, the professor frowned pensively and tucked both hands into his pockets. "Yes. If pressed, I had planned on saying that it was self-defense. But it appears that explanations won't be necessary."

But with those words, Prof. Einstein contorted his face in the wildest fashion, and then smacked himself on the head. "Of course! What a dolt I am! It was self-defense!" The professor gestured at the cooling body sprawled on the deck. A wash of spray crashed over the form, making the limbs move in a gross pantomime of life.

"Don't you see?" Einstein cried, aghast. "That chap was coming at us with a knife! That nullifies everything! The legends clearly state that it must be an act of murder."

Ever so slowly, Lord Carstairs removed the telescope from his eye and pivoted to stare downward at the man. "Meaning that we have got to kill a sailor in cold blood?" he demanded.

"Exactly!"

"B-but we can't do that!" the lord cried out.

"Eh? Why ever not, lad?"

"Because it would be murder! The most horrible act that can be committed!"

In exasperation, Prof. Einstein threw up both hands. "But that's the whole bloody idea, you fool! Besides, you said the crew is obviously composed of Squid God worshipers, so what is the problem?

"I could be wrong," Lord Carstairs hedged, tucking the telescope into the pouch. "It occurs to me that a perfectly innocent sailor might be hesitant about showing himself after his mysterious employers just gunned down a shipmate. That is another possibility."

"Well, maybe," the professor hesitantly relented.

Undaunted, Carstairs continued, "Besides, we do not know that killing them would have any effect. Of course, everyone has heard the legends, but that's all they might be. You are asking me to commit murder, the most serious, heinous crime imaginable, for what may be no reason."

Assuming a Parliamentary stance, the British lord clasped hands behind his back. "I'm sorry, sir, but as an officer and a gentleman, I cannot do it."

"Does that mean it is safe to come out now, *signore*?" a small voice asked as a frightened face rose into view from behind one of the lifeboats. "If it is not too much trouble, I believe that the crew would like to return to port. I have forgotten my wallet."

Numerous cries from behind other lifeboats affirmed that most of the crew had various articles missing and they would be quite lost without the items.

With a hollow feeling in his stomach, Carstairs gave a mighty sigh. "This has been a serious waste of time, sir," he said, then jumped as the sharp report of a pistol cracked across the main deck of the *Bella Donna*.

Flinching from the fiery discharge, Lord Carstairs pulled his own weapon as Prof. Einstein fired twice more in quick succession. Across the deck, a sailor clutched the bloody ruin of his throat and stumbled backwards to fall over the railing and disappear into the choppy sea.

"Keep a watch on them," Einstein said, bringing out the tarantula once more.

Thumbing back the hammer on the Webley pistol for quick action, Carstairs spotted countless sailors ducking out of sight all over the ship. There were more sailors aboard the *Bella Donna* than he had imagined. A lot more. A tremendously lot more. And most of them were now wearing robes. *Oh ho!*

"Sir, I am impressed," Lord Carstairs acknowledged out of the side of his mouth, watching for fresh treachery. "However did you know that fellow was a squid worshiper? Did you spot his dagger?"

"I had no idea, lad," the professor said honestly, tapping his tongue against the crystal. "But the fate of the world rests upon our actions. We needed to murder a man, so I have done so."

In abject horror, the lord lowered his weapon to gape at the elderly professor. "Sir!" he cried, putting a wealth of information and feeling into the single word.

Completely nonplussed, Prof. Einstein continued. "I am quite sure, Lord Carstairs, that the Hells of innumerable religions, both active and forgotten, are already vying for the possession of my soul. I do what I think is best. Now be quiet. There is something out there."

Then softly, as if speaking to himself, the professor added, "And considering how many sacred temples I have defiled and holy men I have annoyed, the Judeo-Christian lot will just have to bloody well take a number to get their paws on me."

Shifting his grip on the Webley, Lord Carstairs muttered something under his breath about the end justifying the means. Then the lord paused in the moral litany as he noticed the lifeboat behind which the dead sailor had been hiding. Upon closer scrutiny, the lord could see that the ocean spray was starting to wash away the fresh paint on the paper patches covering countless small holes bored into its hull. The lifeboat was as seaworthy as a kitchen colander! In a flash, he wondered if the very same thing hadn't been done to every other lifeboat, perhaps even to the main hull of the *Bella Donna*?

"Oh, I say, Professor," Carstairs said calmly. "If the Flying Dutchman is ever to appear, this would be a jolly good time."

"It is close," Einstein stated matter-of-factly, his vision unfocused into the distance. "Yes, very close."

Glancing over the gunwale, the lord saw only empty sea stretching to the turbulent horizon. The storm was coming on fast. More bad news.

"Where is it, sir?" the lord demanded.

Keeping his tongue pressed to the grotesque crystal, the professor pointed a finger off the port side of the Italian steamer. "Over there," he mumbled. "I sense a presence. No, many presences. They have seen us and they are most annoyed. There is great evil, lad. Great evil and great sorrow."

Prof. Einstein removed his tongue from the crystal with a soft pop, as if it had been frozen to a lamppost in winter. "They're here," he whispered, rubbing the crystal clean.

Understandably anxious, Lord Carstairs stared off the port side, but there was only a slight darkening in the air as if an evening mist had risen from the sea. A rustling sound came from behind the man, and Carstairs spun around blindly to fire his Webley into the sky, the booming report sending a dozen armed men back into hiding.

"They had guns on the train. Why don't they use them now?" the lord demanded irritably.

"Firearms did not exist when the Squid God was alive," the professor muttered, lost in concentration. "And now it's too close to the birthing ceremony. As the magic increases, their ability to use guns weakens."

"Ah. Good for us."

"At the moment, yes. But later . . ." Once again, Einstein touched the talisman with his tongue.

"Later?" Lord Carstairs asked worried.

"They're here, directly alongside us, lad!" the professor cried in satisfaction, pocketing the talisman. "Yes, I can see one of them. And . . . and he's seen me! What in the . . . he has something in his hands. Swinging it around and round. Some sort of grappling hook. I . . . look out!" With a cry of pain, Prof. Einstein jerked forward and clutched at his chest.

Keeping the Webley at the ready, Lord Carstairs clutched the professor's arm to keep him from falling overboard. But the limb felt strange, lightweight, and brittle, almost as if it was made of dried leaves.

"What happened, Professor?" the lord demanded. "Are you all right?"

"M-my soul," Prof. Einstein spoke in a ghostly echo, going very pale. "They . . . they don't require my corporeal form, lad, just my soul!"

"Cheeky bounders!"

"And now they have got it," the professor whispered.

In dire consternation, Lord Carstairs furrowed his brow. "And they are preparing to leave?"

Slumping his shoulders, Prof. Einstein nodded bleakly. "They have what they came for. It's over. We have failed again."

"This will not do!" Carstairs stated grimly. Releasing his trembling friend, the lord strode to the railing, took a deep breath, and loudly bellowed as possible. "Ahoy, the Dutchman! Permission to come aboard!"

The entire world seemed to pause at the cry. Even the wind stopped, and the waves froze on the sea.

Moving hesitantly, Einstein placed his tongue to talisman once more. "I sense confusion," the professor murmured. "And a great deal of vulgar language. Ye gods!"

Fading into view from out of the empty air, an ancient wooden gangplank extended to make solid contact on the deck of the steamship with a loud clunk. Without prompting, both Prof. Einstein and Lord Carstairs hopped over the gunwale to land on the ethereal plank.

Screams of rage sounded from all over the *Bella Donna* and a hundred robed sailors brandishing knives, hatchets, axes, and other implements of destruction poured forth from behind the lifeboats, capstan, anchor hoist, coal lockers, bridge, hatchways, portholes, air vents, rope piles, and even the smoking flue. Several of the sailors threw knives, others cast harpoons, and a couple fired arrows from crossbows, but the fusillade passed harmlessly through the ghostly Einstein and Carstairs as they started running along the vanishing plank.

Going further into the mist, Lord Carstairs glanced behind to see the *Bella Donna* begin to fade from sight, the robed crew now silently screaming obscenities and waving an arsenal of weapons.

Sighing in relief, the lord began to choke on the thickening fog, the foul vapor thick with the pungent smell of ancient dust and rotting corpses. With a ragged cough, Einstein covered his face with a cloth, and Carstairs wisely copied the action. By Gadfrey, the reek was horrendous!

Slowly becoming visible ahead of the explorers loomed a gigantic shape, vaguely ship-like, but a vessel whose lines were completely unfamiliar to either of the world travelers.

As Prof. Einstein and Lord Carstairs proceeded closer, a tremendous explosion sounded faintly from behind, and they turned to see most of the main deck replaced with a smoking hole. The *Bella Donna* was already starting to list as it began to sink into the Tyrrhenian Sea. Flaming debris from the blast was still falling from the sky as frantic sailors raced about stuffed cloth into the holes of the life boats, while others clumsily dove into the brine. Seconds later, the building storm broke and the steamship vanished in a lightning flash and torrential rain.

Advancing along the plank with a steady gait, Professor Einstein turned away from the pandemonium. "Well done, lad. How did you know this crazy idea would work?"

"I didn't," Lord Carstairs replied honestly, keeping a steady watch on the shifting plank. "But it certainly had the distinct advantage of never having been tried before. Who would willingly ask to come aboard The Flying Dutchman?"

"Arr," an inhuman voice rasped from somewhere inside the billowing cloudbank. "That be our very question, matey."

ELEVEN

Slow and stately, Big Ben chimed the time across the city of London, its cocoon of scaffolding shaking slightly at each strike of the mighty bell.

Far across town, Mary Einstein sipped a cup of scalding coffee and watched the streets below through a cracked window. A loaded shotgun was cradled in her left arm, and a brace of Adams pistols were tucked into her belt just above the bustle.

Good lord, was it only two o'clock in the afternoon? she thought, barely able to believe it. *The night had been so long, so very long.*

Twelve times the Squid God worshipers had attacked the museum, and each sally had been bloodier, more vicious than the last. With rifle and crossbow, she had eliminated a dozen of the bounders, but still they came on, and on, as unstoppable as army ants, or barristers.

Whatever else you could say about the Dutarian warriors, Mary raged privately, *they most certainly were a precocious lot!*

She had no idea what her uncle would do when he saw the present state of the museum. Much of the building was in ruins, with hundreds of irreplaceable exhibits smashed to pieces, or destroyed by fire. Every window but this one in the living room was covered with boards to hide the missing glass, and gaping holes in the roof had been crudely patched with wooden tabletops. Even the vaunted front gate that withstood The Troubles without a scratch now hung twisted in its battered frame, suspended by a single cracked hinge. The exterior of the museum was dotted with bullet holes, and the pavement was cracked from explosions. The garden was a shambles with a mighty oak tree split in twain, and in a small crater laid a broken sword. A parting gift from a Squid God worshiper she had shot twice in the arse before he would relinquish the dire weapon.

Even the cats were missing, Mary sighed. *Run away, vaporized, or kidnapped, there was no way to know.*

Shifting the shotgun cradled in her arms, Mary craned her neck to see a lone police constable standing on the street corner, whistling and twirling his nightstick. A single copper. But then as the police said, compared to The Troubles, this matter was little more than a Saturday night tosser. Although on a personal note, Mary was starting to imagine that the police considered her uncle little more than a grave robber and really didn't know whom to support when somebody tried to steal back his possessions. How narrowed minded! Even the private detectives she had attempted to hire all turned the job down flat, that is, once they learned for whom they would have been working. Uncle Felix's reputation was finally catching up with him. A pity that the social retribution had to arrive on her shift. Ah well, such is life.

"Miss Einstein, I have been thinking," Katrina said, attaching a new string to her crossbow. "What if all of these attacks were not attempts to kidnap you to use against the professor?"

Moving away from the window so that she would not get shot in the back from a passing cab again, Mary limped across the living room and dropped heavily into a chair.

"But what else could they be?" she asked, plucking poisoned darts from the velvet cloth.

"I have no idea, miss, to be sure," Katrina said, notching a fresh quarrel into the crossbow. "But maybe there is something the Squid God chappies need in the museum, some ancient item, a charm or talisman to finish the ceremony of the rebirth."

"Or something they're afraid of," Mary muttered thoughtfully, throwing a dart into the crackling fireplace. A second later, the flames turned black as pitch, bubbling and gurgling, and then returned to a normal fire once more.

"What a lovely poison," Katrina said in frank admiration, slinging the crossbow over a shoulder. "Almost as nice as our little golden frogs."

"Not quite that powerful," Mary smiled wearily, brushing back a strand of loose hair from her face. Something in the museum, and not her. Bedamned, it was a deuced clever notion. But whatever could it be? Between the public museum, and her uncle's private collection of occult effluvia, anything was possible.

Rising from her settee, Katrina walked to the trolley and poured them both a cold cup of the thick European coffee the professor loved so much. The machine for making it was to have been a Christmas present for the man, but duty calls for all in time of action, and the sludge-like brew would keep a corpse in motion for a fortnight. Longer with sugar.

"What can we do if it is some exhibit they want to purloin, miss?" Katrina asked, starting across the room. "We already have the entire establishment under lock and key, with a constable outside."

Kicking a bent knife on the carpeting out of the way, the cook brought the brimming mug to the exhausted woman, and Mary thanked her with a nod.

"Well," Mary said slowly, flinching as she sipped the acidic brew. "We could always burn the place down."

"Ma'am?" Katrina squeaked, dropping her mug. The cold coffee hit the floor and sizzled louder than the Squid God poison in the fireplace. "Burn the museum . . . b-but this is your uncle's life's work! It would destroy him to see the museum level as a cricket field!"

"Yes, it would," Mary sighed, placing aside the empty mug. "But we may have no choice. How much coal oil and dynamite do we have in the cupboard, anyway?"

"Plenty," Katrina replied in a brogue, a touch of her Irish heritage coming through unexpectedly. "But don't you go be doing anything hasty there, little miss. Let me make a few inquiries first. Perhaps I can get us some assistance for the matter."

"More tigers?" Mary asked curiously, pulling out a pistol to check the cartridges in the cylinder. "Or maybe lions this time? If we use dogs, there better be a bloody great number of them. Or at the very least, they should be exceptionally large hounds. Now I do recall hearing some good things about a certain kennel near Baskerville . . ."

"I have better idea in mind, dear," Katrina said resolutely. "What we need is assistance to guard this modern-day mausoleum."

But the cook abruptly stopped talking when she spied a furtive motion near the window. When Mary looked up and saw the expression on the other woman's face, she instantly jumped out of the comfortable chair to spin about fast. While Mary brought up the shotgun, Katrina did the same with her crossbow. As both of the women prepared to fire, a fuzzy little squirrel scampered along the windowsill, its cheeks bulging with nuts. Ever so slowly, the two women eased their stances, and put the weapons away once more.

"You were saying about getting some help," Mary said, with a weary sigh. "But unfortunately, I have already tried everybody available. The police are too busy, the military says it is not their concern, and the members of the Explorers Club are guarding their own establishment from the rain. Whatever that means! Who else can there be?"

"You'd be surprised," Katrina said in a conspiratorial manner, glancing at the window. "I'll tell you when I get back, miss. Only be a few ticks, ya know."

With a casual wave of dismissal, Mary deposited herself into the chair again. "As you wish. The squiddies rarely attack during the daylight."

"Yes, I know." Laying aside the crossbow, Katrina took a spare Webley .32 revolver from a drawer full of assorted guns, then pinned a wide flowery hat primly in place and departed from the living room at a hurried pace, locking the door in her wake.

Maybe she belongs to some secret society like my uncle, Mary thought in wry amusement. *The International Sisterhood of Cooks and Chiefs. Housekeepers Incorporated.*

Impulsively rising again to make some more of the European coffee, Mary fought back an undignified yawn. She would not be ashamed to accept help from anybody at the moment. Even that oddly secretive Daughter's of Lesbos club that so wanted her for a member, but Uncle Felix stoutly refused even to permit her to attend a meeting.

Rummaging about in a pocket, Mary found a Lucifer and in a very unladylike manner scraped it alive on a shoe heel. Lighting the little alcohol burner underneath the silver urn, she got the blue flame adjusted and soon the coffee began to bubble. Shuffling wearily to a chair, Mary inhaled the pungent fumes, and sent a silent prayer to the universe that Uncle Felix and Benjamin were doing a much better job than she of stopping the impending apocalypse.

* * *

As the fat cook left the museum and rushed down the pavement, the skinny little squirrel spit the nuts out of his mouth. *Egad, what a hideous flavor!* Striding to the street corner, the squirrel inserted two tiny fingers into its jaw and sharply whistled for a cab. As a brougham carriage rattled by without stopping, the squirrel looked at its raised furry arm, and smacked itself in the head right between the pointy ears. The squirrel rushed into a small bush from which then came some inhuman mumbling, a flash of light, a rumble of thunder, and the Dutarian High Priest of the Living Squid God rose from the bush covered with tufts of fur and leaves.

Fighting his way out of the shrubbery, the exhausted High Priest started to summon another cab, paused, and angrily spit an acorn from his mouth. By the Great Lord Squid, the bloody things were everywhere!

Stepping to the curb, the High Priest gave a sharp whistle and the same brougham cab from before stopped this time to let the man climb aboard.

"How did it go, Holy One?" the cabby asked, shaking the reins. The horses whinnied and started forward at an easy trot.

"The silly little skirts are bringing in some help," the priest growled, leaning back in the seat, then frowned and reached into his pants to extract another acorn. This time, he popped it into his mouth and chewed with a vengeance.

"That could be trouble, sir," the driver said glancing sideways. On the street corner a full company of Royal British Marines were walking along in tight formation, a Union Jack fluttering on a pole, while a couple of beefy Scots in kilts expertly made their bagpipes howl in anguish.

"Only for them," the High Priest growled, turning to spit out the remains of the nut cap. *Hmm, not bad. Perhaps acorns were an acquired taste. Like American beer, or human brains.*

Outside the carriage, the marching soldiers started a new tune with great gusto. The priest grimaced at the caterwauling. *Now bagpipes, on the other hand . . .*

"Whatever do you mean, sir?" the driver asked puzzled, flinching from the musical onslaught.

Ripping apart a handkerchief, the thin Dutarian stuffed bits of cloth into his ears. *Ah, better.*

"If the ladies can summon assistance, so can we!" the High Priest growled angrily. "Only let me assure you that our new associates will be much more . . . infernal than anybody they can possibly obtain for hire."

TWELVE

Stepping off the gangplank, Prof. Einstein and Lord Carstairs moved through a hatchway in the gunwale and onto the wooden deck of the strange vessel. When they did, the unnatural mist surrounding the explorers gave a final swirl and faded into nothingness. As the air became clear, just for an instant both of the men thought they had been reduced in size. Then came the startling realization that the sailing ship was huge. Tremendously huge. Mammoth beyond anything they had ever seen.

The vessel resembled an old world clipper ship, with the main deck stretching into the distance like a vast desert plain. Nine immense masts rose into the sky, each shaft thicker than the Tower of London. Ten thousand acres of canvas were laced with miles of rope. There were a dozen capstan rollers bulging with chains, with individual links thick enough to be anchors themselves. The forecastle was larger than the Albert Hall; the quarterdeck could have held army battalion maneuvers, while the main castle was equal to the castle of Buckingham Palace.

There were even more oddities. The dark wood of the ship was deeply grained and, although it appeared solid, when seen out of the corner of an eye, the material seemed to warp in a most disturbing fashion. Plus, there were four gigantic steering wheels, each facing a different direction, which was flatly impossible. Rolling with a terrible slowness, the ship bizarrely moved against the swells of the sea in a most contrary manner, and pervading everything was a low mournful keening. The ghostly moaning came from the very wood of the monstrous vessel.

Then there was the crew standing around Einstein and Carstairs. There were hundreds of crewmen scattered about the deck, and countless more hanging from the rigging like jungle monkeys. British tars stood alongside Vikings, who peered over the masters of Chinese junks. Spanish dandies jostled for position with American slave merchants, while stiffly formal German officers avoided contact with the Australian rumrunners and Eskimo whalers. On a dark night, when the fog rolled in from the sea, bringing with it the smell of salt and rotting fish, these people might well have passed for normal sailors. But only if you were under the stupefying influence of the illegal drug laudanum. They were an ill-dressed lot, surly, filthy, smelly, partially decomposed, and with the stain of their hideous crimes plainly readable upon every unshaven face. Some had their throats cut, others sported elongated necks from hanging, and a few actually had knives buried in their backs, the tips of the bladed peeking out from their shirtfronts.

Only one sailor seemed undamaged, a large bull of a man who stood slightly apart from the leering crowd of murderers. Dressed in fold-top boots and beech skin trousers, the sailor wore a yellow silk shirt with a dirty red bandanna tied about his head. A scar marled his left eye into a dead white globe, and his right ear sported a fat gold ring. Both the professor and the lord identified it as the ragged finery of a buccaneer from a century ago.

"Aye, you're a fine pair!" the big pirate growled, placing both fists on his hips. "Never thought I'd see the day when some damn fool would *ask* to be taken aboard this floating slice of Hell, but here be the two of you! 'Though, I suppose, it is an act too stupid for any one man to accomplish."

"Oh, I say," Lord Carstairs started in a dangerous tone.

"Excuse me, but are you Captain Paul van der Decken of The Flying Dutchman?" Professor Einstein interrupted, stepping closer.

Brandishing a gnarled fist, the pirate frowned, "I am not! The name is John Bonater, Red John to the likes of you. And even if I was the captain, t'would do you no good a' tall! Your soul be ourn!" With a fiendish cackle, he pointed overhead.

Einstein and Carstairs booth looked up, and gasped. High amid the rigging was Felix Einstein suspended from a knotted rope. But it was a younger version of the professor, and he had the same unearthly expression of unlimited woe shared by the rest of the crew.

"Do try to hurry things along, would you?" the soul called down to the professor. "This is extraordinarily uncomfortable."

"Righto," the corporeal professor answered, with a game wave.

Recovering his aplomb, Prof. Einstein addressed the pirate. "I am not terribly interested in that at the moment. My business with the captain is about something else entirely. May we see him?"

Jerking a thumb at his chest, Red John snarled, "Nobody gets to see the captain! Even a pair of queer ducks like you!"

"Why not?" Einstein asked simply.

"Because I say so," Red John shouted defiantly. "That's why!"

Cackling in dark humor, the crew murmured hostile agreement.

Raising a fist to his mouth, Lord Carstairs coughed for recognition.

"Ah, but you see," he spoke loud and clear, "we want to talk to the captain of this ship, not some pox-ridden, milk-sucking, toffy-nosed, sticky-fingered, son-of-a-barrel-boy."

Every member of the crew went pale at that. Even the dead white flesh of the pirate actually turned a faint pink with rage and, with a scream, he whipped forth the cutlass from his belt.

"By the White Christ!" Red John cried, flecks of foam upon his corpse lips. "Give him a sword! I'll carve you into bits so small even the rats won't have you! Give him a sword, I say!"

From amidst the crowd, a scimitar came hurtling end-over-end towards Lord Carstairs. Unperturbed, the explorer neatly caught the weapon by the handle and made a few quick experimental passes.

"Hmm, cheap Singapore steel from the 1820s," the lord muttered, with a grimace. "With bad balance and a poor edge."

A grudging mutter of approval came from the crew.

"And if I win, we get to see the captain?" Carstairs asked, sliding the strap off his shoulder and easing the heavy canvas bag to the deck.

Stripping off the silk shirt, Red John barked a laugh as he dropped the garment, revealing a gaping hole in his chest. "If you win? Oh, aye, if you win. But this is a fight to the death, you Spanish-kissing bastard, and my passing acquaintance with a half pound of French iron has given me a slight advantage, don'cha think?"

Attempting to radiate boredom, Lord Carstairs stifled a yawn.

Without warning, the pirate leaped forward, his cutlass slashing wildly for a quick kill. But Carstairs easily blocked the attacks with a flick of his wrist and thrust the point of his scimitar deep into the pirate's left shoulder. Startled, Red John jumped back.

"Not a bad move for a lick-spittle toady to the crown," the pirate acknowledged, studying the wound. No blood oozed out, only a trickle of clear ichor that smelled of dirty feet and ozone.

"Your mother and a camel," Einstein whispered to his friend.

"Your mother and a camel!" Carstairs said in a booming voice.

Once again, Red John charged in a slashing fury, which the lord easily countered with an overhead block, and side parry. Now the pirate began to move with caution, easing on the hack and slash, and starting to use the point of his cutlass. It was a startling change of tactics. Lord Carstairs barely managed to stop the next charge with a lightning series of blocks. Soon the lord found himself slowly giving ground before the onslaught of undead steel. Again and again, the rusty cutlass of Red John stabbed at Lord Carstairs, once scoring a painful cut on the side of his neck. Sweat stung the wound, but Carstairs ignored the trifling pain as blood trickled into his shirt collar.

Sparks flew as the combatants fought across the deck, the crew moving out of the way and loudly cheering both fighters. Prof. Einstein briefly considered trying to slip away and find the captain while the battle raged, but a quartet of armed corpses stood nearby and were obviously determined to keep the professor exactly where he was.

In a whirlwind of steel, the swords of the two men clanged and banged in relentless fury. Sidestepping a lunge, Carstairs ripped off his coat to gain more freedom of movement. With renewed speed, Lord Carstairs took the offensive, each riposte and slash coming with greater dexterity. Slowly, the grim lord forced Red John towards one of the great masts. Finally, the pirate was pressed flat against the wooden column, parrying desperately.

"Here, matey!" a voice called, and another sword was tossed to the pirate.

Panting from the exertion, Lord Carstairs retreated for distance. "Well then, if this isn't going to be a fair fight, why didn't you say so," he drawled, pulling out the .455 Webley. Stroking the trigger, the lord blasted the blade off the sword in the pirate's grip, damn near taking the hand along with it.

Stunned and angry, Red John threw the pommel and knocked the smoking Webley out of Cartairs' hand, where it slid along the tilted deck and straight into the ocean. The crowd roared its approval.

Equal again, the pirate lunged towards Carstairs, who dodged the thrust and tripped Red John to the deck. Scimitar whirling, Lord Carstairs moved in for the kill. But as he came near, the pirate slashed out at groin level. Just in time to save his descendants, the lord leapt upwards. Spitting fury, Red John scrambled to his feet and the fight resumed.

Standing close to Prof. Einstein, an African warrior in a feathered headdress and loincloth turned to a fat redhead wearing the oilskin coat of a lighthouse keeper.

"Ten gold pieces on the Englishman," the cannibal rumbled.

"Done!" the man cried. The two spit in their palms and juicily smacked them together.

Daintily, the moistened professor pulled out a handkerchief to wipe his face. "Interesting," he said, pocketing the cloth. "Do you often fight amongst yourselves?"

"Of course!" the African replied.

"Indeed. Whatever for? Food? Entertainment?"

"The right to be on deck," a Japanese samurai added somberly.

Dreadlocks bobbing every which way, a blind Jamaican nodded in agreement. "Ya mon, them that loses, must go below."

Prof. Einstein glanced at the deck between his boots. Although the deck crew consisted of several hundred sailors, the number of murders at sea must have easily run into the thousands. Or more. The thought of what it must be like below in the hold to cause such a piteous keening made the professor feel quite ill.

"Come on, lad!" Einstein shouted, feeling just a touch of true panic. "You can do it!"

Bobbing and weaving steadily, Lord Carstairs needed the encouragement as he was beginning to tire, while the pirate was moving as fast as ever. Plus, the ultra-slow rocking of the vessel was throwing off the lord's timing. The motion, the moaning, and the blank sky about them were combining to give a surrealistic, almost dream-like quality, to the deadly serious fight. Shaking the sweat from his eyes, Lord Carstairs tried to conserve his strength by going on the defensive. He met the lunge with parry, slash with block, waiting for a proper opening to end this duel. However, the attack of the undead pirate strangely also began to slow. But it was soon obvious that Red John was now merely picking his targets with greater care. Again and again, the silver snake of the pirate's cutlass lashed out and Lord Carstairs found himself hard pressed to deflect the blade. This gave him an idea.

Making a half-hearted lunge, the lord allowed himself to be driven away in earnest. Sneering in triumph, Red John forced Carstairs backwards, almost into the arms of the cheering crowd. Block, feint, thrust, parry, slash, block, thrust, parry. Lord Carstairs swung madly, seeming to parry the blows of his opponent more by reflex and luck. The lord was clearly near the end of his strength.

Missing a thrust, Carstairs failed to recover in time and stood there, his chest exposed as a perfect target. With a shout of glee, Red John did a running lunge. But at the very last instant, Carstairs swiveled his body just enough so that the deadly cutlass slid past him and speared the chest of a Frenchman in the crowd. Lord Carstairs then pivoted on the balls of his feet and buried his own sword to the hilt in the head of Red John, the force of the thrust driving the corpse to the mast and pinning him there.

The bloodthirsty crowd erupted in shouts liberally peppered with the profanity of the world. Even the Frenchman with the sword in his guts laughed uproariously. "Clever move, *mon ami!*" he chuckled in true Gallic humor. "A good trick that I shall try to remember! *Vrai, pas?*"

"*Oui,*" Carstairs replied, panting for breath.

Without his sword and dangling a good foot off the deck, Red John merely grunted in annoyance. "Aye, a good move it were, true 'nuf."

"Always said you'd hang someday!" another pirate called out in wry amusement.

"Drink bilge water, dad," Red John muttered, trying to focus his eyes on the sword in his forehead.

"Does that mean I win?" Lord Carstairs calmly inquired, staying safely out of the reach of the pirate.

Running a hand through his greasy mane of hair, Red John sighed in resignation. It made an odd whistling sound. "Aye, me hearty. You've won and no man will say you haven't. You and your mate get to see the captain."

This pronouncement, though delivered in a normal voice, instantly silenced the entire crew on the deck, and those down below in the hold.

"Do we have to, Red John?" a Viking hulk asked timidly.

"Yes, by thunder, we do!" the pirate snarled, wrenching the sword out of his face and tossing it to the deck. "When Red John Bonater makes a promise, he keeps it through Hell and high water! Less'n one of you sea maggots thinks ye can beat me." No gaze met his. "Thought as not."

Glad this nonsense was finally over, the professor stepped forward. "Thank you, sir. I am Professor Felix Einstein and this is Lord Benjamin Carstairs."

"A British lord, is it?" Red John grinned, rubbing the hole in his chest. "I should've known ya come by your dirty fighting honestly. Welcome aboard the Flying Dutchman."

"So what is the problem with the captain?" Einstein asked, holding a hand to his mouth for secrecy.

In unison, the crew moaned and covered their faces.

"Mad," Red John whispered, tugging on his beard. "Lord knows the devil himself would be taxed with this crew of whoresons, but Paul van der Decken did it right, he did. Thinks he's every captain who has ever lived, that's what."

With a thumb, the pirate indicated the crew. "It scares the lads more'n anything else, 'cept goin' below." He gave a soulful shudder. "Well, we might as well get it over with."

Following the dead pirate, Einstein and Carstairs headed across the vast deck towards a small cabin almost hidden behind the mizzenmast. Straightening his ragged clothing, Red John knocked softly on the weathered door. "Cap'n, sahr? There be some gentlemen to see ya."

There was only a faint mumbling from within the cabin.

Red John placed his good ear against the door. "Some days, you can almost understand what he's sayin'. But t'day be one of the bad ones, I think."

Thumbing the latch, Red John gave a push and the door swung open with a long slow creak. The room within was dark, a single whale-oil lantern sputtering in a corner gave off a weak yellow light. The cabin was a mess, with broken pottery and rotting food thrown carelessly about. Furniture was smashed and the cupboard was ajar, the doors hanging from broken hinges. A lopsided desk was littered with crumpled papers, the chair splintery and cracked. In fact, the only untouched object in the room was a vast wooden cabinet that completely covered the aft wall.

The professor nudged Lord Carstairs. "There it is, lad."

At this tiny sound, a mound of rags heaved off the bunk. "Is that ticking I hear?" a man's voice rasped. "That's how I know he's near, that damned ticking. Swallowed a clock, you know." The figure giggled and stepped into the light.

Paul van der Decken had once been a giant of a man, but that was long ago. The suggestion of size was still there, but now he was drawn into himself, leaving only a frame of skin and bones. An unkempt mane of white hair fell past his shoulders, his boots had no bottoms and exposed his wiggling toes, and a ragged Dutch uniform hung off him in dirty strips.

Shuffling his boots, Red John noisily cleared his throat. "Cap'n van der Decken?"

Listlessly, the captain stared at the pirate. Then suddenly clasped both hands tightly behind his back and stood at rigid attention. "Mr. Christian!" Captain van der Decken bellowed. "Tie these fellows to the mast and give them forty lashes!"

"Yes, captain!" Red Bones answered smartly.

Shuddering all over, van der Decken then raced out the door shouting, "Damn the torpedoes! Full speed ahead!"

Leaning close to the professor, Lord Carstairs whispered, "I don't think he will be of much help, sir."

"I warned ya," Red John said, taking a chair from the ward table and sitting down.

"We really do not need him, lad," the professor said, opening the lid of the gigantic wooden case at the aft of the cabin. The interior of the chart locker was made of thousands of tiny compartments, each jammed full of rolled parchments.

"Ya don't need'm?" Red John exclaimed, sitting forward with a thump. "Then what the devil did you set him off for?"

Through the doorway, Lord Carstairs could see that the crew was attempting to chase Captain van der Decken from the rigging where he was slashing through ropes with a cutlass. The lord could faintly hear the captain shouting, "Arr! Ya scurvy dogs! Ya dinna kin know the fury of Blood!"

Busy with both hands, the professor was sorting through several maps. Seeing his associate engaged, Carstairs explained, "We are attempting to locate the lost Dutarian Temple of the Squid God. Unfortunately, the only map we knew of was captured by a group of religious fanatics."

Just then, the captain hobbled past the doorway with a belaying pin shoved into a pant leg. "A Spanish gold doubloon for the man who first spots Moby Dick!" he bellowed, stomping along the deck. "Death to the white whale!"

Pausing a moment for quiet to return, Lord Carstairs added, "So the professor had the notion of finding the Flying Dutchman. He postulated that since you sail the world forever, you would have a copy of every map ever created. Therefore, all we had to do was get aboard to find it."

Slumping against the cabin wall, Red John had an unreadable expression on his scarred face.

"Do you get a lot of ideas like this?" the dead pirate finally asked.

"Well, we were pretty much at the end of our rope," Lord Carstairs admitted.

"I should damn well guess so!"

Outside on the deck, the captain was yelling, "And thus, I claim Vesputchiland in the name of Queen Isabelle!"

"Carstairs! I found it!" Prof. Einstein shouted excitedly from within the cart locker, raising a rolled map in victory.

Striding closer, Red John rubbed his scar, "Ye be kidding. Dinna think anythin' could be found in that hog's pile."

"But everything is alphabetically listed," Einstein replied in confusion.

"Ah, magic than, well that explains it," Red John said, shrugging at the mysterious ways of officers and scholars.

"Anyway," Prof. Einstein sighed, displaying the find. "This map lists the location of every major temple in the world. The captain may be mad now, but before his descent into lunacy he compiled an excellent catalogue system."

In a brisk stride, Lord Carstairs brought the oil lantern closer to the table. Unrolling the crackling parchment, Prof. Einstein laid it out flat, placing bits of scrimshaw on the corners to keep the material steady.

"Look at it, lad!" the professor gushed enthusiastically. "Once we deal with the Squid God, this will keep the archeologists of four continents busy for the next century!"

"Bally good show, sir," Carstairs complimented heartily.

Bursting into the cabin, Captain van der Decken snatched the map away. "Analysis, Mr. Spock!" he demanded, shaking the parchment at the pirate.

Standing stiffly at attention, Red John arched a single eyebrow. "It is a map, captain," he replied emotionlessly

"No, by thunder! It be Flint's treasure island, I tell ye! Here, me boyos, look at this chart!" Trailing drool, the captain stormed out again.

"Get that map!" the professor ordered, giving chase.

Nimbly as a mermaid on her first date, Captain van der Decken raced across the deck with Einstein and Carstairs in dogged pursuit. As the two explorers started to gain on him, the captain stopped, twirled around, and grabbed a barrel lid, holding it aloft on his arm like a shield.

"You can't beat America, Red Skull!" van der Decken bellowed, and with a flick of his wrist, the barrel lid flew towards them.

Well-trained from years of dodging jungle spears, Einstein and Carstairs ducked low, and the makeshift projectile spun past them to bounce off a stanchion and hit a Greek fisherman smack in the mouth.

From the deck, Professor Einstein yelled, "You men there, grab him!"

But the sailors did nothing as the gibbering captain scampered on past.

"Now ye be over-steppin' yourself, laddie buck," Red John muttered coldly, touching the knife in his belt. "Mad he may be, but Paul van der Decken is still the captain of this hellship and will be treated as such!"

"But we must have that map!" Lord Carstairs pleaded.

"If you get it, 'twill be because he gives it to you," Red John stated firmly. "But take it by force and you'll answer to the crew. All of us." A low threatening growl sounded from everywhere at that dire pronouncement.

"Ah, I see," Lord Carstairs said acquiescing, with a slight bow. "I believe this is your department, Professor?"

With a pained expression, Einstein rubbed his temples. "Yes, well, then perhaps I had better go talk to him."

Eventually tiring of running amok with nobody giving chase, the captain settled onto the poop deck, resting against the housing that supported one of the great wheels.

Creeping as close as possible, Prof. Einstein called out in flawless Dutch to the tormented figure. "Captain van der Decken? I am here to release you from your curse!"

In open hostility, the captain glared with disdain. "Who cares if there's an iceberg ahead of us? The Titanic is unsinkable!"

Ignoring the babbling, Einstein gradually reached into his shoulder pouch and withdrew a small canvas purse. "This is dirt, sir. Dirt from Amsterdam."

The word hit the captain like hard fists and he recoiled, clearly having trouble breathing.

"The curse says that you sail the seas, never to touch your home port again. But this, sir," Prof. Einstein said, hefting the leather purse. "Sir, this *is* Amsterdam."

A long moment passed, with only the sounds of the souls and sea to mar the thick silence. When Captain van der Decken next spoke, his voice was different, old and hollow.

"How . . ." he whispered softly.

"We knew that once aboard your ship, it would be the only way to get off. I brought it with me from London for just such an emergency." The professor gave a gentle smile. "Actually, I purchased it at a Flea Market along with a rather remarkable copper bracelet."

Slowly extending an arm, Einstein offered the bag, the eyes of the entire crew on the simple act. "Please, captain," he begged, "give me the map."

In growing comprehension, Paul van der Decken gazed at the roll of parchment in his hand as if seeing it for the first time. A violent shudder passed through his body and the captain extended his trembling hand. As soon as the professor had the map, Captain van der Decken's face took on a surprising gentleness. Standing, he did a little dance and jingled a set of keys on his belt. "And where is Mr. Greenjeans?" he asked, skipping away like a kangaroo.

Despite his stout British upbringing, Prof. Einstein felt his heart break at the sight. Whatever crimes Paul Phillip van der Decken had committed in life must surely have been paid for by now. God rest his tormented soul.

Tucking the map inside his jacket, the professor undid the string around the mouth of the bag, and unceremoniously poured the dirt onto the deck of the ship.

He really wasn't sure what to do next. But with a mighty groan, the entire vessel shook, knocking men from the rigging as great cracks splayed out from the tiny pile of dirt. Howls of astonishment sounded from below the deck as the hatches blew off, the sails unfurled, the masts collapsed, and the ship exploded with dazzling light.

Half blind, Lord Carstairs rushed to the professor's side and the men became lost in a whirlwind of tiny glowing spheres, countless thousands upon thousands of ethereal bubbles. As one passed close by, Lord Carstairs saw a tiny grinning sailor inside and realized the truth. *By Jove, these were the souls of the crew!*

The lambent geyser thickened around the explorers, soon creating a fountain of light that poured upward to punch through the dark clouds and radiate outward to illuminate the entire sky! Lifted by the glowing spheres, Einstein and Carstairs found themselves buoyantly floating within a thunderous chorus of free spirits sounding their joy at being released.

A transparent Red John gave Lord Carstairs a friendly punch on the arm before melding into a sphere and rising with the rest of the undamned crew. Streaking into the heavens, the spirit globes went out of sight and the dazzling display of lights slowly dimmed, except for one small sphere that settled inside Prof. Einstein much the same way a man will reclaim a comfortable old chair. Whole once more, the giddy professor barely had time to savor the feeling before he realized they were falling. The Flying Dutchman was gone, returned to the void of nothingness from which it been forged by hellfire and blood.

"Carstairs!" the professor cried.

"Professor!" the lord answered.

Plummeting downward, the two explorers splashed into the Tyrrhenian Sea, going deep underwater before they could arrest their descent and swim back toward the surface.

Erupting from the waves, Lord Carstairs roared in pain as the salt water cleansed the sword cut on his throat. Splashing about with only one hand, Prof. Einstein was struggling frantically to stay afloat and keep something out of the water. Pushing rotten timbers out of his way, Carstairs swam over to his friend to assist.

"Sir, can't you swim?" the lord asked, sounding amused.

"Save the map!" Einstein sputtered in reply, kicking steadily. "The bloody sea water is dissolving the parchment!"

Stroking closer, Lord Carstairs was horrified to see it was true. Grabbing the older man around the waist, the lord shoved Einstein upward and started kicking in a steady rhythm. Safely out of the sea, Prof. Einstein began desperately scanning the smeary surface.

"Well?" Carstairs roared impatiently.

"Eureka!" the professor cried in delight. Then his grin faded and he cried out, "Bloody hell!"

"What is it now, sir?" Lord Carstairs asked from below, riding the rough sea.

"I found the temple. It is on the Island of Dutar!"

"So the island still exists? Excellent!"

"No, it is not excellent."

Treading water, Carstairs snorted to clear his nose. "Whatever do you mean? Is it at the South Pole? At the bottom of the ocean?"

"Dutar Island is in the heart of the Bermuda Triangle!" Prof. Einstein shouted in frustration.

"Of course! Hidden in plain sight!" Lord Carstairs yelled, but then added, "But, sir, Bermuda is over two thousand miles away! How can we possibly get there in time before the moon has finished turning?"

"We can't, lad," the professor stated grimly. "It's over. We've lost. There is no way to travel that far in only a few days."

"Never say never, sir!" the lord yelled, starting to side-paddle. "Once we get back to shore, I know a fellow, who knows a fellow, who knows a fellow who owns a used zeppelin."

"Fly there? Capital idea, lad! Well done!"

"It's only twelve or so miles through shark-infested ocean," Carstairs muttered, keeping the professor and the precious map high above the water. Estimating east from the position of the sun, the lord headed that way while keeping a close watch on the surface for any fins. "By God, I'll get us there even if I have to take a shortcut through Hell!"

Ominous thunder rumbled in the sky at those words. The swimming men looked up just in time to see the amassed glowing spheres pause in their heavenly assent, then spin about and streak back down into the ocean like a rain of golden fire. The souls vanished into the depths of the sea, spreading the light of their lives until the ocean was infused with an ethereal pearlessence.

Then the suddenly warm water below Einstein and Carstairs started to rise. Quickly forming into a swell, the Tyrrhenian Sea elevated the men higher and higher as it built in size and power. Soon their cries of surprise were drowned out by the strident roar of the impossible tidal wave that began carrying them helplessly out to sea and far away from safety of the Italian shore.

THIRTEEN

Still standing guard at the window of the museum, Mary smiled gratefully as Katrina arrived in a black carriage, the cook's arms full of weapons and brown wrapped packages.

"Well done, old girl," Mary chuckled softly, massaging her sore neck. "At least the squiddies won't starve us out . . ."

But her voice faltered as another carriage arrived to stop directly behind the first and Lady Penelope Danvers stepped onto the pavement. She was dressed at the very height of elegance as if for high tea at Hyde Park, but cradled in her velvet gloves was a Holland & Holland .475 Nitro Express elephant rifle that she carried with an air of quiet expertise. Her African maid came next; the muscular Zulu woman was draped with bandoleers of ammunition and carrying a wicker basket of steaming crumpets. Rising over the maid's shoulder was the infamous feathered shaft of a Zulu throwing-sword that had caused the British Army so much bother during the Boer Wars, and had helped England so greatly during The Troubles.

Losing control for a split second, Mary burst into tears at the sight, then pulled herself together and strode purposefully down to the foyer. Kicking aside some debris, Mary threw open the battered front door, the hinges squealing in protest. With shotgun in hand, Mary carefully checked the bushes for any suspicious movements before walking down the front stoop.

"Lady Danvers, how delightful to see you," Mary said politely. "Whatever are you doing here?"

Climbing the steps in a forceful gait, Penelope Danvers embraced the young girl with her free arm, the other keeping a steady grip on the H&H Nitro Express.

"My poor little dear," Lady Danvers said, finally releasing her. "What in God's good name ever convinced you to handle this sticky situation by yourself?"

"Well, I am the curator," Mary started hesitantly, nervously fondling the shotgun.

Delicately pushing the barrel away, Lady Danvers clucked her tongue in disapproval. "Piffle and nonsense, my dear. The Wives of the London Explorer's Club all stand together in times of trouble!" Then she smiled secretly, "As if none of us has ever been attacked before by foreigners seeking revenge because of what our darling husbands have done. Happens all the time!"

"Really?" Mary sighed wearily.

"All the time," Katrina said, returning from the side door of the museum to gather more supplies from the waiting couch.

Wrinkling her nose, Lady Danvers sniffed and scowled. "Land sake's, child, how long has it been since you bathed?"

"Just a few days," Mary admitted, using her shotgun to scratch uncomfortably at the sweat-stiffened clothing. "I was afraid the squid people might attack while I was, um, *au natural*."

"I see," Danvers said with a frown. "A wise choice, they might at that. Dirty little blighters. Well, we're here now, so run off and get a quick wash. You're starting to smell like a man, my dear, and that wouldn't do at all."

"But there's so much to do . . ." Mary started, as a herd of horse-drawn carriages clattered into view from around the corner. The vehicles were covered with heavy boxes, and every window displayed neatly dressed women holding large bore weaponry.

"Ah, the cavalry has arrived, as the colonials would say!" Lady Danvers stated, pushing the girl back into the war-torn building. "Get along! After you have washed and dressed properly, we'll have some nice cucumber sandwiches and pink tea that Towanda packed for lunch, then we'll tell you where all of the new deathtraps are hidden."

Coyly trying to wave away the buzzing flies that had become her unwanted entourage during the past few days, Mary started to protest, then relented and trundled up the main flight of stairs for the bathroom.

Outside the International Museum, the carriages stopped in an orderly line along the granite curb and disgorged a mob of high society ladies, each daintily carrying a wealth of high caliber deathdealers and bandoleers of ammunition.

"And who is the cause of this brouhaha?" Lady Pierpont snorted, viewing the bedraggled museum with disdain. Her gown was brushed velvet, trimmed with fine Irish lace, and strapped about her waist was a hand-tooled leather gunbelt, containing a matched pair of French-designed LeMat .445 pistols.

"I hear they are called Squid God worshipers," Mrs. Foxington-Smythe said, shifting her grip on the Viking war-axe that rested on her shoulder. A bit of cannon fuse dangled from the over-sized cameo on her blouse, and the handle of several daggers jutted from her bustle.

Pulling out one of the titanic LeMat revolvers, Lady Pierpont started to rotate the nine-shot cylinder and check the blackpowder charges. "Never heard of them, but from this mess they seem complete bastards. Look at that flowerbed! Ruined, utterly ruined. And it's far too late to plant any new bulbs now."

"Poor Mary and Katrina handling this all alone," Mrs. Thompkins started angrily, checking the derringer up her sleeve. "It's an outrage. Why hasn't she joined our little group long ago?"

"That crazy uncle of hers," Lady Danvers said bluntly, contorting her face into a mask of disdain.

Swinging a keg of black powder from a carriage bearing her family crest, Lady Pierpont gently deposited it onto the cracked pavement. "Ah yes, Felix the Mad. I must say, all explorers are slightly potty, but he undoubtedly is their king, eh, ladies?"

"Men and their secret societies!" Mrs. Thompkins cried scornfully, dropping a heavy box onto the pavement. It landed with a resounding clatter. "Now, where do you want the bear traps, Penny?"

"Over here," Katrina said, climbing down from the last carriage. "We'll use them to reinforce the coal chute."

"Excellent plan, my dear! But first, we must get those crumpets into the stove to stay warm. Nothing worse than a cold crumpet!"

"Fair enough," Katrina said with a nod. "We must protect mind, body, and spirit."

"Of course, my dear," the lady chuckled. "How else?"

At the exchange, Baroness Edgewaters gave a loud and regal sniff. "And exactly why," she asked, glaring in frank hostility, "are we taking orders from the cook?"

Smoothing her apron, Katrina arched an eyebrow at the comment, then simply turned her back on the aristocrat.

"Indeed, she is the cook. But more importantly, her family name is also Cook," Dame Danvers said in a loud stage whisper. "Sound familiar, my dear?"

As if caught wearing white before Easter, the baroness turned a bright red in embarrassment. "As in Sir James Cook?" she said, her voice rising to a squeak. "The man who circumnavigated the world, discovered New Zealand, stole Australia from the Dutch, and invented a cure for scurvy? *That* Cook? One of the greatest British explorers of all time?"

"I'm his granddaughter," Katrina answered, now lugging a crate of poisoned pungi sticks out of the boot of a carriage. "It was one of the reasons that the professor hired me."

Quickly aflutter, the baroness rushed over to take the box. "My dear, I do apologize. Here, let me help you with that trifle!"

As the growing crowd of women got busy unloading assorted ordnance and ironmongery, more and more carriages arrived, disgorging servants with wicker hampers of food, crates of dynamite, and heavy rolls of the brand-new American invention called barbed wire. Lady Danvers heartily approved of the imported material. It was beastly stuff that could rip off your flesh at a single touch. Simply wonderful for topping fences to hold out impromptu midnight climbers, second story men, and drunken husbands.

"Don't worry about the tigers," Katrina shouted over a shoulder. "They are no longer with us."

"Oh dear, not the Squid God chappies again?" Dame Pierpont asked with a frown.

Lowering her eyes, Katrina primly blushed. "Neighbor's mastiff, actually. Who knew such a thing was possible?"

"Oh well, accidents do happen."

"Move along, ladies! I want the buffet over there, and the dynamite over there," Mrs. Foxington-Smythe ordered gesturing. "Don't dawdle, you know the routine! We have all done this sort of thing before!"

Checking her filigree-covered pocket watch, Lady Danvers loudly clapped her hands. "It's three hours until dark and the bloodthirsty little devils always attack at night. So let's proceed like this was The Troubles, and get moving!"

Exchanging their dainty velvet gloves for sturdy canvas ones, the ladies began stringing the barbed wire, while their maids started hiding the bear traps. In short order, the museum began to resemble the British fortress at the Rock of Gibraltar.

Most impressive! Katrina admitted, standing guard from the open front doorway. But in private, she could only hope it would be enough. Since they had called in friends, it would not be out of the question if the squiddies had done the same, and God alone knew what that could entail!

* * *

The normally dark cellar on Asbury Street, west London, was brightly lit by oil lanterns and full of frantic preparations.

Softly chanting robed figures stuffed clothes, weapons, and equipment into large packing crates. At the middle of the basement, a group of men dressed in white robes was carefully bolting a rubber-edged metal lid onto an iron cauldron filled with blood. A pair of burly masons were bricking closed an alcove containing an antique sword that was bolted to a granite block wall, and draped with stout chains to hold it prisoner. In spite of that, whenever a Squid God worshiper moved too close to the ancient weapon, the chains rattled as the sword strove to burst free and attack. The noises only made the masons move faster with their work as they liberally applied additional cement to the wall.

"You're wrong," a thin man stated, nailing down the lid of a packing crate. "I recommend another frontal attack on the museum. Damn near worked last time."

Standing guard at the only door, a tall woman pushed back her cowl to reveal a beautiful face covered with detailed tattoos. Her facial markings almost exactly matched the runes of power etched into the imprisoned blade across the cellar, only her were perfectly reversed.

"Stuff and nonsense," she snorted in disagreement. "A sneak attack is our only hope."

"Multiple attacks!" a corpulent fellow bellowed, slamming a meaty fist onto a packing crate. "That way at least some of us will capture that bitch alive, and add her blood to the Life Pool."

"Be serious," another woman replied, shaking an arm missing its hand. The bloody stump was wrapped in fresh bandages. "How can we possibly be sure that the group carrying the Life Pool will make it through?"

"We must! The blood of an enemy is great magic, but the blood of a virgin holds even greater power! Possibly just enough to bring forth the Great Squid itself!"

"Huzzah!" they all chorused.

"What contemptible fools," a voice sneered from the top of the stairway.

As the crowd turned, the High Priest walked out of the solid stone wall. The thin man was dressed in the finery of his station, the regal robe bearing an embroidered version of the reverse runes.

"None of that nonsense will be necessary," the High Priest said, sitting down in a chair not visible to the people inside the cellar.

At that pronouncement, excited voices broke out from everybody in attendance.

"But holy one, the defenses at the museum–"

"Surely, we must–"

"Die!"

"Kill!"

Irritably, the priest waved a hand sparkling with demonic jewelry. "Idiots! The defenses at the museum mean nothing. Less than nothing! Soon, our master will live again and we shall set the world on fire, then drown the fire in the blood of our enemies!"

The crowd broke into wild cheering, which caused the usual thumping from the ceiling. With sullen expressions, the Squid God worshipers grew quiet.

Sneering upward, the High Priest screamed, "Enough! The time for secrecy is over! Higgins!"

"Yes, holy one?" a fat man asked timidly.

"Kill that old bat!"

"Oh yes, Holy One!" the fat man cried, drawing a double-bladed dagger. "Thank you!" Shouting a Dutarian war chant, the fellow darted into the stairwell and bounded up the wooden steps.

As the man disappeared, the High Priest waved his flock closer. "What you are going to do tonight," he said slowly, "is simply walk into the precious museum and take the girl alive."

The crowd murmured in puzzlement.

Scratching his head with a cudgel, a squat, burly man bluntly asked, "An 'ow d'yer figga' we're gonna do that, gov'nor?"

In serpentine grace, the High Priest of Dutar spread his arms wide. "Simplicity itself," he answered with a chuckle. "The lady will politely invite you inside. Indeed, she will absolutely insist that you enter!"

"And then . . ." a man in the crowd asked eagerly.

Smiling evilly, the thin priest drew a thumb across his neck with the appropriate sound effects.

At that moment, the thumping from above assumed a frantic tone, and then abruptly stopped.

"Oh yes," the High Priest hissed in delight, rubbing his hands together. "The death of Mary Einstein will be just as simple as that."

FOURTEEN

Meanwhile, the weather across the globe was growing steadily worse. Normally reserved as filler and trivia in newspapers, the bizarre storms were starting to inch their way onto the front page of such conservative tabloids as the London *Times* and the *Wall Street Journal.*

Earthquakes in the Ukraine made the Siberian peasants dance like they never danced before. Volcanoes erupted from calm blue seas, spewing torrents of red-hot lava that cooled and coalesced into patterns reminiscent of the radial arms of a giant sea mollusk. Fires raged unchecked and, indeed, barely noticed in the heart of Australia. A flood drenched the Nile Delta, washing the streets of Cairo clean for the first time in a century. In Holland, the rising sea forced the farmers to frantically reinforce their dikes and alert the emergency cadre of small boys with greased fingers. Icebergs appeared in the Great Lakes. At both the North and South Poles, red-and-white striped shafts suddenly erupted from the permafrost, each huge stone obelisk topped with the figure of a bloated squid. Lightning storms raged across the globe with increasing fury, the electric bolts striking the ground incessantly as if the earth was charging itself for some mighty task, or preparing to cauterize a wound yet to be made. Hail mixed with sand storms in the Sahara Desert, pounding hapless Arabs into the ground like so many tent pegs. Snow frosted the Amazon River Basin, and the flakes were an unbelievable shade of blue, which really didn't bother the local headhunters, as they had never seen snow before.

Violent tornadoes swept through the North American Midwest, but as trailer parks had yet to be invented, little damage was done. An avalanche started at the peak of Mt. Everest, then stopped halfway down and waited, the staggering load of rocks, ice, boulders, flags, and dead yeti just hanging there suspended by nothing visible. Tidal waves raced up, then down, Germany's Rhine River, creating an absolute furor. Aurora Borealis was seen in Spain, Korea, and Panama at the exact same time. The colorful displays filled the night with rainbow splendor, but shed no light on the matter.

Across the globe, wild animals in forests, fields, jungles, and swamps began behaving strangely, as if they also knew a disaster was about to occur. Dogs howled at the sun, while giraffes, which possess no vocal cords, began to croon melodiously. Half a decade earlier, the Seven Year Locust appeared in the Orient for a day that seemed to last a week. Army ants and killer bees formed a military pact to attack the Andes mountain range, yielding no effect whatsoever. Rainbow trout were found swimming in the Dead Sea. In spite of their every effort to the contrary, chameleons shifted into a shocking plaid pattern and stayed that way. Hordes of pigeons rose into the air and were never seen again, not that anybody really cared. The always-skittish ostrich reached an all-time high for burying their heads in the sand, reaching unheard-of depths. Squids and octopi gleefully bubbled in anticipation. A lion lay down with a lamb and only a burping lamb was left by dawn. Lemmings didn't bother to leap from their favorite cliffs; they simply exploded. Sperm whales started to sing the blues, while what the blue whales did is best left undisclosed.

Things were even worse in the world of the occult. Crystal balls clouded over, no longer able, much less willing, to foretell the future. In slaughterhouses, the entrails of goats began to take on new and sinister meanings to the normally immune butchers. Every tea leaf at the bottom of a cup in England suddenly became a repository of arcane knowledge. The normally nimble platens of Ouija boards fused into place atop the symbol for the moon. No matter how often they were thrown, Tarot cards always landed face down and made small whimpering noises. Palm readers closed their hands and shops. Indian shamans woke from fevered nightmares of being squeezed. Psychics got headaches. Fakirs went home to their mothers. Hoping for revelation, Druids sacrificed a bush to the Great Tree, but the act proved fruitless. Pagans burned with eagerness. Gurus went ohm. Soothsayers got the sack. Astrologers consulted with each other, no matter what their birth dates. I Ching readers flipped coins and decided to interview numerologists, who had been counting on them for an answer. Phrenologists rushed to put their heads together.

In the unseen world, leprechauns put away their bottles, while genies hid inside theirs. The fairy queen traded in her throne for a one-way ticket to New Jersey and the Loch Ness monster put on a disguise.

* * *

Deep within a bubbling hell of its own creation, noxious chemicals mixed with human blood, to cook, swirl, and combine to form primitive protein chains. Chains that coalesced into living cells that joined to build organic groupings that began to forge the nebulous infrastructure of an extremely large cuttlefish, or squid.

At present, it was a non-sentient beast, merely an animal. But ever so slowly, a spinal column commenced to grow, delicately attaching itself to the pulsating brain stalk of colossal proportions. Very soon, it would no longer be a mindless brute, but an intelligent creature firmly entrenched in the world of the physical and yet able to draw upon the limitless power of the ethereal plane. A thinking monster armed and armored with magic.

Most of the people in the world would merely curse it as a demon. Others would hail it as a god.

FIFTEEN

Bathed in silvery moonlight, London was unusually quiet that night. River fog filled the streets, and every window was shuttered tight against the possibility of a coming storm. Great Britain was famous for its bad weather, but recently it was becoming so bad that no ships dared to go to sea, and every sailor watched the turning moon with growing suspicion.

The cobblestone streets of the great city were deserted, the cabbies locked inside the carriage houses with their nervous horses. Toffs and toughs did their drinking at home, and hundreds of thieves had turned themselves in to the police to spend a safe night in jail. Even the lusty whores of Whitechapel were staying safely tucked in their beds to conduct business. Occasionally, a dog would start to howl, but then abruptly stop.

Alone in all of London, only Wimpole Street had no fog, the flickering gaslights clearly illuminating the International British Museum and its surrounding grounds.

". . . and amen," Mary said, closing the small black Bible and making the sign of the cross.

Standing before a roaring fireplace, the freshly scrubbed young curate was wearing trim riding clothes and knee-high leather boots. An Adams .32 pistol jutted from a holster on her right hip and a short sword in a restored Roman scabbard was belted about her trim waist, while a quiver of arrows rested comfortably on her back next to a Chinese longbow.

"What were you just doing, dear?" Lady Danvers asked from a nearby desk where she was sharpening an American Bowie knife. Lying displayed on the table before the woman were four loaded crossbows, a stack of iron quarrels, two Colt revolvers, and a sturdy wooden box full of half-sticks of dynamite, the flat ends of the waxed tubes expertly crimped with the stubby fuses ready for action. Close at hand, the deadly H&H .475 Nitro Express Special leaned against the wall.

"Blessing the museum," Mary replied, placing the Holy Bible on a bookcase full of religious volumes. "If the squiddies try any magic tonight, perhaps this will slow them down, or at least hinder their entrance."

"Interesting idea," Lady Danvers said, tucking the blade up a lacy sleeve. "But I do not know if a Christian prayer will work against these ancient heathens."

"Praise the Lord, but pass the ammunition," Baroness Edgewaters muttered, pouring a cup of coffee from a steaming silver urn. A well-used Henry .50 rifle was slung over her shoulder, along with a bandoleer of ammunition crossing her ample bosom. A deadly Spanish machete was strapped at her side.

"Quite so," Mary agreed, picking up her Remington shotgun once more, and resting the wooden stock on a pert hip. "So just in case, I also performed the Catholic ceremony, as well as those of the Hebrews, Moslems, Buddhists, Druids, and Egyptians." Then she frowned. "I would have also done the Norse, but I could not find a live goat to sacrifice to Odin."

Peeking out the shutters of a window, Lady Pierpont was dressed as if on a safari; khaki shirt and pants, black Hoby boots and a brace of LeMat .44 pistols.

"Fair enough, my dear," the lady said, drawing a revolver to spin it once in her palm and holster it again. The action was done so effortlessly it seemed to have been performed without conscious thought, only the speed and grace belying her expertise. "The ceremony may not help, but it certainly can't hurt the situation."

"My thoughts exactly," Mary Einstein said, brushing away a loose strand of damp hair from her face. Washed and fed, with a full hour of sleep, she felt enormously refreshed. The camaraderie of the other women had bolstered her sagging spirits, and she felt ready for anything.

Just let the squiddies rally tonight, Mary raged privately, *and they will get a taste of real English spunk!*

Along the far wall was a line of emergency provisions, the bulging haversacks containing maps, candles, knives, British pounds, French gold sovereigns, tinned meat, hard tack, spare rope, and extra pistol ammunition. Katrina had even included a canvas medical kit; containing an electric lantern, a vial of powdered arsenic, needle and thread, some French condoms and a bottle of Scotch whiskey. Although slightly askance at the assortment, the other ladies decided it was always best to err on the side of safety and to be prepared for anything, from wholesale destruction to a seduction. The entire world was at stake, but even more important, England itself was in danger!

Careful of casting her shadow on the window and making a target for snipers, Mary went to the shutters and scrutinized the shiny new gate attached to the battered fence. Held in place with barbed wire, the gate was merely there for show, but every little bit helped. However, the oak window shutters were firmly nailed closed. The back and side doors were barricaded with barrels full of dirt on the outside and stacks of heavy furniture inside the building. Bear traps filled the lawn, barbed wire festooned the top of the iron fence, and there was a roaring fire in the hearth, along with more than sufficient coal to last through the night. It was the best they could do, and hopefully enough.

"Stay safe, dear Benjamin," Mary whispered softly, sending the heartfelt prayer to the evening wind.

By the ticking of the clock, time passed in a slow and steady procession. Eventually, the coffee was gone, and the pile of sandwiches reduced to a scattering of crumbs. Each of the women was lost in private thoughts by then, and thus nobody paid any attention at first when the crystal chandelier in the ceiling started to tinkle softly. But the noise steadily increased until it was discernible above the crackle of the fireplace.

Then a second wave of vibrations shook the museum, and a glass of water fell from the desk to crash on the floor. Instantly alert, the women pulled weapons and prepared for an attack.

"Penny, check the back door!" Mary snapped, thumbing back the hammers on her shotgun. "Katrina, more coal on the fire!"

Suddenly, the whole room began to quiver, then the entire building! Pictures danced off the walls, books shifted, and andirons fell over in a clatter that was lost in the steadily growing rumble coming from outside.

"Is it a mole machine?" Mrs. Foxington-Smythe asked, kneeling to place an ear to the floor. "No, it's not coming from below."

Dashing to the window, Mary threw open the wood shutters and peered about while the double barrel of her Remington scattergun mimicked her actions. On the streets below, people were running around shouting, a cab rolled past without any horses, and then came a team of horses galloping by without a carriage. *Now how the deuce did that happen?*

A fresh quake shook the city, and windows cracked for blocks in every direction. The gas lamps on the street corners flickered and pulsed like mad things. Roof tiles began to rain down upon the pavement, and Big Ben started to chime non-stop.

"Could this be an earthquake?" Mrs. Thompkins hazarded, conceiving of no other possibility. The matronly lady twisted her hands nervously on the worn shaft of her Viking war axe.

Her pale face turned to ivory from the bright moonlight, Lady Danvers frowned deeply. "Impossible. Britain does not have earthquakes."

"The queen would never allow such a thing," Baroness Edgewaters snorted, her gray eyes scanning the horizon as she pulled a cartridge from the bandoleer and slid the greasy brass round into the open receiver of the Henry rifle. "But what else could possibly be doing this?"

"I think I know," Mary said softly, just as the whole of England seemed to shudder.

The women could hear ten thousand more windows smash outside, then they heard Mary gasp in horror and rushed to her side. Following her pointing finger, the ladies were stunned to see a curved object slowly rise on the distant horizon. Soon it was taller than the houses, the bridges, the churches, and still the mysterious object swelled in size. Even in the flickering glow of the tortured streetlights, the ladies could see vast clouds of dust billowing around the base of the structure. Listening closely, they could just barely discern the faint sound of smashing masonry mixing with splashing water.

Like a mountain lifting from the sea, the gigantic object began to loom above the metropolis, dwarfing even Big Ben and the Tower of London to the status of mere toys. On it expanded, going higher, getting larger, until it seemed the stars overhead would be smashed aside, or the city crushed beneath.

"It's!" Mary squeaked.

"The!" Lady Danvers gasped.

"Ark!" Baroness Edgewaters finished in a strangled croak.

At those words, a thin line of flame raced up the keel of the titanic Biblical vessel, arched over the bow, and then down the other side along the gunwales. In mere seconds, the whole craft was ablaze, the writhing flames casting London into a hellish midnight dawn.

Dropping her crossbow, a wild-eyed Mrs. Foxington-Smythe scampered across the foyer for the front door. "The Explorers Club is burning!" she cried in horror. "We must help our husbands!"

Grasping the latch, Mrs. Foxington-Smythe yanked with frantic strength, but the portal remained firmly closed, held in place by the strong hand of Baroness Edgewaters.

"Louisa, regain your composure!" the baroness scolded. "This might be a trick to lure us outside!"

Unheeding and uncaring, Mrs. Foxington-Smythe planted a dainty boot on the jamb and put her back into the job, but the door refused to budge. Rushing forward, Mary grabbed the hysterical woman about the waist, and tried dragging her away to no avail.

"The men can take care of themselves!" Mary grunted, heaving with each exertion. "We have to stay here!"

"My love is in danger!" Louisa Foxington-Smythe stormed in reply, shaking the latch furiously. "Nothing else matters!"

Dropping her weapon, Mary redoubled her efforts to free the woman, but it was to no effect. Finally, Lady Danvers took hold of Foxington-Smythe by the shank of her hair and forcibly turned her head to speak face to face. "Nothing else matters," Lady Danvers repeated angrily. "Not even saving the world?"

The panting woman stared in agony, conflicting emotions crossing her features at lightning speed. Then, ever so slowly, her grasp on the latch eased, her shoulders slumped, and Mrs. Foxington-Smythe stepped away.

"My sincere apologies," Mrs. Foxington-Smythe said to the others in the room. "I . . . I lost my priorities for a moment."

Mary gently squeezed her shoulder consolingly. "Think nothing of it, Louisa. I might have done the same if Bunny was there."

"Bunny?" Duchess Farthington chuckled, a shiny twinkle of amusement in her blue Saxon eyes. "Are you perhaps referring to Lord Benjamin Alexander Julius Carstairs?"

Completely caught off guard, Mary could only stutter and stammer a few random words of total gibberish.

"Ah, I see," Baroness Edgewaters smiled tolerantly. "So it's love then. Good show, my dear. Welcome to the Explorers' Wives Club."

As the rest of the woman gathered around to hug the newest proto-member of the circle, there came a polite knock from the other side of the front door.

"Penny, stay by the fireplace," Mary ordered, suddenly all business, the brief moment of intimacy gone. She grabbed the shotgun off the floorboards and cocked both hammers. "Baroness and Katrina with me. Let's make sure that everything is kosher."

With a nod, Lady Danvers clicked off the safety on the Nitro Express in solemn expectation. "Absolutely, little sister."

"Kosher?" Lady Pierpont asked in confusion, drawing the massive LeMat. "Whatever does that mean?"

"It is an Americanism," Katrina explained softly, notching a fresh arrow into her crossbow. "Meaning spot on, or shipshape."

"Ah. Deuced clever those colonials."

Standing to the side of the front door, Mary used the muzzle of the shotgun to flip open the conversation hatch. When nothing came rushing through, she eased the weapon into the hatch and carefully peeked out.

"Good evening, Miss Einstein," a smoldering man said politely.

Standing on the front stoop was a disheveled man in torn and smoking livery, but still ramrod straight with a calm and almost serene countenance. Behind him stood an army of people in tattered clothing, carrying wooden planks containing bedsheets draped over piles of lumpy objects.

"Good evening. Who are you, sir?" Mary demanded, angling the Remington towards his waist, the perfect height for blowing a man in half.

"Allow me to introduce myself, madam," he said in a gravelly voice. "I am Carl Smythe, the replacement head butler for the Explorer's Club until my dear cousin, Jeeves Sinclair, returns."

Inexplicably, his voice sent a shiver down Mary's spine, and she heard Lady Danvers cock both of the hammers on the Nitro Express. Mary had heard about Jeeves going on sick leave and about the replacement butler, and yes Carl Smith, or Smythe, was the correct name. But something about this genial servant greatly disturbed her. Some instinct honed from years in the bush traveling with her uncle bespoke of untold danger here. Yet it was only a butler.

"And?" Mary prompted coldly, slightly tightening the pressure on the trigger.

If the action was seen by the man, he did not openly react. "There has been a most unfortunate . . . incident at the club, Miss Einstein," Carl said, coughing slightly. "Some masked hooligans blew up the water mains and soaked the Ark, you know about Noah's Ark, I presume, yes, of course you do. Well, the resulting flood of waters . . ." He turned to glance at the burning Biblical goliath dominating the London skyline.

"Well, it is quite a mess."

In spite of her reservations, Mary relaxed a bit at the man's professional demeanor. *An incident, he called it? Good show.* Now she noticed the other people were the staff of the club. Gingerson, Alberts, Coltrain, she knew them all by sight.

"What are they carrying?" Mary demanded,

"Well, madam," Carl continued. "The staff managed to save most of the journals from the fire, but several of the club members were hurt in the falling masonry, and I took it upon myself to decide that a hospital was too dangerous a location for recuperation. What if those masked men returned? So I was wondering if we could use the museum for a make-shift camp for tonight."

Oh God, it was the wounded explorers under the sheets! "Of course!" Mary gushed, lowering her weapon. "Come inside right away."

Sliding off the bolt, Mary threw the door wide. "Katrina, get the medical kit! Ladies, watch the shadows for any suspicious movements in case the servants were followed!"

"Let me inform the police that it's fine to let you through," Lady Danvers said, grabbing a lantern from the table.

With a boot on the threshold, Carl stood in the doorway and blocked the way. "I saw no constables about, madam," he said, with a slight nod. "If I may venture a guess, I would imagine they are presently at the club trying to control the growing riot."

A prickly feeling was at the back of her neck, but Mary could still find nothing wrong with the tale. She must simply be jumpy from the previous attacks. *Plus all that damn European coffee. Nerves, that's all it was, a simple case of battle fatigue.*

"Yes of course," Lady Danvers said, stepping aside. "Quite right, Carl, well done."

Glancing over a shoulder, Mary called out, "Stay sharp, ladies! This may be a diversion. We had best be ready for trouble."

"Righto," Mrs. Thompkins calmly replied, slipping a dynamite-tipped arrow into the notched receiver of her crossbow.

Under the watchful gaze of the heavily armed women, Carl directed the other servants to bring in the litters of wounded men. Staying near the smashed window, Mrs. Pierpont kept a pistol in her free hand as she bolted the wooden shutters to keep out the night air. On the horizon, the ark continued burning fiercely. The sound of fire bells filled the night and the thick plume of smoke was starting to blot out the turning moon and twinkling stars.

As each litter passed by, Mary felt foolish as she dutifully lifted the covers to check the faces of the burned and bleeding explorers underneath. The men moaned at the bright light of the oil lamps, and she quickly covered each in turn. So far, Mary recognized every member from the social gatherings and speeches at the Explorer's Club. Thankfully, none of the wounded men was the husband of any of the ladies present.

Then Mary froze at the realization, her stomach tightening as if standing on a booby-trap deep inside an Egyptian pyramid with tons of stone about to crash down upon her head. *Not one of the wounded men was related to the ladies present.* But that was patently impossible. These were the wives of the senior-most members, men who were always at the damn Club. Their lack of attendance was beyond impossible, it was absurd, and more important, suspicious as all bloody Hell.

Taking a lantern from the table, Katrina headed towards a curtained doorway. "I think the litters should go in the workshop," she directed. "It has plenty of space, and we must keep the front room clear in case of trouble. Follow me, please."

"Of course, dear lady," Carl said with a smile, sounding extraordinarily pleased.

Warily studying the butler as he walked past the roaring fireplace, Mary tore her vision away from the moaning wounded and looked at the opposite wall. She involuntarily gasped at the moving shadows. Instead of the outlines of weary servants carrying litters of wounded men, there was only the murky penumbra of robed men and women carrying a steaming cauldron. Mary had no idea what the iron pot contained, but the robes she knew on sight.

"It's a trick!" Mary cried, swinging the shotgun around and firing from the hip. "They're squiddies!"

The blast rocked the cauldron and the servants shimmered as their magical disguises melted away. Triggering her weapon again, Mary blew two of the Squid God worshipers out of their boots and directly into the fireplace.

Snarling curses, the rest of the squiddies protectively surrounded the cauldron as they pulled out knives, crossbows, dynamite bombs, and hatchets. The women cut loose with pistols, rifles, and crossbows, just as the invaders charged. Explosions and screams filled the room as the fight escalated into total chaos! The thick clouds of billowing gun smoke masked the rampaging battle, and soon the floorboards ran with blood. . . .

SIXTEEN

A deep and peaceful topaz blue, the Caribbean Sea was smooth and calm. Not a wave broke the surface, nor a breeze disturbed the perfect serenity of the marine expanse.

Then a tiny bubble rose from the cool depths to pop on the surface. More bubbles came next, larger, louder, dozens, hundreds, thousands, millions, until the sea was roiling wildly, a churning, thrashing chowder of primordial frenzy.

Shifting, the salty blue began to move around a central axis, swirling about faster and faster to form a whirlpool. Building in power and speed, the sides of the whirlpool sharply rose as the middle descended, going all the way down through the murky depths of the tumultuous sea. Schools of fish raced from the area in terror, and even the clouds seemed to balk in awe of the rampaging eddy on display.

Exactly on cue, the horizon heaved upward, and a tidal wave crested into view with the tiny screaming figures of Prof. Einstein and Lord Carstairs still riding atop the impromptu Italian tsunami.

The roaring wave rushed towards the rumbling whirlpool, and then roughly whipped forward to cast the two men down into the gaping maw of the aquatic storm. Tumbling head over heels, Einstein and Carstairs could only stare in wonder as they became ensconced in darkness, hurtling down the funnel of the stentorian whirlpool.

"Professor, I do believe that this is the Bermuda Triangle!" Lord Carstairs bellowed in surprise.

"That would also be my estimation, lad!" Prof. Einstein yelled over the sea and wind.

"We made bloody good time!"

"Indubitably!"

Dimly seen below the plummeting men, strange mists started to form at the rocky bottom. Savage lightning crackled from out of nowhere in a pyrotechnic explosion of color and pain as Einstein and Carstairs entered the thickening clouds. Bracing themselves for a shattering impact, the explorers were surprised to still be falling, ever falling, far beyond any possible sea depth.

Now they noticed that the whirlpool was gone, replaced by the swirling clouds, and the professor and the lord slowly realized that their angle of flight had shifted. They were no longer going down, but flying sideways, ever building in speed as lightning crashed around them in an oddly familiar manner.

"By Gadfrey, lad, this is a transdimensional vortex!" Prof. Einstein cried, losing a shoe. "It must be the secret entrance to Dutar Island!"

"Exactly the same as in the Vatican!" Carstairs shouted in delight. Cupping both hands to his mouth, the lord turned to bellow at the sky. "Oh I must say, well done, Captain van der Decken! Good show!"

"Sailors always pay their debts, lad! The Dutch doubly so!"

"Righto, sir!"

Now joyfully hurtling through the magical maelstrom, Einstein and Carstairs noticed the mists were changing into a strobing tunnel of blue light. But the further they proceeded, the more difficult it became to breathe. A bitter chill swept over the men, and ice formed on their damp clothing. Suddenly, they began to move apart, the gap widening with every passing second.

"Benjamin, we're caught in an ethereal drift!" Prof. Einstein cried in desperation, fighting a shiver. "Captain van der Decken knew the doorway, but only you have seen our destination, the temple of the Squid God! Concentrate, lad! Use your mind to guide us there!"

Scowling darkly, the freezing lord threw every facility of his prodigious mind to the task. Almost instantly, the mists ahead of the men began to thin and Einstein and Carstairs discovered themselves moving to the left along a horizontal tornado of wind and thunder that stretched off to an impossible distance.

Appearing at the extreme far end of the ethereal force tube was a black castle situated on top of an icy mountain. A dozen robed figures were moving around the misty edifice of evil; one of them was wearing robes of blood red and a golden mask shaped like a screaming squid.

There could be no doubt as to the identity of the masked man and, facing their true enemy at last, without question or pause, Prof. Einstein and Lord Carstairs drew their handguns and opened fire at the High Priest. Several of the robed servants clutched their chests and fell off the mountain peak, but the High Priest only recoiled at the sight of the two explorers running out of the stormy sky.

"You!" the High Priest screeched, pointing a finger, as the rest of the Squid God worshipers dove for cover.

As Prof. Einstein and Lord Carstairs paused to reload, the High

Priest raised an ebony staff crackling with energy. Taking a dramatic stance, the High Priest started intoning a spell while Einstein and Carstairs commenced firing and running once more. Thunder crashed as the weapons discharged and the glowing staff was nicked by a bullet, the ricochet cracking a stone step near the priest's sandals. Then a small round zinged off the golden mask, as a large caliber bullet grazed the High Priest's shoulder, blood spraying from the wound.

Leaning on the staff, the High Priest sagged. Prof. Einstein and Lord Carstairs cheered in victory as they reloaded on the run, then started firing as fast as possible. Twice more the High Priest was hit and he sagged to a knee, dislodging the golden mask. As it fell away, the High Priest faced the men directly with a trickle of blood flowing from his contorted mouth.

"Son of a bitch!" Lord Carstairs shouted, waving the Webley about to disperse its smoke before shooting again.

"You traitorous little bastard!" Prof. Einstein bellowed, out of control in his rage.

Lifting himself painfully with the ebony staff, William Henry Owen spit a curse at the two explorers, his words swallowed by the howling wind and never-ending lightning.

Surging forward with renewed speed, Einstein and Carstairs focused their weapons on the High Priest and Owen was hit twice more before the rest of the Squid God worshipers rushed forward to form a living wall around their priest.

"A nice try, Professor!" Owen screamed above the strident storm, making a rude gesture. "But now it's time to die, Christian fools!"

Stoic as grenadiers, the British explorers replied with a flurry of gunfire.

Sneering triumphantly, Owen waved his staff and it pulsed with power, the nimbus of light expanding to fill the universe. In a twinkling of colors, the transdimensional tube vanished and Prof. Einstein and Lord Carstairs found themselves unexpectedly falling from the empty sky.

On the horizon, the black castle was gone, replaced by a range of tall mountains and a dense forest that were coming towards the explorers at a frightening speed.

"Try for the lake!" Lord Carstairs screamed, spotting a flash of blue amid the dense greenery. Extending his arms, the lord started flapping madly, and incredibly he moved slightly to the right. *By jingo, it was working!* "Go limp! It'll soften the impact!"

If there was a response from Prof. Einstein, it was lost as seconds later the men painfully crashed into a thick layer of leafy boughs, punching straight through to hit the crystal clear water. With a tremendous splash, they went below the surface, closely followed by an avalanche of broken tree branches. Crashing waves crested high on the icy water, ripples spreading out to the rocky shore. But soon the lake was serene once more, and displayed no signs whatsoever of its uninvited guests.

SEVENTEEN

The body lay sprawled on the sloping bank of the mountain lake, the motionless figure covered with mud, kelp, and wind-blown leaves.

Groaning as if an experiment of some crazed German scientist coming to life for the first time, Lord Carstairs stiffly rose from a watery depression in the sandy ground. Every inch of his body felt bruised, and there was a nasty dirty copper metallic taste in his mouth, as if he had been sucking on a halfpenny.

Gingerly, the lord felt about and discovered the source of the blood was a badly split lip. It was uncomfortable, but hardly life threatening.

Standing painfully, Carstairs glanced around. He was situated alongside a small lake, standing in a Lord-Carstairs-sized hole in the mud. Extending over the lake, there was a ragged hole in the leafy canopy of tree branches that went all the way through to show a clear sky. The details of his arrival came flashing back and the lord flinched at the memory of his landing. It was a miracle that he was still alive. The trees must have slowed his descent just enough to let him survive the impact into the lake. Having seen the famous cliff-divers of Mexico, Lord Carstairs knew that from a great enough height, a person would splatter when he hit the water, as if the liquid was solid stone. Very nasty.

Hawking to clear his throat, the lord now noticed a most unpleasant buzzing noise mixing with the sounds of the forest. *Hornets? No, wait, that was somebody snoring.*

"Professor?" Lord Carstairs called out hesitantly.

The buzzing abruptly stopped. There came a rustling of leaves and a nearby bush shook as Einstein clumsily rose into view.

"God's navel, we survived!" the professor muttered, holding the side of his head. "How are you doing, lad?"

"Damaged, but alive, sir," Carstairs replied, gingerly feeling for broken bones under the mud and leaves covering his arms. "Apparently, that Owen fellow was able to disperse the vortex prematurely."

"Prematurely for us," Prof. Einstein wheezed, removing some kelp from his head. "Although . . ." Glancing downward, the man went pale, and screamed.

Charging forward, the lord caught a glimpse of a pink professor ducking out of view. "What is it, sir?" Carstairs demanded, then suddenly realized that the mud was falling away to reveal that he was stark naked.

"Bugger!" Lord Carstairs cried, diving back into the prickly bushes.

"This must be an unfortunate side effect of leaving the vortex before reaching its end destination," the voice of Prof. Einstein postulated from somewhere amid the greenery.

"Sir, we could get arrested for this!"

"If there are any police to do so, lad."

Staying low amid the bushes, Carstairs gave the matter some thought. "That's true. I did not see any signs of civilization as we were falling and I am unable to identify any of the plants near us."

Pulling a leaf free, Einstein examined it closely. "This bush resembles an elderberry, but it's wrong. Too thick, too dark."

Doing a brief study of the local flora, Lord Carstairs was forced to admit that all of the dense vegetation about them was strange. The carpeting of grass was more like moss, and jungle vines hung from trees resembling a combination of oak and juniper.

"This whole place feels . . . different," Einstein added, after a long tense moment.

"Originally, I had attributed that to my lack of trousers," Carstairs said dryly. "But now I think it rather more likely that the island of Dutar is not hidden inside the Bermuda Triangle, but in some distant place and the Triangle is merely the gateway. Quite possibly a land where even Her Majesty's forces have yet to penetrate."

"Sound reasoning," Prof. Einstein said, pulling more kelp away from a most inappropriate location. "Unfortunately, that means we are truly on our own."

"Quite so, Professor," Carstairs called back. "Then we had best get to work!"

* * *

A few hours later, the explorers emerged from the bushes dressed in simple grass skirts, hats of woven weeds, and treebark sandals. Prof. Einstein also carried three stones bound by lengths of tree vine into a crude South American bolo, along with a rough stone dagger. Lord Carstairs was armed with a primitive boomerang and a stout tree branch with the bark removed, making a most formidable club.

"Borneo?" Prof. Einstein asked, surveying the throwing stick.

"Australia," Lord Carstairs corrected, holding it for display. "Simple and deadly at fifty yards. I developed a knack for the things while investigating the hidden rooms inside Ayers Rock. Oh, I say, nice dagger."

"Thank you. The first thing my old archeological master insisted on was our learning was how to knap stone tools," the professor said with a touch of pride, offering the razor-sharp weapon for inspection. "I could not find any flint, only some low-grade quartz to work with, but it will suffice for the nonce."

"Should have made one for myself," the lord said wistfully, returning the blade. "Perhaps later, eh?"

Carefully sliding the blade into the vine hem of his skirt, Einstein inhaled deeply through his nose and held the breath. The forest air smelled of pine, elderberry, cedar, and fresh animal droppings. How lovely to be back in the woods again! A majestic range of mountains edged the horizon, most of them snow-capped, although one was smoking in the manner of a sleeping volcano. By Gadfrey, just how large a landmass was Dutar Island?

"Now the question is, which direction do we take?" Prof. Einstein queried aloud, rubbing his chin thoughtfully.

Dropping to a knee, Carstairs carefully studied the crumpled markings in the muddy shoreline. Then standing tall, he peered upwards at the damage in the treetops. "Well, sir," he said slowly, testing each word for flaws, "if there is any correlation between the angle of the fall and our original trajectory, then I would venture to guess that we might head in the direction of that singular mountain." He pointed with the club.

Looking in the indicated direction, Prof. Einstein saw the mountain was noticeably taller than the rest, and the only one not capped with snow or alive with volcanic steam. However, the dark stone of the peak appeared to be black as coal. *Just like the mountain peak of the temple of the Squid God. Bingo! As his Catholic friends liked to say.*

"That does seem to be our goal, lad," Einstein agreed, hitching up his skirt. "If it's a clear night, hopefully we will be able to determine where we are from the stars."

"Then we should be off," Lord Carstairs said, lifting his hefty weapon and taking the lead along a natural path through the thick bushes. "*Tempus fugit!*"

"You can say that again," the professor grumbled, taking up the rear guard.

* * *

Surrounded by a tapestry of greenery, a sphinx sat atop a grassy knoll and hungrily viewed the approaching human morsels. People lost in the forest were a beacon to her senses, and she could not have resisted coming to them if she tried. How delightful was the aroma of their fear! How satisfying the anticipated crunch of their bones! How convenient their clothing for flossing! Although, the sphinx did notice that these poor bastards were pretty much dressed in leaves and weeds. Ah well, it would not hurt to have a bit of salad with your lunch. Diet was so very important.

Striving for maximum effect, the sphinx waited until the humans were just about to reach her clearing, then she jumped straight up into the air. Seconds after, as they exited the bushes, she landed directly in front of them with a ground-shaking thump.

"Halt!" the sphinx roared, raising a paw.

In utter amazement, Prof. Einstein and Lord Carstairs stared at the huge sphinx filling the clearing. Built along classic lines, the being had the head and breasts of a beautiful woman atop the body of a lion with a serpent's tail, and a pair of great white wings fluttering from her wide shoulders. Most definitely a mammalian female; thankfully, there was a golden breastplate covering her ample bosom. The sphinx stood a good ten yards tall and some twenty yards long and, while her voice was quite loud, it was also remarkably pleasant.

As circumspectly as possible, the professor leaned over and whispered, "I am beginning to believe that the vortex might have taken us a bit further than we had first suspected."

"Quite," the lord replied. "But then, perhaps this is the true home of . . . you know what."

"Indeed so, lad, you may have struck upon the truth with that theory."

"Thank you, sir."

Twitching her haunches and flexing her talons, the sphinx frowned unhappily. These mortals were surprised, but the heady aroma of terror was blatantly absent. An angry growl began to well within her throat. That would soon change!

"Greeting, humans!" she boomed. "What are two nearly naked men doing in my forest?"

"We're lost," Einstein answered promptly. "And what are your next two questions?"

Her hackles rising, the sphinx spit in ill-controlled rage, the tiny globule of moisture hissing through rock and soil.

"Impudent toads!" she snarled, both mighty breasts heaving. "Very well! What walks on four legs in the morning–"

"Man," Carstairs interrupted.

Blinking hard, the sphinx gave a long pause. "You have heard these before?" she finally asked.

"Yes," the professor replied, turning away. "That is three for three. Goodbye."

"HOLD!" the giant sphinx thundered, blocking their path with a paw the size of a divan. "You must now ask me three questions and if I can answer them all, then death is your reward."

Turning their backs on the female monster, the two explorers quickly conferred for a moment.

"Question number one," Lord Carstairs said, turning around once more. "In terms we can easily understand, please detail to us exactly and precisely, in increasing orders of magnitude, where we are currently located."

The sphinx frowned at that. This was clearly not the sort of thing she normally encountered. "Ah, well, hmm, you are in the forest of Woodmote, in the satrap of Quithshard, in the county of Hixlap, in the country of Kooopashtahl . . ." The sphinx began to sweat, this question could literally take forever to answer! ". . . on the continent of Dutar, on the world of Lurth, in the orbit of the star Pol, in the third spiral arm of the galaxy 3457J9, which is in the pocket dimension of magic, which is–"

"Wait!" the professor cried, raising a palm. "Elucidate on that last bit and you can stop." It was not a question.

With a sigh of relief, the sphinx accepted the alteration. "This is the dimension where magic rules, not the laws of physical science. Despite the fundamental difference in its basic construction, the only real deviation is that, here, time flows twice as fast as anywhere else."

In dire consternation, Einstein and Carstairs exchanged glances. They now knew why the Squid God had retreated to this dimension. Recuperating from its wounds here, the beast had only been asleep for two thousand years, not four thousand. Unfortunately, it also meant that it wasn't five days until the rebirth, but two and a half. Maybe less.

"Question two," Lord Carstairs said hurriedly, shifting his grip on the wooden boomerang. "In an easily comprehensible manner, give us the exact location of the being that we seek, known to us as the Squid God."

Raking a clawed paw through her golden tresses, the sphinx stared hard at the two humans dressed in their ridiculous salad clothing. "An interesting line of inquiry. The Colossus resides in a temple atop that distant mountain."

The sphinx pointed, and following the direction of the talon, the explorers saw she was indicating the bare rock peak, standing alone amidst the range of taller snowy mountains.

"Excellent," Lord Carstairs sighed. "That was the one we were already heading for."

"Spot on, lad!" Prof. Einstein agreed. "We're closing in fast."

"And now, little ones, ask the last of your questions," the sphinx sneered, licking her bristling cat-whiskers with eagerness. She had been worried at first by their boldness, but the sphinx felt that she was back in control.

"As you wish, madam," Lord Carstairs replied. "Question number three: with the weapons and resources immediately available to us, what is the surest, fastest, and easiest way for us to kill you?"

With an audible clunk, the beast dropped her jaw to the rocky ground, then closed it with a snap. For several minutes, her fangs ground against each other as she engaged in furious thought.

"Gosh, what a good question," she finally admitted in a friendly voice. "I have no idea. You win! Goodbye." With a bound, the sphinx went sailing over the trees and was gone from sight.

"Sometimes, it really pays to have a classical education," Lord Carstairs noted, starting to walk again.

"Quite," the professor laughed, but then abruptly stopped. "However, lad, if this is the homeland of the Squid God, and his worshipers know that we have arrived, then we can expect hostile magic to be directed our way. Perhaps even magical creatures; such as werewolves, dragons, or basilisks."

At that pronouncement, the lord lost his smile and hunched his powerful shoulders in preparation for an attack as the explorers tramped through the thick woods, tightening their grips on the crude weapons.

EIGHTEEN

The alien sun was directly overhead as Prof. Einstein and Lord Carstairs pushed their way through some nasty thorn bushes to discover a beaten dirt path that headed towards the mountains. Following the smooth path, their speed increased greatly, and soon the dusty men began to pass cultivated fields of wheat, corn, and softly-whistling zucchini.

Tired and hungry, Einstein and Carstairs liberated a small repast of non-musical food from the lush croplands and wolfed it down raw. Feeling greatly refreshed, the explorers continued their cross-country trek. As the day began to ebb into evening, the men stopped at the sight of a walled city in the distance.

"Eureka!" Lord Carstairs cried in delight.

"Weureka," Prof. Einstein corrected primly.

"Quite right, sir," the lord chuckled. "We both discovered it at the same time. I do apologize."

Following a serpentine trail to the crest of a low hillock, Einstein and Carstairs found they could see past the adobe wall and into the city proper. It was a squalid affair of ragged tents and crowded buildings, with chimneys that belched out thick black fumes. The reek from the billowing smoke smelled so horrendous that it brought a homesick tear to the eyes of the Londoners. Ah, civilization!

"That seems to be our best bet," Lord Carstairs said, resting his club on a tan shoulder. "We must find proper clothing, supplies and, most importantly, hard information."

Tucking the bolo into his skirt, Prof. Einstein agreed. "I have yet to see any buildings outside the city, which says there must be a good reason for the wall. Which further suggests that we might not want to spend the night out here in the wild."

As the explorers trudged closer, they could see that the wall was made of huge stone blocks joined without mortar and reaching some ten yards high. It would be much too difficult to scale; definitely not the sort of barrier built on a whim.

The dirt path ended at a paved road bustling with people, animals, and wheeled wooden carts. None of whom paid any attention whatsoever to the semi-naked explorers. The paved road went directly to a large archway in the wall, the opening protected by an imposing gate of thick iron bars.

Stepping into the flow of traffic, Einstein and Carstairs observed that while the majority of the crowd was humanoid, some of the beings were most definitely not. Drunken centaurs hoisting bottles staggered out of town, while a squad of singing dwarfs swaggered inside. Exiting the city, a hulking lizard in silver armor barely managed to squeeze through the archway. On top of its head was perched a small stuffed bunny riding in a position of authority. Whether the rabbit was an ornament, or the driver, was impossible for the men to discern.

And the humans! All of them were dressed in an amazing variety of fashions: Oriental kimonos, fur cloaks, bamboo armor, and linen tunics. The majority of the people seemed to be of a mid-European stock, but skin tones ranged the full spectrum of colors from Hottentots to Swedes.

Most of the pedestrians leaving the town did so without hindrance, but all of the beings entering were briefly stopped by the four guards standing before the gate. Large, muscular men covered with scars, the guards were clad in chainmail shirts that reached to their knees, tight leather trousers, and spiked iron helmets. At their hips hung curved swords possessing a very-well-used and dangerous appearance.

"The people seem to be a strange mixture of several different races and cultures," Lord Carstairs stated, rubbing his unshaven jaw to the sound of sandpaper. "The language is a polyglot, but seems to be primarily based on the idiomatic sub-tongue of Hellenic Greek. Very similar to the language carved into that broken stone banner from Atlantis you have."

"You're quite right, lad," Einstein sighed in relief. "At least we shall be able to converse with the natives."

"We had no such trouble with that sphinx, sir."

"Ah, but she was magical. That's a whole different set of linguistic rules, based upon the second secret Mother Tongue of Humanity, and all that." The professor, hitched up his grass skirt. "Well, there is no sense in delaying the inevitable. They aren't very suspicious of strangers, sir. Shall we try the direct approach?"

"Very well," the lord agreed, flexing his muscular shoulders. "But be prepared to run if necessary."

With forced casualness, the explorers started whistling a tune and strolled to the gate. As expected, the first guard raised a hand as they approached. The whistling stopped, and both men smiled.

However, the guard curled a lip at their outfits. "Two coppers to enter," he said in a businesslike manner.

In a mimic of every religious official he had ever annoyed, Prof. Einstein tried to appear holy. "But my son, we are holy men traveling under a vow of poverty."

"A vow of what?" the guard snorted. "Never heard of such nonsense in my life. It's two coppers, or you can't come in."

"But we really do not have any money," Lord Carstairs said, filling his voice with honest sincerity.

"Cow flop," the guard retorted, pulling his sword. "What are you two trying to smuggle inside?"

Bowing his head, Einstein followed suit. "We are only poor monks from the distant mountains, why don't you . . ."

"Mountain monks!" the guard screamed, turning pale. He raised an arm to hide his face. "Unclean! Get away! Vamoose!"

Caught by surprise, Einstein and Carstairs could only blink in response. "What was that?" the professor began. "Look sir, we are not–"

"I don't want to hear about it, ya murdling freaks!" The guard yelled as the other guards scrambled out of the way. "Get in! Get out! I don't care. Just don't touch me!"

Not quite sure how to take this reaction, the two explorers decided to seize the golden opportunity and scurried through the gate. Moving quickly along an alleyway, Einstein and Carstairs found a bustling marketplace, with wheeled carts full of produce lining the street on both sides. Chickens cackled in little wicker cages, and fish loudly barked from slopping buckets. Farmers were selling their crops at the top of their lungs, a butcher hawked fresh red meat from a bucket, and several bakers carried steaming pretzels on iron rods, the delicious aroma doing the selling for them. Coins were exchanged as sales were made, a modified form of Pakistani tally sticks used to add the totals.

Taking refuge behind a truly impressive, though hairy, tomato, the two explorers caught their breath.

"Mountain monks?" Lord Carstairs queried, glancing backwards at the city gate.

Adjusting his weed hat, Prof. Einstein shrugged. "I have no idea, lad. But perhaps it is something we can use to our advantage."

"How do you figure that? That guard most definitely did not wish to continue our association."

"Ah, but he did let us in without paying, Carstairs. Many societies have beggars that they spurn, but are forced to care for due to a religious or sociological ethos. It can not hurt to try."

Lord Carstairs frowned, but did not disagree. In a casual stroll, Prof. Einstein approached a man who was polishing a pile of plump purple fruits.

"Greetings, my son," the professor smiled. "I am but a humble Mountain monk and–"

A juicy fruit hit the professor with a splat, and he wiped his face clean to see the farmer raising another one to throw.

"Help! I'm being attacked by a Mountain monk!" the grocer shouted, in clear panic. "Help! Guards!"

Across the market, everybody screamed and started throwing things; mostly foodstuffs, but a few rocks were included in the barrage aimed at the splattered professor.

"There he is!" a man screamed, heaving a brick. "A dirty, stinking, Mountain Monk!"

"Herd 'em towards the town center!" a woman added, raising a flaming torch.

"Don't touch them!" another warned.

"Hey! There's two!" somebody cried, gesturing at Lord Carstairs.

A big butcher brandished his meat cleaver. "Then we'll just need twice as much wood to burn 'em!" he bellowed.

As the howling crowd advanced, rotten fruits and gobs of nightsoil pelted the lord like a sneeze from Satan. Galvanized into action, Carstairs yanked loose a pole that was holding up a tent, causing the cloth to collapse on the mob. Then kicking over a fruit cart, the lord scooped up the professor under an arm and ran madly down an alleyway, turned down another alley, turned again, hopped a fence, and then another, until he was standing in a quiet courtyard.

Holding his breath, Lord Carstairs waited as the sounds of the mob went past the courtyard and faded away into the distance. Whew! He hadn't done anything like this since his initiation night at Harvard!

Easing the professor to the ground, Carstairs studied the courtyard. The walls were of alternate red and black bricks, giving an odd harlequin effect, and the ground was dirt covered with loose gravel. A few hexagonal barrels formed a pyramid against the rear of what appeared to be a warehouse, and in the corner was a large horse trough full of greenish water. As Carstairs walked for an inspection, a cat-like creature sprang onto the trough from the shadows, gave an annoyed moo, sprouted wings, and flapped away into the darkening sky.

Turning away from the scummy water, Lord Carstairs threw away his befouled hat. "Brilliant move, Einstein," he rumbled. "Now what do we do?"

"I'm thinking, lad," the professor sagely muttered, when a rotten fruit struck the nearby wall with a juicy splat.

Again? The explorers spun around at see a group of grinning youths entering the courtyard through a door masked by the shadows. The clothing of the teens had obviously been chosen for dramatic effect, but the weapons in their hands were strictly utilitarian, staves and long knives with blades that gleamed evilly in the failing light.

"Well-well, what have we here, my grunties?" a tall youth asked, with a jaunty leather codpiece tied to his head.

"Mountain monks!" a fat one chuckled, a gold ring through his nose. "Fun time!"

"Under a sentence of death, they is," the leader smiled, displaying cracked stained teeth. "To anybody who finds 'em."

A lad sporting a pair of horns brandished a short piece of rope and started tying a noose. "So let's have a bit-o-fun," he suggested, the squeak of puberty marring the otherwise ominous statement.

Totally nonplussed, Lord Carstairs thoughtfully rubbed his chin. "What do you think, sir?"

The professor shrugged. "No sense looking a gift horse in the mouth, lad."

"Any chance they might be Squid God worshipers?

"Highly unlikely. Not even William Owen would be desperate enough to enlist these poltroons."

"Agreed," the lord said, crackling his knuckles. "But only unconscious, correct?"

"That would be wise," Prof. Einstein agreed. "There is no purpose in arousing the local constabulary."

By now, the gang was glancing in confusion, and a burly redhead wearing a gaudy rainbow vest stepped forward. "Here now," he demanded rudely. "Aren't you Mountain Monks?"

"No," Prof. Einstein said, pulling out the bolo. Spinning it to a whistling pitch, he aimed and let it fly.

The entangling strands caught three of the gang and the spinning stones knocked one completely unconscious. As there was insufficient space for a proper return throw, Carstairs hurled his boomerang straight into the gang, bringing two more to their knees. Then the British lord waded into the moaning group with his bare fists and the fight was over before it had really begun.

After tying up the teenagers with some of the vines from their jungle clothing, Einstein and Carstairs went to the water trough and tried to wash off the worst of the fruit juices. This resulted in their acquiring a slight greenish tinge, which they glibly accepted as additional disguise. Stuffing their makeshift garb into an empty barrel, they stripped the gang naked and began to don what they could of the appropriated clothing.

"Whatever is wrong, lad?" Prof. Einstein asked, struggling with a pair of boots. "Feeling bad about thievery?"

Lord Carstairs gave a snort. "Not from the likes of these. I was actually struggling to recall the appropriate quote."

"'Stealing from thieves is not a crime,'" the professor supplied, "'only irony.'"

Tugging on the largest set of pantaloons, Carstairs smiled. "Ah, yes. Don Quixote, by Cervantes."

"Really? I always thought it was the Queen's tax assessor. How very interesting."

When they were finished, Prof. Einstein was dressed in boots and trousers of blue leather, a cotton shirt, and the rainbow colored vest. Fortunately, Lord Carstairs was able to find a pair of boots comfortably large enough for his feet, but the biggest pair of pants clung to the man in a most alarming manner and none of the shirts could be properly buttoned closed.

"Leave the shirt unbuttoned to the waist and drape a belt over a shoulder," Einstein suggested, sliding a stolen knife into his waist. "It will give a nice pirate effect."

As if listening to his batsman, Lord Carstairs dutifully followed the suggestion, and laid a belt across his hairy chest. By Gadfrey, he did look like a bloody pirate! *No offense meant, Red John.*

"How much money did we get?" the lord asked, getting back to business.

Pulling a fistful of coins from his pocket, the professor jingled the mixture in his palm. "Twenty copper pieces, two pewter, and one silver. And judging by the city gate tax, this isn't much. We will need a great deal more to buy anything useful."

"Quite so. Very well, first we must raise additional funds," the lord said, using stiff fingers to comb back his damp hair. "And for that we need a bar."

"A bar?"

"Bar, saloon, tavern, beer hall," Carstairs stated with a shrug. "Anything of that sort will do nicely."

"This is no time for drinking, lad," Prof. Einstein decried, with a waggling finger.

"True enough, sir. However, a tavern is the very best place to start a real fight," the lord explained, flexing his massive hands.

"Ah, of course," the professor answered, trying valiantly to hide his complete lack of comprehension.

NINETEEN

Walking out of the courtyard and onto the street, Einstein and Carstairs saw that night was falling across the nameless city. Strange constellations were appearing in the purple sky, and bright lamps were beginning to glow on every street corner. But instead of the flickering gas jets of London, on top of the bamboo poles were glass balls about the size of a melon, filled with schools of tiny iridescent fish. In passing, the men could distantly hear a faint bubbling.

The hustling crowds of people were mostly gone, and yawning merchants were closing the shutters of their shops, while sleepy vendors packed away their carts. Moving through the darkness were happy faces illuminated by the soft, red light of smoking pipes. The city gates were closed, the earlier destruction cleared away, and the town was a peaceful sea of tranquility.

Strolling along the pavement, the professor nudged Lord Carstairs and indicated a building. It was a rather shabby, single-story brick structure, with smoky light pouring from the windows and the universal sound of laughter wafting from the swinging doors. Hanging from an external beam was a wooden sign in the shape of a bucket, with glowing symbols that melted and changed under the explorers' gaze to reform into letters spelling out in English 'Big Bob's Boozarama.'

"How about that?" Prof. Einstein asked, with a gesturing palm.

Thoughtfully, Lord Carstairs rubbed his prominent jaw. "Acceptable, but not perfect."

Just then, the window exploded as a body came crashing through to land sprawling onto the street. With a crisp sucking sound, the falling shards of glass wove an intricate pattern in the air, and then were abruptly sucked back to reform once more into a window. The drunk in the gutter muttered an obscenity, rolled over, and began to snore.

"I stand corrected," the lord smiled. "It is ideal!"

"Really?" Quite reluctantly, Prof. Einstein let Lord Carstairs lead the way to the establishment and through the swinging half-doors.

Once they were inside, the place seemed hardly different from any low-class drinking establishment across the ghettos of the world. It was noisy and crowded, the floor near the front door was sticky, and the air smelled of stale beer. The gray plaster walls were decorated with lewdly suggestive posters, and there was a pristine dartboard that apparently nobody had ever hit. The single notable difference was that this tavern was well illuminated with clusters of the glass balls filled with fish hanging from the rafters of recessed ceiling. The illumination was clear, and the ever-present bubbling merely added to the assorted clamor.

Approaching the counter, the explorers' feet crunched with every step as the floor was covered with a thick carpeting of green and blue peanut shells. As they expected, there were no proper stools at the counter; the customers placed an order and drank it standing, or walked away. The counter itself was a massive slab of wood, apparently hewn from a single incredible tree. On the staggered shelves behind were the usual assortment of bottles, flasks, jugs, and casks. But some of them were hissing, while others trembled for no discernable reason.

Wiping a pewter tankard clean with a damp rag as if he had been doing it forever, the fat barkeep sported a scruffy moustache and wore a cracked leather apron over a stained tunic and breeches. Off to a side of the counter was a small green lizard slurping at a bowl of milk. On the wall nearby hung a crooked mirror with a thirty-piece orchestra inside, playing a snappy tune that was vaguely familiar.

"Is that Mozart?" asked the professor, scratching his head.

"Liszt," Lord Carstairs corrected.

As could be expected, the patrons were an unappetizing collection of snoring drunks, shifty touts, toothless whores, boisterous toffs, and several deadly serious drinkers. Even in his feckless youth, if Einstein had walked into such a place all by himself, the scholar would have used the momentum of his entrance to wheel about and leave immediately.

Spotting an empty chair by the stairs that led to the mezzanine, Lord Carstairs directed the professor to take a seat. Then flexing his hands, the lord sauntered into the middle of the tavern and loudly announced. "I can beat any man in this bar!"

A stunned hush fell over the room, then a grinning bear of a man stepped into view from behind one of the thick beams that supported the ceiling. Wearing only baggy trousers and thick-soled boots, the bald giant was covered with scars, and had a gold chain looped from a cauliflower ear to his broken nose.

"Is that a challenge, stranger?" the Goliath asked politely, waving the small cask he was been using as a mug.

With forced bravado, Lord Carstairs sneered contemptuously.

"What? Are you stupid as well as ugly?"

Two of the tavern patrons fainted on the spot, and another looked embarrassed as a splashing sound came from under his table.

"Hey, no need to get nasty," the mountain of muscle said, laying aside his drink. "And the name is Crusher, Skull Crusher d'Colinquet on formal occasions like this."

"Lord Benjamin Carstairs," the explorer stated loudly and clearly, while he advanced closer.

Crusher moved forward, and the men met in the middle of the tavern to face each other eye-to-eye. That was a new experience for the British Lord, and not a pleasant one. They were of precisely equal height and girth.

Seeing that he was not having the usual effect of raw terror on this weirdly dressed newcomer, Crusher noisily cracked his enlarged knuckles.

"Now if you wish to die," Crusher said in a friendly manner, "I'll be happy to just kill you. No charge."

"Ah, but I am betting that you can't," Lord Carstairs said, pushing a chair out of the way to make some combat space.

Interested murmurs now rose from the onlookers, and faces started to smile with avarice. The band in the mirror began playing a dramatic military tune, and the bartender started placing the more delicate glassware safely under the wooden counter.

"Oh, you wanna disguise the suicide as a bet?" Crusher said, tightening his belt a notch. "Fine. Name the figure."

This was not going as Carstairs had planned. In the background, several patrons had taken positions of safety on the railed balcony over the barroom, while others had simply tilted their tables sideways, forming impromptu barricades to hide behind.

Drawing in a deep breath to gain time, Lord Carstairs chose an amount at random. "Ten gold pieces?"

"Done!" Crusher grinned, displaying a gold tooth. "Mighty generous of you. What about weapons?"

The lord arched an imperious eyebrow. "Well, if you need a weapon, I suppose. . . ."

"Bare hands it is," Crusher smiled, nodding his head. Then without another word, the bald man charged forward, every slam of his boots making the floor shake.

Waiting until the very last possible moment, Carstairs nimbly side-stepped the man's rush, then smashed the fellow in the side of the head with a powerful right jab. With a startled cry, Crusher went sailing sideways to land on a table. The bar furniture smashed into kindling under his weight, and the hairless giant crashed to the dirty floor.

Wild cheers exploded from the crowd.

"Do it again, my gruntie!" a drunken man called from behind a palisade of empty bottles.

"Aye!" a leering wench added, plumping her ample wares. "To me!"

Doffing his hat to the laughing throng, Lord Carstairs turned to assist his bleeding opponent off the floor. For a second, it seemed as if Crusher planned on continuing the fight. Then he sheepishly rubbed the back of his neck and smiled.

"Now that was a new dirty trick, ya scum," Crusher muttered unhappily. "Where'd ya learn that?"

"Oxford debating society," Lord Carstairs said, proffering an open palm. "My winnings, if you please."

Lowering his head, Crusher scuffed his boots about in the colorful nutshells. "Well, y'got me there," he muttered. "I . . . I only have two silvers."

Instantly, the shouting, drinking, and laughing crowd went deathly quiet. Then all of them turned to frown at the obviously embarrassed Crusher.

A little fellow with a metal pot on his head finally spoke. "Crusher, you made a bet without having the money to cover?" he demanded askance.

Looking like a whipped dog, Crusher made feeble gestures with his scarred hands. "Well, ya see I . . . the thing is . . . damn it, I've never lost before!" he offered as an excuse.

"Cheater!" the customers screamed in loose unison, the cry echoing to the rafters.

Swarming upon the bald man in a savage mob, the patrons pounded Crusher until he fell. They hauled his broken body out the swinging doors and into the street. Rushing to the window, Prof. Einstein and Lord Carstairs watched in growing horror as the howling villagers threw a rope over a tree branch and hanged Crusher without pause or ceremony.

Feeling sick to their stomachs, the explorers stumbled away from the window and sat down in some empty chairs. Murdered over a bar bet? Incredible! Unthinkable!

Casting a glance at the window, Einstein and Carstairs could see the patrons now using torches to set fire to the swinging corpse, while others pelted it with stones pulled from the street. After a while, the muttering crowd filed back into the bar and angrily returned to their abandoned drinks.

Somehow or other, the professor found the power to speak, "I say, lad, good thing you won," Einstein whispered.

"Rather," Lord Carstairs agreed, rubbing his aching hand. "These chaps take gambling even more seriously than a Greek jailer."

"Different lands, different values," Prof. Einstein muttered, watching the patrons set the tables right, and return to their former seats. "It's rude in Sweden to brag, and I once got badly beaten by a cabby in Japan for giving him a tip."

"Ah, yes. That is quite an insult over there."

"Indeed, it is, my friend. Even more so than licking your lips after a meal in–"

"Hey, you two!"

Braced for anything, the explorers slowly turned at the summoning, and saw the fat bartender waving them over. Exchanging glances with each other, Einstein and Carstairs decided to take a chance, and crunchingly walked across the floor to the counter.

"Since the honor of my tavern is at stake, I will pay the ten gold pieces that Crusher owed ya," the barkeep stated, displaying a gap-toothed smile. "In credit, of course."

"That sounds quite acceptable," Prof. Einstein said.

"No, it is totally unacceptable," Lord Carstairs countered smoothly. "Since it is in credit, wouldn't fifteen gold pieces be more appropriate?"

In grudging acceptance, the bartender curled a lip, and offered his hand. "Done and done. Shake on it."

"Of course, rather than fifteen credits, I'd happily settle for five in hard cash," Lord Carstairs quickly amended, also extending his hand.

Recoiling slightly, the bartender underwent a variety of facial expressions before exploding into laughter. "By the Oracle, you argue as well as you fight. Five it is, hard and clean." Reaching into a pocket of his leather apron, the bartender produced the coins and placed a mixed stack of gold and silver disks on the stained counter top. "Agreed?"

"Indubitably, sir," Lord Carstairs answered politely.

Tilting his head, the puzzled barkeep stared at Carstairs.

"Yes. Agreed," the lord translated, and now the two men attempted to crush each other's hands for a while before finally parting.

"Now will ya be wanting to purchase anything with your winnings?" the bartender asked, resting an elbow on the counter as he slipped into professional mode. "Fighting and arguing makes a man mighty thirsty, eh?"

"Naturally, barkeep," Lord Carstairs smiled. "We'll start with a drink, for me and my friend."

"Fair enough," the bartender said, reaching under the counter to operate a spigot. When his hands returned into view, each carried a large pewter tankard of frothy beer. "And the name is Red Jack."

"Really?" Prof. Einstein said in surprise, taking the heavy container. "Any relation to the pirate of the same name?"

"Not that I know of," Red Jack said, placing the mugs down. "But then I know three more folks with the same name, they be a bootblack, a blacksmith, and alchemist. Nice fellows all."

Then Red Jack leaned closer to add softly, "But I don't suggest ever stopping by for dinner at the alchemist if he's having one of his 'brain fevers', if you knows what I mean."

"Quite so," Lord Carstairs politely chuckled, raising the frosty tankard. "Chin chin, old bean!"

Sniffing the contents first, the explorers experimentally sipped the amber brew, and were pleasantly surprised to discover it was ordinary beer, although slightly chilled. Cold beer? What kind of barbarian country was this island of Dutar?

Without any warning, the orchestra in the mirror swung into a rousing rendition of the exact same song they had been playing ever since the two men had first entered the bar.

"Is that all they know?" Lord Carstairs asked, using a handkerchief to wipe his lips.

Drawing another beer, Red Jack sighed. "Sadly, yes." He shoved the pewter tankard down the length of the counter; another patron made the catch and sent a coin rolling back. Red Jack caught the coin, bit it, then tucked it away into his leather apron for safekeeping.

"By the way, your mirror is crooked," Prof. Einstein said, using a sleeve to wipe the residue from his lips. He had a spare handkerchief, but instinctively knew its use would not be met with universal acceptance in this class of establishment.

"That be normal," Red Jack replied, gathering a dirty mug and tossing it over a shoulder to splash into a barrel full of soapy water. "The tuba player is fat. Will there be anything else?"

"We could use some weapons," Lord Carstairs stated, placing down the empty tankard. "Swords, crossbows, anything like that."

"Plus some medicinal chemicals," Einstein added ever so coolly. "Sulfur, charcoal, potassium nitrate. . . ."

Scratching his head, then his arse, Red Jack grunted steadily at the monumental effort of hard thinking. "I sell drinks. Weapons you got to buy from the City Chancery in the Mayor's Office," he said, plucking a mug from the soapy water and starting to dry it with a rag that had seen better days. "As for them other things, I have no idea. Sorry."

Einstein and Carstairs exchanged weary glances. Oh well, there went the idea of blackpowder bombs and French petards.

A customer at the end of the counter called an order and Red Jack pulled drafts into a pair of pewter mugs. The same motion that set the drinks sliding along waved the explorers closer.

"Tell ya what," Red Jack whispered, looking about warily. "I got a book of magic I can sell ya. Never been used, she is. Nice an' clean."

Although born and raised in London, Einstein had heard this dubious description applied before to everything from young girls in Mexico, to gold bullion in Russia. He hadn't believed it then and he certainly didn't believe it now.

"May I please see this alleged book," the professor demanded suspiciously. "I own several and don't want to buy a book that I already have at home."

"Sure, sure! No problem!" Red John beamed, heading into the back room. "Just a tick, eh?"

Listening to the exchange, Lord Carstairs decided to play the devil's fool and stay out of the conversation until needed. Radiating a casual air, the lord gently stroked the lizard on the counter. It gave a goofy smile.

"Nice," the lizard said in a high voice.

Snatching back his hand, Lord Carstairs almost went airborne. "By Agamemnon's shield, it talks!"

Stepping back into the room, Red John barked a laugh. "Well, of course, he talks. Say hi, Winslow."

"Hi, Winslow," the lizard obediently replied.

"Er, hello," the lord replied in strained courtesy.

As the lizard slurped at the bowl of milk, the level dropped enough for the lord to see that most of the bowl was filled with small rubies.

"Great Scott, what are those for?" Carstairs asked askance.

Winslow stopped drinking and glanced at the man as if he was stupid. "Pretty."

Feeling like a fool, Lord Carstairs tried to hide a grin. "Of course, forgive me."

"S'right," Winslow replied amiably, returning to his interrupted meal.

Laying a wrapped bundle on the counter, Red Jack folded back the flaps of cloth, revealing a small leather book. "Ah, here she is! Careful now, it's untouched," he said passing the book to the professor.

First inspecting the binding, Prof. Einstein wet a finger and leafed through the volume. "Impressive," he said. "But how do we know that these will actually work?"

"Why, them spells is genuine," Red Jack cried out, placing a hand on his heart. He sounded genuinely hurt. "And every one works, too. I seen 'em! Ya got my word of honor on it."

Glancing out the window, the professor saw the still burning figure hanging from the tree, small children were jabbing the charred body with sticks. "Mmm, yes, well, we accept your word of honor of course," Einstein said with strained emotions. "Yes, I believe that we are interested in obtaining this particular volume. How much are you asking?"

"Obviously, I couldn't let it go for less than two gold pieces for such a rare and valuable item as this," Red Jack stated, blinking innocently. "Take it, or leave it."

"One," the professor replied, holding out a coin.

Red Jack eagerly snatched it away. "Done!"

As Prof. Einstein and Lord Carstairs bent over the curious volume, Red Jack turned away to bite the coin in private, before stashing it away. This was the easiest two silvers' profit he had ever made. *Ah, tourists. Ya gotta love 'em.*

"How very interesting," Lord Carstairs said thumbing through the book. "The table of contents is in a recognizable form of English, but the rest of the book, hmm."

"Ah, well, there's the rub," Red Jack said, polishing the bar top with a rag. "If you want it translated, that's another matter."

"No thanks," Einstein said, petting the lizard who began to purr.

"We can read it perfectly fine."

As if hit by lightning, Red Jack dropped the rag. "What was that?" he whispered softly, his eyes threatening to leave his body. "B-but you're not supposed to be able to read it! Nobody can read the damn thing!"

In wry amusement, Professor Einstein stopped stroking the happy reptile. "Really now," he scolded. "I should think the book highly useless if we could not read it."

"Quite simple, really," Lord Carstairs announced, flipping through the pages of cryptic scrawling and ideographs. "The book is written in several languages, the majority of them dead, secret, or antiquarian. But no real problem." Suddenly, a light dawned on his face. "Or is that the scam?" Carstairs demanded.

"Aye, it is," Red Jack conceded, pouring himself a quick shot of a green liquor that radiated visible lines of force. He tossed it back and shuddered. "The book costs a gold piece, but the Magicians' Guild charges a hundred gold pieces to translate every page."

Closing the volume, Lord Carstairs gave a chuckle. "So the book itself is a loss leader." He saw the lack of understanding on the bartender's face. "A come-on, a tease," the lord explained lugubriously. "A ruse to generate business for the Magician's Guild."

"Yar, that be it," Red Jack sighed, starting to clean the shot glass. "Everybody in town has a copy. But there be more. After ya reads a spell, the words disappear from the page."

"A cheap book filled with terribly expensive, one shot, magic spells," Prof. Einstein muttered, looking at the book with marked disdain. "No, I don't think we wish to do business with this Magician's Guild."

"Thieves is the term we use," Red Jack whispered, glancing about quickly to see if anybody was within hearing distance. "But not very loud."

With a crash, the swinging doors slammed aside and in walked a group of battered young men wearing only underwear.

"There they be!" the black-eyed leader shouted.

"Thieves!" another shouted.

"Let's kill them!" the boy with the horns added, smacking a metal bar into his hand.

Pivoting, Einstein grabbed a bottle and smashed it on the counter. Still holding the glass neck, the professor gestured with the jagged broken ends towards the teens.

"On the count of three," Carstairs said, lifting a solid oak chair above his head.

"Don't try it, lads!" Red Jack cried out, raising a warning hand. "They got a magic book. And kin read it!"

"Cow flop," the leader muttered, taking a step forwards.

"A demonstration then," Lord Carstairs offered, lowering his chair. "If you so please, Professor?"

Placing his makeshift dagger on the counter, Einstein lifted the book and read from the cover. "The Al A. Kazam Big Book of Magic. Copyright–The Year The Mayor Got Stomped by the Giant Toad." He flipped to an inside page. "Attention, Seeker of Wisdom! Whom so-ever holds this volume has in his hands a thing of great and terrible power, dark knowledge known only to a few who have dared to face the infinite and guaranteed to be sure fun at parties, fetes, and galas."

Half of the street gang was gone by now, while the customers were loudly betting on the outcome of the confrontation.

"Bah. P-phooey," the leader quaked, tugging his stained shorts into place. "E-everybody knows that page. It's the one the Guild does for free!"

Controlling his anger over being refuted, the professor riffled through the pages and chose another. "Page 147: To Summon A Demon From Hell," Einstein read, making a weird gesture. As his hand snaked about, the professor's left pinkie created a glowing contrail in its wake, the pink lines soon forming an inverted trapezoid suspended in the empty air. An ominous moan of power filled the tavern, and the air grew noticeably cooler.

"First, you place your two knees close up tight," Prof. Einstein echoed in stentorian tones. "Then you swing them to the left, and then you swing them to the right–"

A scream interrupted the incantation as the remainder of the gang took flight, most of them using the door, but two departed through the window. As before, the glass repaired itself with a bizarre sucking sound, and the crowd of patrons erupted into applause.

"Splendidly done, sir!" Lord Carstairs cried, slapping the professor on the shoulder. "What else does this book contain?"

Recovering from the friendly blow, Prof. Einstein straightened his knees. *Zounds, the man was strong!* "Here, lad, read this secret table of contents for yourself."

Briefly, the lord scanned the listing. "Ah, then we won't need to buy weapons. Excellent."

"Magical weapons?" Red Jack gasped aloud, seeming to have trouble breathing. *There were weapons listed in the book*? "Wait! Let's the three of us talk straight dagbloon and no by-products!"

It was suddenly obvious to the two British gentlemen that the local bartender was about to start lying on an unprecedented scale. With a curt gesture, Professor Einstein cut off the barrage of incoming horse feathers, accidentally leaving a brief pink contrail behind. Oops.

"Look here, my good man, we've had a busy day, so I'll tell you what we're going to do," the professor said, patting the book. "You're going to direct us to a reputable stable and give us enough gold to pay for quality horses and to purchase supplies, along with a map of the fastest route to that big mountain to the west. In return for this, you will select one spell from this book, and if it is a spell that we can do without, then you shall have it."

In righteous indignation, Red Jack silently demanded a better deal with a hurt expression, then woebegone, and finally pitiful, but the professor remained adamant. There followed a hushed discussion as to which spell would be used. Steadfast, the bartender overruled the professor's suggestions of 'Water Into Wine' or 'Instant Sobriety' and finally decided upon 'Golden Touch', despite the misgivings of Lord Carstairs.

The deal was cinched and money exchanged. Lord Carstairs kept the other patrons away, as Prof. Einstein guided the bartender through the complex spell, and even helped Red Jack to make the appropriate motions. As the last cryptic word was spoken, the spell book gave off a pyrotechnic burst of colors and, with an audible pop, the page went blank.

"Is that it?" Red Jack asked, inspecting his glowing hand.

"Touch something and see," Prof. Einstein said, sliding the book away. "I modified the spell slightly so that it would not work on living flesh, so there's no danger of you sneezing and becoming a statue."

"A-are you a wizard?" the barkeeper asked in awe.

"Good lord no! Just an amateur linguist and member of the Southbank Good Grammar Society."

Hesitantly looking about for a test subject, Red Jack stopped and grinned. With his hand visibly twinkling with ethereal magic, he touched the counter. In a rippling motion of color, the wood transformed into solid gold, shining as if freshly forged.

"Yes!" Red Jack cried in delight, grabbing his face in delight. The man froze in horror, but when nothing happened, he exhaled in relief.

Then frowning slightly, Red Jack felt a rush of panic as he started to rise above the counter. Good lord he was becoming a giant! No, the counter was sinking lower. And lower . . .

"Watch out!" Lord Carstairs cried, grabbing the professor and hauling him away.

With the sound of splintering wood, the mega-ton metal counter thunderously crashed through the old wooden floorboards, leaving a perfectly rectangular hole behind as if cut from a toolmaker's die. A second crash closely followed, along with an assortment of minor smashing and the shattering glass.

"Whee! Do again!" Winslow called from somewhere in the murky darkness of the cellar.

Clutching his chest, Red Jack fainted and toppled over, his solid gold shirt slamming against the floor with a strident clang.

With a wordless roar, the rest of the patrons rushed closer, carefully skirting the gaping hole in the floor, and gathered around the moaning barkeep to start pressing small items into his glowing hand. As the object became gold, the owner rushed away and another took his place.

"Time to go, sir," Lord Carstairs advised sagely, edging towards the door. "By tomorrow morning, this whole village will be on the silver standard, and our gold coins will be worthless."

Hugging the book, the professor blinked at that. Egad, he hadn't thought about the devaluation aspect.

"Think we can make all of our purchases tonight?" the professor asked, as they ran along the empty street.

"With a bag full of gold?" Carstairs asked, moving past the burning corpse swaying in the breeze. "Most certainly."

Just then, the ground shook and, in gradual stages, the dark city became infused with a brilliant amber radiance. Casting a furtive glance backwards, the two explorers stumbled as they saw the entire two-story tall tavern was now solid gold, and beginning to sink into the soft ground. Scrambling out of the second story windows, patrons started jumping to the pavement with small golden items in their arms, then they frantically ran away in every direction.

"But we'd better be quick about it, sir," the lord stated earnestly, increasing the pace of his stride.

TWENTY

Racing to the other side of town where the hubbub and clamor of the sinking golden tavern could not be heard, Prof. Einstein and Lord Carstairs searched for a stable with living quarters directly above. This was a much nicer section of town, where the prostitutes had teeth and uniformed guards patrolled the neatly paved streets.

After locating a suitable establishment, the explorers woke the owner by loudly banging on his door, and then appeasing his fury over being awakened with a lot of jingling coins.

Purchasing the needed supplies and horses only took a few minutes, but clothing was a problem because of the unusual size of Lord Carstairs. A tailor was summoned, and his stock ransacked under the musical urging of the jingling coins. Soon enough, the professor and the lord were comfortably dressed in soft leather boots, black pants, and tan tunics.

Paying off the merchants, Einstein and Carstairs checked the saddles on their horses, and looked over the bags of supplies. Their saddlebags bulged with tack, gear, food, and battered tin canteens of cheap watered wine. They had observed that the sanitary facilities of the town were not very impressive, and decided that a touch of alcohol in their drinking supply might indeed be a wise precaution.

By the time they were ready to depart, excited people were on the street talking about something odd happening at the Boozarama across town. Taking that as their cue to leave, the explorers mounted their horses and rode directly to the west gate. The guards waved them through without incident. Once they were in the clear, Einstein and Carstairs took off at a full gallop into the night. When they were out of view of the city guards, the explorers crisscrossed their trail a few times just in case of pursuit. The local constabulary did not seem very formidable, but since this was the home dimension of the Squid God, anything could be coming after them next. Literally. The notion was quite, well, unsettling.

On through the night, Einstein and Carstairs traveled at a brisk pace, resting the horses only when necessary. They knew that only a day and a half remained in the real world before the moon would finish turning, and then. . . .

To save time, the lord and the professor ate and slept in shifts, each guiding the other's horse as a strange trio of different sized moons rose in the black starless sky. The motion of the animals was not a problem as any decent archeologist could sleep soundly astride a racing horse. Although for true comfort, it was a well-known fact that a hippopotamus made the best ambulatory bed.

In gradual stages, the wild forest thinned to lush fields of grass, and finally into barren scrub with only a few gnarled weeds dotting the landscape. By dawn, the weary explorers reached a dry riverbed; on the opposite side was a shifting expanse of sandy desert, the dunes stretching to the horizon where jagged mountains rose into the azure sky.

As Einstein and Carstairs slowed the horses to a walk and took them across the cracked mud of the riverbed, a jet of dust shot up to form a geyser on the opposite bank. Spreading wide, the spray hardened into a large rectangle atop a pole. Dumbfounded, the explorers watched as a glowing green line scrawled across the board:

WELCOME TO THE BADLANDS,
EINSTEIN AND CARSTAIRS.

"I think before progressing any further we should see about those weapons," Lord Carstairs sagely suggested, dismounting and using the leather reins to tether his beast to the ground.

"Indubitably," the professor said, with a straight face.

Sliding off his mount, Lord Carstairs chuckled at that.

Tethering their mounts to a scraggly bush, Carstairs kept guard with the newly purchased crossbow, while Einstein chose a comfortable rock to use as a chair and opened the book of magic to study the list of incantations.

"Ah, here we go," the professor said after a few minutes. "Chapter seventeen, 'A Spell to Summon the Most Powerful Offensive Weapon'."

Biting off a chunk of honeybee jerky, Lord Carstairs chewed thoughtfully before swallowing. "Is it possible to alter the spell to read 'The Most Powerful Offensive Weapon Tailored to My Personal Abilities and Limitations?'"

"Good thinking, lad!" Prof. Einstein said, flipping through the book. "Umm, yes, there is a hidden addendum in 'Appendix B'."

Finishing the jerky, Carstairs lowered the crossbow and extended a hand. "Do you mind if I try it first?"

"Any reason?"

"In case of a mishap, I am less prone to damage than you."

"Ah. True enough."

Accepting the book, Lord Carstairs carefully followed the chart, made the necessary corrections with the wording, and rattled off the spell with the appropriate hand gestures. As he finished, there was a crackling explosion of light and colors. When the smoke cleared, the page was blank and Carstairs had been radically changed.

His crossbow and the clothing from the village were gone. Now the lord was wearing a sort of military uniform composed of mottled forest colors, high top black boots, and a round metal hat. A canteen and knife were strapped to his waist, along with a holster and angular pistol of extraordinary size. A huge, rectangular pack covered his back from neck to hips. From the top of the backpack came a silvery metallic belt that looped downward to the bulky weapon strapped to his chest. Supported by a body harness of steel braces and shiny black straps was some sort of gun, or cannon, with multiple barrels set to rotate about a central mechanism. On the top of the machine was an enclosed handle with a trigger set towards the rear.

"Good heavens," Lord Carstairs whispered, staring at his new accoutrements. "What in the world is this device?"

Retrieving the magic book from the dust where it had been dropped, a distant memory flared for the professor from a lecture he had caught at the British War Museum.

"That is a Gatling gun!" Einstein cried in delight, slapping the book clean on his thigh. "By George, these spells don't play cheap, do they?"

"Actually," Carstairs said, reading from a tiny manual attached to the handle, "this is a United Kingdom, Mark 17, electric Vulcan minigun, firing 10mm caseless, armor piercing, high explosive rounds with a maximum discharge of 8,000 rounds a minute."

"Bah, that's scientifically impossible," Prof. Einstein said, leaning in close to see the pamphlet. "You must be reading that wrong."

"It is in American," Lord Carstairs admitted. "But I do have a passing familiarity with the language."

After reading the little manual twice, the professor shrugged in resignation. "I don't understand a lot of that technological jargon," he admitted. "But it does sound most impressive."

As he started to hand the booklet back, Einstein gaped at the rear cover. "Merciful heavens, lad, this pamphlet is copyrighted 2018!"

"You mean the year 2018?" Lord Carstairs asked, checking it for himself. It was true. "Fantastic! Do you think we should get another?"

Patting the book of magic, Prof. Einstein shook his head. "The spell vanished after you read it, remember? Besides, if you have a physical weapon, then I should acquire a magical one. We would be better balanced."

"Good point, sir. Oh, another thing."

"What?"

"Observe."

Squinting, the professor could only see the dust trails of the departing horses.

"How totally inconvenient," Einstein cursed, then started flipping through the book. "Maybe we can find a spell for making horses. Perhaps flying horses! That would be nice. Once in Persia, I had to capture a winged horse to save a blind princess from a one-legged . . ."

"Weapons, first, Professor. Amazing tales later."

"Oh, I suppose."

Finding the appropriate page in the book, Prof. Einstein performed the required ritual. Once more the explosion came, but this time when the smoke cleared there was revealed only a simple sledgehammer standing upright on the sandy soil.

"That's it?" Lord Carstairs asked in disbelief.

In consternation, Prof. Einstein looked at the blank page, then at the hammer again. "Well, it is supposed to be magic, lad, so we must not judge these things for their appearances alone."

Grabbing the handle experimentally, the professor tried to lift the masonry tool, but it refused to budge.

"Allow me," Lord Carstairs offered, cracking his knuckles.

Waving the lord onward, Einstein watched as his friend proved equally unable to budge the hammer so much as an inch. Then in a flash on comprehension, the professor pulled his grunting friend away.

"Don't bother, lad. A hundred men couldn't move that weapon," Prof. Einstein stated sadly. "Unless, I miss my guess, we have conjured Mjöllnir."

Lord Carstairs arched an eyebrow. "The hammer of Thor, the Norse god of Thunder?"

"A weapon with the storms of nature at its command. Rain, blizzards, lightning, tornadoes, etcetera."

"Well, that is a splendid weapon!"

"If only I could use it," the professor noted sourly.

Rolling up both sleeves, Prof. Einstein took hold with both hands, bent his knees, and put his entire body into the effort. But the thunder weapon remained motionless.

"It must not consider you holy enough," Lord Carstairs suggested, tilting back his metal hat.

"Guess I am not, at that," Einstein admitted, finally letting go. The man flexed his hands, trying to restore circulation. "I am not Norse, nor do I worship Odin."

"Forget 'tailored to your abilities and limitations,' eh, Professor?" Lord Carstairs chided softly.

Rolling his eyes sheepishly, Einstein admitted it was true.

"Is there another magic weapon spell?" the lord asked.

Thumbing through the pages, the professor checked the Table of Contents. "Yes and no."

"Explain that, please."

"There is a spell for magic swords, but it requires the caster to sacrifice five years of his life."

Lord Carstairs frowned. "Indeed. How old are you?"

"Fifty six."

Setting the safety on his massive weapon, Carstairs reached for the book. "Then I will do the spell for you. Shouldn't be too difficult to make the spell a gift."

The softly moaning desert air blew over the two men as the professor struggled to speak. "Lad, I'm flabbergasted by your offer. What can I say as thanks?"

"Piffle, sir. I am only 29, five years won't harm me a bit."

"I will never forget this, Benjamin," the professor said with unaccustomed frankness.

"Think nothing of it, sir," Lord Carstairs replied gallantly.

Besides, he added privately, *it never hurts to have your future father-in-law owe you a favor.*

Studying the book, Carstairs made the proper corrections, took a deep breath, and spoke the words of power. There was the usual pyrotechnic thunderclap and, as the smoke cleared, Prof. Einstein was wearing a plain bronze crown on his head, with a sword in a dull scabbard belted about his waist.

Very hesitantly, Einstein drew the sword free, the silvery blade singing as it left the scabbard. Nearly a full yard in length, the straight blade shimmered in the daylight like an oiled gem. But the handle was wrapped in old leather, worn and sweat-stained. It was a weapon that had seen much use on the battlefield somewhere.

Doffing the crown, Prof. Einstein saw that it was similar in design to the Iron Crown of Italy, only this circlet bore a coiled dragon about the rim. It was very familiar, and Einstein felt positive that he should know the crown and sword. There was something at the back of his mind about such a pair of famous weapons . . .

"Does it feel magical?" Lord Carstairs asked hopefully, studying the blade. The sunlight glinted along the edge as if it was sharp as a surgeon's scalpel.

"Not really, lad," Prof. Einstein replied forlornly, turning his wrist to inspect the sword from different angles. "The balance is excellent, and it's as light as a feather, but so is my bamboo fishing rod." He swung the sword at a nearby rock for a glancing blow in order to listen to the song of the steel. A crude but effective way to test the tensile strength of the blade. Unfortunately, he seemed to miss, as the sword passed by the stone without a sound.

"Now that's odd," the professor commented with a frown. "How could I miss at this range?"

With a gritty rumble, the boulder split apart at shoulder height, the upper chunk sliding off to tumble to the ground with a heavy thud. The interior of the boulder was mirror bright, as if polished by a glazier. The two men stared at the rock for several seconds.

"Good enough!" Prof. Einstein noted happily, checking the blade for nicks or scrapes. But there were none, the blade was perfect.

"Rather," Lord Carstairs agreed, giving the word two syllables.

Prof. Einstein pulled out the sword once more and held the blade to the sun to read the symbols etched into the bloodgutter that extended down the middle.

"By Gadfrey, this is the sword of Alexander!" he cried out in delight. "The real sword! The one I could never find!"

Carstairs gave a long whistle of astonishment. "So it is, Professor," the lord agreed, very impressed. "I thought it looked familiar! I have a copy in my collection that I bought from the Spanish War Museum a few months ago. Wretched thing, but it's deuced similar to this."

Turning his face away, the professor hid a smile. So that's where the copy ended up! The world of professional archeology was very small indeed.

"Well, we can't get much better than this," Prof. Einstein stated, sheathing the famous blade. "Let's be off and try to find those horses, eh?"

"Righto, sir!"

Shifting the packs on their backs more comfortably, the beweaponed explorers trekked into the desert after the runaway mounts.

* * *

As the two humans disappeared behind a sand dune, the blue sky shimmered and then ripped apart to reveal the starry blackness of deep space.

"There you are!" a loud voice rumbled and, from out of nowhere, a giant mailed hand descended and reached for the tiny sledgehammer. The weapon magically swelled to full size in the great fist. With a crash of thunder, both were gone from the realm of Mortals.

* * *

Standing on top of a cloud, a powerfully built, red-haired man in leather armor and wearing a winged helmet fondly caressed the hammer. "There, there, pookums," he cooed softly. "You're back with daddykins now."

Then turning to face the universe, the redhead gestured with the hammer, making the mighty pillars of the heavens shake. "And who dared to disturb the rest of Mjöllnir?" Thor boomed furiously.

There was no answer to the challenge, except for a faint distant chuckling. It could have been a singing bird, or a splashing waterfall.

"Loki, it must be you!" Thor declared, his noble face nigh purple with fury. "Prepare for battle!"

Pausing in the act of marking a deck of poker cards, the thin god loosened a poisoned dagger in his boot. "No, wait! I didn't do it this time!" Loki cried in forced innocence.

"Liar!" Thor boomed, and the storm god charged at his ancient foe, the mighty hammer whirling above his helmet.

Ducking out of the way, Loki countered with some itching powder and a Morningstar mace to the groin. He missed, and soon the heavens rumbled with the clash of steel and the crash of thunder, the divine battle punctuated with the occasional yelp of pain.

* * *

Hunched against the stinging breeze, Lord Carstairs paused and waited for the panting Professor Einstein to catch up.

Behind the men stretched a trail of boot prints already partially filled from the shifting sand. Unfortunately, the horses had bolted back towards the forest, and there were no spells of Summoning in the magic book, nor were there any for making beasts of burden. With no other recourse, the men had started walking into the burning desert.

Cresting a low dune, Einstein and Carstairs looked down upon an ancient pavilion of crumbling stones hidden inside a ring of obelisks. It was almost an exact duplicate of Stonehenge, only in much better condition.

"How odd," Lord Carstairs remarked. "Just a moment ago, I could have sworn this valley was empty."

"Me too," Professor Einstein agreed, placing a hand on the grip of his sword. "Stay sharp, lad."

As they started towards the structure, there was a hiss and from out of the stone pillars stepped a giant red scorpion. The armored body of the monster stretched more than ten yards long, the deadly barbed tail was arched high as if ready to strike, and the pair of lethal pincers clacked as they mauled the empty air.

"Greetings, foolish mortals!" the scorpion hissed over the howling desert wind. "Prepare to die!"

Having heard something similar only yesterday, Lord Carstairs flicked his wrist to release the safety on his weapon and tightened his grip on the handle. The eight barrels of the Vulcan mini-gun started to rotate, and a split-second later a strident stream of flame and steel vomited forth. The armor-piercing shells punched a line of holes through the crimson chitin of the giant scorpion, the explosive charges detonating inside like a string of firecrackers. The monster shook as it was torn apart from within, bits of shell and blood arcing into the sky.

After a good, long burst, Carstairs released the handle and silence returned so fast his ears rang. All around the explorers, a gentle patter of scorpion meat fell to the sand in wet smacks. Amid the smoky destruction of the alien Stonehenge, there stood several pairs of crimson legs, which the dry wind finally pushed over to fall upon the ground with the clatter of old bones.

"Good shooting, lad," the professor complimented, daintily removing a bit of shell from his tunic.

"I hate scorpions," Carstairs stated, as the rotating barrels of the ungainly Vulcan slowed to a halt. "The nasty little buggers always crawl into your boots at night."

"First a sphinx, and now a giant scorpion," Prof. Einstein said, adjusting his bronze crown. "I have a bad feeling, lad, that the closer we get to the black mountain, the more things like this we shall encounter."

Frowning in agreement, Lord Carstairs started walking forward once more, keeping clear of the dripping corpse of the colossal arachnid. Just for a moment, he hesitated. *They were low on supplies now, and scorpion meat smelled exactly like lobster . . . no. It had talked. There were limits.*

Hours slowly passed, and their walking soon became trudging. But the explorers had trekked through most of the major deserts of the world, and the techniques of marching through shifting sand soon returned and their speed increased.

However, the desert seemed to stretch endlessly before them, the black mountain never coming any closer. The blazing sun was oppressively hot and, while his odd metal hat gave Lord Carstairs some measure of protection, Prof. Einstein only had his crown. Soon the professor was forced to tie a handkerchief over his gray hair for some much-needed shade.

As the long day progressed, the sun reached its zenith in the azure sky, and the heat was becoming unbearable, every breath labored. Forcing themselves to take only sips from their tin canteens to stretch the flavored water, the men were astonished to discover that both of the water containers had unexpectedly become empty at the same moment.

"But there was plenty of water remaining," Lord Carstairs said, looking unsuccessfully for holes in the canteen.

Drawing his sword, Professor Einstein glanced about uneasily. "I have the feeling, lad, that we are in for another attack. Since brute force has already been tried, be prepared for subtlety."

As the explorers crested the next sand dune, they were met by a deliciously cool breeze. They saw two large water fountains surrounded by a soft carpet of emerald green moss. Made of multiple tiers of marble, the identical splashing fountains were filled with crystal clear water.

Approaching with extreme caution, Einstein and Carstairs stepped onto the moss and abruptly stopped as a small cloud promptly precipitated in the form of a grinning skeleton clothed in long flowing black robes.

With a flick of his wrist, Lord Carstairs had the Vulcan ready, but Professor Einstein raised a hand to restrain his young friend.

"Let him talk first, lad," the professor said out of the corner of his mouth. "We need information. Besides, you might damage the fountains and we need that water."

Sighting his target, Lord Carstairs simply nodded in response and eased his grip on the trigger mechanism.

With the wind whipping his loose clothing about, the skeleton bowed at the waist, the gesture causing him to make a comical rattling noise. "Greetings, weary travelers!" it said. "You have come to the long sought Fountain of Immortality. Congratulations on your success!"

"But there are two fountains," Einstein noted pragmatically.

"Ah! The other is the Fountain of Instant Death," the skeleton replied, thrusting out its jaw in lieu of a smile. "Nobody really goes out of their way to find that. Not much call for it, you know."

"How interesting," Lord Carstairs mused thoughtfully. He could see definite military possibilities in both. "So, which is which, sir?"

With a flourish, the skeleton raised a bony finger into the air. "Now that's the question, isn't it? You must decide, and drink! Eternal life, or sudden death!"

"Neither then, thanks," Carstairs said.

"Goodbye," the professor added.

Upon turning to leave, the men found themselves facing the fountains. Spinning about, the explorers incredibly were again staring at the fountains. Conferring in private, Einstein and Carstairs tried looking in different directions at the same time . . . and still found themselves facing the two fountains.

"Well, I shall be jiggered," the professor cursed in frustration.

Merrily splashing, the cool waters gurgled down the multiple tiers of the marble structures into the deep basin.

"No rush," the skeleton chuckled evilly, crossing its bony arms. "I can wait *forever!*"

Frowning in annoyance, the explorers once more spoke in private for several minutes, and even drew a couple of sketches in the sand, before coming to a decision.

Taking the professor's canteen, Lord Carstairs strode to the first fountain and filled the canteen halfway. Then he walked over to the other fountain and filled his own canteen halfway.

Cackling in delight, the skeleton danced about on the sand. "So one of you shall live, and one will die! Could it be that . . . hey! Stop that!"

Unperturbed, Lord Carstairs poured the contents of one canteen into the other. He then capped the full canteen, shook it, twisted off the cap and took a healthy slug of the mixture. When nothing happened, the lord then handed it to the professor who gratefully swallowed several gulps. Vastly refreshed and no longer the least bit tired, the explorers turned to leave, their steps firm and strong once more.

"So long," Lord Carstairs called in farewell.

"Our thanks, sir!" Prof. Einstein added, politely. "Much appreciated!"

"That's not fair!" the skeleton screamed furiously, stamping its bony feet on the lush moss. "You have to choose!"

"We did," Einstein retorted, glancing backward. "Really now, if you are going to give people puzzles to solve then you must pay closer attention to how you word the rules."

Continuing out of the valley, the explorers left the skeleton behind, cursing and kicking at the ground.

* * *

Several hours later, the sun was beginning to set as Prof. Einstein and Lord Carstairs finally reached the barren foothills of the black mountain. The sand gave way to hard stone, and their pace increased dramatically until the men reached a cliff overlooking an enormous chasm, the bottom lost in rolling banks of cool mist. Faintly from below they could hear the roar of a wild, whitewater river.

"This is much too far to jump," Lord Carstairs said, licking a finger to test the wind blowing through the abyss. "We'll have to find another way across."

"Over there, lad," Prof. Einstein said, starting to the left.

Just a short distance away was a wide stone bridge built across the yawning chasm. The center of the span was masked in fog, and the explorers had their weapons at the ready as they approached. Sure enough, the moment they stepped foot on the stones the fog lifted to reveal a knight dressed in a suit of red armor.

The style of the armor was a wild mixture of a dozen cultures, but every aspect was designed for offense. And held by this dire guardian was a long sword over three yards in length, the point cutting into the granite blocks forming the bridge. The blade was made of a shiny black material, the edges feathered with ripples so that it glistened like a thousand razors in the light of the setting sun.

"Sir, I do not think this gentleman will be amenable to visitors," Lord Carstairs noted, once more flipping off the safety of the Vulcan mini-gun.

Removing the handkerchief from under his bronze crown, Prof. Einstein returned his sword to its scabbard. "Let's find out first," he suggested, "before doing anything rash. 'Softly, softly, catchee monkey,' as Kipling would say, lad?"

"This is no primitive chimp, sir," the lord growled dangerously.

Standing as motionless as a statue of a Royal Beefeater on sentry duty at Buckingham palace, the red knight seemed oblivious to the cautious approach of the two men. That is, until Einstein and Carstairs came within a few yards, then the knight smoothly lifted his weapon into an attack stance.

"Hold! None may cross without the password," the knight stated firmly, his voice booming in a most impressive manner.

For a while, the only sound was the words echoing again and again into the depths of the rocky chasm below.

"Afraid we don't know the password," Professor Einstein answered politely.

"Really?" the knight said, lowering the sword. "Then go and battle the Moon Scorpion, if you dare, and he shall whisper the password as he dies."

"Sorry, we seem to have missed him," Lord Carstairs lied smoothly. In truth, he had done everything but miss him.

In response, the knight stiffened in his armor. "Then while I live, you shall not cross."

"Fair enough," Carstairs said in a monotone, bracing himself against the weapon's recoil and clicking off the safety again.

As if sensing danger, an exact duplicate of the knight stepped out from behind the first. Then another, and another. In perfect synchronization, the four guardians raised their dire swords.

"Wait!" Prof. Einstein cried, moving between the five warriors. "A question first, please, Sir Knight, ah, Knights."

The swords of the four red knights neither dipped nor wavered. "We are programmed to respond to questions," they replied in perfect harmony.

Programmed. What did that mean? "Is there no other way we can get across?" the professor inquired hopefully. "Pay a toll, or pass some test of wits?"

That seemed to give the knights pause. "Actually, there is."

"Excellent!" Einstein beamed in delight. "What is it, pray tell?"

"Immortals, gods, and sorcerers may come and go as they wish," the knights answered rigidly. "So we have been commanded, and so it shall ever be."

Grinning in triumph, Lord Carstairs flipped the safety on. "Bingo! We have drunk from the Fountain of Immortality."

"A noble try," the four responded, looking at the Englishman. "But not half good enough."

"We have a lovely book of magic, and a magic sword," Prof. Einstein offered hopefully. "A legendary sword, actually. Powerful stuff, me laddies."

"Bah, the merest trifles!" the guardians intoned. "Listen and learn, mortal travelers. Untold ages ago, a conclave of magical beings forged us from the living metal core of this planet. The spell took years to create and months to cast. During it, the Time/Space continuum shuddered, and the stars in the heavens changed their courses for all eternity."

Their voices raised in timbre and volume. "*We are the ultimate sentry, invested with the combined power of a thousand masters of destruction, beings whose merest glance would wither you like grass in the sun.*" The knights repeated the Ritual of the Swords. "You shall not cross without the password!"

With an expression of relief, Prof. Einstein walked right to the knights and doffed his crown. "Thanks ever so, but we don't need it. Because I am a god, you see. The name is Einstein. Professor Felix Einstein."

"You . . . are unfamiliar to us," the four said hesitantly. "Identify, please."

"Check the pantheon of the Beeta-Bora tribe of the island

Tookawee," the professor said glibly. "I was the first European to contact them. When they saw my lantern and matches, I was proclaimed a god." Einstein turned to Lord Carstairs and added, "As the natives would have eaten me otherwise, I accepted the position."

"Accessing files," the four knights murmured and a faint whirring noise could be heard. "Micronesia, Polynesian file, Beeta-Bora, main pantheon, sub-pantheon." The crimson guardians gave choking noises. "Prof. Einstein, the white god of fire and fertility."

"Fertility?" Lord Carstairs repeated, amused.

Feigning innocence, Einstein blushed and said nothing.

Bowing respectfully, the titans separated to either side of the bridge. "Pass, milord," they intoned together.

Dashing across, Einstein paused to indicate Carstairs. "And what about my acolyte here?"

"Acolyte?" they echoed in shock. "He is your High Priest?"

Taking the cue, Lord Carstairs did a little dance and waved his hands about in the air.

"All hail the great and powerful Einstein!" the lord sang. "Bringer of fire and flame! Roaster of meat! Giver of light! Pleaser of women!"

Slumping slightly, the red knights gave a four-part metallic sigh. "Pass," they muttered sullenly.

Wasting no time in further niceties, the lord held onto his steel hat and scampered across the bridge, not slowing until reaching solid ground on the other side of the chasm.

"Fast thinking there, lad," the professor panted. "Where did you learn to lie like that? Parliament?"

"Of course. But I was also a member of the Drama Club at Oxford," Lord Carstairs added proudly. "I even played Puck in 'A Midsummer Night's Dream'."

Stunned, the professor stared at the six foot six, two hundred and fifty pound slab of muscle. "You played an elf? How the deuce could you play an elf?"

"Superbly," Lord Carstairs said, twirling an imaginary cape about his shoulders.

Trying not to show his annoyance, the professor kept a neutral expression. He often had the same problem with Mary. Actors! They were almost as balmy as novelists.

Looking over the great expanse of the ragged mountains, Lord

Carstairs abruptly turned and returned to the very edge of the chasm. "Hail guardians of the bridge!" Carstairs bellowed, through cupped hands. "We need to speak!"

Fanning himself with the crown, Prof. Einstein stopped and frowned. "What in God's name are you doing, lad?" he demanded.

"Asking directions," the lord answered over a shoulder.

Without bothering to turn their bodies, the four knights rotated their heads. "Yes, Puck?"

Oh, they heard that, eh? Damn. "By any chance, do you know the whereabouts of the Dutarian Squid God?" Lord Carstairs asked politely.

"Actually, we are trying to find its temple," Prof. Einstein clarified. "It's supposed to be somewhere around here, and we would like to get there before the squid awakens."

A faint rattling could be heard from the guardians. "Y-you m-mean, the c-c-c-colossus is about to rise?" Their strange multiple voices reached a high note on the last word.

"Why, yes," Lord Carstairs answered truthfully. "Is that a problem?

With a clatter of armor, the four knights coalesced back into one figure that drew itself stiffly erect. "Gotta go," it said, vanishing in a puff of orange smoke.

"Oh, bloody buggering hell!" the professor complained, jamming the crown back on his head. "Every time I start to feel good about this mission, something like that happens!"

"At least we now have a clear path of escape if necessary," Lord Carstairs said cheerfully, turning towards the mountains again. "Positive thinking, sir. That's the ticket!"

"Oh, do shut up, lad."

Proceeding along a wide ravine, Lord Carstairs led the way as the two followed a meandering path. Small arroyos branched off from the main passageway constantly, and the side paths were ideal locations for an ambush. Checking their weapons, Einstein and Carstairs tried to watch in every direction for more sentries, guards, booby-traps, and anything else they could think of that might bar the way. But there were only the broken rocks, and the low moaning wind.

Sloping upward, the rocky path curved along the exterior of the steep mountain, forming a spiral to the very pinnacle where they found a dark cave. Digging into a pocket, the professor pulled out a miner's candle purchased in the city. Shaking the candle vigorously, Einstein made the hexed wick obediently burst into a tall flame. Just as a precaution, Carstairs did the same with another candle.

But entering the cave, the men found that the candles were insufficient to the task of illuminating the vast interior of the mountain passage. They were not in a tunnel, but a subterranean cavern; its upper reaches were lost in shadows and stalactites, and stalagmites hid the presence of nasty holes in the rocky ground that almost seemed to have been designed to break the ankles of unwary travelers.

Proceeding with extreme care, Einstein and Carstairs walked in the center of the cave, the footsteps of their boots, oddly, not making any echoes. They moved in utter silence. The effect was most disturbing, and the explorers moved slightly closer together for protection. As they followed a bend in the cave, the dying light of the setting sun was cut off completely, and the darkness became pitch black. Suddenly, the explorers were standing in a small halo of candlelight amid the eerily still passageway.

"Well, it could be worse," Lord Carstairs said, trying to enliven the mood.

"Really, how?" Prof. Einstein asked, just as a gust of wind from nowhere blew out both of the candles.

"Never mind, sir," Lord Carstairs said from the darkness. "Damn, mine isn't working. Shake your candle, Professor?"

"I am, lad, but nothing is happening!" Prof. Einstein replied angrily. "Do you have another?"

"Not that I can easily reach."

"Bollox. Wait a second, maybe I have something better than a candle. Hold on."

For a few moments, nothing happened, then the cave became bathed in a golden glow as the professor drew the Sword of Alexander. The two men sighed in relief, then froze motionless at the sight of dozens of winged demons hanging upside-down from the ceiling in countless rows upon rows. Snapping open their slated yellow eyes, the inverted hellspawn looked directly down at the started explorers, who stared right back at them in equal surprise.

"By The Great Squid!" a big demon screamed, gesturing with its talons. "It's them! The Englishmen we were told about, Lord Einstein and Prof. Carstairs!"

"I think that's Prof. Einstein . . ." another demon sniffed primly.

"Who cares? Kill them!" a horned demon interrupted, brandishing a barbed trident. "Rip out their hearts and drink their blood!"

Dropping from the vaulted ceiling, the snarling demons spread their wings and flew to the attack, screaming exactly like a bunch of bats out of Hell.

TWENTY-ONE

"For Queen and country!" Lord Carstairs yelled, triggering his weapon. The roar of the Vulcan mini-gun filled the cavern.

The fusillade of steel tore into the demons, the explosive charges hurling black blood, flesh, and rock splinters about in a horrid spray. A cloven hoof thrust downward and Prof. Einstein jerked aside, swinging his sword in response. At the touch of the enchanted blade, the creature burst into flames. But more demons replaced those who died, and the battle raged on in rapidly increasing levels of violence.

* * *

In a side alcove, a fat demon, wearing a light blue, two-piece leisure suit, stopped banking the fire beneath his evening meal. Dripping butter, the live spider roasting on the spit gave a sigh of relief. Curiously, Vognol the demon waddled toward the main tunnel. What was that bizarre noise? Could it be another wayward traveler? He glanced at the meal roasting above the sulphurous flames. It was always nice to have more company for dinner!

Humming a heretical hymn from the fifteenth Century, Vognol reached the main tunnel just in time to get smacked in the face by a lump of meat. Scraping off the slab, he was startled to realize it was the face of Brindrexil, one of the few demons who knew how to play a decent game of bridge.

"Brindrexil!" Vognol cried. "What in Heaven is going on?"

The disembodied demon face scowled. "Trouble! Go tell the boss!"

Tucking his friend into a pocket, Vognol started to go, but could not resist his streak of curiosity and crept forward to steal a glimpse of the battle. Peeking around a stalagmite, Vognol saw the last of his brethren annihilated by a noisy device strapped to a large pink human wearing a metal bowl on his head. Then Vognol's narrow eyes widened to human normal as he recognized the two mortals. It was Lord Einstein and Prof. Carstairs! *Oh yes, this was definitely not the place to be right now.* Turning tail, Vognol tucked the barbed appendage into another pocket of his suit and scuttled off. The High Priest of the Great Colossus would pay a good price for this sort of information!

* * *

Drenched in black blood, Lord Carstairs was busy scanning the roof of the cavern for more inhuman foes, but the ceiling appeared to be empty, at last. "All clear here, Professor!" he called.

"Just a moment, lad." Doing a perimeter sweep of the ground in case of any flank attacks, Professor Einstein saw a fat little demon racing away down a side passage. Purely out of reflex, the professor raised his sword arm and shouted, "Stop!"

Obediently, the Sword of Alexander pulsed with light, and then a lance of flame leapt from its tip to engulf the escaping monster. With a crackling flash, the demon was vaporized and only the gray ash of its weird clothing remained to float gently to the rocky floor.

"All right, that should be the last of them," Einstein stated confidently, waggling the sword in victory.

"I must say, Professor, that flame lance was a jolly good trick," Lord Carstairs said, resetting the safety on his mini-cannon. "What else can that bally sword of yours do?"

"To be honest, I have no idea, lad. That was as much a surprise to me as it was to you." Respectfully, the professor inspected the blade. "I wonder if Alexander had this built to do anything else that we should know about?"

"A pity it didn't come with an instruction booklet similar to the one that came with my gun," Carstairs observed.

Turning the glowing blade about for inspection, the professor frowned. "That's true, you got instructions. But if this is as sophisticated a magical device as your gun is a technological device. . . . Sword, what can you do?"

There was a ripple in the air, and a floating papyrus scroll formed before Prof. Einstein. Slowly, the scroll spread wide and began to unroll, gilded words forming in ancient Macedonian on the ancient paper. The syntax was odd, but the professor had little trouble reading the list and was quite impressed. No wonder Alexander the Great had conquered the known world!

"This is astounding, lad!" Einstein cried in delight. "Come see for yourself! What can't this sword do? It is indeed a weapon fit for the king of the world!" Softly, almost as an after-thought, the professor added, "So why in Hell am I holding it?"

Glancing about the dim cavern, Lord Carstairs could only see Prof.

Einstein standing there, holding the sword.

"What is astounding, sir?" the lord asked pointedly.

"What? Don't you see anything?" asked the professor, halting the scroll with a thought.

Stepping over a demon corpse, Carstairs moved through the floating paper. "Nothing unusual, sir."

"Interesting," Prof. Einstein muttered, his mind whirling with the limitless possibilities of this new information. "Very interesting, indeed!"

Lord Carstairs began to tap his boot impatiently, and the professor quickly explained what was happening.

"Fantastic!" the lord said at last. "It seems logical that since the sword was designed to unite the world in peace, which was the true dream of Alexander, then it must be more than eager to wage war on those who would enslave the world."

"Thus I am its master purely by default," Einstein murmured. Then he stiffened as a silent voice shouted into his mind.

"Beg pardon, sword. I am its chosen *champion* by default," the professor quickly corrected. "Fair enough, I suppose. The enemy of my enemy, and all that."

"Let us push on, sir," Lord Carstairs said, checking the feed on his mini-gun. "*Carpe diem!*"

"Oh, stop with all the Latin, would you, lad?"

"Do you prefer Swahili?"

"Oh yes, please, that would be lovely."

With the shining sword leading the way, Prof. Einstein and Lord Carstairs probed deeper into the hellish cave, bypassing a small campfire with a very unhappy spider tied to a rotating spit. They set the insect free, and it joyously sang their praises before limping away for home, leaving in its wake a squishy trail of herb-flavored butter.

After stomping out the fire, the explorers pushed onward and soon saw a dim light coming from around a sharp bend. Hugging the wall in case of attack, Einstein and Carstairs listened for any breathing or movements past the turn, then boldly stepped around the corner.

Down a short passage was the mouth of the cave, the opening filled with an unearthly light. Exercising extreme care, the men crept forward and stepped out of the mountain cavern and onto a small ledge. A dry lifeless breeze tugged at their clothing, as a dour-faced Prof. Einstein and Lord Carstairs surveyed the great valley spread before them. The landscape was illuminated by the cold blue light of the triple moons and, upon closer inspection, they saw that valley was circular and rather resembled the mouth of an extinct volcano. Scarred and jagged, the world below was composed of only crumbling rock and burnt soil. Bare twisted trees, little more than gnarled sticks, were scattered about like the long-dead corpse of a once great forest.

Drifting along the bottom of the crater were misty tendrils of swirling fog that were eerily similar to the clouds of the transdimensional vortex. Perhaps this was the wellspring of those evil portals. Not a creature could be seen moving in the forlorn crater; there wasn't even the lonely wail of vampire bat to break the horrid silence. Never had the two men imagined a land so totally devoid of faith, hope, or love. It was worse than Liverpool.

In the center of the crater was an oily-appearing lake, its dirt shoreline lapping at the base of a titanic obsidian peak that rose high into the midnight sky. There was no visible road or pathway to the summit, yet atop the forbidding ebony spike stood a marble building with Doric columns. At first glance, it appeared to be built in the style of ancient Rome. But upon closer inspection, Einstein and Carstairs could see the domed roof was decorated with eerie staring eyes and the marble columns were detailed to resemble writhing tentacles.

"Behold, the temple of the Squid god," Prof. Einstein said, speaking as if torn between relief and disgust. "Exactly as we saw it from inside the transdimensional tunnel."

"Ghastly place. A most fitting home for the beast," Lord Carstairs agreed, using a tone of voice that he normally reserved for the operators of opium dens.

"Quite so, lad," the professor agreed. "I feel the need for a hot bath just by looking at that lake."

Advancing to the edge of the rocky ledge, Lord Carstairs looked down the side of the mountain. Directly beneath them was smooth stone extending for countless yards. Taking a gold coin from his pocket, he flicked it over the cliff. Closing his eyes in concentration, the lord softly counted as the coin fell, patiently waiting to hear the ring as it hit bottom so that he could calculate the distance. But either the coin never reached the bottom of the crater, or the ground was so far away he could not hear the sound.

"How ever will we get down?" he wondered aloud. "The demons

obviously flew."

"I'd say that we must climb down, lad," Einstein said gruffly. "At least it will be easy going. Plenty of handholds."

"True," the lord agreed cautiously. "However, during our descent, we will be highly visible. And if attacked by more winged demons, we would be at a marked disadvantage clinging to the side of a bally mountain."

"Quite so," Prof. Einstein said with a frown, then laughed through his nose.

"All right, what trick do you have planned?" Carstairs asked, pushing back his steel hat. "Any chance we can also fly down?"

"Me? Oh, yes, but not you. So we'll have to use a disguise spell," the professor said, mentally summoning the scrolling papyrus once more. "Yes, that will do nicely. I can conjure an optical illusion of the two of us masked as winged demons. Normally, the sword could not do this for somebody other than the wielder; but if we're smeared with fresh demon blood, this will be easily accomplished."

"If that is the only component required, sir," Lord Carstairs replied, gesturing at his blood soaked military uniform. "Then I am more than ready."

Tugging at his clothing, the professor scowled at his clean tunic and pants. Not a bloody drop of inhuman blood on the whole outfit. Drat!

"However, I am not similarly anointed, lad," Einstein countered, starting back into the cave. "And I had best hurry before this dry atmosphere leeches away what moisture there is from the corpses."

"Well, it was certainly nice of the creatures to supply us with so much raw material to work with," Lord Carstairs added, squinting to make his eyes adjust to the dimness. "Although they hardly did so willingly."

Inside the cavern, the men found a particularly juicy corpse and used a torn wing as a sort of brush to paint the professor all over, not forgetting his back and scabbard. The brackish liquid was very sticky and dried quickly, so they had to move fast. Once Lord Carstairs was satisfied with the professor's condition, Einstein checked the lord over and did a little touch-up work to make sure Carstairs was also liberally smeared. Finally ready, Prof. Einstein waved the sword and nothing seemed to happen.

"Oh I say," Lord Carstairs frowned in annoyance. "The spell only worked on you, but I am unaffected."

"No, it only worked on you," the professor started. "Oh, of course. Others see us as demons, but we see our true selves."

"Indeed? Well, I am looking at a little old demon carrying a stick."

"And I observe a gigantic demon carrying a log."

"Good show, then!" Lord Carstairs said, gesturing at the ledge. "Shall we go?"

Returning to the outside, the professor sheathed the sword once they were in the moonlight. The men waited for a few precious minutes to see if the illusion would hold with the weapon in its scabbard. When there was no apparent change, Einstein and Carstairs eased themselves over the edge of the cliff and started climbing down the side of the volcanic ridge.

* * *

A few hours later, they reached the layer of strange mist near the bottom. Experimentally, the lord dropped a coin through and heard it hit the ground this time. Then the professor tested the composition of the mist by dipping the toe of his boot into the fog and withdrawing it quickly to see if there was any change in the leather. The boot appeared to be unaffected, so Einstein and Carstairs climbed down into the mysterious mist. But the explorers still wisely held their breath until they came out the other side and reached clear air once more. *Ah, better.*

The bottom of the crater was only a few yards away and they reached the ground without any incident, aside from a few scraped knuckles. Flexing their aching hands, Einstein and Carstairs studied the weird mist floating over their heads. It was constantly moving as if stirred by unfelt winds, and the vapor shone with the reflected moonlight casting an almost ghostly illumination across the crater. Spotting the fallen coin atop a boulder, Lord Carstairs suddenly felt the frugal presence of his long-deceased father and retrieved the gold to tuck it away in a pocket.

"Waste not, want not, eh, lad?" the professor chuckled.

"Well, we are here to save the world," Lord Carstairs said, securely buttoning the pocket in his military uniform. "But afterwards, life goes on."

"If we are successful," Einstein muttered under his breath.

Carstairs heard the comment, but did not reply. His cool bravado was for show only, as he knew the terrible forces of evil they would soon be facing. The words of the old papyrus scroll from the professor's London museum rang unbidden in his mind, "*A thousand armies of a thou-*

sand men were naught but toys to the dire squid . . ."

Then Lord Carstairs set his jaw. Mary would have to face that alone if they failed. Totally unacceptable!

Nothing was said as the men double-checked their weapons, then moved out from behind the boulder to do a covert reconnaissance of the crater. Illuminated by the murky glow of the strange mist and triple moons, there was a network of flagstone paths creating a kind of spiderweb pattern on the ground. Rows of gnarled tress lined each path, the leathery branches hanging low and dripping with thousands of knotted whips. Nobody had to tell them that any unauthorized trespasser would be brutally thrashed to death.

Carefully avoiding the beaten path, Prof. Einstein and Lord Carstairs kept low among the outcrops of rock and stealthily worked their way closer to the edge of the oily lake. No trees grew in the dank waters, and the men played a quick game of one-potato-two-potato to see who would step on the first flagstone.

Lord Carstairs won, or lost, depending how you looked upon the matter, and braced himself before treading on the oily stone. Nothing happened, so he moved to the next. Again nothing occurred. Feeling bold, the lord simply walked straight across the lake and onto the bottom of the wide staircase leading up into the obsidian column.

A movement at his side made the lord tense, but then he saw it was just a little demon carrying a stick and Carstairs relaxed. Then he scowled and looked directly at the other being.

"Oddbotkins, of course it's me, lad. Calm down," the monster whispered in a familiar voice, studying the tremendous set of stairs.

"Quite so, sir. Just checking."

Carved into the living rock, the steps reached halfway up the spire to culminate at a large iron door. Staying low, Einstein and Carstairs ascended the stairs and reached the door in a few short minutes. However, the metallic portal proved to be sealed with a brand-new padlock crafted by Culvers and Son Locksmiths, West Sussex, London. *Damn!*

Trying to hold his Vulcan mini-gun more like a log, Lord Carstairs stood guard while Prof. Einstein removed his crown and used one of the points to pick the antique lock. With a subdued click, the mechanism yielded and the door swung aside on well-greased hinges. Beyond was total darkness.

As Einstein put the crown back on, the blackness was banished as ten thousand torches flared on the walls of a gigantic hall. The place was filled with hundreds of smiling people wearing crimson robes. There were dozens of huge tables piled high with food and mounds of gaily-wrapped gift boxes, and across the rear of the hall was a gigantic banner that read, in ancient Dutarian, 'Happy Birthday.'

"Surprise!" the crowd raggedly cheered, throwing a snowstorm of human-fingernail confetti into the air. Then the joyful throng went deadly silent.

"Hey, that isn't the Great Squid!" shouted a robed man in marked disappointment.

"Oh for the love of Hell," a woman griped. "It's just a couple of those Mountain monk demons."

Einstein and Carstairs tried not to show their reaction to that. No wonder the locals feared Mountain monks so much!

Pushing his way to the front of the sad throng, a thin man raised a glowing monocle to his eye. "Now see here, our High Priest specifically told your master that . . ." He stopped, goggled, then recoiled in shock. "By the blood of living Lord Squid! It's . . . it's Einstein and Carstairs!"

"Who?" some timid soul squeaked in puzzlement.

"Kill them!" the rest of the crowd bellowed, rushing forward.

Knowing escape back up the cliff was impossible, Prof. Einstein drew his sword and braced against the oncoming tidal wave of homicidal lunatics. "How many of them are there, do you think, lad?" the professor asked, licking dry lips. The floor shook under their pounding boots.

"About two thousand," Lord Carstairs said readying his mini-gun.

"And how many rounds do you have?"

Quickly, the lord checked the digital read-out on top of his ungainly weapon, as the war cries of the squiddies reached nearly deafening levels. "Just about two thousand!" he bellowed above the turmoil.

With a dramatic flourish, Prof. Einstein pointed the sword at the screaming mob. "Then make every shot count!"

TWENTY-TWO

A final shot from the Vulcan mini-gun rang out loud and clear in the great hall, and the last of the knife-wielding fanatics fell sprawling to the floor, his poisoned dagger merely nicking the polished toe of Lord Carstairs' army boot.

"Got him, sir!" Carstairs announced grimly from behind a yard-tall pile of robed corpses. As he released the trigger, the rotating barrels of the empty Vulcan began to slow.

"Thank God for that ricochet," Prof. Einstein commented, sheathing the sword.

With the smoke from the weapon clearing, the professor could see that the hall was devoid of living enemies, the room carpeted with twitching bodies, awash in a sea of gore. The banner hung from the wall in tatters, knives stuck out of the walls, and smashed birthday gifts lay everywhere. Even the huge, Earth-shaped birthday cake had been reduced to no more than a pastry mash on a tilting wheeled cart.

Then the professor sadly glanced at the burning ruin of the magic book on the floor. A Squid God worshiper had ripped it from his hands during the fray and the book, well, retaliated. Afterwards there had not been much remaining of either the thief or the volume. Einstein postulated there was a protective spell placed on the book by the local Magician's Guild to deter any thieves from attempting freelance wizardry. *Such a pity.*

Climbing over the palisade of dead, Lord Carstairs slapped the buckle on his chest harness. As the strap disconnected, the ammo pack dropped off and the red-hot Vulcan slid to the filthy floor with a loud clatter. Giving a thankful groan, the British lord straightened to his full height and stretched.

"By George, that device weighs a bloody ton," Carstairs stated, massaging his neck.

"However, you are now defenseless," Prof. Einstein observed frowning. "Well, there are certainly enough swords, axes, and such lying about for you to choose from. Pity the book is gone or we could summon you another whatever-that-was again."

"Actually, sir, I still have these," Lord Carstairs remarked, producing a pair of sleek, angular pistols with oversized maws. "The pamphlet listed them as Smith & Wesson .44 AutoMagnums."

Working the slide atop the pistol, the lord ejected a brass round. The cartridge was thick and long, shiny with a steel coating. In professional admiration, Carstairs smiled. How lovely. Ammunition like this could easily blow the head off a man!

"And what are those?" the professor asked pointing.

With the removal of the Vulcan, a pair of small spheres was now exposed attached to the left and right suspenders that supported the military gunbelt around the lord's waist. Each of the globes was about the size of an orange, had a crisscross diamond pattern cut into the surface, and was topped with a handle and pull-ring assemblage.

Holstering a pistol, Lord Carstairs pulled one of the spheres loose and turned it about for inspection. "I have no idea," he said honestly. "The pamphlet referred to them as R-47 napalm, but did not explain the term."

"Napalm?" the professor said slowly, tasting the word. "It sounds Greek, but I have never heard that word before."

"Nor I. But apparently, the spell considered the whole outfit to be a single unit."

Accepting one of the objects, Prof. Einstein scrutinized the napalm ball without touching the pull-ring on top. That was obviously the operating device, childishly simple, but what happened once the pull-ring was removed was unknowable until the device was activated.

"Curious," the professor said thoughtfully, weighing the sphere in his palm. "No explanation indicates that they are very common in the 21st Century. Decorations, perhaps?"

"Considering the utilitarian nature of the rest of the outfit, I find it highly unlikely," Lord Carstairs countered, taking the mysterious sphere back and attaching it again to the web harness of his gunbelt rigging. "Shall we go? There may be more squiddies on the way."

"Do you really think there are any more?" the professor demanded, gesturing at the sea of corpses.

Carstairs made a face. "Well, no, actually. But we cannot be complacent."

"No, of course not. You're quite right, lad. Let's push onward."

After a brief reconnoiter of the great hall, the explorers discovered that the only other door was on the far side. The armored portal was sealed with an array of heavy padlocks, but those were easily undone, then the door itself stood slightly ajar. As carefully as possible, Einstein and Carstairs squeezed through the crack without moving the door, only pausing a moment for the professor to grab the monocle from the still hand of the bony Squid God worshiper. He chanced a peek through it at Lord Carstairs and saw the man, not the demon disguise. *Excellent, it was still operational! The monocle would fit nicely into the museum's display of cursed optics and occult eyewear!*

Straight ahead of the men rose an endless staircase, lit by flickering torches set into wall alcoves.

"Stay sharp, sir," Lord Carstairs said, working the slide on each of the S&W .44 AutoMags to chamber a round for immediate use. "It appears that we have some serious walking to do." The lord had recently read an article in the *Times* about the American gun manufacturer Colt Arms working on such a pistol, and that was how their weapon was primed.

"I'll take the lead this time, lad," Prof. Einstein said, wiggling the monocle into place around his left eye. Scrutinizing the steps, he moved to the left, then the right, and started climbing upward in a geometric zigzag pattern.

* * *

Leaping around the last corner, a panting Einstein and Carstairs landed on the top level of the stairwell with their weapons drawn.

Ahead of them was a long empty corridor with yet another set of doors. Yet neither explorer took any solace in the fact that they were alone. Each of the battered men was soaked with sweat, bruised, reeking of gun smoke, their backpacks gone, clumps of hair missing, and their clothes badly ripped. Prof. Einstein had a gouge in his crown and Lord Carstairs carried an arrow sticking through his left sleeve.

"Anything?" Lord Carstairs asked, poised to leap.

"Looks clear," Einstein reported, squinting through the cracked monocle. "Let's go."

"No, wait!" the lord commanded, grabbing the older man by the arm.

As if cast in bronze, Prof. Einstein went motionless with a boot paused in the air. "What is it?" he whispered.

Gently lifting the professor, the lord placed him safely aside, then dropped to his hands and knees. Crawling about on the marble floor,

Lord Carstairs gave a subdued cry of success, and oh-so-very-carefully draped a handkerchief over a thin black thread stretched across the entrance of the corridor.

"Good going, lad," Prof. Einstein exhaled. "How ever did you spot it?"

"Simplicity itself," Lord Carstairs said, rising and dusting off his hands. "This is exactly where I would have placed a trip wire. If anything, these Squid God chappies are extraordinarily audacious."

"At the very least," Einstein agreed heartily, casting a glance over a shoulder. "That climb up the stairs is something I shall have nightmares about in the future. Trap doors in the floor, swinging blades from the ceiling, flames from the walls, a giant boulder that rolled up the passageway while a flood of water poured down, then a maze of mirrors, arrows from the stairs, and now a trip wire. Heaven alone knows what it would have unleashed."

"Only more of the same, I'm sure," Carstairs agreed, yanking the forgotten arrow from his sleeve and casting it aside. "But then, you can always rely on fanatics to be unreasonable."

"It's their one saving grace, my boy," the professor chuckled, brushing the loose hair from his face.

"Infidels!" an inhuman voice throated in a bizarre scream.

Spinning around fast, Einstein and Carstairs saw a large hairy creature charge out of a hidden doorway in the middle of the long corridor. Ambush!

"A werewolf!" Lord Carstairs sighed, triggering the two massive handguns. "Damnation, and we have no silver aside from a few useless coins!"

The booming rounds from the S&W .44 AutoMag plowed a bloody path of destruction through the werewolf, blowing bones and guts out its back in a grisly explosion. But as expected, the creature only staggered, then stood upright once more, stuffed the beating organs back into its chest, and lunged for the explorers again while howling like a primordial nightmare!

Blowing military hellfire at the werewolf, Lord Carstairs continued firing the pistols with devastating, if only temporary, results.

"This may take some time, sir," the lord said, grunting from the recoil of the thundering handguns. "You'd best proceed and try to stop the birth ceremony by yourself. I'll be along soon."

"No, we strike together, Benjamin!" the professor cried, drawing the sword. With a gesture, he sent a lance of flame to engulf the beast, but the magical fire slid off the inhuman fur without doing any damage whatsoever.

"I'll go to the left!" Lord Carstairs said with a wink.

Nodding in understanding, Prof. Einstein went to the left, the reverse maneuver catching the werewolf by surprise. As the manimal paused in confusion, Lord Carstairs shot it point-blank in the ear, blowing out its brains onto the marble wall, as Prof. Einstein hacked off a hairy leg.

Falling to the floor, the yowling monster thrashed madly about in agony! But it was a trick. Rolling atop the leg, the werewolf stuck it back on as if donning a boot, and its brain wiggled up an arm to enter through the ear and snuggle back into its proper place.

"Impossible!" Prof. Einstein cursed. "Incredible!"

"Duck!" Lord Carstairs yelled, as the snarling creature lunged for the professor. Cutting loose in a non-stop barrage with the booming AutoMags, the lord drove the thing tumbling along the corridor, leaving a grisly trail of animated entrails.

Spearing a heart with the sword, Prof. Einstein cried out as a spine wrapped around his leg. For a delusional moment, the professor felt that he was trapped in a combination anatomy class and puppet show. This was like something from a Hieronymus Bosch painting! Shaking free the heart, Einstein hacked off the spine, almost removing his own foot in the process.

"Sir, the very purpose of this beast is to slow us down!" the lord muttered, dropping the spent clips as the *Times* article had described, and clumsily inserted the last spare ammunition. "Leave me behind, Professor! Stop the ceremony! It's almost time for the rebirthing!"

"We don't know that for a fact!" Prof. Einstein retorted, casting a double-death spell upon the healing werewolf. It went stiff, fell over, trembled, and rose once more, if anything looking even angrier than before.

"Can we take the chance?" Lord Carstairs said between each booming round. "Remember, sir, if the enemy wants you to go down, then speed is your only hope!"

Einstein growled in agreement at that. It was the most basic military strategy of all.

"Get moving, my friend, save the world. I shall not let the werewolf past!"

"We stand as one!" the professor cried defiantly, brandishing the sword. A thousand years of Anglo-Saxon heritage surged within the elderly professor, and he felt like Nelson at the Battle of Copenhagen when the admiral held a telescope to his blind eye and cried out. *'Ships? I see no ships!'*

"Felix, if you stay, then Mary dies!" Lord Carstairs snapped. "Is that your wish?"

Casting a blizzard at the werewolf, Prof. Einstein faltered at that remark, his face torn with indecision.

"It is time to go, Felix," the lord said calmly, watching the beast thaw. "Save your niece. Protect the queen."

The queen! That did it. British to the bone, Prof. Einstein could not betray his nation. Lord Carstairs was correct, this was another trap set for intruders, and the most insidious one of them all, a waste of precious time.

With a heavy sigh, Prof. Einstein lowered the sword, spun about on a boot heel, and sprinted down the long corridor.

"Godspeed!" the professor shouted over his shoulder, then crashed through the door at the end, leaving it wide open.

Moving into the middle of the corridor, Lord Carstairs took a stance and started placing each round into the icy werewolf to inflict maximum damage and buy as many seconds as possible.

Shaking itself free, the creature sprang for his throat, and Carstairs blew off a hairy limb. The werewolf dropped, temporarily disarmed. Seizing the opportunity, Lord Carstairs fired both magnums in unison and severed its neck with a shot.

As the furry head went flying, the magical beast staggered about blindly and stepped on the trip wire at the top of the stairs. With a whispery sigh, a blade swung from the ceiling and cut the werewolf in half. Vivisected, the disassembled monster went tumbling down the stairs. Soon there came the sound of sound of arrows, flames, rocks, and countless explosions.

Smiling in triumph, Lord Carstairs started to holster his hot guns when more hidden doors in the walls swung open and out charged a dozen more werewolves. Only these beasts were armed with javelins and rode astride spiders the size of draft horses. Lord Carstairs cursed at the sight. *Calvary! The archenemy of all foot soldiers.*

Firing both of the AutoMags steadily, Carstairs backed down the corridor until he reached the door. Pausing only a split second to yank it closed, the lord put his back to the portal and waited for the things to come closer.

"None shall pass," Lord Carstairs whispered softly, tightening his grip on the handguns. Then he began shooting again, and shouted the phrase as a battle cry. "None shall pass!"

Howling their own war chant, the werewolves and spiders rushed the lord, and the deadly battle commenced in earnest.

* * *

Maintaining a steady pace, Professor Einstein raced up the next stairwell and soon the sounds of gunfire faded into the distance. Shaking his head to clear it of unwanted thoughts, Prof. Einstein concentrated on watching for traps as he climbed the steps. It was obvious by now that William Owen was a powerful sorcerer, and while Alexander's sword possessed an extensive list of spells, Prof. Einstein was lacking essential basic training in the occult arts. That placed him at a crucial disadvantage. But whatever the cost, Einstein knew that he must be victorious. There were too many lives depending upon the outcome.

At the top of the stairs, the professor found another bronze door, this time unlocked and slightly ajar. The room beyond pitch black, and not a sound could be heard aside from his own breathing. *What, no sign saying 'insert booby-trap here'?*

Keeping flat to the wall, Prof. Einstein squeezed through opening without touching the portal or the jamb. Reaching the other side, the professor expected to see some sort of a hidden explosive charge, or a spring-loaded bear trap, but instead there was only bucket balanced atop the door. The slightest touch to the door and the bucket would fall dashing out its contents. Whatever those were, he wanted no part of them.

Sniffing hard to try and detect any telltale odors from the bucket, the professor almost gagged on the foul reek of fresh blood filling the air. Good lord, he hadn't smelled anything that bad since working at the sewage plant in Bombay, India! Covering his nose with a handkerchief, Prof. Einstein glanced at his clothing, but the earlier rush of water in the booby-trapped stairwell had washed him clean of the demon blood. So where was this awful stink coming from?

Raising the glowing sword higher, the professor could see that he was standing in an alcove set between two carved pillars. Advancing past them, he saw silvery beams coming from the ceiling and looked upward to see the triple moons shining weakly through a transparent dome.

Glancing downward, Einstein saw that the marble floor was inlaid with a huge mystical rune in the shape of an engorged squid that pulsed like a living thing in the moonlight. Good enough. There could be no further doubt that this was his goal, the temple of the Squid God, as he had seen it atop the black mountain. But if this was their temple, then where were Owen and his cadre of worshipers? Was he too late? Had the Squid God already been born?

Squinting at the ebony shadows outside his circle of light, Einstein demanded maximum illumination; the sword responded by increasing its glow to a nearly blinding level. As the temple became filled with the clear white light, the professor almost gagged at the sight of all the dead bodies lining the walls. The horrible reek he smelled was coming from the dozens, no, the hundreds of corpses stacked like cordwood between the external pillars forming a sort of crude wall around the temple.

Every robed man and woman had a slit throat, the rivulets of dark crimson dribbling onto the marble floor to trickle into the rune and flow along the lines like burgundy wine in an aqueduct. Suddenly, the professor had a flashback to the blood on the floor of the exhibit hall of his museum. He took a glance through the cracked monocle and saw thick, evil magic everywhere. Fresh spilled blood must be a prime ingredient for the summoning of magical power for these heathen lunatics. Prof. Einstein snorted at the phrase. Lunatic. Never before had the word been used so accurately.

Stepping over the trickles of blood, the professor moved into the rune and the illusion of empty air shimmered away to reveal a large stone altar draped in a tapestry adorned with strange mystical symbols. Placed prominently on top of that altar of evil was a bubbling iron cauldron, connected to the rune by strands of silver wire. But was the rune powering the cauldron, or vice versa? Trying the monocle once more, the professor cursed as the glass shattered from the overload of dark forces in the area. *Blast!* He cast it away, and licked a cut finger.

Expecting attack from everywhere, Prof. Einstein eased closer to the altar, and the silver-blue moonlight changed to a silvery-green. The professor went motionless. Had he just triggered some spell, or spoiled it? There was no way to tell. Then again, since his task was to stop the ceremony of the rebirth, perhaps some plain, old fashioned smashing about would do the trick. Tally-ho!

As Prof. Einstein leveled the sword to unleash general destruction, a lightning bolt crackled down from the ceiling to knock the blade from his hand. Einstein cried out in pain as the sword went tumbling through the air and hit the floor with a loud clatter. Immediately, its golden aura began to fade.

Massaging his stinging hand, the professor spat a curse as William Owen floated out from inside one of the support columns to land near the altar. The Dutarian High Priest was wearing a hooded black robe edged in the finest filigree; on a gold chain about his neck hung a duplicate of the rune on the floor, and in his right hand was a tall staff made of carved human bones.

Horrible! But then Prof. Einstein spied a medical plaster on Owen's neck covering the wound he had received from the bullet fired by Lord Carstairs. *In spite of all his magic, this is only a mortal man*, Einstein reminded himself, sneaking a hand into his pocket. *And anything that can be hurt, can be killed.*

"So you made it here alive. Well done, old man," Owen sneered, clenching his undamaged left hand into a tight fist to shake it at the professor. "I really didn't think you and the royal lump would get this far. Yes, indeed, I must admit that you do remind me of a blind whore."

Raising both eyebrows, Prof. Einstein stared back at the man in total confusion.

"I've got to hand it to you," the High Priest finished with a fiendish cackle.

"Spoken like the true lower class trash you are," the professor spat contemptuously. Then, moving fast, Einstein threw a fistful of gold coins at the priest as a distraction and desperately dove for the fallen sword.

Sliding across the bloody floor, Prof. Einstein was almost to the sword when a blue flash engulfed him like an explosion and he was brutally thrown aside. Tucking and rolling as he had been taught by his old judo master in Japan, the professor smoothly rose to a standing position, pressed against the wall of human flesh that was jammed between the stone pillars.

"You can forget that wretched toy," Owen continued, lowering the crackling staff. "While I find you pitiful, I have a healthy respect for the Sword of Alexander. You taught me about its abilities, remember? Such a pity that you couldn't find the ancient sword of Dutar. With that you might have actually stood a chance against me."

"A camel and your mother," Prof. Einstein snarled, hoping to trigger a blind rage. An angry opponent, was a weak opponent. That bit of wisdom coming from the Oxford snooker club, winners of the Grand Master Award for ten straight years. Or was it Sun Tzu? Blast, he often got the two confused.

"Oh yes, they do it often," Owen snickered. "And what's more, I like to watch."

"Well, those that can't do . . ." the professor said, leaving the astonishingly rude sentiment unfinished.

Going livid, the Dutarian High Priest shouted in a strange language, and a lambent field of rainbow light enveloped the professor. Unexpectedly feeling as if he weighed a ton, Einstein was forced to his knees, and discovered that he could no longer draw in a breath. His temples began to pound as a burning sensation filled his laboring chest. With fumbling hands, the heaving professor ripped open his collar, but to no avail, and the temple started to become blurry.

"Goodbye, Prof. Einstein," William Owen snarled, as the rainbow glow increased around the explorer until the light seemed to fill the universe.

TWENTY-THREE

With both lungs pumping furiously, Prof. Einstein spit his last breath at the High Priest in a virulent curse. Unexpectedly, the pressure suddenly dissipated and the professor was able to draw in a breath of cool, reeking air.

Feeling his strength rapidly return, Einstein attempted to duplicate the gesture that was filling his mind, and as he did, the rainbow glow around him vanished completely.

Gurgling in shock, Owen staggered backwards and clutched a fistful of his own hair. "Impossible!" the High Priest croaked, attempting to hide behind his magical wand. "Incredible!"

"Neither, you simpering dolt," Prof. Einstein wheezed menacingly. Slowly standing, the professor touched the battered bronze crown still on his head. "Apparently, your cowardly attack has awakened the Crown of Alexander, and it yearns to once more battle against evil."

Suddenly radiating a protective bronze shine, a rather tan-looking Prof. Einstein took a determined step forward. "Which means you, old boy," he added in dire explanation.

"It's a trick," Owen muttered, and thrust his wand forward. A shimmering blue beam lanced from the tip to hit the bronze field fluctuating around Einstein. But it only ricocheted off to strike the floor and leave a thick patch of ice.

Rolling up his sleeves, Prof. Einstein listened to the voice astride his head, and made a fast series of complex finger movements. Across the temple, the Sword of Alexander rattled alive, and then flew through the air to land in the professor's outstretched hand with a firm smack.

With both of the magical items awake and reunited, the professor could mentally hear them converse. The magic book from the nameless city had played fair. The sword working together with the crown constituted a single weapon. How very interesting! The professor briefly wondered if something similar to this had been the origin of the legend of Merlin. Had he been a wizard, or merely the voice of the crown that King Arthur wore? Now there was a neat puzzle to solve some other day!

Duck to the left!

Moving fast, Prof. Einstein dodged an incoming barrage of ice balls from the wand of the High Priest. Whew, that had been close.

Thank you, he thought at the crown.

No problem. Now, have at thee!

What? Oh. "*En garde*!" Prof. Einstein snarled at his enemy.

As Owen shifted about like a boxer ready to slip a punch, Einstein spun the sword in a complex pattern and cut loose a dazzling beam of force. As it shot across the temple, a swirling pattern of crackling energy appeared about the gesturing High Priest, and the ray was deflected to strike a marble pillar, vaporizing a massive chunk of stone. Weakened beyond endurance, the column fell and a score of corpses tumbled away to reveal the mountain crater outside. On the horizon, the triple moons were just starting to align themselves in a straight row, one behind the other.

Oddbotkins, a conjunction here must mean a full moon on the true Earth! the professor deduced. *This was it, the rebirthing will commence at any moment!*

So kill him, the crown urged.

Most sensible advice. I shall!

Rummaging about in his robes, William Owen dropped some acorns on the floor, then pulled an Adams .32 pocket-pistol and fired. But the Sword of Alexander blocked the incoming lead with childish ease.

Gesturing with both his free hand and the sword, Prof. Einstein tried to freeze the mouth of his enemy, but the Staff of the Squid God neutralized the conjure. Shouting incantations at each other, the two men advanced and blinding polychromatic lights filled the temple. Death spells collided with the sound of slamming anvils. Mesmerisms swirled hypnotically in the boiling air, and each man just barely missed having his sanity stolen by the other. Clothing burst into fire, only to regenerate precisely behind the moving bands of flame. Flying knives swirled about the two combatants in a hurricane of edged death. A slimy blob appeared next to the professor, but it was promptly eaten by a miniature Tyrannosaurus Rex. Banshees raked sonic claws across aching eardrums, countered with wads of magical cotton. Deadly Black Mambo snakes slithered across the glass-dome of the ceiling, only to be killed at the mere touch of a Golden Arrow frog hopping about. Soon, the bloody floor was crawling with deadly insects, and fanged leprechauns got crushed underfoot. Passing angels clucked disapprovingly at the wanton display of violence, while summoned demons merely laughed and took photographs. Briefly, the angry ghost of Red John Bonater appeared, waving a naked scimitar, but the avenging specter vanished a heartbeat later as the High Priest opened a transdimensional portal and sent the spirit hurtling down into the fiery abyss of Hell. A split second later, the transdimensional vortex opened wide again, and the pirate was kicked out.

"No sailors, or actors allowed!" a demon shouted, and slammed the portal shut permanently.

A giant transparent hammer pounded ineffectively on Owen's head, while an ethereal mousetrap snapped without damage on the Prof. Einstein's adamantine body. Arrows shot from their open palms, cannon balls volleyed from their knees, and steam shot from their ears as the scholars battled for control of the world. The priest and the professor alternately grew and shrank in size to distort each other's aim. Waves of unreality crashed about the men, sparkling darkness swallowed throbbing sunlight and, in the air above the combatants, a giant pair of hands thumb-wrestled in deadly sincerity. Balls of blue fire bounced madly about the room. Lightning bolts crackled everywhere. The hundreds of dead Squid God worshipers arose as a zombie army. But a thundering avalanche of kosher salt poured into the temple, and set them tumbling into the crater. Yet the ethereal maelstrom did not even ruffle the hair of the wildly gesturing enemies. The temple shook at the passage and the partially open door in the alcove slammed shut, dislodging the bucket on top. It crashed to the floor releasing its watery contents, the fluid hissing and sizzling as acid began to dissolve the marble.

The sound caught Einstein's attention for a moment, and he gasped in horror at his reflection in a patch ice on a column. He looked older! Years older. Apparently channeling this much magical force through his physical form was taking a terrible toll. The professor was aging at a phenomenal rate. His bushy gray hair was receding from a wrinkling brow. Liver spots now dotted both hands, and every joint began to hurt with advanced rheumatism. Even his vaunted eyesight was beginning to blur, and the voice from the crown was starting to dim. This magical battle was literally sucking the life out the professor, yet there was no other choice. He had to fight on.

Working together, the crown and sword of Alexander countered a fresh wave of attacks from the snarling Owen, then blocked a returning series of death spells. Next, the temple was rocked by a powerful earthquake, the floor starting to crack open wide before it was repaired by a giant translucent staple gun. That was when Prof. Einstein noticed that the High Priest of Dutar had not aged one single bit from the battle. *How could anybody still be fresh and young after this level of expenditure*? On that subject, the crown was ominously silent.

Feeling his teeth starting to loosen, Einstein knew that he had to do something deuced clever soon, or else Owen could simply wait until the professor died of old age and win by default. But what could he try that had not failed already?

Maintaining the attacks, Prof. Einstein tried to analyze the situation, replaying the previous fight in his mind. The answer came immediately. The rune on the floor! That had to be it! No matter what was happening, Owen refused to move from his original position. On the other hand, Prof. Einstein had run around quite a bit in order to dodge various attacks. But Owen would rather take damage rather than leave the immediate vicinity of the mystic rune. What to do? What could he do?

Meanwhile, transparent vipers tried to spit poison at Owen, only to be consumed by a giant mongoose. Then a golden wolf ate the mongoose; a red bear consumed the mongoose, only to be squashed by a belly-flopping golden whale, the impact cracking the marble floor.

Concentrating on the rune, Prof. Einstein observed a slim wire leading from the boot of the High Priest to the edge of the mystic symbol. Hells bells, the clever bugger must actually be siphoning off magical energy from the ethereal matrix within the rune! Every attack by the Sword of Alexander was fueling the High Priest's continued youth! In spite of everything, Einstein had to admit it was a damn clever strategy, and one that he could do nothing about.

Getting tough, the bronze crown decided to switch tactics and offered a new battle plan. Maintaining a shimmering shield with the outthrust palm of his left hand, Prof. Einstein leveled the sword at Owen, and from its tip, a massive power beam erupted. It struck the staff of the High Priest, and tried to alternately burn-boil-bore its way through. In response, Owen grabbed the seal of the Squid God hanging about his neck, and the bone staff stiffly resisted. Using more and more of his life force, Prof. Einstein increased the attack. A stream of vitriolic gold splashed against an immaterial barrier of shimmering blue, and the temple became awash in the lethal vibrations of the Technicolor battle.

Looking frightened, Owen was muttering defense conjures, as his staff now began to smolder slightly. Then the defensive aura about the High Priest started to shrink, and the man gasped for breath, literally cooking in the awful heat. Knowing he was on the verge of victory, Einstein grinned in delight, then staggered as he felt a hammer-blow to his chest and he recognized the symptoms of a coming heart attack. *Bloody hell, not now!* But a wave of weakness washed over the aging professor, and he fell to his knees, barely able to keep the sword erect.

Unexpectedly released, Owen clutched the Great Seal and redoubled the output of his own staff. The temple shuddered under the iridescent by-products of the irresistible force meeting the immovable object in a dazzling pyrotechnic display. The marble cracked, and the tapestries draped over the altar vanished in a sheet of flame, the additional heat only increasing the fierce bubbling in the cauldron of blood.

With sweat pouring from his pain-wracked body, Prof. Einstein struggled to maintain some kind of defense against the brutal ethereal assault. The temperature of the temple was steadily rising and, with a flash, a pool of lava surrounded the professor, the little island of marble floor directly beneath his feet shrinking in the molten stone. Grinning in triumph, Owen laughed uproariously. Raw hatred of the mocking foe welled from within Prof. Einstein and inspiration came. Horrified, the bronze crown vetoed the outlandish idea, but the professor refused to listen this time, and charged.

Now instead of deflecting the incoming barrage of enemy magic, Einstein ordered the sword of Alexander to devour it, re-channeling the excess into his dying body. The sword rebelled at first. But the professor demanded its obedience in the name of Alexander! Reluctantly, the sword obeyed, writhing at the foul taste of the dark magic. In a welling of new strength, a glorious fire raced through the veins of the professor and his heart began to beat strong and steady once more. The age spots vanished, his vision cleared, and Prof. Einstein launched the final leg of his assault. It was all or nothing, now. This, as the Americans liked to say, was the proverbial It.

With a convoluted double-gesture, Einstein created a coiled spring under his boots and launched himself forward like a circus performer. Flying across the temple, the professor smashed into the startled Owen, driving the High Priest away from the rune, and the silver wire attached to his boot snapped free. Dropping his staff, Owen convulsed in screaming agony as blood began to flow from his eyes. As if in response, a deafening thunderclap shook the temple, and the mystic rune on the marble floor flared with a surge of primordial energy.

"The matrix!" Owen shrieked, going pale. "You fool! It's been activated too soon!"

"Excellent!" Prof. Einstein grinned in triumph, expertly swaying to the motion of the temple.

"We'll both die, you old fool!"

"Just as long as you go first, traitor!"

Rampaging completely out of control, a violent flare of magic engulfed both men, and a swirling hurricane of mystical energy horribly tore them apart, literally disintegrating their bodies into their component atoms. Bit by bit, organ by organ, each man was painfully rebuilt with pure elemental magic incorporated into every fiber of his quivering body. The pain was beyond imagination, and Einstein prayed for the release of death. But then with a strident thunderclap, the agony ceased, the aura faded away, and a woozy Professor Felix Einstein found himself standing alongside William Owen inside the cooling pentagram.

"We should be dead," the High Priest muttered in confusion.

"As you wish, old boy!" the professor growled, swinging the sword with all of his renewed strength, not in some magical or special gesture, but simply as a length of sharpened metal.

With a sound beyond description, the Sword of Alexander cut the High Priest in half, cleaving him from shoulder to belly.

Still hideously alive, William Owen staggered backwards, and the sword spat forth a fireball that exploded the priest into grisly rain of smoking gobbets. Unabated, the energy ball continued onward to punch a hole through the marble pillar behind the dead man, and then streak across the crater to violently impact on the distant mountains with spectacular results.

"Church of England doesn't sound so bad now, does it, Willy, my boy?" Prof. Einstein gloated, wiping the hot sword clean on the pile of smoldering rags. Allowing himself a small smile of victory, the professor started to head for the altar when he felt a strange tingling in his toes. *Eh? What was happening this time? Surely, not another heart attack!*

The bronze crown howled a warning, and Einstein realized that the magic stored in the body of the dead priest was beginning to flow back into the rune on the floor, and then into the professor, the only available living human.

Frantically, Prof. Einstein tried to leap for safety, but it was too late. The magic poured into him like quicksilver charged with electricity. Unfortunately, he was already full, packed solid with ethereal energy, without an inch to spare!

It was only an awkward trickle at first, then a searing rush that changed into a sizzling torrent! Helpless, Prof. Einstein could only scream from the pain of having even more titanic power jammed-pounded-shoved into his writhing body. Reeling with unbearable agony, Einstein fought to retain his sanity as he became saturated with potent ethereal energy. But that proved impossible, and stray leakage radiated from his every orifice, no matter how inappropriate or embarrassing.

A loud slam from across the temple caught the professor's attention, and he turned to see Lord Carstairs dash through the doorway. The lord was armed with a bent .44 AutoMag in one fist, and the other glistening from the silver coins held tight between his fingers, bits of brains and fur clinging to the coins. A bleeding gash bisected the lord's right leg and his left arm was supported in a makeshift sling torn from his own gory shirt.

Stepping out of the alcove, Lord Carstairs could only gape at the strange and terrible sight of the glowing professor floating in the air near a sort of tribal altar holding an iron cauldron whose contents gave off the most repellant fumes. Sheet lightning crashed about Prof. Einstein, and he appeared to be in tremendous pain as the temple of the Squid God insanely bucked and writhed, the marble floor and walls flexing and convulsing as if living organic matter.

"Professor!" Lord Carstairs shouted above the storm, limping forward.

Intent upon reaching his friend, the lord did not notice the patch of ice on the floor and he slipped and fell face first into the pool of acid. His features dissolving, Carstairs rolled away, going directly into a ghostly bear trap. The hinged jaws slammed shut on the man, nearly cutting him in half.

"Benjamin, no!" the professor shouted, reaching out for his friend. Instantly, a searing power beam struck the lord and a sphere of the purest light enveloped him in a soothing cocoon. Gently, the lord was lifted off the floor . . . only to be brutally dashed against the nearest marble column. The white sphere vanished, leaving the lord sprawled on the floor panting for breath.

"Sorry, lad!" Prof. Einstein boomed. "I can't . . . control . . . there's too much . . . !" Just then, another spasm took the professor as the domed ceiling exploded, the tinkling pieces flying away into the night sky. Now the light of the triple moons flooded the temple, and the rune flared making the cauldron on the altar furiously boil, the rising fumes soon taking on the aspect of a ghastly squid.

Going pale at the sight, Prof. Einstein summoning his every ounce of British pluck and mentally composed the most all-encompassing spell of death and destruction that he could possibly imagine, using every piece of biological, scientific, historical, and mystical information that he had ever learned.

"*Die!*" the professor commanded, the words transforming into visible letters. The altar stones cracked under the assault, the cauldron turned white-hot, and the temple of the living Squid God vanished in a staggering detonation of mono-atomic flame.

The entire mountain crater shook as the lambent maelstrom of cosmic power extended beyond the atmosphere and into space. Earthquakes shook the entire world. Mountains rose and fell. Oceans parted. The pillars of heaven trembled. The whole Time/Space continuum shuddered. Dimensional walls cracked, and stray bits of awesome ethereal blast shot off into neighboring vibratory planes of existence.

* * *

In another world, in another time, a husband and wife stopped rocking their wooden chairs on the porch of their Iowa farmhouse and gasped at the astonishing display of lights that filled the evening sky.

"Well, hoot," the old man said, spitting a chaw of tobacco into the rose garden. "Will ya look at that, Marge! What d'ya think . . . Lucas?"

With her white hair reflecting ten thousand colors, the old woman shook her head. "Naw, gotta be Spielberg. He likes those fancy cloud effects."

"Yep, I reckon you're right, uh-huh."

* * *

In the Dutarian temple, there immediately followed a volcanic implosion of starkly indescribable power, and everything reversed. There was a dark flash, followed by a rude sucking sound that ended in a crescendo of silent thunder!

Falling to the cracked floor, Prof. Einstein heaved for breath, utterly amazed that he was still alive. Forcing himself into a kneeling position, Einstein looked around to see that he was on a circular piece of marble that was surrounded by a field of fused glass. The only other objects in sight were a panting Lord Carstairs lying face down in the smashed alcove, and the noisily bubbling cauldron on the cracked altar.

Dropping his jaw in shock, Prof. Einstein simply could not believe that the cauldron was still intact! Starting towards it, the professor could not get close enough to tip it over, as the iron pot was incandescent with heat.

"S-sir?" a familiar voice groaned.

Spinning about, Einstein rushed to the side of his friend. "Lad, you're still alive!" the professor cried in delight. The lord's clothing was in tatters, but there seemed to be no blemish on him, much less bleeding wounds.

"T-that is a m-matter of opinion," Lord Carstairs moaned, sitting upright. "W-what the H-Hell happened?"

Grasping an elbow, Prof. Einstein helped the lord to stand. "I hit you with a healing spell, lad," he explained. "Albeit, a more powerful version than the one I originally asked for. I must have absorbed more magic than I imagined."

"And what of Owen?" Carstairs asked, glancing about the smashed temple. Smoldering debris and pieces of bodies lay scattered everywhere. "I see that you have been busy, but what was the outcome, sir?"

"William Owen is dead," the professor said, glancing at the sizzling hole in the pillar. "Of that fact, I can assure you."

"Excellent!" Lord Carstairs smiled, rubbing his smooth face. The lord flinched as a memory of the acid came rushing back, but the pain was only a memory. There didn't even seem to be a scar on his cheeks. Actually, he felt rested and strong, as if he had just spent a weekend fishing in Scotland, instead of battling the forces of evil. "A healing spell, you say, sir? Well, I must admit that . . . professor! What happened to you?"

"Why, what's wrong with me?" Einstein demanded, touching himself all over to check for wounds or burns.

"Sir, your hair!" Lord Carstairs stated cryptically, but then he was interrupted by a loud booming noise that came from the boiling cauldron.

As the explorers turned, a thick geyser of black blood shot high into the sky, then spread out in an umbrella formation to rain down around the cauldron, only to rise up again. As the cycle accelerated, another resonating boom sounded and from out of the depths of the iron pot, and a slim green tentacle arose, its underside lined with suckers. The wriggling limb fondled the air for a few moments, its suckers making wet smacking sounds. Then the tentacle extended from the radiating cauldron until it was five yards long, eight, ten, twenty yards long!

With a grim expression, Lord Carstairs reached for the AutoMag, but only slapped his bare hip. Blast and damn! Bending down, the lord grabbed a jagged piece of fused marble from the broken floor and brandished it as a crude dagger.

"All right, let's finish the job," he said resolutely.

"Righto!" Prof. Einstein cried, going for his sword, but the weapon and scabbard were not at his side. A quick touch to his head found only hair. The bronze Crown of Alexander was also gone. *Of course,* he realized unhappily, *they had been summoned for the specific task of fighting the High Priest. With their task completed, the magical weapons must have departed back to their original realm.* It was deuced bad timing, but Prof. Einstein wished them both well for the assistance provided. Unfortunately, his own battle with evil was not yet finished.

Spying a dagger in the disembodied hand of a dead Squid God worshiper, the professor rushed over to obtain the weapon. But the rigor of death had tightened the fingers into a vise. With no other choice, the professor used a piece of marble to smash the fingers apart in order to obtain the dagger.

Once more armed, Prof. Einstein stood in triumph, when a sharp whistle came from Lord Carstairs calling for his attention. Turning around, the professor frowned to see another tentacle slithering into view from the cauldron. Then came a third, forth, fifth, sixth, more! The white-hot rim began stretching like taffy to accommodate the monstrous limbs. The umbrella of blood stopped as a bulbous mass rose from the center of the tentacles, a single great eye looking about with a fierce intelligence. Spreading beyond all credibility, the cauldron squealed as a second eye joined the first and a pulsating head slid upward, closely followed by the slimy body of a gigantic green squid. Stepping out of the rune, the towering creature flexed its tentacles about in every direction. Its job done, the exhausted cauldron gratefully crumbled into dust.

Nearly filling the temple, the Squid God stood thirty yards tall, its horribly human eyes rotating in opposite directions as it looked about the smoking ruins. The mottled skin of the colossus was a nauseating green, with an undertone of purplish-blue, rather reminiscent of a festering bruise.

In ghastly majesty, the squid looked at the triple moons in the sky just starting to break formation and, for a while, the only sound discernable was a faint clacking noise coming from a parrot-beak mouth located under the beast and set amid the undulating tentacles. Giving a regal nod to the unearthly satellites, the Squid God now glanced around the temple and finally noticed the two tiny humans standing nearby. It smiled.

Supported by its nest of tentacles, the squid smoothly undulated closer, accompanied by a barrage of juicy smacking sounds from its suckers on the marble floor.

With a sigh of resignation, Prof. Einstein extended a hand to his friend. "I fear we were too slow, Ben. Well, goodbye, it has been a true pleasure working with you."

In a rush of unaccustomed emotion, Lord Carstairs took the offered hand and solemnly shook. "So long, Felix. At least we gave the bloody thing a run for its money."

"*What-ho!*" the squid rumbled, the stentorian voice coming from the parrot beak in its belly. "*Greetings, my loyal worshipers!*" The language was Dutarian, but the meaning was crystal clear to the scholarly explorers.

Rising to his full height, Prof. Einstein glared in unbridled contempt at the hideous monstrosity. "By gad, sir, we are no—"

Moving fast, Lord Carstairs clamped a hand over the professor's mouth. "Greetings and salutations, mighty one!" the lord shouted. "We were afraid that you might not actually appear!"

"*Yes, it has been a long time,*" the squid admitted, turning both eyes to look upon the humans. "*And yet you two remained faithful. I'm touched. Really, I am.*"

Raising two tentacles, the beast exposed a smile. "*As a reward, I will allow you both to live in this dimension for the rest of your natural lives.*" It paused, then added, "*After which, I will come back and totally destroy everything here, so be sure to have lots of tasty children!*"

Nearly insane with anger, Prof. Einstein struggled to get free, but

Lord Carstairs easily overpowered his friend. "Your wish is our command, Great One!" the lord yelled. "Please accept our humble thanks!"

"*Think nothing of it,*" the squid chuckled, giving a merry flip of a tentacle.

Flowing away from the explorers, the squid called out terrible words of power while gesturing with multiple limbs. With a crash of thunder and lightning, a long transdimensional vortex appeared. But then the tunnel contracted into a shimmering oval no thicker than an inch.

Utterly flabbergasted, Prof. Einstein and Lord Carstairs could see downtown London only a few feet away on the other side of the portal. Although it was midnight at the temple, dawn was just starting to break over the city. The full moon was setting behind Big Ben, its long-hidden side now revealed to be the face of a snarling squid. Clattering along, a horse-drawn cab rolled past the magical window without seeming to notice its presence. Strolling on the pavement, a man and woman in formal clothes were laughing about the strange phenomenon in the starry heavens.

"*So this is the mightiest city in the world,*" the squid said, the words punctuated by the clacking of the beak. "*Hmm, really doesn't look like much, but I have to start somewhere.*"

As daintily as a ballerina, the colossus began to step-step-step through the dimensional doorway, crushing the cab flat in the process. On the pavement, the man cursed and the woman screamed in terror.

"*Farewell!*" the squid bellowed, the words echoing slightly as the portal started to close. "*Keep the faith!*"

Without hesitation, Einstein and Carstairs sprinted across the temple, and dove after the departing squid just as the vortex slammed shut.

TWENTY-FOUR

In a wild explosion of colors, Einstein and Carstairs appeared on the London street. The inertia of their dive sent them plowing into the rubbery backside of the colossal squid, and the explorers bounced off to land painfully on cold cobblestones. That was when the men rudely discovered that they were, once more, stark naked.

"You know, sir," Lord Carstairs rumbled, grabbing the opera cloak off the stunned gentleman standing aquiver on the pavement, "this will never become a popular mode of transportation."

"Agreed!" Prof. Einstein muttered, helping his friend rip the cloak in half and wrapping his piece about his middle in the fashion of a Burmese nappy.

Busily munching on the horses, the Squid God ignored their arrival. With a soft burp, it finished the repast and began picking through the ruins of the hansom cab to stuff the dead driver into its parrot-beak mouth.

"*Ummm*!" the squid crooned, the noise echoing along the city street. A dozen windows slammed open in response, angry heads popped out, jaws dropped, screaming commenced, and the windows slammed shut.

"This way, lad," Einstein whispered, dashing into a nearby alley, his skinny shanks moving with surprising speed.

As the explorers zigzagged through the back alleyways of London, the Squid God undulated along the cobblestones to survey its new domain.

So this was the currant pinnacle of civilization, eh? Spurting gas flames dimly illuminated the bumpy streets of stone. The buildings were stacked together with no consideration given to safety or comfort; few trees were in sight, and the smell! There must be hundreds of thousands, if not millions, of people jammed into this dirty city. The air stank of coal soot, and the nearby river was contaminated with sewage and industrial chemicals. Overlaying everything was the stench of sex and unfamiliar drugs. The squid gave itself a little hug out of sheer pleasure. *Lovely!*

Rounding a corner, the monster came to a halt as it spied a crowd of people congregating around a building that fairly reeked with alcohol.

Must be either a tavern or a temple, the squid decided wisely.

"Hey," a pieman cried. "H'its a bloody great octofish!"

Squinting in an attempt to focus her vision, a charwoman gave a hiccup in disagreement. "Nyah, yawr balmy, mate. It's one'a them things they makes chutney outta."

"Oh!" the pieman cried, very impressed. "I never seen a whole one'a them. How do they get 'em into them 'ittle jars?"

"I dunno. Hammers maybe."

"Think it came from the circus?"

Annoyed at their cavalier attitude, the Squid God shot a pillar of flame into the sky, expecting the primitive humans to faint from sheer terror.

Instead, the crowd broke into applause and started cheering.

This gave the demon pause. In its long absence, humanity had obviously become remarkably sophisticated. They were no longer easily swayed by the simple tricks that had served it so well in Dutar. Okay, fair enough.

Hooting like a thousand tortured banshees, the Squid God expanded its eyes and sent out twin death rays to sweep the crowd. Dozens of people exploded into vapor at the contact, and the rest ran shrieking into the night, their cries only adding to the chain of chaos radiating throughout the city.

Watching the growing pandemonium, the Squid God used the tip of a tentacle to wipe away a bead of sweat from its brow. *Whew! Tough crowd.*

Scooping a few of the least dead humans into its mouth, the Squid God messily munched on the bodies as it wriggled along searching for something tastier. The colossal demon paused at the sight of a burnt skeleton of a wooden vessel that was large enough to accommodate a hundred Squid Gods. After a minute of scratching its head, the squid gave a rippling shrug of confusion and moved on. How very odd. He would have to remember to ask somebody about that.

* * *

In the kitchen of the museum, Mary Einstein clumsily lit the gas stove and set the kettle on the flame. It was most inconvenient walking with a cast on her left leg, but she had been very fortunate to receive only a broken bone in the firefight with the squiddies. Most of the other ladies had been seriously wounded and required surgical attention. However, every one of the Squid God worshipers had been killed, except for one fellow disguised as William Owen who escaped with that big black pot of blood. Why in the world the squiddies wanted that, Mary had no idea, but she was sure that it bode ill for England.

For the past two nights, Mary and the few undamaged survivors of the London Explorer's Club, Ladies Auxiliary had stood guard in the museum, but there had been no further attacks. Perhaps there were no more Squid God worshipers in England, or at least in London. Thankfully, ever since the appearance of the burning ark, the police had established a protective cordon around the museum. *Ah well, better late than never.*

Pouring herself a nice cup of tea, Mary started to spoon in some sugar, but then paused to listen to the museum. Had there just been a knock at the side door? Katrina was in town buying some new tigers, and Lady Danvers was standing guard on the rooftop with the portable cannon she called an express rifle, so Mary was alone for the moment. Even with the army of police constables outside, this would be a prime time for the squiddies to attack again.

Again the knock came at the back door, much louder this time.

Lifting the Remington 12 gauge shotgun, Mary warily stomped across the kitchen. "Who is it?" she called out sweetly, trying to sound old and frail as she cocked back the hammers on the shotgun.

"Darling, it's us!" the voice of Lord Carstairs called.

Having been fooled that way before, Mary was supremely suspicious. That certainly sounded like her Benjamin, but there was something different about the voice. *Fool me once, shame on you. Fool me twice, and shoot me for being an idiot, as her uncle liked to say.*

Tightening her grip on the shotgun, Mary carefully flipped over the conversation hatch and peered outside. Dark shadows masked two people standing under the rose arbor. The size and shape of them were correct for her uncle and Lord Carstairs, but there was something odd about their clothing.

"Step into the light," she demanded.

"Actually, I would much rather not," Lord Carstairs demurred.

"That was not a request, sir," Mary stated in a dangerous tone, leveling the shotgun out the hatch.

Raising his hands in surrender, Lord Carstairs stepped quickly to the hatch and placed his face in the opening. Snatching the man's nose, Mary tugged hard, until his eyebrows rose in consternation.

"Oh, I do say," Carstairs murmured.

Releasing the noble proboscis, Mary lowered the shotgun and placed a hand on the bolt, but paused once more. "How did you get past the police?" she demanded.

"Hells bells, girl, I own this property!" Prof. Einstein snapped from the shadows. "Why shouldn't they let me pass?"

"Although they did have a bloody good laugh," Carstairs added with a grumble. "Cheeky bounders."

The professor gave a snort. "Actually, we're the cheeky ones, lad."

"How very droll," the lord drawled sarcastically, glancing sideways. "Have you ever considered vaudeville, sir?"

Scowling, Mary kept her hand on the bolt. Now what was that nonsense all about? Just because it looked and felt like the men was not conclusive proof of identity against the camouflage of a magical glamour.

"What's my middle name?" she demanded, releasing the bolt and fingering the trigger on the weapon.

"You have two, Elizabeth and Victoria," Prof. Einstein snapped in reply, going on tiptoes to peek through the hole. "Both coming from your cousin's step-daughter who died of the flu on your second birthday! There is a scar on your left resembling Bolivia from where the dog bite you, and I once caught you making sand castles inside the Arc of the Covenant. Now open the damn door, please, we're freezing out here!"

Good enough! Lowering the shotgun, Mary pulled back the bolt. "Thank God, you're both alive!" she cried, stiffly limping aside to swing the door wide. "I have been so worried about you both!"

Moving fast, the two men squeezed through the narrow opening and dashed past Mary, sprinting across the kitchen. Automatically assuming that they were being pursued, the woman slammed the door, threw the deadbolt, turned, screamed, and spun about again.

"You're naked!" Mary shouted at the wallpaper.

"Semi-naked," Lord Carstairs corrected, sounding very embarrassed.

"Sorry, lass," the professor said in a husky tone. "Our lack of clothing is entirely an accident of our travels."

There came scurrying sounds, muffled grunts, and the rattle of dishes.

"My dear, your leg!" Lord Carstairs cried out, from the other side of the room. "Are you all right?"

Using the shotgun as a crutch, Mary waved the trifle aside. "A simple fracture of the tibia, nothing serious."

"Really?"

"Well, not serious for me. But it cost the Squid God some twenty worshipers who are now permanent guests of the Royal London Morgue!"

"Good show, lass!" Prof. Einstein added. "See, lad? I told you that she was a wonderful curate!"

"Indeed you did, sir."

"Well, I had help," Mary started, studying the design of the wallpaper. "Decent yet?"

"Semi-decent," Lord Carstairs rumbled.

Turning about very slowly, Mary relaxed slightly at the sight of her uncle covered in one of Katrina's cooking aprons, while Lord Carstairs had draped himself with the tablecloth in the manner of a Greek toga. The dishes on the kitchen table were still trembling from his nimble extraction.

Although thrilled by their return, Mary started to speak, but then found that she could only stare at her uncle. Or rather, whoever this was that sort of resembled her esteemed relative.

"Uncle Felix?" Mary asked hesitantly, swinging her cast forward to awkwardly step toward the man.

"Something wrong, niece?" Prof. Einstein asked timidly, trying to shift the apron to hide his secret tattoo. He always knew that drunken night in the West End would came back to haunt him one day. Damn Dr. Hyde and his silly chemical experiments!

"Your hair!" Mary said, gesturing with a vague wave. "And your face!"

"Yes, what about it?" he demanded, rolling his eyes in an effort to look at his own features.

Reaching into a pocket of her dress, the woman pulled out a small mirror and passed it over. Examining himself in the looking glass, the professor gasped in surprise. His stock of white hair was now glossy black, with just a touch of silver at the temples. His features were the smooth face of a man in his early forties, and curling back a lip revealed a full set of teeth. Even the hole in his ear from being tortured in Rome was repaired! A fast glance down underneath the apron made him gasp in delight. *The tattoo was gone. Hurrah!*

"How is this possible?" Prof. Einstein demanded of nobody in particular.

"Apparently, when your healing spell repaired me, sir, it also rejuvenated the caster," Lord Carstairs said, running a hand over his smooth chin. Every previous scar was gone. "No offense meant, sir, but you were a tad out of control there at the end."

"No offense taken, lad," Einstein replied with a growing smile. "And unless I miss my guess, you've gotten those five years back as well."

"Really?"

"Yes!"

"Splendid!" Overcome with joy, Lord Carstairs gave a whoop of celebration and grabbed the professor. Laughing like loons, the two explorers danced about in the kitchen, rattling the dishes in the cupboard and the silverware in the sideboard.

"Will you two please get dressed!" Mary bellowed, covering her eyes. "This is most unseemly!"

Lurching into action, the men dashed into the hallway and closed the hinged partition.

"Ah, where are the spare travel bags, my dear?" the professor called out from behind the louvered doors.

"In the washroom!" Mary answered, valiantly trying to hide a smile. "I stored the bags there with my own kit in case you summoned me to join you in the field."

"Stout girl!" Lord Carstairs boomed in delight. There came a scuffling sound and then a striking match. "Ah, I have the lamp lit, Professor!"

"Good show, lad," Einstein said. "The washroom is this way."

"After you, sir."

As their voices faded, Mary carefully slid her plaster-coated leg under the table and gratefully sat down in a chair. She took a sip from her cup of tea, only to find it tepid. Then in spite of the situation, she secretly smiled at the memory of the two partially naked men waltzing around the room. She would drink cold tea for that anytime!

Giving the men a few moments of privacy, Mary stiffly rose and set about making sandwiches, and put a fresh kettle on the stove. When the food was ready, she stomped to the hallway door and listened. She could faintly hear the muffled grunts of men getting dressed in a hurry.

"So wherever did you go?" Mary asked loudly. "What happened?"

"Italy first, and then we were transported to another realm, where magic ruled instead of science," Lord Carstairs said emerging from the hallway. He was in safari khaki again, and dripping with firearms. "Aside from that, rather a dull place, actually."

Going to his side, Mary rested a hand on his arm, and Benjamin reciprocated. For a few delicious moments, neither of them spoke, each savoring the wonder and majesty of the other's presence.

"But Uncle is now younger?" Mary asked, breaking the spell. "And you were wounded somehow?"

"Indeed he was, my dear, and very badly," Prof. Einstein said pushing the louvered door aside. His khaki shirt was improperly buttoned and appeared to be a size too small. But the professor was also sporting a small arsenal of lethal ironmongery. "Luckily, I was able to use the local magic to repair him for you."

Suddenly aware of their scandalous position, Lord Carstairs and Mary Einstein lost their smiles and slowly looked at the professor. Their hands still touching, Lord Carstairs blushed and cleared his throat, while Mary tried to speak, but no sound would come.

"Yes-yes, I know, you're in love. Wonderful," the professor said irritably. "Niece, you have my permission to marry. He's a fine man."

"Thank you . . . Uncle," Lord Carstairs said, removing his hand. Then the lord went down on one knee, "My darling, I know this is not the most appropriate moment . . ."

"No, it most certainly is not, Bunny," Mary interrupted, gesturing at the kitchen chairs. "Try formally asking me tomorrow after we have gotten some much needed rest." *Along with a ring. Men, sheesh!* Taking a seat, Mary rubbed her aching hip. "Right now, I want to hear all of the details. How did you stop the Squid God?"

As the lord rose, the professor shuffled his boots, and the two men exchanged covert glances.

"You did stop it," Mary demanded, tapping the shoe on her good foot. "Correct?"

A distant explosion filled the night.

"Library," the professor said urgently.

As quickly as possible the three ran down the hallway and into the next room. Prof. Einstein yanked back the drapes, exposing a panoramic view of London. A goodly portion of the city was on fire and, revealed in the terrible light, was a monstrous squid standing taller than Big Ben. The squid uprooted a small building and shook out the residents to fall into its gaping maw.

"Dear God in Heaven," Mary whispered, clutching the back of a chair for support.

The sound of a large-bore rifle firing came from the roof of the museum, closely followed by several more reports.

"What is that?" Professor Einstein demanded, glancing at the ceiling.

"Sounds like a Holland & Holland .475 Nitro Express," Lord Carstairs stated, cupping an ear. "Old brass, hand loads, using the formula for cordite favored by the Explorers Club."

"So it does, lad," Einstein murmured thoughtfully, although he could not detect any of those details. However, it did sound like a very big gun. "Niece, is Lady Danvers walking our parapet, by any chance?"

Unable to wrest her eyes away from the view of London, Mary simply nodded in reply. "She is standing guard on the widows-walk to watch for any Squid God worshipers," Mary answered, hugging her shotgun. "I have no doubt that she was unpleasantly surprised to spot the infamous squid itself."

With a tingling sensation in his stomach, Prof. Einstein had to admit he was quite impressed. Walking the roof all by herself, eh? That Penelope Danvers was quite a woman!

The flames from the city were growing higher, and the leviathan squid began juggling horses, popping each one into its mouth like gumdrops. Shuddering in revulsion, Lord Carstairs closed the drapes. Placing an arm about Mary, the lord tenderly helped the crippled woman back into the kitchen. A few seconds later Prof. Einstein joined them, his face a grim mask.

"It's a lot larger than it was before," he said, stumbling to the table.

Taking command, Carstairs poured them each a hot cup of tea and everybody drank a round posthaste. It helped, but not much.

"Any whiskey?" Lord Carstairs asked.

Prof. Einstein jerked a thumb. "In the cupboard, lad."

"All gone," Mary countered. "Katrina used it to make a firebomb."

"Egad, did it work?"

"Tied to a coal oil lamp, the results were quite spectacular."

"Good show! I really must remember that trick," the professor said, glancing about the kitchen. "By the way, where is our cook?"

Mary turned a sullen face towards the living room. "Doing some shopping downtown."

The professor glanced in the direction of the library as another explosion came from London.

"Oh dear," he said softly.

From the roof, the H&H Nitro Express rifle fired again and again. Then something rattled down the shingles, the eaves, musically bounced off the gutters and landed on the flagstone walk with the telltale metallic tinkling of spent ammunition.

"What a brave woman," Prof. Einstein said, peering upward. "I really should have married Penny when I had the chance, but such is luck."

"Tommyrot!" Mary snarled, slamming down the cup and cracking the china saucer. "We make our own luck, Uncle. All right, what should we do now?"

"As I see it," the professor said, taking a bite of a cucumber sandwich. "We have two options."

"Three," Lord Carstairs countered, buttering a steaming scone.

"I wasn't counting running away, lad."

"Neither was I."

"Really? Then you go first."

Devouring the pastry, Carstairs picked up a mug of tea and took a deep swallow. Ah, tea! For any true Englishman, it was like blood to a vampire.

"First, we could try to return to the dimension of magic," the lord said, leaning closer. "Procure another magic book and find a way to bring it here with us. Although, I personally think that plan is unworkable."

From outside came the sound of a building crashing, followed by hundreds of screams. In response, the Nitro Express sounded in a thundering double-report of both barrels being fired at the same time.

"I quite agree," Prof. Einstein said, hunching closer. "Now as I see it, due to their ethereal nature, all demonic creatures have a material weakness. Something that binds them to the physical plane. Vampires can be killed by wood. Werewolves with a silver bullet–"

"Actually," Carstairs interrupted with a delicate cough, and flexing the fingers of his left hand into a fist. "Werewolves have two weaknesses."

"Really?" the professor asked. "Sounds fascinating, lad, but tell me about it later."

"Of course."

"Anyway, our second option would consist of systematically hitting the squid with weapons constructed of every chemical compound we have. By trial and error, we may eventually discover something useful."

"I think it extremely unlikely that we'd discover anything soon enough to be of any benefit to London," Mary said, nervously scratching under the cast, her exposed toes wiggling in harmony. "What's our third option?"

Draining his mug, Lord Carstairs brushed the crumbs from his shirt. "There is always the chance that the military will kill the beast. The British Army is the best equipped, most dedicated fighting force on the face of the Earth!"

The mournful wail of a fire engine joined the cacophony of distant noises. Another boom came from the roof, followed by more rattling cartridges tossed away.

"No, seriously," Mary said urgently. "What can we do?"

From the very depths of his soul, Prof. Einstein heaved a mighty sigh. "I honestly have absolutely no idea, Niece."

Without comment, Mary reached out to clasp Benjamin's hand, her dainty fingers almost lost in his grip. Toying with a spoon, the professor put an ungentlemanly elbow on the table and listened to the growing sounds of the destruction of London.

"This could be the beginning of the end of the world," Prof. Einstein admitted glumly.

* * *

Charging up the pavement, the breathless police constable slammed open the door to Metropolitan Central.

"Oy!" he shouted to the boisterous mob of policemen milling about inside. "There's a bloody great squid tearing up Waterloo Road!"

"We know," a burly sergeant said, tossing over a carbine rifle.

Making the catch, the constable could only stare aghast at the weapon. He hadn't touched a rifle since training days!

"This also," the sergeant added, passing a bulky shoulder bag made of military canvas.

The bag was surprisingly heavy and the constable opened it to discover a dozen boxes of ammunition. *Bloody hell!*

"What are my orders, sir?" the constable managed to ask, while working the bolt to load the weapon.

"Maintain order, and prepare for an evacuation," the sergeant said brusquely. "Plus, shoot any looters. And if you get the chance, pop a few rounds towards the Loch Ness monster."

In ragged stages, the room became totally quiet.

"Cor blimey, tain't really, is it?" somebody asked, above his knocking knees.

Breaking open his Webley revolver to check the load, the old sergeant scowled. "Who knows? I don't care if it comes from Mars or the Bermuda Triangle! Our task is civilian control. The military will do that nasty up a proper treat."

The faces and hearts of the constables lightened at that pronouncement. Yes, indeed. What invader could possibly stand against the might of the Royal British Army!

TWENTY-FIVE

Ripping the roof from a warehouse on College Street, the Squid God gobbled the raw fish and sides of beef, using two ropy limbs to shovel the food non-stop into its mouth. *Ah, until you come back, you never realize how much you miss home cooking!*

On the ground, a group of shouting men smashed lanterns onto barrels of oil and soon the warehouse was ablaze. The shouting changed to cheering as the fire spread, and the disgruntled squid knocked down a burning wall and sadly moved on. *Fried food? Bleh.*

Lumbering across the Humberford Bridge with bits of stonework splashing into the river in its wake, the squid reached the Charing Cross embankment. Lifting an overloaded row boat from the shore, it slurped down the sailors like an oyster from its shell, then swallowed the boat as well for a bit of roughage. Ignoring the Authors Club as unworthy, the squid ate a milk cart, complete with driver, horses, and the glass bottles, and then proceed down the street until it encountered Cleopatra's Needle. *Hmm.*

Languidly, it wrapped a tentacle about the lower half and pushed. The stone cracked in half, and the squid began using the monument as a pick to clear something caught in its beak. For some reason this seemed to annoy the locals more than anything it had done so far. *How very odd.*

At breakneck speed, a steam locomotive charged straight at the squid as it started across the railroad tracks. On board, the engineer and stoker together shoveled more coal into the roaring engine already under full steam, the boiler ready to burst from the mounting pressure. Rocketing along the tracks, the juggernaut was almost upon the Squid God, when the monster flicked out several tentacles and snatched the train off the tracks. With a hoot of delight, the squid grasped the main driving wheels and chuckled as the locomotive spun about like a child's whirligig. Soon tiring of the toy, the squid gave a twitch and the locomotive went sailing away high above the city.

Seeing no more trains to play with, the squid wriggled further along the river, eating horses, people, and small buildings in a non-stop orgy of inhuman gluttony.

* * *

On a main street, iron shod hooves clattered on the cobblestones as a full company of Royal Dragoons rode into view. Pausing at an intersection, the white-faced riders straightened their green coats, leveled their deadly six-yard long lances, and prepared to charge. Frowning, the major stared through field glasses to find the enemy, then almost inhaled his moustache at the sight of the squid.

"We're to use lances and swords against *that*?" the major screamed. "Are those fools on Downing Street mad?"

Without waiting for an answer, the fat major turned and bellowed, "Dragoons, retreat!"

"You stinking coward!" a corporal screamed, releasing his reins. Drawing a pistol, the soldier shot the officer dead.

"Dragoons!" the corporal bellowed, waving the smoking gun. "Charge!"

However, the trumpeter sounded retreat anyway. Unfortunately, the lancers and soldiers were busy fighting to keep control of their mounts, the horses screaming and bucking in raw terror at the grotesque sight of the towering squid now looming above them . . .

* * *

A major on a nearby rooftop grimaced at the sight of chaos below. *Damn the cavalry!* "Lieutenant," he shouted, "have the 104th and the 57th take positions on these roofs! Horses are worse than useless. The Highlanders will have to hold the road! Send a runner to the field headquarters; we'll need bloody cannon to kill this thing!"

Blaring bugles relayed the orders, and soldiers raced to obey.

Meanwhile, the troopers on the street had begun firing upon the monster as it ripped apart an orphanage searching for a little snack.

"Company, cease independent firing!" a color sergeant shouted furiously, his bristle moustache quivering. "You will fire upon my orders! Form two columns for volley fire!"

With oft-practiced ease, the soldiers quickly formed a double line across the road, leaving the pavement clear for the hordes of civilians to run past them.

"It's the apocalypse!" a man shouted, waving a Bible.

Another fellow knocked him down, stole the Bible, and was promptly shot by a constable.

Hundreds more people streamed by in every conceivable stage of dress. A clean chimney sweep, a butcher with cleaver in hand, a bare breasted woman, a gang of ragged children, and a group of men and women carrying a tall man holding a whiskey crock.

"Wha' y'mean it's really there?" the drunk demanded. "Shitfire! Leg it, lads!"

"We are, mate!" shouted one of the people carrying him. "Now shut up and keep still!"

The crowd seemed to take heart as they saw the soldiers standing at the ready, and many gave a 'hurrah' as they passed by at a full run.

"Steady on," the sergeant ordered in a soothing voice. "Doomsday, or not, you'll follow orders, or answer to me."

Most of the civilians were past the soldiers as the squid finished rooting through the cellar. The creature consumed one last pit bull, gave a polite burp, and turned in the direction of the soldiers.

Ah, the demon squid thought gleefully. *I just love a man in uniform.*

"Fire!" the lieutenant cried, and the front row of guns boomed. "Advance!"

In sharp response, the first line knelt to reload, while the second line took aim.

"Fire!" the major cried, and the second row of guns discharged in perfect unison.

"Advance!" The second line stepped in front of the first, knelt, and began to reload. The first line stood.

"Fire! Advance!"

"Fire! Advance!"

"Fire! Advance!"

In wry amusement, the Squid God watched the maneuvers. Sure and steady, the troopers moved up the street, their rounds hitting it with machine precision. The rooftop gunners joined the battle, and a series of continuous volleys now struck the hellbeast from every direction. Then even more troops joined the assault. The volley became a barrage, a fusillade, a bombardment!

Furrowing its mottled brow in concentration, the squid roughly calculated that the soldiers would march into the range of its tentacles in five minutes. That was rather impressive for a suicide ritual. So it relaxed to watch the show and wait for dinner to arrive.

* * *

In the War Office at Whitehall, the general in charge of Her Majesty's Royal Forces raised his head from the war map as striding footsteps sounded from the hallway. Then the door slammed aside and in strode Prime Minister Benjamin Disraeli.

"Well?" Disraeli snapped, sidestepping a group of scurrying clerks. "What the devil is happening out there? Report!"

"The situation is poor, Prime Minister," General McTeague said, glancing out the nearest window. "The civilians are stampeding and rioting. The police have been armed to help stop any looting. Five thousand troops fill the city and the reserves have been activated. The Horse Guards have been divided, half sent to help patch any holes in our defensive arc, and the rest are on the way to Buckingham Palace."

"Sounds good," the Prime Minister said resolutely. "Well done!"

"No, it is not," McTeague countered angrily. "We had established emergency medical facilities at several locations, but so far there has been no need for them."

"How can that be? That monstrosity has ravaged several square miles of the city!"

"Because, Mr. Disraeli, the creature devours anybody it encounters. There are no wounded."

That somber observation caused the Prime Minister to signal for a chair, and a corporal delivered one posthaste.

"What about deploying the Navy?" Disraeli asked sitting down heavily.

Surrounded by a mob of scurrying military aides, General McTeague walked over to a large map of London tacked to the wall. "Four iron-clad gun boats, two destroyers, and ten gunnery ships are on the way from the yards. As you can see, the thing is still close enough to the river that the Navy should be able to hit it fairly easily with their large guns."

"Wouldn't that simply drive the creature inland?"

"No, Prime Minister. Because we have already set cannon positions at St. Clements, Blackfriars, Leicester, and Charing Cross," the general said, indicating the positions on the map. "The monster will be caught in the crossfire, without any place to run."

"Excellent!"

Scowling darkly, McTeague returned to the strategy table. Colored markers and tiny flags showing troop locations covered the map of London, with a large ball of twine sitting prominently near the Strand

Hotel to mark the current spot of The Thing. They had markers for German gunships, Russian balloons, even American Calvary, but who could have foreseen this?

"I only hope this is enough," the general added softly.

"Whatever do you mean?" Prime Minster Disraeli asked, accepting a cup of tea from an aide. "It sounds like a rather good plan!"

"But you haven't seen this bloody thing, sir," the general said, gazing at the smoky city. "And I have."

* * *

A sweaty officer slashed downward with a saber and the blindfolded draft horses were cut free from the wheeled cannon. Another officer shouted orders, and teams of frantic soldiers positioned the weapon on the road before St. Clements Church, while privates carefully unloaded 12-inch shells from a straw laden lorry. There were forty assorted cannon filling the intersection in a broad semi-circle, including ship cannon, garrison pieces, siege guns, and even some massive field artillery.

Dozens more wagons were constantly arriving, carrying shells and powder, even though there were already enough explosives at the barricade to sink Gibraltar. The big guns, garrison and siege class, were aimed west on the Strand, the monster's most likely avenue of approach. The ship's cannons, backed by field artillery, were pointed northwest on Aldwych and south on Milford Lane, just in case.

Taking a brief swig from a canteen, the colonel in charge of the artillery post knew that similar batteries had been formed at other critical intersections, and he could only guess at the defenses of Buckingham Palace. Thank God the animal was heading in the wrong direction.

Soon stripped empty of their deadly cargo, the lorries were rolled into position and toppled over to form a crude barricade. Razor-sharp pikes were placed in clusters between the wheel spokes, and barrels of fulminating guncotton with fast-burning fuses were hidden under crates of nails.

Several blocks away, a small building collapsed and the Squid God began picking through the rubble.

"Does that bloody thing do anything else but eat and kill?" a sergeant demanded of nobody in particular.

"Not so far, Sarge," a corporal replied. "You would think by now it might need to use the loo."

"It's getting bigger," a private said, shifting his grip on a Henry rifle. "The more it eats, the larger it becomes. Not fatter, mind you, bigger in size."

The other soldiers paled at that news, but continued their work with a renewed determination.

"Bring about the other guns!" the colonel bellowed, ignoring the trickle of sweat running down his back.

Moving in unison, grim soldiers swarmed over the other cannons and swung them around until every weapon was pointing at the monster mollusk.

"In position and loaded, sir," a lieutenant said with a salute.

"Fire!" the colonel shouted, brandishing a fist.

The barrage of shells hit the squid, along with several nearby buildings, the missed rounds blowing off chunks of granite and liberally peppering the creature with shrapnel. When the smoke cleared, the squid was dripping green blood. Strangely, it appeared to have only taken damage from the shrapnel and none at all from the shells that had hit it directly.

Radiating a monstrous fury, the Squid God turned to glare hatefully at the massed troops. Once more, the death rays lanced from its bulging eyes, and the first row of men simply exploded into a bloody mist.

Frantically grabbing shells and shot, the rest of the terrified troops quickly reloaded. The colonel tried to speak but could only manage a high-pitched squeak. His batsman handed over a canteen of Scotch whiskey and the officer took a quick swallow. Invigorated, the officer now managed to bellow, "F-fire all g-g-guns!"

In ragged stages, the cannons loudly spoke again. This time, every shell precisely hit the oncoming squid and created no visible damage. Hooting a war chant, the squid increased its speed and, as it moved over the barricade, the hidden barrels of guncotton were detonated. As the blast filled the street, the whole body of the squid visibly rippled, its eyes bugged out, and wisps of smoke shot out of its previously unnoticed ears. The behemoth wobbled, then it weebled. The cadre of soldiers held its breath. Then the squid's eyes uncrossed and swiveled in their direction. Raising two tentacles to expose its underside like a saucy French can-can dancer, the squid then spat a cloud of nails out of its beak, the hellstorm of bent iron cutting down squads of soldiers. Men shrieked, gunpowder charges detonated, and the squid advanced.

Engulfing the intersection with its tentacles, the squid cut off any possible escape by pulling up chunks of the roadway. Completely trapped, but not yet defeated, the British soldiers bravely emptied handguns and rifles into the beast, while others used swords, lances, and pikes.

Quite unaffected by the metal weapons, the squid simply swept the struggling men into its insatiable maw with long fluid motions. Munching the tasty treats, the squid considered the actions of the humans. *If they were making this big a fuss, then it would seem logical that the ornate building over by the small lake must be where their leader lived. Excellent! Eating the emperor would add greatly to the confusion and fun.*

When no more soldiers remained, the titanic squid licked its beak clean and headed in a westerly direction, wriggling straight towards Buckingham Palace.

* * *

From the second-story window of a private home, a tall thin man contemplated the increasing devastation.

"Doctor, come quickly!" he shouted, laying aside his Meerschaum pipe. "A giant squid appears to be ravaging London!"

"Come off it, old man," a somber voice replied from inside the flat. "It's just another of your cocaine delusions."

"No, I swear! A colossal squid!" the thin fellow said, peering at the monster through a spyglass. "Dutarian, I'd say. About four thousand years old."

"Nonsense!" a fat man snorted, waddling in from the other room. "Now how the hell could you possible know its age from just looking at the thing?"

"Elementary, my dear John. You see–"

But the dissertation was interrupted by the arrival of a steam locomotive dropping out of the sky and crashing onto the apartment. The meteoric impact flattened the entire building, leaving only a group of howling urchins standing in the street and the smell of fresh baked bread.

* * *

On the other side of London, a platoon of soldiers struggled to carry a lumpy, canvas-wrapped object along a dank alley behind Morley's Hotel on Trafalgar Square. The item was larger than a pregnant cow, and seemed heavier than original sin. Over the rooftops of the brick buildings lining this street, only the smallest part of the monster squid could be seen.

Very briefly, Lt. Curtis checked a map. "This is it. The Lion and Eagle tavern. Sergeant, break down that door."

A single hard kick from Color Sergeant MacScott rendered the portal passable and the platoon of soldiers swarmed inside. The storage room was empty, and the bar itself was completely deserted. There was money lying on the counter, and a spilled beer still dripped onto the sawdust floor.

Crossing to the front shutters, the lieutenant gently swung them open just enough to see several of the mottled tentacles of the invader filling the street outside. Perfect!

"Move these tables," Lt. Curtis whispered, pointing around the bar. "There, and over there! Quickly now, lads! Double time!"

In short order, the platoon created a clear area before the window and their cargo was set down with grunts of great relief.

Taking a small can from a canvas bag at his side, Corporal Moorehouse went about oiling the hinges on the shutters, while the rest of the platoon busied itself cutting the ropes and peeling back the canvas to reveal the shiny mechanism of a brand new Gatling gun.

Supported by a heavy tripod of cast iron, the massive weapon consisted of a cylindrical firing chamber fronted by eight barrels joined in a circle. An open box on top fed in the shells, and a large crack on the side operated the deathdealer. In the light of the coal-oil lamps, the superweapon gleamed like a gift from Heaven.

"Bring some barrels from the cellar," the lieutenant ordered. "They will offer a bit of protection from flying glass."

Turning about, Curtis added, "You four! Take cover behind the bar, be ready to give protective rifle fire in case of a mishap."

The soldiers moved with all due haste, and started loading their weapons.

Stepping close to the window, Sgt. MacScott tugged nervously on his muttonchops. "What is the plan of attack, sir?" he asked softly.

"We are going to cut off a limb," Lt. Curtis said, watching the work in progress. "Here now, tighten that bolt, lad, or the first round will be our last!"

Scratching under his cap, the sergeant seemed ill at ease. "Begging your pardon, sir, but is this wise? A wounded animal will be much more dangerous."

"It's heading for Buckingham Palace and the Queen! And we do not intend to wound the beast, but kill it! These bullets are coated with an anti-coagulant."

Furrowing his brow, MacScott paused before replying, "But of course, sir. I see."

"The blood won't clot and the creature will soon bleed to death," Lt. Curtis explained.

"Bally good show!" Sgt. MacScott cried with a snort, then quickly lowered his voice. "Our science boffins really pulled a wowser out of their hat with that trick!"

Kneeling on the sawdust, the lieutenant helped a private attach the ammunition box. The brassy cartridges were streaked with an oily substance. "Actually, the chemical compound is a German invention," Curtis replied. "Something they came up with during The Troubles."

"Oh," Sgt. MacScott frowned. "Well, jolly good idea, anyway, sir."

In short order, the top hatch was closed and locked in place, the bolt thrown, and the handle freed from its mooring.

Outside the tavern, the sounds of battle steadily increased until they became an endless roar.

"Ready for operation, lieutenant," Corporal Moorehouse stated, giving a crisp salute.

Standing and brushing the sawdust from his pants, Lt. Curtis primly tightened the chinstrap of his helmet. "Proceed, Mr. Moorehouse."

Putting his back into the task, the corporal began wildly cranking the huge handle. With a loud ratcheting, the eight barrels started to rotate. A split second later, the top muzzle vomited forth a stuttering, banging stream of high velocity lead. With a mighty crash, the windows disintegrated and the tentacle in front of them was torn apart under the strident fury of 400 rounds a minute!

* * *

Ripping a gargoyle off a nearby building to toss at a particularly bold cannon crew, the squid felt an itch at the base of tentacle four and flexed a muscle to remove the minor annoyance.

* * *

A battering ram of flesh came crashing into the bar, toppling the gun and crushing the soldiers as it plowed through to reach the alleyway.

"Retreat!" Lt. Curtis shouted, drawing his saber.

Unstoppably, the tentacle smashed into the bar sending bottles crashing and bodies flying. Trapped in the corner, a soldier shot his rifle at the thrashing limb, and accidentally hit an oil lamp. Covered with flames, the tentacle quickly withdrew, destroying more tables and men in the process. As the ceiling timbers groaned and the walls began to collapse, the few remaining soldiers fled from the ruined pub, shooting their weapons at the thing every step of the way.

Reaching the alley, the soldiers took stock of their losses, counted the dead, and reloaded with professional efficiency.

"Hellanddamnation," Corporal Moorehouse stormed, angrily throwing his hat to the cobblestones. "Doesn't that beastie have any weakness?"

"Fire," a panting private volunteered, leaning against the wall. "It . . . don't like . . . fire."

"Explain that, old son," Moorehouse demanded, and the soldier complied with what few details he had witnessed.

Slowly standing tall, the resolute corporal smacked a fist into his palm. "By Gadfrey, if only we had some kind of Greek fire thingy to hose the monster down with!" he raged.

On the other side of the burning tavern, the squid moved along the street, always accompanied by screaming and booming cannons.

"An 'ose," a private echoed, rubbing his chin. "What 'bout a fire hengine loaded with coal oil stead of wat'r?"

Bursting into laughter, Corporal Moorehouse clapped the man on the shoulder. "Brilliant, my son! We'll save London yet and it'll be the Victoria Cross for the lot of us! Come on, boys!"

Grinning like fiends, the soldiers took off with hands on their hats and spread out to search for the nearest fire station.

* * *

Lacy white clouds lazily moved past the British hot air balloon, HMS *Cloud Runner.* The balloon was draped with a colorful Union Jack and stout netting that was lashed with ropes to a simple wicker basket.

Inside the basket were two British soldiers, several wicker hampers, and a pressurized tank connected to a burner unit situated underneath the open bottom of the balloon. A quivering gauge on the tank showed the pressure of its gaseous contents, and a hissing flame jetted up from the burner to force a column of superheated air into the taut balloon. An actual flying machine, *Cloud Runner* was the marvel of the age, and the most deadly weapon in the renowned British arsenal of scientific war machines.

As the balloon drifted leisurely along on the afternoon breeze, Major Braithwaite carefully shifted his balance in the gondola and scanned the horizon with binoculars. Meanwhile, PFC. Youngerford notched a steel-tipped quarrel into a military crossbow and prepared to shoot.

"Ah, here he comes. Tethering line, ready?" the major asked, one hand on the wicker rim of the basket.

Angling against the wind, the private carefully adjusted the aim of his heavy crossbow. "Aye, aye, Skipper!" Youngerford answered. The Royal Air Corps wasn't really part of the Navy, but using salty nautical terms made him feel better.

"Then do it, lad," Major Braithwaite ordered brusquely, lowering the binoculars.

Giving a nod, PFC. Youngerford pressed the release lever. With a sharp twang, the crossbow bolt whizzed through the air to thump into a tree trunk in the park near the statue of Lord Nelson. As the line grew taut, the balloon stopped with a gentle bounce.

Although greatly pleased, Major Braithwaite did not compliment the shot since superb marksmanship was why the lad was here. Well, that and the fact that he was the only applicant who hadn't gotten airsick during training.

The smoky city of London sprawled below the HMS *Cloud Runner*, and madness seemed to rule the streets. Only Trafalgar Square was strangely empty of civilians or soldiers, and the major suspected a trap for the squid.

Well, it wouldn't be needed after they were finished with the nasty bugger! Braithwaite thought, without fear of contradiction. *By Gadfrey, he used to eat mounds of fried squid every Saturday while he watched the local shinty game. And now one was smashing up the capital of the kingdom? Unacceptable!*

Raising the binoculars once more, Major Braithwaite adjusted the focus and swept the scene for details. Small fires were burning everywhere, many buildings seemed to be missing, and there was general destruction left in the wake of the gigantic squid. Looking further afield, Braithwaite saw hordes of civilians choking the streets as they tried to get away. Only a single plump woman dressed like a cook stood her ground near an exotic pet shop and was firing a pistol at the titanic beast. *Good show, miss!*

However, even at this height Major Braithwaite could hear the shouts and screams of the population, along with the sounds of continuous gunfire and explosions. The major gave a weary sigh. Not so very long ago, a similar London scene had caused him to join the army in the first place. Adjusting the field glasses, Braithwaite frowned. How deuced odd. He should have been able to spot Cleopatra's Needle from this height. Was he facing the wrong direction?

"Skipper, the monster has almost reached the square!" PFC. Youngerford said with calm urgency.

"Why so it has, lad," Braithwaite replied, watching the city below. "Give me a reading on our height, please!"

Leaning dangerously out of the bobbing basket, the private read the markings on the tether rope. "One hundred yards, sir."

"Good show. Then cut me a ten, and a six second fuse, and hop to it!"

"Aye, aye, sir!" Kneeling alongside a wicker hamper, Youngerford brought out a roll of stiff green cord. Using military scissors, he neatly trimmed the fuse to the needed lengths. Closing the hamper, the private went to a wicker basket near a wicker chair. Choosing several dynamite bombs from the array inside, he oh-so-carefully inserted the fuses. To save space and weight in the *Cloud Runner*, there were no sandbags attached as ballast to the hot air balloon, the bombs served that purpose. After the mission was completed, the aero-pilots would simply turn off the gas jet and float back to the Earth like a homesick soap bubble.

With a thundering crash of masonry, the squid oozed into Trafalgar Square, the street churning with tentacles and dotted with explosions. Petulantly, the colossus began ripping apart the buildings, but it found them all empty. Obviously, the prey had already fled.

Snorting at the obvious distress of the monster, Major Braithwaite lowered his binoculars. "Cigars," he ordered brusquely.

Removing a pair of panatelas from an inside coat pocket, PFC. Youngerford passed one to his commander. Striking matches, the soldiers lit the cigars and puffed the tips to a bright cherry red. Exhaling smoke through his nose, the major looked over the arsenal of deathdealers and made his selection.

"We'll start with a brace of the short-fused dynamite sticks," he decided. "No, make that the iron balls. Those will give it a nice dose of hot shrapnel. We can then follow up with a couple of bottles of nitroglycerin to widen the wound and then we'll finish it off with a steady pounding of dynamite, six stick groupings, 90%, waterproof fuse, for deep internal damage."

Supremely confident, Major Braithwaite puffed on the cigar and grinned in satisfaction, "Then back to barracks in time for dinner and hurrahs."

"Aye, aye, sir!" Youngerford cried eagerly, rushing to the task. His hands became a blur of activity.

"Steady on, private! We'll do this by the numbers," the major chided formally. "Now, ready one and two, for my mark."

"Ready, sir," PFC. Youngerford said, moistening a finger. "Wind is south by southeast, two knots."

Inhaling sharply, Major Braithwaite grabbed the central array of ropes supporting the balloon above. "Light the fuses . . ." he ordered slowly. "And drop them . . . now!"

* * *

Strolling along the Strand, the Squid God had paused to beat a dead horse in order to tenderize the snack, when a thunderous explosion occurred on top of its head.

Eh? What in Dutar was that? Glancing upward, the squid saw the hovering balloon and wicker basket. *A flying house?*

Quite puzzled, the colossal monster studied the weird apparition until something was tossed overboard to land directly between its eyes. There followed a loud explosion. *Oh, just more enemies.* Giving a hoot of amusement, the squid gestured with a tentacle and threw a lance of fire at the floating annoyance.

The distance was too great for the magical fire to reach the balloon, but it did ignite the wicker basket hanging underneath.

Encased in flames, the mooring line burned through and the *Cloud Runner* drifted away on the morning breeze. Beating at the spreading fire with their jackets, the British aero-pilots tried to keep the blaze from reaching the basket of bombs and the pressurized tank of natural gas.

The blast lit up the sky for miles.

* * *

Standing on the roof of the Admiralty Building, a team of Army Engineers watched the defeat of the Royal Air Corps with some serious dismay. On the streets, a battalion of troopers jogged into the square, keeping a constant stream of rifle fire at the squid, which followed along behind, eating any stragglers or heroes.

Near the edge of the roof of the Admiralty Building, a team of technicians was working feverishly to assemble a metal framework that rather resembled an oversized coat rack. However, resting against the rack were twenty-four, state-of-the-art, Congreve black powder rockets. Each Congreve was a full yard long, thick as a haunch of meat, and situated on top of a wooden pole two yards long that it used as a stabilizer.

"Check elevation," an officer commanded brusquely.

Only a short distance away, the squid was nibbling on the towering stone arch erected to honor the Admiralty. In astonishment, the officers watched as the behemoth tore the top of the monument free and placed the archway on its head as a sort of hat. The squid turned about, almost as if searching for a mirror to check the fit.

"Insolent dog!" the officer cried, thumbs tucked into his gunbelt. "What is the wind, please?"

"South by southeast, two knots," a corporal replied.

Doffing its granite chapeau, the squid began to wriggle in their direction.

"Ready-aim-lock-fire!" the colonel shouted as a single word.

With shaking hands, privates lit the fuses and ducked. Spraying sparks and clouds of thick black smoke, the mighty Congreve rockets streaked across the city to hit the squid with satisfying accuracy. The steel-tipped rockets punched through the monster and burst out the other side. The iron-tipped missiles burrowed deep inside the creature to detonate, but only produced a sort of rude burping effect.

However, the barbed anti-ship rockets sank into the squid and stayed there, securely anchored by their hooks designed to entangle the rigging of an enemy vessel. The attached mooring lines were sturdy steel chains bolted to the granite cornerstone of the Admiralty Building's foundation.

"Ah ha, now we have you!" a major cried in delight. "It's trapped like a rat in a whatchamacallit."

"A rat trap, sir?" a private bravely asked.

"Exactly!"

Ever so gently, the squid probed at the exit wounds with a few tentacles. With their jaws dropping, the Army Engineers watched in dismay as the wounds began to close and soon were gone.

Now turning to face the soldiers atop the Admiralty Building, the squid formed a mouth around each chain and started sucking them inside like cooked spaghetti. As the cornerstone was yanked away, the building began to collapse underneath them. With sad faces, the Army Engineers did not say a word. There was really nothing they could say.

* * *

In stunned horror, Prime Minister Disraeli watched as the Admiralty Building broke apart and tumbled down into a pile of stones and rubble. Closing the curtains, Disraeli adjusted his morning coat, smoothed his hair, and briskly walked out of the War Room and down the main corridor of Buckingham Palace.

Armed guards were everywhere, Beefeaters mixing with Royal Marines, Dragoons, and common foot soldiers. But each trooper in turn passed the PM without question. A Gatling gun was being assembled in the middle of an intersection, and doors were being nailed shut everywhere.

Little good those will do, Disraeli mentally admonished. *But it was always important to keep the troops busy, even when the work was pointless.*

Reaching the main dining hall, the stiffly formal guards saluted at the approach of the Prime Minister and threw open the double doors.

"Your Majesties," Prime Minister Disraeli said, entering the royal dinning hall and giving a bow.

Seated at the extremely long table stacked with food, was a short dumpy woman in a plain black dress and a gold crown, and a tall smarmy man in a spotlessly clean military uniform.

In casual concern, the two glanced from the staggering breakfast repast of eggs, toast, bacon, sausage, potatoes, kippers, steak, roast quail, smoked ham, a roasted turkey, grilled tomatoes, fried mushrooms, porridge, oatmeal, coffee, tea, milk, biscuits, butter, scones, and a hundred different types of jam.

"Has the animal been killed yet?" Queen Victoria asked, stirring the

India tea in her Royal Dalton cup with an Irish silver spoon.

"No, your majesty. In fact, I fear the creature is almost upon us," Prime Minister Disraeli said with some force in his voice. "Once again, I strongly recommend evacuation to Scotland."

"Out of ze question," Prince Albert snorted, holding half a sausage on a fork. He did an excellent impersonation of a rutting pig before adding, "Ve stay und fight!"

Looking up from the table, Queen Victoria paused in the act of breaking the yolk of her egg. "Oh dear," she said. For a moment, the Prime Minister was unable to tell whether she was reacting to the situation or to the broken yolk. "Then I suppose we must use the Black Squad."

"Vunderbar!" Albert shouted eagerly, nearly bouncing in his chair. German by heritage, the prince-consort fairly tingled at the prospect of someone else doing battle. "Let us show dot monster vhat ve English are made of!"

A true diplomat, Prime Minister Disraeli merely arched an eyebrow and dutifully replied, "Quite so, my liege. The Black Squad it is."

* * *

A few blocks away from the palace were the parade grounds of the Palace Horse Guard. Behind a tall brick wall, impatient soldiers milled about a stable that oddly smelled of motor oil and coal dust.

"By thunder, I can't stand it!" Sgt. John Barta raged, kicking a spanner across the stable. "That thing is out there destroying London and we sit here on our duffs!"

Muttering agreement, the soldiers snapped their suspenders and stomped about, much too full of energy to sit still.

With a loud crash, the stable doors slammed open and in walked a young lieutenant swinging a swagger stick.

"Ten-shun!" Sgt. Barta cried out, standing at attention.

Regardless of what they were doing, all of the other soldiers instantly did the same.

"At ease, men," Lt. Stephen Donaldson said, walking across the straw-free floor. "What is our status, Sergeant Barta?"

"Sir!" the sergeant shouted, giving a crisp salute. "All units are fueled, armed, and ready to go, sir. I have taken the liberty of ordering the crews to begin stoking the boilers."

The lieutenant narrowed his eyes. "Have you now?" Lt. Donaldson said sternly. "Well, sergeant, since you are so bloody eager to be off. . . ."

Knowing he had seriously overstepped his authority, the sergeant braced himself for a formal denouncement, swiftly followed by getting his arse chewed off in private. But instead, the lieutenant laughed and slapped him on the back.

". . . I suppose we shall have just to go and stomp that squid into jelly!" Lt. Donaldson announced with a fierce grin. "The word just came from Buckingham Palace. We're to engage the creature immediately!"

Wildly cheering, the soldiers threw their hats into the air. Some hugged, others brandished fists at the sky, while one Welsh fellow broke into an impromptu jig.

"All right, my roughriders, mount up!" Lt. Donaldson called, tightening the chinstrap on his plumed helmet. "Soon enough, that bleeding thing will meet the greatest fighting force ever forged by the entire human race."

"The Black Squad!" the soldiers cheered defiantly.

TWENTY-SIX

Shouting hurrahs, the soldiers and officers of the Black Squad raced to the tents at the rear of the stable. As the soldiers separated into teams, Lt. Donaldson and Sgt. Barta joined the troops heading for the first tent.

As the men of Alpha Team darted through the canvas flap, they slapped the shiny metal oval for good luck before stepping through. Once inside, the soldiers moved to their stations with subdued gestures. Space in the dome was at a premium for the twelve-man crew.

Crossing the corrugated iron floor, several of them paused to grab tools or insulated gloves from pegs welded to the riveted iron wall that curved upward to form the high domed ceiling. Clanking and clamoring, various machines filled the aft portion of the dome. In the center of the strange room was a trio of huge ball bearings set in a protective ironwork cage. At the front was a long curved window with a complex control panel and three high-backed chairs.

Turning around from the third seat, a sergeant in grimy overalls nodded in greeting, his hands never leaving the controls.

"She's ready to go, sir," the sergeant-engineer stated proudly. "We've got plenty of steam, fresh water, and coal, sir. Stocked to the gills, we are."

"Thank you, Chief Higgins," Lt. Donaldson replied, glancing around professionally. Everything seemed to be shipshape. "Carry on."

The other soldiers settled themselves into the chairs at their battle stations, with two going through an alcove at the rear of the machine. Shifting their gunbelts about, Lt. Donaldson and Sgt. Barta took the vacant chairs at the control board and strapped themselves in tight. Very tight. Nobody ever made the mistake of leaving the harness loose more than once.

Humming a battle tune, Lt. Donaldson worked the levers and dials on the board. "By the numbers, gentlemen!" he called, over a shoulder. "Sharply now, lads!"

"Boiler at 3 point 2 atmospheres!" a private shouted.

"Electric generator, smooth!" a corporal shouted.

"Gyroscope, stable!" a private whispered, massaging his sore throat.

"Pistons, primed!" an engineer shouted.

Sgt. Barta bellowed, nearly drowning out the growing thumps from the machinery in the rear of the dome. "We are good to go, at your command, *shar!*"

Moving his hands with the grace of a concert pianist, the lieutenant deftly began throwing switches. Indicators became illuminated on the control board, gauges flicked into life, and several small panels began to radiate a soft glow.

"Half power, Chief Higgins, and watch the oil flow to number three piston," Lt. Donaldson said, twisting a brass rod to unlock it before plunging the control deep into the board. "Beginning primary sequence . . . now!"

Through the front window, the lieutenant watched as the interior of the stable smoothly flowed past them. Reaching the outside, Donaldson turned the dome about to watch the other three tents glide from the barn like circus ghosts.

"We're going hard!" Lt. Donaldson announced, touching a button.

Now the view in the window rose dramatically, and he could see the other tents lifting ten yards into the air, the canvas sheets sliding off the shiny machines underneath. Based upon the original design of the Venusian invaders, each machine was a flat-bottomed dome set on a tripod of jointed metal legs that ended in huge splayed disks.

Some refugees and soldiers passing by in the littered streets stopped to point and cry out in horror. A man, wearing only his nightgown and top hat, jerked to a halt at the sight that had been filling his nightmares since The Troubles strode through London destroying everything they found.

"Ye gods, they're back!" the man screamed, clutching at his chest.

Turning away from the rampaging squid, a hundred soldiers raised their rifles to fire at the Venusian war machine.

"No, by gum, look!" a dollymop cried out, pointing a stiff finger.

Brightly lit by the flickering orange glow of the burning city, the crowds could see that the walkers were painted a glossy black, with bright silver trimming the edges, and a plate was fastened to the front of each displaying the Royal Seal of England in pure gleaming gold. Painted along the side of each tripod was its name, just like any other ship in the Royal Navy: HMW *Avenger*, HMW *Revenge*, HMW *Justice*, HMW *Destroyer*. Then a flexible pole shot upward from the top of each machine, and the glorious crossed bars of a Union Jack unfurled.

"By jingo, they be ours!" a man cried, tears of relief pouring down his flabby cheeks. "Hurrah!"

"HMW?" a solicitor asked confused.

"Her Majesty's walker!" a blacksmith shouted proudly, puffing out his chest.

With grace and power, the Black Squad strode smoothly past the Horse Guard parade grounds, and splashed through the small lake to reach the Strand. Constantly in motion, the tripods of legs stretched out and contracted with the gentle hiss of escaping steam. Everywhere they went, the Royal walkers were followed by startled, and then cheering crowds.

Almost appearing to float, the towering tripods daintily stepped over a barricade of massed cannon and troops barring an intersection. At the sight, a victory shout broke out from the soldiers, a glorious cry that built in waves until the noise was almost tangible.

Defiantly, a major shook a fist towards the colossal squid in the distance. "Ah-HA! You big bastard! Eat . . ." Words failed him. What did they fire again, lead? Steel? Lightning?

"Eat it raw!" he ad-libbed with a flourish.

"Twice!" a brash young captain added fervently.

Beaming smiles, troops got their nervous horses out of the way as the Royal walkers strode by, their great steel feet sinking a yard into the cobblestone street with each step. Somewhere in the city, a familiar keening started building into a moan, then became a strident musical wail! As the gates slammed aside, an entire company of Scottish bagpipers marched smartly from the parade grounds to follow behind the British war machines. That alone was sufficient to bolster the confidence of the soldiers and civilians. Damn the impudence of the squid! Once more Great Britain would carry the day.!

As the raucous Highlander musicians passed, a tweedy man turned to his neighbor, who hid the fact that he had just finished picking the other fellow's pocket.

"If nothing else, those pipers should throw a scare into that nasty blighter," the victim chuckled.

"The music drives 'em mad, it does," the thief agreed.

* * *

Without much ado, the sun crested the sky and the moon officially arrived above the war-torn the city.

Munching happily, the Squid God paused in the act of consuming the last of Her Royal Majesty's 56th Fusilier Company and looked curiously around. *Now what was that lovely music?* Then the squid saw the first of the tripods stepping over a low building. The sight caused the squid to forget about the remaining soldiers–who quickly used the precious opportunity to scurry to freedom.

Scowling darkly in concern, the squid stared at the armored things coming its way. *Those looked suspiciously like fellow demons*, the squid hooted thoughtfully. By the turning moon, he had not endured four thousand years of boredom just to share the goodies with a bunch of upstart newcomers!

Preparing to attack, the squid slowed. That was a good point to consider. He had been gone for four thousand years. Perhaps these approaching devils merely needed to be reminded of whom they were dealing with, the dreaded Colossus of Dutar! Fair enough. Humming softly, the squid began the first swaying movements of the traditional 'Fight or Scram' war dance.

* * *

Through the front windows of the HMW *Revenge*, Lt. Donaldson, Sgt. Barta, and the gunnery officer could only stare at the waltzing leviathan.

"What the deuce is it doing?" the gunnery officer muttered as the squid began to execute a flashy series of moves along the broken street.

"Who cares?" the lieutenant replied savagely, throwing more switches. "Let's kill the smarmy thing."

"Magnetic lenses at medium aperture," Sgt. Barta announced, calmly adjusting some dials. "Range?"

"Four hundred yards and closing!" a corporal stated.

"Power?" Lt. Donaldson demanded, moving levers.

"Accumulators at 99 per cent!" a private answered.

"Prepare to fire," the lieutenant commanded. "On my mark!"

In spite of their safety harness, the crew grabbed convenient wall straps and prepared for the coming onslaught.

"Ready, and fire," Lt. Donaldson said calmly.

The gunnery officer pressed a switch with his thumb.

A tiny hatch flipped open at in the front of the *Revenge* exposing a complex set of crystal lenses that started pulsing with light, and then out lanced a brilliant rod of quasi-solid lightning. A burning, mauling power ray of raw atomic energy so thick and heavy, the walker actually recoiled from the thrust. Onlookers watched, dumbfounded, as the scalding beam shot across the sky towards the jitterbugging behemoth.

The *Avenger* and the *Destroyer* followed suit, the black domes bucking with each eruption of boiling plasma. Dodging between the burning buildings, the *Justice* circled inland and shot the gargantuan squid squarely from behind.

The four energy beams struck the squid dead center, and the monster became lost in the incandescent fury of the atomic barrage. Two of the rays accidentally touched each other and a few drops of superheated matter sprayed outward to rain across the city. Falling onto rooftops, the tortured nuclei sizzled through stone and steel as if they were cheap French cheese; one of those nasty types that got soft at room temperature, and smelled of dirty feet. Caught in the backwash of the mauling power beams, a nearby church melted into lava. Green trees visibly wilted from the titanic outpouring of heat and, just for a moment, the thermal updraft cleared the smoky London sky.

As the searing beams were turned off, the population of the bedraggled city blinked a few times to clear their eyes, and then goggled in astonishment at the unbelievable sight of the giant squid still standing there. It appeared to be completely undamaged, and extremely annoyed.

"Sweet Jesus, Mary, and Buddha," Sgt. Barta whispered, going pale.

"Did we somehow miss?" Chief Higgins asked, loosening the top button on his starched collar.

"Must have. There is no other explanation," Lt. Donaldson stated, twisting the steering yoke. "What is our power status?"

"Accumulators at eighty per cent, sir!" a private answered.

"Give me a status check," ordered the sergeant.

"Boiler pressure, steady!"

"Generator, steady!"

"Charge!"

* * *

With every limb flailing, the squid nimbly executed a particularly graceful leap, then slipped on the molten church and fell on its face with a loud unpleasant smack, like a duck being crushed by a cinderblock. Furiously embarrassed, the squid stood upright on all eight tentacles. *So much for the niceties of society! Now this was personal!* Spitting flame, the Squid God advanced upon the row of hissing metal tripods.

* * *

"Full power!" Lt. Donaldson ordered, twirling dials on the focusing mechanisms to minimum aperture.

In the window, he could see the other walkers, thick black smoke laced with red sparks pouring from the rear vents of the silver dome. In the aft of his own machine, a cursing team of privates was shoveling coal into the main boiler until it was stoked to the danger level.

"Fire again!" Donaldson shouted, through clenched teeth. "And again, man!"

The volcanic beams lanced out once more, but the oncoming squid now actually seemed to absorb the energy blasts.

Gritting his teeth, Lt. Donaldson released the safety switches. "Continuous fire!" Donaldson commanded.

"Sir?" Sgt. Barta cried out in disbelief.

"Just do it!"

At point-blank range, the four burning rays of destruction slammed into huge beast. No mere burst this time, but steady streams of boiling plasma, the nuclear liquid trying its best to bore directly through the devilish squid! The towering monster disappeared as it became encased in a hellish nimbus of radiant power!

Then with a sputter, the beams stopped, and cold air from the river rushed inward to soothe the cooked atmosphere.

"Accumulators empty, sir!" a private announced, as the ceiling lights dimmed, closely followed by the indicators of the control panel.

"Battery power!" the sergeant brusquely ordered.

At his station, a corporal threw a heavily insulated switch with an audible clunk. In gentle pulsations, the ceiling lights returned, but the control board stayed dark.

"On battery, sir!" Sgt. Barta reported.

"We need a minute to recharge," Lt. Donaldson said, thinking out loud. "All right, prepare for docking maneuvers!"

This was not the time to ask for explanations, so the sergeant simply did as commanded, and fervently hoped the commander knew what the Hell he was doing. Docking maneuvers?

"Dock-ing man-neu-vers, hut!" Sgt. Barta chanted in a military cadence from his sweaty chair.

Tearing off their safety harnesses, the crewmembers rushed to the master control bank. In trained groups, the soldiers grabbed the huge levers and strained at the Herculean task of pushing them into the desired positions. With steam hissing from every joint in the telescoping legs, in slow, ragged stages the Royal walker eased into a kneeling position and gently leaned against a smoldering building.

"Dead silence," the lieutenant spoke softly. "First man to speak gets sixty lashes."

That truly startled the crew. It was the first time he had ever threatened any of them with corporal punishment, and the soldiers heard the note of urgency in his usually calm voice. Could the situation already be that bad?

Retreating past their fallen comrade, the rest of the Black Squad maintained a constant barrage of short bursts as they steadily walked backwards. The weakening power rays splattered against the mottled hide of the squid with no noticeable effect.

* * *

Moving into the clearing between the Constitutional Club and Victoria Hotel, the squid eagerly started for one of the metal tripods when it was unexpectedly pummeled by a bombardment of high velocity shells from a flotilla of ships in the river. Again and again, the sixteen-inch guns spoke their violent language of destruction.

With explosions dotting its body, the squid blinked in surprise. *The retreat had been a trap*? Suspiciously, the monster looked down at the dead metal thing leaning against the burning building.

* * *

Instantly tilting the dome upward, the crew of the HMS *Revenge* let the beast have a fully recharged power blast directly in the left eye! Jerking its head out of the way of the sizzling beam, the squid ducked low, and then coiled a couple of tentacles about the legs of the machine. Lifting it high, the infuriated monster rushed forward and wildly hammered the other tripods with the one in its grasp as if it was a club. The ringing cacophony of the attack was beyond deafening.

In a shower of glass, the front window of the *Revenge* shattered and dead soldiers fell out to hit the ground with a sickening thud. Even while falling through the air, Lt. Donaldson showed true British bravado and fired his Webley .455 service revolver into the towering beast until he landed on a surprisingly soft and spongy mat. *Egad, he was standing on a tentacle!* Emptying his pistol, the lieutenant drew his sword and charged along the limb, hacking and slashing.

Swatting at tentacle six with the smoking tripod, the squid brushed away the annoying little thing, and resumed brutally smashing the other machines.

Spinning at full RPMs, the gyroscopes of the walkers tore free from their stout housings and burst out of the machines to spin away like mad tops. As the squid continued savagely pounding away, the domes cracked, generators shorted out, and fat blue sparks crackled over the Royal Walkers until they went dark. Soon, steam could be seen wafting from the gaping rents in the dome, closely followed by the stink of roasting human flesh.

The squid sneered in contempt. *Yeah, right.* Not falling for that old trick again, the monster continued to hammer all of the walkers until the things fell apart. Then the squid danced on the broken pieces until there was nothing remaining except crimson-smeared debris.

* * *

Standing on the front lawn of the museum, Prof. Einstein, Mary, and Lord Carstairs used field glasses to watch the ghastly end of the unequal battle. The billowing smoke from the carnage rose to form a horrid funeral shroud over the doomed city.

"This is absolutely amazing!" Professor Einstein muttered, lowering the field glasses. Biting a lip, the professor pulled out a spare keychain to rub his new lucky dinosaur tooth. "Our heat rays are capable of reaching over two thousand degrees Kelvin. That's the surface temperature of the sun! There is no possible way any organic matter should be able to withstand that kind of thermal assault!"

Lowering the glasses, Mary arched an eyebrow. "But, uncle," she began slowly. "I thought that you had said the creature is magical . . ."

Interrupting her with a cry, Lord Carstairs cast away the field glasses. "Great Scott, my dear, that's it!" he gushed excitedly. "The Dutarian legends said that the Squid God was invulnerable to man-made weapons!"

A loud *cra-ack* of a large caliber rifle sounded once more from the rooftop. Lady Danvers' supply of ammunition seemed endless. But if her efforts were yielding any results, it was not apparent amid the warfare filling the city.

"I don't see the point," Prof. Einstein said, gesturing at the rampaging squid. "The walkers are Venusian inventions."

"Exactly the point, dear Uncle," Mary said, shifting position to keep her cast on a flagstone and out of the dewy grass. "The Royal Army tripods are copies of the Venusian designs. They were only designed by aliens, but every piece of these machines was actually forged by English mechanics."

"Made by men," Einstein whispered, going pale. "Oh dear."

Loudly and bitterly, Lord Carstairs cursed in fourteen different languages, including Dutarian and lower Welsh.

"By thunder," the lord cried, returning to English. "If only a single one of the original Venusian war machines survived intact, we'd show that beastly thing some British spunk!"

Pivoting about clumsily, Mary stared at the professor. He grinned innocently, and turned away to start whistling.

"Uncle Felix . . ." Mary said in a very dangerous tone of voice.

Looking skyward, the professor began to study a passing cloud of smoke riding the noon breeze. "Yes, too bad we don't have any of those," Prof. Einstein said to nobody in particular. "Such a pity. How sad."

Sensing the futility of further discussion, Mary took Lord Carstairs by the hand and started pulling him along. "Benjamin, come with me!" she ordered.

"Whatever for?" the lord queried, politely following.

"Just come along," Mary repeated, shambling quickly across the damp lawn. "And I'll show you!"

"No, wait!" Einstein cried, dropping the dinosaur tooth. "It's, ah, no, I mean, the key! The key is lost!"

"Then we'll break in!" Mary tossed over a shoulder hobbling along steadily.

In moral anguish, Prof. Einstein weighed the balance between the total destruction of the world and damaging his prize exhibit. His prized, secret, illegal, contraband exhibit.

"Oh, hell," the professor muttered in resignation and started after them. "Wait for me!"

TWENTY-SEVEN

As the trio hurried along the grassy lawn, Lord Carstairs could see that they were heading for a large carriage house just past the ruins of the rose garden. The bushes were trampled, the sundial toppled over sideways, and the gazebo was reduced to little more than busted kindling. This was obviously the result of the Ladies' Auxiliary tangling with the Squid God worshipers.

Stopping at the side door of the carriage house to catch her breath, Mary impatiently waited for her uncle to arrive.

"Come along!" she urged, snapping her fingers.

As the professor redoubled his speed, Lord Carstairs looked over the carriage house. The red brick building was unusually large for a family of only two people and a small staff.

The steeple was made of heavy gray slate and edged with barbed iron spikes, and the large wooden door at the front seemed to be permanently nailed shut. Thick iron bars covered the closed oak shutters, and the only visible door was draped with so many lengths of linked iron chains it appeared to be wearing medieval chainmail.

How very curious, the lord pondered. *The building more resembled a small bank than a simple carriage house.*

"I'm here! I'm here! Don't break anything," the professor chided, pulling a key from his vest pocket.

Impatiently, Mary snatched the key from her uncle and started releasing the collection of heavy padlocks. As each lock was disengaged, she yanked away the accompanying chain and tossed it over a shoulder into the rose garden.

As the iron-plated door was finally revealed, Prof. Einstein replaced his niece at the door and spun the combination dial to his birthday, height, and the number of times he had been arrested in Tokyo. With a solid clunk, the internal bolts disengaged, and Einstein pushed open the armored door.

The inside of the carriage house was pitch dark.

Striking a match on the doorframe, Mary shuffled into the blackness and pulled down an alcohol lantern hanging by a length of chain from a rafter. Sliding up the flue with a thumb, she lit the wick and turned the clear blue flame up all the way.

As the light filled the building house, Lord Carstairs could see that the walls were lined with tools and workbenches, in the corners were barrels of grease, along one wall was a steam-powered lathe of clever design. But his inspection stopped dead at the sight of a Venusian war machine squatting in the middle of the carriage house.

Only a sort of gurgle escaped his slack lips. There was no way this infernal device could possibly be mistaken for one of the British-made counterparts. The catch-basket at the rear was a mess of twisted hoops, but the dome was the color of smooth, burnished silver, although marred in hundreds of spots from the ricochets of British bullets. The infamous telescoping legs were compacted to a mere yard in length, a wooden stepladder giving easy access to the open hatchway in the side of the alien dome.

Involuntarily raising an arm to block the sight, Lord Carstairs had a flashback to the war when he had stood helpless amid the blood and thunder of the cackling alien conquerors. The war for the world. The terrible nightmare that the newspapers of the planet took to calling The Troubles after it was all over and Humanity the winner.

Shivering from the adrenaline rush, the British lord inhaled deeply as he stood proudly erect and walked over to spit on the vile machine in raw hatred.

Shuffling closer, Mary squeezed his muscular arm. "I understand, my love. But the machine belongs to us now and could mean the survival of Humanity."

"Yes, of course. I understand," Lord Carstairs said through clenched teeth. "But, by God Almighty, how I hate those damn creatures!"

Closing the outside door and locking it again, the professor gave a snort. "That's why keep we it well hidden, lad!"

"Stop wasting time," Mary said, clumsily starting to climb the ladder. "Let's get going!"

Taking her about the waist, Lord Carstairs gave the woman a boost through the oval doorway of the dome. Squaring his broad shoulders, Carstairs summoned his resolve then also entered, although his stomach gave a flip at the thought of doing so under his own volition.

Slowly, the lord stood in the dome, wary of hitting his head against the low ceiling designed for its non-human creators. The fetid smell of the aliens was long gone, replaced with the homey aromas of grease, leather, and some sort of lemon waxy polish. Interestingly enough, the dome still had its original flooring of a woven material that was as soft as lambs wool, but as resistant to fire as concrete. However, the lord noticed with marked satisfaction that it was badly stained in numerous spots, as if green ink had been tossed about randomly. The Venusian crew must have died hard before surrendering their craft. *Good.*

While Mary and the professor rushed about the interior turning on various machines, Lord Carstairs studied the craft, comparing it to the few pieces of smashed wreckage on display at the Royal War Museum. Glowing softly, the curved wall was lined with gauges and meters, labeled in the aliens' angular script. A ceramic lattice at the rear of the dome closed off the engine room containing the bizarre power source that English technicians had sadly never been able to duplicate.

Spanning the front of the craft wall was a blank sheet of shiny material that dimly reflected the three explorers like a frosted mirror. Underneath that murky mirror was a curved panel covered with a multitude of controls, levers, dials, switches, and countless triangular buttons. Attached to the bottom of the control panel, as if grown there, were two oddly shaped chairs, festooned with power cables, hydraulic pistons, and the infamous 'feeding' tubes.

Going to a wicker hamper, Prof. Einstein tossed a fluffy pillow to Lord Carstairs. Going to one of the chairs, the professor arranged the pillow over the spiked gap in the bottom, and carefully sat down. With a faint whine, the chair automatically molded itself to the contours of his human anatomy.

Grabbing a tuning fork from a wall bracket, Mary kept a firm grip on the dangling ceiling stanchions and hobbled away to disappear behind the ceramic lattice.

"Here we go," Einstein muttered, pressing a button.

A low hum rose from the belly of the alien war machine and the shiny panel above the control board cleared to become totally transparent. Now they could see the interior of the carriage house with astonishing clarity.

"Amazing," the British lord breathed, watching tiny geometric figures scrolling along the side of the viewscreen. "I've never seen a war machine in such an excellent state."

"Not surprising, considering how the mobs tore them apart. What you see is the result of a lot of hard work by Mary and me," Einstein said, running his hands over the control panel with the ease of long practice.

"We found it in the yard of the Museum where it had been hidden from the clean-up squads. It was quite badly battered. But we managed to surreptitiously salvage parts from several other wrecks."

"You have done a superlative job."

"Thank you. Now if only the damn thing works," Prof. Einstein muttered, fiddling with a large dial.

Using the pillow, Lord Carstairs took a seat. "Eh? What was that, sir?"

"Oh, nothing, lad. Nothing at all."

With a stuttering hiss, a section of the floor separated into several pieces and Mary crawled into view. Her long hair was now tucked under a cloth cap bearing the logo of the Orient Express, and she was wearing a canvas engineering apron composed almost entirely of pockets filled with tools.

"We're ready to go, Uncle," she said, limping to a chair near the lattice. "We have more than sufficient allotropic iron fuel." As the woman sat, a section of the curved wall irised open, exposing a full set of alien controls and some twinkling circuitry that musically hummed.

"Good show, lass!" the professor beamed in delight. "By any chance, Lord Carstairs, do you know how to operate the steering mechanism?"

"I am familiar with the basics," Carstairs acknowledged. "My family happens to be a patron of the Venusian War Museum and I spent a great deal of time in the simulators."

"Superb! I helped found that establishment," the professor said, twisting a button and sliding a dial. "Nice to know it's been useful."

Scowling in concentration, Carstairs studied the jerky writing on the dashboard before palming buttons and levers. "This, and this, should do it," he said confidently, and a throb of power from below answered in a positive manner.

"Energy levels are?" the professor asked.

"Nine over nine and steady," Mary said checking a pulsating meter while strapping herself firmly into place with a purely human-designed safety harness.

"Beginning primary sequence, now!" Lord Carstairs announced, flamboyantly throwing a trip bar. Instantly the machine quivered all over and a shower of sparks sprayed from a box on the wall. The lord quickly reversed the switch.

"Cursed thingamabob shorted out," Prof. Einstein snarled, rising from his seat. "Just be a second."

As the professor headed for the rear of the craft, Mary tossed him a shiny copper wedge topped with a corkscrew. Making the catch with one hand, Prof. Einstein disappeared into the rear engine compartment and there came the sound of hard banging.

Studying the exposed circuits inside the wall, Mary slid some noisy components into new positions as if operating a four-dimensional abacus. In response, the twinkling lights changed color and hue.

"That has it fixed, Uncle," Mary shouted, over a shoulder.

"Well, for the time being, at least," Prof. Einstein stated, walking back into view, the copper wedge severely dented.

Very displeased, Mary scowled at the sight of the damaged tool, and the professor could only shrug as he gave it back.

"I really was gentle as possible," he apologized.

"Of course," Mary murmured, dropping it into a box bolted to the floor. Inside were a dozen more of the tools, each one equally disfigured. *Men!*

Resuming his seat, Prof. Einstein tightly buckled on the safety harness. "Try it once more, lad."

With some trepidation, Lord Carstairs eased a slightly different switch into position, and the war machine violently lurched, smashing straight through the wooden door of the carriage house in an explosion of splinters.

As the machine rampaged across the lawn, Carstairs thumped a dial, and the tripod eased to a rocking halt. With direct sunlight bathing the craft, the viewscreen automatically polarized to remove any unwanted glare.

Feeling the eyes of his two companions on him, the British lord sheepishly smiled over a shoulder. "Sorry. Bit out of practice, you know."

"Well, the door needed replacing anyway, lad," Prof. Einstein said with a shrug.

Cracking his knuckles, Lord Carstairs began caressing the controls with both hands. Creaking loudly, the dome rose to its full height, the telescoping legs extending in a staggered series of burps and hisses. On the floor between the two men, a small screen slid out from the control panel to display a view directly below the tripod. Craning his human neck, Lord Carstairs could see that all three of the thick columns were streaked with rust and one had a large welding patch holding it together.

But the alien machinery seemed to be working fine, in spite of all the noise and trembling.

Flipping switches and turning knobs, Lord Carstairs started the tripod walking forward at a more reasonable pace. Rattling at every step, the walking machine awkwardly clumped past the Museum. As she came into view, a grinning Lady Danvers on the rooftop paused in her reloading efforts, and gave them a game thumbs-up of encouragement.

"What a splendid woman," Prof. Einstein sighed in resignation.

Daintily stepping the tripod over the barbed-wire-topped iron fence, Lord Carstairs eased the machine along Wimpole Street towards the distant fighting. Unfortunately, the lord was finding it almost impossible to maintain an even keel as the huge, segmented shoes at the bottom of the telescoping metal legs kept shimming at every minor bump in the road.

"Sir, are you sure this machine is battle worthy?" Lord Carstairs demanded, fighting for control of the alien walker.

Privately wishing for the original shark tooth, the professor nervously fondled the replacement lucky dinosaur fang. "Have we a choice?" he asked bluntly.

"No, not at all," Mary said, holding on for dear life.

Despite the best efforts of Lord Carstairs, the tripod wove drunkenly down the road, the city on the viewscreen constantly bobbing about maddeningly. Luckily, the jerky swaying had little effect on the stalwart constitutions of the veteran sea voyagers.

Squinting to see through the blanket of smoke swirling in the outside air, Prof. Einstein caught a glimpse of the squid dismembering a full battalion of Royal Dragoons, chunks of men and horses flying everywhere. A hard lump formed in his throat at the carnage, but the professor forced it back to the proper location. *Here we come, old chap!*

"Target in sight!" Prof. Einstein announced, feeling a surge of cold fury.

"Range is, ah, eighteen *frukongs!*" Mary said, reading figures off of a teardrop-shaped gauge.

While steering the tripod, Carstairs did the mental conversion to metric. *So that would be . . . one hundred twenty three point four yards. Close enough.* "Ready the heat ray!" he ordered.

"Affirmative," Einstein said, pulling a lever and pressing three buttons in ascending order.

On a small viewscreen, Mary watched as from the top of the dome a round portal irised open and out lifted a skeletal limb of interconnected metal braces. At the very end was a squat box-like apparatus, vaguely reminiscent of an American magic lantern projector, a louvered grill covering the large crystal lens.

* * *

At the sight of the non-British walker, the fleeing civilians turned chalk white and dogs began to howl. Grown men screamed, women cursed, and horses fainted. Without a thought, all the soldiers in London turned their weapons toward the old and hated enemy, the rampaging squid momentarily forgotten. As the tripod staggered towards the river, dozens of shells began whistling past it in a steady rain of high explosive death.

* * *

"Professor, this is terrible!" Lord Carstairs snarled, as two shells collided in mid-air. The resulting double-explosion showered the walkers with hot shrapnel making the sound of a winter hailstorm.

"Just what I was afraid might happen," the professor said grimly, running his fingertips over the control panel.

"They think we're Venusians!" Mary realized, holding onto her hat with one hand. "Bunny, do something!"

With a sharp metallic bang, a dent appeared in the side of the dome near the oval hatchway. As the depression popped out again, the wall lights dimmed, and only very slowly returned.

"Good shooting, lads!" Lord Carstairs complimented, brandishing a fist. "And at this range, too! That really is quite impressive, sir."

"Too bad we're on their side," the professor grumped, hunching lower in his chair.

"Easily solved, sir," the lord said, playing the control panel with both hands. "Let's just show them which side we are on. Boost iron flow! I want full power!"

"Done!" Prof. Einstein replied, flipping buttons. "Engines at twenty over twenty."

"Battle stations!" Mary loudly commanded.

As Lord Carstairs labored to weave a safe path through the incoming bombardment, Professor Einstein referred to a small journal chained to the wall and threw several switches on the control board. One of the scrolling figures along the bottom of the viewscreen rose to become a tight series of concentric circles. Fumbling to operate a joystick mechanism not meant for human hands, the professor struggled to place the circles on the colossal beast, but the erratic weaving of the walker made his task nigh impossible.

"Stand still for a moment, lad," Einstein ordered, biting a lip.

Pushing this and rubbing that, Carstairs brought the machine to a rocking halt. Immediately, the artillery shells started exploding closer to them. Jiggling the lever with both hands, Einstein managed to center the innermost circle of the targeting system on the distant squid.

"*En garde*, demon!" the professor growled, squeezing a lever.

TWENTY-EIGHT

From the battered box dangling at the end of the metal arm there lanced out a pale ray that struck Nelson's Monument and melted the bronze statue into a glowing puddle.

"Damnation!" Prof. Einstein muttered, releasing the lever. "The calibration must be off. Never thought I'd use the machine in a fight!"

"Sir, until we've established our bona fides, I really don't want to give them a stationary target," Lord Carstairs said through clenched teeth, as a nearby water tower was blown apart from the barrage of shells. "Or the squid, either."

With nightmarish speed, the colossus was wriggling towards them, its deadly tentacles writhing about like a nest of insane snakes.

"All right lad, let's try that again!" the professor stated confidently and pulled the lever again.

* * *

Once more, the feeble alien heat ray reached across London heading for the giant squid. But this time it hit. In a flash of superheated vapor, two of the beast's tentacles literally disintegrated under the onslaught of the power beam.

Reeling from the pain, the Squid God gave a high-pitched shriek that cracked glass and sterilized chickens for a dozen miles in every direction.

* * *

"God's teeth, it worked!" Lord Carstairs shouted, starting the walker into motion once more.

"Jolly good shot, Uncle," Mary said, inserting a new blue thing into the wall where the old blue thing had cracked into dust and sprinkled to the carpeted deck.

* * *

"Cease fire!" a general shouted, trying to focus his binoculars on everything at once.

As the cannons ceased their roar, the officer was not exactly sure what was happening. *A functioning Venusian war machine had staggered from the north side of London and joined the fight against the giant squid? Were the two vying for supremacy?*

The general scowled. *No, that made no sense. Only one answer was possible. An antique machine appearing from the general vicinity of Wimpole Street could only mean the International British Museum for Stolen Antiquities. Well, the owner may be a certified balmy, but he was loyal to the core.*

"It's that madman Prof. Einstein!" the general shouted to a nearby lieutenant. "Spread the word! The damn thing is on our side!"

"Yes, sir!" the lieutenant replied crisply, and raced to find a sergeant to get the job done.

Within moments, semaphores were flashing the incredible message across London. Soon, flags began to wave a warning, then flares shot skyward, and bugles began tooting musically.

Rather loath to accept the bizarre orders, the soldiers were slow to turn their cannon away from the hated tripod and back towards the giant squid. But as always, the British Army blindly obeyed orders and allowed the alien war machine free and unrestricted rein across the capital.

* * *

With the walker clattering at every step, tiny bits of rust flaking off from a rent in the bottom, Lord Carstairs drove the tripod in a bold advance towards the trembling squid. Furious at being confronted, the angry demon hooted a challenge, the horrible noise sounding like a cat caught in a mechanical reaper.

Inside the dome, a wire-mesh-covered box on the wall blurted, *"Tu'end deouhf? gohb Wspfm dgfudbcs jax!"*

Both of the Einsteins and Carstairs glanced at each other in total shock.

"That's Venusian," Mary identified in wonder, wrapping some tape around a leaking pipe.

"There must be some form of mechanical translator," Lord Carstairs postulated, twirling two dials in unison.

Working the aiming lever, Prof. Einstein nodded in agreement. "Didn't know the walkers had that ability," he said, squeezing the firing mechanism. Then he softly added, "I wonder what else this bloody thing can do that we don't know about?"

* * *

Barely visible in the morning light, the alien death ray shot over the rooftops to strike the squid again. Trying to dodge out of the way, the beast got only a glancing blow. But on contact, a thick slice of the creature disintegrated into radiant steam. Hooting in agony, the squid tried to hide behind a church, but the beam struck it again annihilating another chunk of its pulsating anatomy.

Although cruel, vicious, bloodthirsty, and cheap to friends on their birthdays, the Squid God was no fool and knew real danger when it arrived. Determined to take out this new adversary as quickly as possible, the crazed mollusk did the only logical thing. It charged straight for the dilapidated machine.

* * *

Inside the dome, the translator box finally switched over to English and gushed forth a stream of vulgarities, mostly involving anal orifices and a sharp stick.

Not good, most definitely not good. "Evasive tactics!" Lord Carstairs shouted, shoving a finger into a hole on the control board and scratching the interior surface.

With a lurch, the alien walker pivoted about in a wobbly circle, its legs almost twisting into a knot as it twirled out of the path of the monster's headlong rush. Carried by its own momentum, the squid missed the tripod and crashed into Westminster City Hall, stone blocks and office furniture flying into the smoky sky. As the dizzy squid untangled itself from the smashed building, the heat ray swept across the slimy torso and more of the hellspawn beast was painfully atomized. Mad with desperation, the squid raised a chunk of the building as a shield. But with incredible accuracy, the pale ray went through one window and out another to strike it smack between the eyes.

With a chunk of its brain gone, a terrible chilling truth came to the squid as it realized that it was on the verge of losing the fight. Which translated into d-dying! Turning to flee, the squid only made it a block before the heat ray hit yet again to shear off a fourth tentacle. Thrashing about mindlessly, the smoldering rope of muscle dropped to the street, ironically crushing a beer wagon and a temperance hall at the same time.

While the tripod paused to vaporize the limb, the wounded squid took advantage of the lull to frantically cast a dozen healing spells upon itself.

Ah, better, it sighed in relief. Then a boiling wave of mollusk madness filled the demon, and it rallied to the attack.

Circling each other in the manner of prizefighters, the two outlandish combatants warily searched for an opportunity to end the deadly fight quickly. Although, the squid had repaired all of the damage incurred so far, it was now reduced to its original size from the sheer amount of tissue lost.

The squid lashed out a tentacle, and missed the dome. In response, the heat ray swept the neighborhood, setting a dozen rooftop fires and catching the beast squarely in the left eye.

Overwhelming pain filled the Squid God as the orb burst into oily fumes. Half blind, the squid decided that was enough. Even the final demise-from-which-there-was-no-return would be preferable to this humiliating death by inches.

Spinning about in a waggle of limbs, the squid called upon its mother moon for aid, and then insanely tapped some of its own life force to cast an incredibly deadly spell. With a gesture, a hoot, and a pyrotechnic flash, the squid unleashed a sparkling rod of elemental destruction from its remaining eyeball.

Streaking across London, the ravening beam annihilated the very air as it headed for the enemy war machine.

* * *

Every alarm, bell, and jingling toot, the Venusian walker possessed sounded in warning at the approach of the incoming energy surge.

"Duck!" Lord Carstairs yelled, flipping a button.

Hissing steam, the legs retracted and the dome dropped lower, but not quite fast enough. The effervescent death beam caught the dome full in its hellish glare! But the scintillating dagger of magic stopped a scant yard away from the surface of the alien machine and splayed out harmlessly, like water hitting an invisible steel plate.

Inside the dome, the humming of the equipment was the only sound for a while.

"Absolutely incredible," Prof. Einstein exhaled, unable to tear his sight away from the fantastic light display outside.

"We seem to be protected by some sort of energy blister," Mary rationalized, studying the effect on her little viewscreen. "Similar to the field of force around a magnet."

"It does make sense that the Venusians would have a defense against energy weapons," Lord Carstairs smiled grimly, tightening his grip on the steering yoke. "Bally good show! This inviso-shield thingy gives us a formidable advantage!"

Inviso-shield? "For Queen and country!" Prof. Einstein cried, brandishing a fist, carried away by a rush of patriotism.

Raising the dome to its full height, Lord Carstairs eagerly started forward while Prof. Einstein lashed out with the heat ray again, and again, and again! But in spite of the relatively short distance separating the combatants, the pale beam faded to nothingness before reaching the cowering squid.

"Oh, what is wrong now?" the professor demanded petulantly, pounding on the control panel.

"Power is at ten over ten," Mary stated, staring aghast at a gauge. She tapped it with a rubbery fork, but the reading stayed the same.

"Well, boost iron flow, girl!" Prof. Einstein ordered.

"I already did that, Uncle!" she retorted. "It's no use. The protective energy blister is consuming too much energy. We cannot fight and keep the blister at the same time."

"Then cut the inviso-shield," Lord Carstairs said calmly, cracking his knuckles as a preparation to rejoining the battle.

Inviso-shield? "Be glad to," Mary snorted, gesturing at the overlapping circuitry of the alien controls at her station. "After you tell me how!"

"Hmm, good point," the professor acknowledged sadly. "Any suggestions?"

"Give me a minute," Carstairs said, staring at the control panel, his inner sight lost in his dimly remembered days at the war college.

"Sorry, lad," Prof. Einstein said, pointing out the viewscreen, "but it appears that we don't have a bloody goddamn minute. Look!"

* * *

Although woozy from the massive expenditure of magic, the squid decided to try a different approach. Lifting its front tentacles, the squid exposed its beak and vomited a combination of fire and acid at the street below the tripod. The purely chemical spray passed without hindrance through the defensive shield to form a puddle on the ground that started dissolving the granite cobblestones.

As the tripod's segmented shoes began to sink into the scummy lava, it started to tilt. Seizing the opportunity, the squid quickly swallowed the rest of the venom, and breathed out a wave of bitter cold. Snow and ice hit the tripod, but it was already out of the pool of molten rock and onto solid ground. However, the tripod wobbled with each step as its shoes were now coated with irregular lumps of hardened stone.

* * *

Stepping out from behind the ceramic lattice, Mary triumphantly waved a severed cable. "The field of force is off!" she cried, casting away the crystalline tube.

"Excellent," the professor growled, immediately firing the heat ray.

This time the pale ray reached the squid and there was an eruption of flesh as a vast section of the monster disintegrated. The battered squid wailed so loud that banshees answered from distant Ireland. A torrent of blood gushed from the gaping wound, then the break slammed shut and closed to heal without a trace of a scar.

The sight was amazing! But more importantly, Prof. Einstein, Mary Einstein, and Lord Carstairs could see that the monster squid had been reduced in size again by the loss of flesh. Now it stood a scant ten yards in height, almost the exact same height as the Venusian walker.

"A fair fight at last!" Mary yelled, working the controls in savage glee. "Time to die, squiddie!"

As if also realizing this fact, the Squid God vented a squeal of pure aquatic fury, and lunged for the tripod with every tentacle writhing.

Trying to dodge, Lord Carstairs sent the walker spinning away like a Whirling Dervish turned ballerina, but it was to no avail. A slimy green tentacle wrapped around a rusty metal leg and latched on tight. Again the heat ray spoke, burning deeply into the squid. The creature ignored the destruction of its own flesh, and undulated closer to coil all of its remaining tentacles about the dome and squeeze. Squeeze!

Alarms sounded all over the Venusian walker as the booming beat of the giant squid's heart filled the dome like wild jungle drums; the status lights on the control panel changed from puce to mauve, and read-outs changed from flowing lines to sharp angularities.

"I can't move the walker!" Lord Carstairs growled, his hands starting to bend the control yoke. "We're trapped!"

The mottled belly of the squid filled the viewscreen, its snapping beak chipped at the dome, then a forked tongue licked hungrily along the exterior, leaving behind a trail of sizzling puce-colored slime.

"Same here, lad!" Prof. Einstein shouted, smacking the control. "I can't focus the heat ray on the beast when it's this close!"

Checking her little viewscreen, Mary saw that the mechanical arm supporting the heat ray was pinned to the dome under a thick tentacle, the hundreds of suckers along the writhing limb slurping at the alien metal. Then a section of the tentacle accidentally moved directly in front of the heat ray box.

"Uncle, shoot right now!" she ordered.

"Righto!" the professor cried, triggering the weapon. But he was a split second too late. The tentacle had moved and the beam stabbed into the sky to only hit nothing a few clouds.

"Damnation!" Lord Carstairs snarled, leaning in closer for a better view. *Come on, squiddie, do it again.*

With a gasp, Mary recoiled from the viewscreen as the delicate manipulator arms, formerly used to grab victims and toss them into the rear hamper, came to life of their own volition, and reached out to try to repair the larger mechanical arm.

Holding her breath, the woman watched in hopeful expectation. But the effort proved fruitless as a tentacle crushed one of the tiny manipulator arms. Rallying to the defense, the other arm beat feebly at the monster with pitiful results.

Groaning under the strain, the dome bent slightly and a cluster of cables snapped free to whip across the interior, spraying out sparks and pinkish steam. Diving for cover, Prof. Einstein and Lord Carstairs hit the floor as the cables lashed past. Wildly yanking gooey alien fuses from the wall, Mary managed to cut the power and the cables went dead, falling to the deck as impotent as the Flemish Army.

"Clear!" she called, just as the alarms went silent. Now the alien craft was filled with the pervasive hum of the generators and the steady pounding of the squid's inhuman heart pressed against the dome. The effect was unnerving.

Scrambling back into their chairs, Einstein and Carstairs needed no encouragement as they frantically threw switches and pressed buttons, then pressed levers and twirled switches.

"I must admit, this is a deuced clever ploy," Lord Carstairs stated in an annoyed tone. His fingers danced on the controls in an effort to vent the spare allotropic iron onto the squid. But the vent would not open under the pressure of the ever-tightening tentacles.

"Sadly, I concur," Prof. Einstein said, struggling to shunt power from the engines and electrify the hull. Some sort of automatic feedback device kept stopping him, and finally it shut down that section of the control panel to prevent further attempts. Bloody automation!

With a terrible creak, the inner supports started to bend, then the hatchway buckled, jamming the exit door firmly into place.

"If any of us also feels deuced clever," Lord Carstairs added releasing the useless control panel, "please speak quickly or forever hold your peace!"

For a full minute, the only sounds were of groaning struts and a ghastly chuckling from the embracing squid.

"By jingo, I have it!" Mary said, releasing her safety harness and grabbing a ceiling stanchion to stand. "We can take the blighter with us!"

Spinning around in his chair, Prof. Einstein stared aghast at the woman. "Are . . . are you suggesting that we *deliberately* explode the engines?" he demanded.

"Yes, I am."

"My dear girl, that is sheer brilliance!" the professor shouted joyfully, yanking off his own harness. "When that Venusian walker exploded in Belgium near the end of The Troubles, the resulting blast leveled a whole city block!"

Already out of his chair, Lord Carstairs swayed to keep his balance in the tilting walker. "A capital idea!" he said over the increasing noise of beast and machine. "A detonation of that magnitude should be more than sufficient to blow this thing back to whatever Hell it originally came from."

"To the hold!" Mary shouted brandishing a heavy spanner, and started for the rear of the dome.

Scrambling around the ceramic lattice, the three explorers dashed through an hourglass-shaped door. Entering the engine room, they slowed and were very careful where they stood. There was no proper floor here, only a nigh incomprehensible maze of wires, pipes, tubes, conduits, cables, coils, and bus bars that completely filled the engine room in every direction.

"How do we make the power plant detonate?" Carstairs asked anxiously, looking over the complex maze of flexing machinery.

"The trouble has always been to keep the foolish device *from* exploding," Mary corrected, rolling up a sleeve. Choosing her target, the woman began banging the spanner on a rack of delicate crystals, smashing each of them in turn.

Grabbing a hammer, the professor assisted in the destruction. "Come on, lad! How often do you get a chance to vandalize a priceless artifact while still on British soil?"

In spite of the circumstances, the lord grinned. *By Jove, that would be different!* Ambling over, Carstairs appropriated a heavy wrench and joined the task.

After cracking a green glowing tube, Mary shoved the spanner deep into the works of a delicate matrix made of silver wires combined with a flowering shrub. There was a flash, the stink of ozone, a spray of hot sap, and the steady humming of the machinery began to rise in tempo and tone until it became a harsh keening.

"That's done it," Mary said cheerfully, dusting off her palms. "We have about a minute before it goes, maybe less; so let us depart."

Tossing away the hammer, Prof. Einstein grasped the handle of the emergency escape hatch and pulled, but the metal plate refused to move. Trying once more, he noticed that the rim of the doorway had been buckled, either by the squid, or by a detonating British artillery shell.

In stuttering fury, the riveted seams in the dome popped open sounding like machine gun fire, and the squid hooted even louder as the whine of the alien engines took on a deadly urgency.

"We're doomed," the professor said, slumping his shoulders. "There's nothing in heaven that can possibly force that hatch!"

TWENTY-NINE

With a screech of tortured metal, the portal swung aside and Lord Carstairs tossed the broken handle into a corner.

"Then again, I could be wrong," Prof. Einstein finished lamely.

Looking through the open hatchway, the sweating people could see the writhing tentacles entwined about the rusty legs. Groaning in protest, the struts began to bend.

"Quickly now, follow me!" Lord Carstairs said, climbing through the hatch.

Swinging his body back and forth to gain momentum, the lord sailed through the air to grab a metal leg and rapidly slid down to land atop a mottled tentacle. Scrambling past the smacking suckers of the writhing limb, Carstairs safely tumbled to the lawn of a flattened house. Looking up at his friends, the lord waved them on.

Without hesitation, Mary dove through the crimped hatchway and clumsily repeated the movements, except that her journey ended with a gentle thump in the arms of Lord Carstairs. As they stole a brief kiss, Prof. Einstein bounced to the ground at their feet.

A shadow engulfed the three explorers and they turned to see the Squid God blocking out the sun. Shooting death rays out of its eye, the squid breathed fire from its mouth, while the writhing tentacles slapped the softening dome harder, and ever harder. Pink steam shot out of the open hatch of the engine room, just as the interior of the dome began to glow red-hot.

Exchanging brief glances, the three explorers turned and ran for their lives.

"Head for the river!" Prof. Einstein yelled, his skinny legs pumping. "The water should offer some protection!"

"Exemplary, sir!" Lord Carstairs shouted.

"Shut up and run!" Mary ordered, ripping off the encumbering engineer's apron. Scandalously hitching up her skirt, the woman took off at a full sprint in spite of the heavy cast on her leg.

Properly raised British gentlemen, both Einstein and Carstairs averted their gaze from her naked knees and concentrated on heading pell-mell for the nearby Thames River.

Out of the corner of his vision, Prof. Einstein saw a team of horses pulling a fire truck along the bank of the river. Jammed in the back were a dozen soldiers holding torches and oil lanterns. Stopping for a precious second, the professor tried to wave them away, but the group was too far away to hear. With a heavy sigh, Prof. Einstein turned his back to the brave soldiers and resumed his mad dash. *Any second now. . . .*

An enormous hoot split the air, and somehow Lord Carstairs got the feeling it was directed at them. Checking over a shoulder, the lord was chilled to see the Squid God coming their way with the vibrating Venusian war machine still entangled in its suckered limbs.

With a Herculean burst of speed, Carstairs rushed forward to grab the elderly professor and the wounded Mary in his arms. Hugging them close, Lord Carstairs charged for the river, as the shadow of the giant squid cast them into darkness. His legs pounded against the hard ground, and his heart felt as if it was going to burst out of his chest from the strain. Honor demanded his all, but love asked for even more, and Lord Carstairs pushed beyond the pain, forcing himself to go faster, ever faster, until the world became a blur of motion. There was no passage of time. No sound, except the pounding of his shoes.

Unexpectedly there came the strong smell of gardenias from Mary's tousled hair. *No wait,* the lord frowned, *that was from the professor's pomade. Now that was a rather fey perfume for a proper British gentleman to be using. Rather!*

Suddenly airborne, Lord Carstairs realized he must have gone straight over the embankment. Looking down, the lord saw the shimmering expanse of the Thames River just as a blinding flash of light filled the world.

A rush of air slammed into the falling explorers, shoving them into the water even as a growing peal of thunder reached intolerable levels. Plunging beneath the churning surface, Einstein, Carstairs, and Einstein separated and stroked deep into the river. Bright lights from above streamed into the murky water, closely followed by a wave of tingling warmth that spread downward only a scant few yards in their wake.

Reaching the river bottom, the explorers headed for the rusted-out hulk of a sunken tugboat. Lying on its side, the craft offered easy access through its smoke stack. As the humans swam inside, a school of trout darted out and was decimated by a rain of debris falling from the surface. The tugboat was hit by a piece of the dome, and the wooden hull exploded into silt and splinters. Something hard bounced off the iron smokestack, and the submerged explorers covered their ears from the strident ringing. Each clang rattled their teeth, and made them shake in an unpleasant harmonic response.

Outside the mouth of the iron tube, Prof. Einstein, Lord Carstairs, and Mary Einstein watched as glowing chunks of twisted metal and semimolten stones streaked past. Leaving contrails of bubbles in its turbulent wake, the wreckage impacted the riverbed with countless dull thuds. The meteoric strikes stirred up dark clouds of mud that eerily rose like inhuman hands, only to bend with the gentle current and stretch out of sight.

Bizarre lights continued to play along the surface of the river. But the maelstrom of destruction soon slowed, and finally stopped completely. Their lungs were bursting at this point, but the explorers forced themselves to stay below as long as possible.

Another minute, then two. Starting to turn slightly blue, the three nodded at each other and gamely swam for the surface. Heading for the opposite bank, they thrust only noses above the water and greedily sucked in the fresh air.

When their hearts had stopped pounding, and the black spots left their vision, the trio swam under the water until reaching the reeds along the opposite bank. Carefully emerging among the muddy plants, the dripping explorers saw that the far embankment was a swirling hellstorm of smoke and fire, with a mushroom-shaped cloud rising into the sky. The booming echo of the titanic blast still rumbled through London like thunder in a distant valley. Buildings had been flattened for blocks, and a dozen more structures were burning out of control. But there was no sight of the Venusian tripod, or of the Squid God.

"Looks good. But we better check to make sure," Mary said stoically. Diving back into the water, the woman began swimming across the choppy river, leaving a milky contrail from the dissolving cast in her wake.

"Lord, I certainly hope it's dead," Prof. Einstein muttered, starting after his niece in a stately dogpaddle.

"Bloody well has to be," Lord Carstairs growled. "What could possibly have survived that blast, eh?"

The statement was logical, but the professor kept a close watch for any untoward movements along the disheveled shoreline, as they got closer.

Reaching the smashed embankment, the explorers crawled along a jagged crack and finally reached what had formerly been a street. Dripping wet, the three people clambered over heaps of rubble to reconnoiter the steaming blast zone. The smoke grew thicker as they approached, then cleared away completely to reveal a huge crater in the ground, the yawning depression filled with bubbling molten lava.

"*Finito,*" Prof. Einstein sighed in relief.

"Good show, my dear," Lord Carstairs stated, straightening his sodden necktie. "Your plan worked flawlessly."

"Like Hell it did!" Mary cried, pointing a finger. "Look there!"

The men turned and gasped. Only a block away was a two-foot tall Squid God weakly crawling along the ruined street.

"You son of a bitch!" Prof. Einstein cursed, drawing his Adams .32 pocket pistol and pulling the trigger. But the river had seeped into the cartridges, rendering them as useless as votes in a monarchy.

With a single bound, Lord Carstairs leapt upon the monster in a rugby tackle and pinned a tentacle under his boot. More surprised than hurt, the squid thrashed about and hooted angrily. Grabbing another tentacle, the lord whirled the squid around and dashed it to the ground. Completely unharmed by the impact, the creature bounced off the cobblestones and came back to smack Carstairs right in the face. The lord staggered away with blood gushing from his broken nose.

Landing on its eight tentacles, the squid started racing for the river. With a savage shout, Prof. Einstein tackled it hard, carrying them both across the broken pavement and through the remains of a glass window. Rolling about on the floor of the clothing shop, Prof. Einstein ignored a pair of scissors and, instead, grabbed a shard of window glass to stab the squid viciously. But only red blood flowed from his own cut hand as the makeshift dagger rebounded from the magical creature.

Like green coals in the dark, the two eyes of the little squid glowed with hatred, and soft beams shot out to engulf Einstein; he could feel his very life force, his soul, dwindle under the twin death rays. Dropping the glass, the professor raised a hand as a shield and the squid smashed him in the knee, the bones breaking audibly. Biting back a cry of pain, Prof. Einstein fell sideways and kicked out with his good leg to drive the beast away.

It was a noble effort, but the furious squid snatched another shard of glass and advanced upon the helpless professor.

Appearing through the smashed window, Lord Carstairs shoved the stainless steel barrel of the Webley .44 into the mouth of the monster and pulled the trigger. The massive handgun boomed, the blast making its eyes bulge out. But then the squid crunched on the barrel with its parrot-beak. Caught in the act of firing, the gun exploded and Carstairs was thrown backwards to land sprawling on the street, bleeding from the hand and chest.

From out of nowhere, a decorative garden rock flew through the air to smack the Squid God directly in the head. With an inhuman burble, the stunned monster dropped and went limp.

"Uncle, help me!" Mary cried, throwing her only other rock. The rough projectile caught the squid between the eyes and it crooned woozily in pain. Grabbing onto a tentacle, the woman tried to keep her weight on the good leg. Walking was becoming very difficult as pieces of the cast were peeling away from the soaking in the river, exposing the wooden sticks and leather straps underneath. But that was merely a framework to hold the plaster, and not designed to support her.

As the squid started to rouse, the professor hobbled closer and grabbed another limb to spread the beast wide. Outraged over the simplistic ploy, the squid struggled wildly in their grasp.

"Get a weapon, lad!" Einstein yelled, bracing himself with his undamaged knee. "Kill this damn thing before it escapes!"

Rising weakly from the cobblestones, the lord looked for the previously used garden rock, but it was nowhere in sight. Stumbling along, Carstairs searched the decimated suburb for some kind of a natural weapon. Nothing made by the hand of man would do. Cobblestones were carved by hammer and chisel, bricks were baked in an oven, house timbers were cut by saws, broken glass, frying pans, forks, an axe, boot scraper, horse whip . . . *Damn, civilization! Were there no more ordinary rocks? Was there nothing natural and not formed by the hand of Humanity that he could use? Nothing at all?*

Inside the crumbling building, Mary and the professor were starting to lose the tug-o-war with the outraged squid. The deadly beak in its belly snapped at them both, nipping cloth and skin, while the horrible eyes threw out sparks that singed painfully. It was blatantly obvious that the squid was starting to regain its strength, unlike the rapidly tiring humans.

Oozing slime from every pore, the squid wriggled in their grasp, the suckers on its tentacles making hungry wet noises. Prof. Einstein struggled to maintain his balance, but the pain of the broken joint was excruciating. Slipping on a broken roof tile, the professor lost his grip and landed sprawling on the floor. Free at last, the squid brutally smacked Mary to the ground; the breaking of her ribs made a horrible noise.

For a precious moment, the squid looked down at its fallen adversaries, its beak snapping hungrily in triumph. Then the monster turned away to undulate toward the window and the world outside. *Freedom was more important than a snack right now. Revenge would come later. Oh yes, nothing could stop it now!*

As the squid climbed over the windowsill, a bare-chested Lord Carstairs charged inside the store, brandishing a burning tree limb held in his cloth-wrapped hands. Roaring in unbridled fury, the lord rammed the jagged end of the untrimmed branch into the squid until it came out the other side.

Skewered like a shish kebab, the dangling squid went stiff, every twitching tentacle splaying outward. Its parrot-beak emitted a keening howl of anguish. Green blood gushed from the hideous wound, the viscous fluid igniting into flames as it touched the burning branch.

Snarling grimly, Lord Carstairs held onto the branch, his grip involuntarily going weak from the mounting waves of heat that emanated from the spreading fire. Soon, the flames covered his bandaged hands. The pain was incredible, and Lord Carstairs felt the urge to retch at the smell of his own roasting flesh. But surrender was not an option for the lord. Carstairs knew that the fate of the world was being decided right here, and right now. Nothing could make him stop!

"For Queen and country!" Lord Carstairs snarled, lifting the branch higher, hoping the flames would consume the squid before destroying his hands.

An unexpected telepathic plea for life reverberated in the lord's mind, closely followed by offers of countless riches, unlimited power, eternal life, absolute knowledge, and all the mates he could ever wish. *Anything! Everything!*

In utter contempt, Lord Carstairs filled his mind with thoughts of sweet Mary and slammed the squid against a brick wall to grind the flaming branch in deeper.

Reaching out with every tentacle, the squid pulled loose bricks from the wall and hurled them at the lord, breaking a rib and cutting open his bare shoulder. Spitting in the eye of the squid, Lord Carstairs ruthlessly moved the sharp end of the branch around inside the beast, seeking its evil heart.

More blood gushed from the wound. Screaming and hooting, the squid again sent a telepathic plea for its life, along with a promise of eternal friendship, then of ruling the world together! Concentrating all of the power of his Harvard-trained intellect, Lord Carstairs mentally told the beast exactly where it could jam the offer without the use of any decent lubricant.

Growing weaker, the squid feebly beat at the lord with its tentacles. Then it insanely ripped open its own wound to squirt blood onto the branch, sending the flames back towards Carstairs. Angling the stick, the lord searched for the heart higher in the head of the horrible thing, crushing and smashing every organ he could find.

Wildly flailing, the squid cast a miniature lightning bolt at the bleeding shoulder of the lord. Literally galvanized, Lord Carstairs hissed at the searing contact, but stood his ground as his flesh sizzled and charred.

Suddenly, the squid turned partly invisible, then became a miniature Venusian, and next a weeping human baby!

Ruthless as a Lord High Executioner, Carstairs slammed the squid against a nearby tree, and then against the brick wall once more. Again and again, the lord jabbed the branch into the thrashing body. With a rippling visual effect, the illusion of a baby vanished and the squid was revealed once more, blood dribbling from every orifice. Twisting the fiery branch like a drill, Lord Carstairs ignored the pain in his fingers and stabbed once more into the beast.

Shuddering all over, the squid violently spasmed, its eyes rolling upwards into the misshapen head. There was an incoherent telepathic scream, its tentacles flexed, and the Dutarian Squid God went completely limp.

Yeah, right. Scraping the rubbery corpse off the tree limb with his boot, Lord Carstairs decided to take no chance of another trick from the clever mollusk and proceeded to stab as many more holes as possible into the nightmarish animal lying on the pavement until it started to resemble old chutney.

Still not satisfied, the lord keep going until the jagged end of the branch splintered on the paving stones from the heavy blows.

"W-well d-done, lad," Prof. Einstein said weakly, shuffling through the open doorway of the destroyed store. "I t-think you c-can stop now."

"We want nothing to remain of the thing!" Carstairs mumbled through his broken nose. "Can't chance another regeneration."

"Burn . . . in the store," Mary panted, hobbling closer with both arms wrapped around her chest. "Accidentally blaze . . . natural heat . . ."

"Yes!" the lord cried. Lifting the slimy corpse on the branch, Carstairs shambled inside the building.

The endless bolts of fabric revealed that this was a dressmaker's shop; the blast from the exploding Venusian tripod had set the place ablaze. Perfect. The cloth was man-made, but the fire was accidental and should fulfill the requirements of a natural weapon.

Finding the largest pile of flaming dresses, Lord Carstairs thankfully released the branch and let it fall into the lacy conflagration. The remains of the pulped body sizzled like rancid lard before puffing into greasy smoke.

With a clatter of bells, a fire engine came charging round the crumbled frame of a factory down the roadway. The horses were gone, so the fire-wagon pumper was being hauled by a rag-tag crew of dirty soldiers.

"Too late, lads," Prof. Einstein panted, leaning on the doorway of the building. "It's all over."

Shrugging off the horse harness, a filthy corporal looked at him with a puzzled expression. "What was that, sir?"

"I said it's over," the professor replied. "The monster is dead."

The corporal cupped a hand to his badly bruised ear. "Eh?"

Oh lord, the blast had made them deaf. Hopefully it was just a temporary condition. "I said it's dead!" Prof. Einstein bellowed, trying not to move his hip. "The beast is dead! Dead! It's dead, I tell you. I tell you it's dead!"

"It is quite dead," Lord Carstairs added, walking from the store, his hands, raw as butcher's meat, hanging at his sides.

"Oh, so it's dead," the corporal said finally in comprehension. "Burned it up, did ya? Good show. But let's not take any chances, eh?"

Approaching the smashed store, the soldiers rolled the fire engine through the missing front window. Leaving it in the middle of the largest blaze, the soldiers dashed out of the dressmaker's shop just before the reservoir tank of six hundred gallons of coal oil whoofed into a volcanic tower of flame, the lambent fireball rising up through the missing roof and flaming through every window.

As the exhausted explorers retreated for safety, the soldiers tossed their loaded rifles and ammunition belts into the blazing store. Detonating from the heat, the brass cartridges cut loose a near continuous fusillade, the hot lead ricocheting off the brick walls to become its own crossfire. Spreading out to hunt for more fuel, the soldiers began tossing into the pit any loose lumber they could find from other nearby buildings.

Soon enough, the dressmaker's shop was a towering pyre, a crackling inferno with white-hot heat that rivaled the very pit of Hell itself.

That was when the entire British Army arrived and started building a real bonfire.

EPILOGUE

A week later in Buckingham Palace, trumpets blared in glorious harmony as Professor Felix Einstein, Lord Benjamin Carstairs, and Mary Einstein were escorted by liveried servants into the throne room.

Although covered with plaster swatches and bandages, the three explorers were dressed in their finest clothing; the men were in formal gray morning coats, and Mary was in a beautiful gown resplendent with jewels borrowed from the Egyptian section of the Museum. On the fourth finger of her left hand glittered a diamond ring of truly exquisite taste. The ring had come from the private vault of the Carstairs Estate, and not from any of the professor's nefarious displays.

Confined to a wheelchair, Prof. Einstein used his bandaged hands to push himself along the red velvet carpet. His broken leg jutted straight out on a wooden platform, and the professor's smashed knee was encased in a lump of plaster painted black to match his pants.

With his left arm in a sling and the other hand swathed in bandages, Lord Carstairs looked like the walking dead. There was a bloody bandage around his neck and fresh stitching across his forehead. One eye was swollen nearly shut and severely discolored in spite of the adroit application of fresh leeches. In addition, the lord was encumbered with a truly impressive white cross on his face, the strips of adhesive plaster helping to hold his shattered nose in shape. Inhaling via the wounded appendage caused a most impolite whistling effect, so Lord Carstairs did his best to breathe through his mouth without drooling. Sadly, this goal was proving more difficult to achieve that originally planned.

Limping alongside the two men, Mary Einstein appeared to be the least damaged. But that was because much of her oversized jewelry had been deliberately chosen to mask the woman's collection of bruises and contusions. The long sleeves and high collar of her gown hid a wealth of plaster strips, and the lacy bodice disguised the yards of lumpy bandages wrapped around her cracked ribs. Walking was quite difficult for the woman, breathing even more troublesome. However, everybody in attendance simply assumed that her rigid posture came from a proper British education. Or maybe it was just a saucy French corset.

As the Royal Philharmonic Orchestra swelled into a stirring rendition of 'Rule Britannia,' the explorers stiffly walked down the carpet in the traditional march of step, pause, then step, pause. Subdued murmurs of approval rippled through the huge attendance of political dignitaries and aristocrats. Every personage of high blood or noble birth in the whole of the British Empire was present, along with the entire membership of the London Explorer's Club. Included were several explorers whom everybody thought had been dead for years, and one chap still had an arrow sticking through his pith helmet, so quickly had been his egress from the wilds of Borneo and subsequent return to England.

Situated proudly amid the explorers was Jeeves Sinclair, a gold membership pin on his lapel for all of the precious books he had saved from the rioting and fire, and a somber black armband on his sleeve for the departed Carl Smythe.

Dressed completely in black and wearing veils, the members of the Explorers Club's Ladies Auxiliary stood demurely alongside their infamous husbands. Everybody present thought it only polite to ignore the arsenal of weapons hidden in the folds of their clothing. By the unanimous consent of Parliament, the female warriors had proved their loyalty to the crown beyond reproach, and thus had been awarded the distinguished right to stay armed while in the presence of the Queen.

With an honorary L.A.L.E.C. membership pin on her blouse, Katrina Cook stood alongside Edward Crainpoole, the rarely seen assistant to Lord Carstairs. The burly manservant was casting furtive glances at the pretty cook, and she was returning the secretive looks with unabashed interest.

Hoping that nobody noticed, Lord Carstairs broke protocol to wink at the family retainers on the sly. The man turned beet-red with embarrassment, and Katrina had the presumption to giggle. *Damn the woman! What a splendid wife she'll make for Edward. He'll need at least two weeks' holiday for the honeymoon. Oh, stuff and nonsense, a month!*

"I would suggest a matched set of His and Her Webley pistols for a wedding gift," Mary whispered softly out of the corner of her mouth.

Radiating dignity, Lord Carstairs said nothing, but the twinkle of amusement in his eyes brightened to a barely stifled gale of laughter.

Pausing only for a moment to oil a squeak out of his new wheelchair, Prof. Einstein ignored the others and tried to contain his excitement. *So this is it. The day of days. Oh joy, oh rapture divine!*

The orchestra swelled the music perfectly in synchronization with the three explorers stopping at the base of the royal dais, upon which rested the throne of England.

Short and dumpy, almost resembling a fat old man rather than a middle-aged woman, Queen Victoria Hanover contained the absolute resolve of a born leader, her bright eyes missing nothing that transpired in the throne room. In the background, Prince Albert was chomping on a roast beef sandwich and getting gravy all over his silken finery.

Normally dressed in black, today the queen was in bright cheery colors in an effort to lighten the mood of the war-torn city. There was even a garland of fresh flowers in her crown, and a corsage on her left wrist. However, her hard black shoes rested on the crudest of footstools, a lumpy block of rock known as The Stone of Destiny. Stolen from Edinburgh Castle centuries ago, the rock was the symbol of Scottish independence, and the subtly of its location was lost on nobody.

"Such a pity," Mary sighed under her breath, performing an awkward curtsy.

"It's a fake," Lord Carstairs replied while bowing. "I stole the original years ago and gave it back to the Scots."

Flushed with pride, Mary turned to face the man directly. "I love you," she declared in a clear loud voice.

The ten thousand people in attendance immediately started coughing in embarrassment at the unseemly outburst. A small army of butlers and maids rushed into the throne room and connecting galleries to distribute baskets of linen handkerchiefs in an effort to explain the coughing, as if this was the height of the flu season. The diplomatic ruse worked and, although it did take a while, eventually normalcy returned to the proper levels of haughty dignity.

"Lords and Dames," a herald bellowed, standing forward on the carpeted the dais. After a pause, he loudly banged the Royal Staff of England ritually twice on the dais. "Gentlemen and Ladies! The supreme ruler of the United Kingdom of Great Britain and Ireland, Empress of India, her most royal majesty, Queen Victoria Hanover!"

The loyal crowd erupted in cheers as Queen Victoria nodded in response and gave a small wave. Nothing else could be said or done for a while until the jubilation quieted down.

Standing off to the side of the throne, Prime Minister Disraeli scowled darkly at the three explorers waiting on the red carpet, while General McTeague surreptitiously gave them an approving thumb-ups sign.

Stepping a little closer to his fiancée, Lord Carstairs caught sight of an antique sword hanging at the general's side and was shocked to realize it was the long lost Holy War Sword of Dutar!

"Now where did he find that thing?" the lord muttered askance.

"I heard Excalibur told them," Prof. Einstein replied softly. "Some building fell over and it tumbled into the street."

"Probably walled up by the squiddies."

"Quite so, lad."

"That certainly would have come in handy yesterday," Mary whispered, massaging her aching ribs.

As the general shouting and assorted hurrahs subsided, the Lord Chamberlain walked to the queen and extended a plush cushion upon which rested an engraved silver sword. The room became hushed at the sight and all the people held their breath.

Taking the weapon by its jeweled handle, Queen Victoria arose from the throne and walked to the edge of the dais.

"Kneel, Prof. Einstein," she commanded, then paused. "Ah . . . wheel closer, Professor."

Pushing his chair to the very bottom of the steps, Prof. Einstein bowed his head before his sovereign lady. Overcome with emotion, happy tears flowed down his cheeks. *At last, after all these years, this was it!*

Using the flat of the sword, Queen Victoria tapped the professor gently on each shoulder. "In the name of St. Michael and St. George," she intoned, "we dub thee Sir Felix Einstein, knight errant and protector of the realm."

The castle shook as the crowd roared its approval. As the queen returned the sword to the Lord Chamberlain, a liveried page stepped forward holding a golden tray. Lifting a necklace from the tray, Queen Victoria showed the room that it carried the Great Seal of England. As the cheering slowed, the queen leaned over to place the golden chain and seal about the professor's bruised neck. Einstein winced at the weight, but said nothing.

"You may now rise . . . er, sit upright, Sir Felix!" Queen Victoria said, formally announcing his new title.

Tears of joy streaming down his face, the knight raised his head to thunderous applause.

With a formidable lump in his throat, Sir Felix had to swallow a few times before being able to speak. "Your majesty, I . . . I, really, I don't know what to say."

"Then do not say anything," the queen replied quietly. "Besides, sir knight, there is more."

That caught Einstein off guard. *More? The Lord Chamberlain hadn't said a word about anything more at the rehearsal this morning.*

From the behind the throne, a somber Minister of State approached holding a small wooden box. Removing the garland of flowers from her crown, Queen Victoria opened the lid of the box and withdrew a rectangle of black cloth. As she placed it upon her head, the throne room went deathly silent. In the extreme rear, a stunned seamstress dropped a pin and the impact rang louder than Big Ben at noon on Guy Fawkes Day.

"In accordance with the law of the land, and by royal decree," Queen Victoria announced in a hard, clear voice. "Your name is to now be stricken from the rolls of honor for the heinous crime of *treason*."

A gasp rose from the assemblage and Felix Einstein turned white. His mouth moved, but not a sound came forth.

"Your crime, the illegal possession of a Venusian war machine and the rebuilding of same machine to full working condition," the queen continued, scowling at the suddenly pale man in the wheelchair. "By English law, the punishment is death."

The world seemed to start spinning, Einstein felt himself go weak, and he slumped over the arm of the wheelchair. Rushing closer, Lord Carstairs took hold of his friend by the elbow to keep the man from sliding onto the floor.

"Your Majesty, if . . . if I may speak in his defense," Lord Carstairs started in a desperate rush for clemency.

"However!" Queen Victoria interrupted loudly. The crowd held its breath. She let them feel the terrible power of her wrath, then allowed a small smile to touch her lips. "Due to your recent services to the crown, you are hereby fully pardoned, *Professor* Einstein."

Exhaling so forcefully in relief that the tapestries on the wall fluttered, the crowd made sympathetic noises.

Handing back the necklace of his all-too-brief knighthood to the liveried page, Prof. Einstein bid it a fond farewell. *Oh, well, easy come, easy go.*

With a worried expression, the professor leaned forward as far as he could. "Your majesty," Einstein whispered tensely. "I don't suppose there is any chance that I will be able to keep the remaining walker parts that I have already collected?"

"Do not push your luck, Felix," Queen Victoria replied barely above a hush. "The Lord Mayor wants your head for destroying his residence, and Prince Albert is not fully convinced that this whole incident is not your direct responsibility."

Wiping his mouth clean on a sleeve, the Royal Consort glowered at the professor in clear and open dislike.

"Yes, I see," Prof. Einstein murmured sullenly. "Then I thank you for your incredible lenience, Your Majesty."

Unseen by anybody else in the castle, the queen gave him a gentle kick. "Oh, stop sulking. I know that you are innocent, and you will be knighted again next week after the ruckus has died down. Now be a good fellow, wheel aside and look very solemn."

Really? How excellent! Masking his elation with a woebegone face, Prof. Einstein pushed himself off the red carpet, a classic figure of dejection and misery. Several people in the crowd wept at the pitiful sight.

Nodding approval, Queen Victoria motioned for Lord Carstairs and Miss Einstein to approach. The lord forced himself to bow in spite of the pain, and Mary did the very best curtsy possible under the circumstances.

"Lord Benjamin Carstairs and Mary Elizabeth Victoria Einstein, it appears that there is little we can give as a reward for your services to crown and country," the queen pronounced loudly, making a regal gesture with a small hand. "Lord Carstairs is already a knight of the British Empire for his valiant efforts during The Troubles, and holds a Victoria Cross for his actions during the Boer War in Africa."

Shifting her stance, Queen Victoria smiled down at Mary. "And you, my dear, will soon become Lady Carstairs, a position we find ourselves envying you to some small degree."

Applause broke from the Ladies Auxiliary of the Explorers Club, but a single stern glance from the queen ended that foolishness quickly. *What a rowdy mob of hooligans!* Victoria thought. *I really must give them my patronage as soon as possible.*

"Thank you for the compliment, your majesty," Mary said, trying to curtsy again.

"Oh stop that, girl, I can see you're in pain," Queen Victoria commanded gently. Then she spoke in a loud commanding voice, "Therefore, we beg the boon of Mary Einstein and Lord Carstairs to accept our offer of hospitality, and to hold your wedding here at Buckingham Palace."

Nothing short of the end of the world could have possibly stopped the attending crowd from making noises of astonishment, delight, shock, and unbridled jealously at that pronouncement. Even though he was supposed to be acting chastised, Prof. Einstein grinned like a drunken loon. Mary flushed and even Lord Carstairs was flustered at the incredible honor.

"Oh yes, please, your majesty!" Mary gushed, gingerly taking the bandaged hand of her fiancée. "Thank you, yes!"

"It is my pleasure, child," Queen Victoria said, giving a rare smile. "We shall have tea next week, my dear, to discuss the details. Agreed?"

Mary nodded.

"Excellent!" the queen stated. "Then let it be so!"

In response, the Lord Chamberlain thumped the Great Staff of the Empire twice upon the dais, officially sealing the deal.

"Now in regard to the damage caused by this, rather more unpleasant matter," Queen Victoria said, addressing the crowd. "We have decreed that a one-pound tax is to be levied on everybody in the entire commonwealth to aid in the restoration of London, and a bronze statue will be erected at Trafalgar Square for the soldiers and citizens who so valiantly died during the, ahem, Occurrence."

Occurrence. The word was whispered a thousand times across the throne room and into the galleries. Good choice.

"Also, all forms of calamari are now forbidden within the land of Britain until further notice!" she added with some note of vengeance.

Precisely on cue, the Lord Chamberlain banged the Great Staff twice. "God save the Queen! This audience is over!"

With a crash of brass cymbals, the Royal Philharmonic started to play a rousing march. Chatting excitedly among themselves, the crowd began to shuffle for the exits in stately procession.

Amid the throng, several members of the Explorers Club and Parliament rushed over to console Prof. Einstein about the loss of station. Stepping out of the shadows, the cabby, Davis, blocked their progress with a lower-class scowl. Pushing his wheelchair like mad, the professor took advantage of the distraction to roll nimbly across the throne room and into a small alcove.

"Sergeant Oltion?" Prof. Einstein asked breathlessly, breaking to a squealing halt. "Are you Color-Sergeant Trevor Oltion? My contacts in the military said that you are to be the fellow in charge of my Venusian machine parts, I believe?"

In cool and frank appraisal, the British Marine stared at the professor and slowly, ever so slowly, lifted a disdainful eyebrow.

"Sir, those parts, enough to build another machine, I might note," Sgt. Oltion said with growing fervor, "are not, quote, yours, end of quote, but are the sole and exclusive property of her majesty's government!" The professor's wheelchair actually moved back a few inches under the verbal assault.

"Sir," the sergeant added, almost as an afterthought.

"Of course! That's what I meant, Trevor, old boy! But couldn't you simply leave the parts in my protective custody?" Prof. Einstein asked hopefully, rifling through his wallet. "I am an honorary member of the North Cumberland Dragoons!"

"No." The single word broached no further discussion.

Einstein plowed on anyway. "I am also a full corporal with Scotland Yard."

"Pulls no weight with me, sir," Sgt. Oltion sniffed, crossing his muscular arms to display the tattoos of a dozen wars.

"I am also an operative of the British Secret Service."

"How nice."

"A bishop in the Church of England?"

"Don't care," the sergeant yawned.

"Once, long ago, I traveled from a far land," the professor said, brushing off his lapel with one hand, and rubbing his wrist with the other in a complex gesture.

The sergeant stared at the professor blankly.

Oh, drat. "Wealthy and unscrupulous?" Prof. Einstein asked in desperation, pulling from his coat pocket a flawless blue-white diamond the size of a cricket ball.

The soldier dropped his jaw.

"It's from the lost mines of King Solomon, you know," the professor said teasingly, turning the diamond about to let the light sparkle on its many facets. "And there are more. Oh, there are a lot more of these."

Beaming in delight, Sgt. Oltion placed a friendly hand on the professor's shoulder. "Cor, an why didn't ya say so in the first place, old bean!" the soldier chuckled, unable to take his eyes off the massive gem. "Let's go have a nice cup of tea and finish this little chat in the confines of my private office . . ."

* * *

Many hours later, when the long day finally ended, the sun began to set and a full moon rose into the starry heavens. Once again, its inhuman arse was safely turned away from the sight of Humanity, and the man-in-the-moon smiled peacefully upon the slumbering Earth.

If that face seemed slightly altered and now vaguely resembled a very startled Prof. Felix Einstein radiating a wild explosion of magic in some primitive temple, that surely was a matter of the purest coincidence.

THE END

Printed in the United States
21499LVS00001B/326